christic

CODES

christic CODES

book one

Ana-Maria Theis

Christic Codes

Published by Ana-Maria Theis
www.anamariatheis.com

ISBN 978-0-9966875-6-0 (Paperback)
ISBN 978-0-9966875-1-5 (eBook)

Library of Congress Control Number: 2015912984

First Edition: September 2015
10 9 8 7 6 5 4 3 2 1

To everyone who has known and experienced darkness
(in its various forms), and managed to rise above it.

11.17.2015

To Marcella,

I'm incredibly happy that I am able to share with you this particular moment of my journey through life.

If imagination is not (yet) your best friend, make it so ☺. And make your life as magical and wonderful as you like !!!

Blessings & best wishes,

chapter / ONE

Breathe, just breathe. You're safe. You're back in the body. Breathe…in and out…in and out…in and out…

My chest was rising and falling, unable to slow down. I was starring for the millionth time at the ceiling, lying down on my back in bed, trying to compose myself. It was that time of the night, when sleeping would be the last thing I would do.

It happened again…for the nth time. I lost count. I should've gotten used to it by now. But an attack was not something I would take lightly, especially, not when someone or something was trying to suck the life out of me. Literally. In my sleep.

I like to tell myself there won't be another time…

I bent over to my right and touched the floor next to my bed where I would usually keep my cell phone—a.k.a. alarm clock—to check what time it was. *I know, I am weird.* Normal people kept their time telling devices on the night stand. But not me. I tried to convince myself to buy a small one, but was always afraid that I would be late for work or other stuff. So instead, I stuck with my cell on the floor next to my bedside…trying to minimize the exposure to radiations. I knew, it didn't seem realistic or much of a difference…but I felt it. And that's not all I could feel.

It's 3:04 a.m… Great. Another night in the trenches.

Jan was working again all night in the lab, so naturally, I was left alone to fight with my… fears. And attempting to sleep with the lights on in the hallway—which was far

1

from ideal. But it *was* one of those nights when he was working on some crazy-long hours experiment, which in the morning might turn out to be another waste of time, and for me another... *fun* night. For which, I would pay in the morning when actually, I was supposed to finish the presentation for my newest client—Mr. Tellman. A very quirky man, loaded though, and willing to do whatever would take, to please his youngest daughter Clara, who was getting married in eight months time.

The house that I was designing for him, was in fact a wedding gift for his daughter. It was suppose to be a surprise, a really good one. Because from what he had told me, I'd gathered, his daughter was even more peculiar than him. So I'd better pull out my magic and deliver some brilliant house design for the newlyweds.

To be honest, I was kind of surprised how Mr. Tellman had found me, and basically from our first meeting, had decided to give me the commission for the house. Which by the way, in these parts of the world, this would be considered a rarity. Usually, business decisions, or job decisions, easily, could take up to three months. Minimum. As a foreigner—Romanian—living in Hamburg, and having a few years of experience on the German working market, I could testify to its inflexibility.

Assimilation versus integration. Fit the norm versus free expression.

Especially and unexpectedly, in the highly qualified arena. Welcoming culture in Hamburg was definitely, still low. Hence, truly unfortunate for me, since I was currently residing here, with my boyfriend...soon to be husband.

Yes. I was getting married, too.

Three months ago, we were coming back from the city, walking toward home, and figuring out some day to day stuff, when out of nowhere, the marriage proposal happened.

"Let's do it! " he said, holding my hand a little tighter.

"Do what?" I asked, entirely confused.

"You know...get married. It feels right. It is right, so let's just do it!" Jan replied, with a contagious enthusiasm.

"So, that's it?! That's the best I will get out of a marriage proposal?"

He shrugged. "Well, you've got to admit, this is pretty romantic, not to mention spontaneous..." He blinked a few times theatrically, those happy gold-brown puppy eyes of his. Yeah, it was hard to argue with that.

I burst out into laughing, and a warm feeling expanded my insides. "Yes, it is!" A very gentle kiss, stopped me before I could comment any further.

Sometimes I'd wondered how my life would have turned out, if I hadn't come to Germany. It was a question that probably would never get answered.

I had followed my boyfriend at the time, who got a job here, right after he'd finished his PhD in a very particular branch of Mathematics. After many years of commute between Romania and Germany, we'd decided it was time to be together more than a month—both in the same place—every other three or four months, or seeing us only for holidays and vacations.

We had stretched ourselves, until no more was possible. So after I was done with my studies, I was the one who was going to be more flexible with home and work. After all, I had an international profession. I was an architect. So when he'd called me, after he'd got his contract renewed, *I* was the one who had to move. I basically, hated it. I had a life in Bucharest. I had friends, a great job, working as a freelancer, making lots of money…I was doing well. I was riding my wave.

I came to Germany, and all that went away. I had lost everything that I had worked for, everything that resembled normal, in my life. Adding to that, my relationship went up in smoke. My boyfriend became my Ex.

In less than a year since I'd moved to Germany, my old life had been completely dismantled. I wanted to run back to Romania, to forget everything, and start over. I had nothing left, to keep me here. But I was stopped by a friend who told me that, maybe it wasn't the best thing to do anything radical, and give it some time, continue whatever I had started here—which was a prep year for a PhD, something combining architecture and media— and later see, if I still had the same desire to escape.

I was *so* tired and over with studying upon my arrival here: two years at the Art Academy, then six years Architecture School, then a year here of intensive learning of German—I had some previous knowledge of it since my secondary school, so it wasn't completely new, but German was German…not easy. Because our plan was not to stay here very long, while I was here, instead of taking a crappy job, the better alternative was to stay in the academic world until things would crystallize in other

3

directions, for both of us.

What I had realized, the day we'd separated, was that I had basically put my entire life on hold. My career, all those hard working years of studies, and all my life plans. Waiting to live my life. At the age of twenty-seven, it was a pretty tough wake up call.

Looking back at those moments in time, I understood it was for the best. I mean, living between worlds was hard enough, but when you would have to hide it from your partner, it made it that much harder. By now, I could truly appreciate the saying: 'ignorance is bliss.' Not for me, though. I wanted to know no matter what. But for people like my Ex and others, which were the majority, living in complete oblivion, it was indeed a blessing. I knew that, because whenever I had the impulse to give away a little bit more information about...me, well, I would find myself in very awkward situations. It had ranged from: weird looks, rolled eyes and raised eyebrows, to downright aggressive. The inertia that most people lived in, was so thick…like a drug. An addiction so deep, that when you would try to break it, the response would automatically be defensive.

It wants it back.

To break free from it, when you were chained that heavily, it could get quite dramatic. Literally. It's like the world you knew, would crumble right before your eyes. Your beliefs, your values, your identity, everything that makes up the fabric of *your* reality, would instantly get pulverized. *Puff. Gone.*

My journey of awakening had begun many years ago. In my childhood actually, while listening to a story of my cousin Laura's grandma. She was telling me about heaven.

"You know Ariana, when people go to heaven, they actually go to this beautiful garden. Their bodies are made out of wax like texture, and—"

"What do they do, all day long?" I asked almost annoyed, being more interested in the doing, than in the being.

"They lie in the grass, or next to a tree, and sing praises to God," she answered undisturbed.

"That's all, they do?!" I felt, I was choking. Mentally, I couldn't quite grasp that. I was eight, and to me that was mind numbing boredom. I mean, I loved God, but that was too much for me. I thought that the afterlife was supposed to be fun, especially, if you went to heaven.

"Yes. They praise and serve the Lord."

That did it for me. I could never do that, sit all day and do nothing, just sing and praise the Lord. That right there, was the moment when I took charge of what I believed about God. Inside me, a voice would always nag me that there was more to it.

Time, research and personal experiences proved me right.

I was fourteen when I'd discovered Radiesthesia. By then, I had read dozens of books about spirituality, metaphysics, occult sciences, lost civilizations, and many other subjects...and found myself attracted toward understanding how life worked. How we fitted in the bigger picture. So when that came into my life, I was very happy to see the immediate applicability of the knowledge in one's life.

Through Radiesthesia, one could access information about people, places, objects, basically everything of animate or inanimate nature, by establishing resonance with their energy fields using the vibrational fields of the human body, with the help of specially calibrated instruments and a scale of measurements to decode the information.

It might sound very complex—and I wouldn't deny, that in fact it is—but once you'd learn what to do, and having enough practice to be accurate in translating the data, this becomes easy and fun, not to mention helpful. It's like having a very cool gadget that would provide all sorts of information about virtually everyone and everything. The only difference would be, you are the gadget, and the more experience and training you would gather, the more precise your info would be.

Throughout high school and after that, I had developed a special relationship with a teacher of mine. She was my math tutor. In my home country, high school was always serious business, especially with subjects like math, and if you were like me having a major (we call it profile) in math and physics, then it was actually expected of you to prepare outside school, to meet the high standards set out by the teachers. So in order to solve some crazy homework—international math competition crazy...—well, basically everyone would get a math tutor. Unless you were beyond genius. But even those that were super gifted at math, would choose to have one. As a mentor, or like a coach to train with.

In my case, it was simply to go through the craziness... I had other aspirations and talents, that I put my focus on. However, this experience brought me close to a very special person that was more than just a teacher, she was my friend, she was like family to me. Mrs. Tudose.

She and I shared this passion for all things metaphysical, spiritual, and hidden. But from a more scientific perspective, than most. At least in those times, middle of the 90's. When subjects like those, were still pretty much in the underground arena.

Before and mostly after math sessions, or during private visits, we'd used to have these long talks about different books we'd read, interesting experiences we had, exchanging ideas, books, personal problems... It was very magical. We created a sacred space for us and for those like us in our circle, who shared this passion.

I remember visiting her one time—I was already a student at the university—when she told me: "You know, last month I bumped into Mrs. Munteanu."

"Mrs. Munteanu as in the Physics teacher?!" I added, surprised.

"Yes, and she was upset. We've been quite good friends for years, but never did she once opened up herself to me, as she did that day."

"Mhm..." To be honest I wasn't surprised, the woman looked always very unhappy.

"She told me a bit about her family. She complained that she and her two grown up sons don't really get along. Translation...she doesn't really approve the women in their lives, and the fact that they choose to ignore her calls. And on top of that, she has some nasty health issues to deal with at the moment. Anyhow...I ended up recommending her some books to read. You know, to enlarge her perspective on things. And somehow I lent her those two books you gave me last time you were here."

"Really?!"

That was BIG.

"Yeah...I told you, I was really surprised myself. But what was even more astonishing, was the fact, she actually read them." Mrs. Tudose smiled, pleased with herself.

"Wow...that's something."

"And you know what else I told her, after she read those books?"

I could only stare, expectantly.

"I told her that those were your books. And you and I share common passions and we are friends, and we talk about this stuff all the time. She was really impressed with you."

"Again…wow!" Because last time I saw her, she was the opposite of that. During my high school years, I used to be part of the Brainstorming Club, ran by another Physics teacher. For those times, she was extremely cool, and really open minded about a lot of things. Everyone would come up with different topics, like U.F.O.s, fringe science stuff, poetry, art, and even some life after death, which was my very own special contribution.

Every year for the anniversary of our school, she would select a few of us to each give a talk about these kinds of subjects. Naturally, I was one of those people. So when my turn came, I had quite an audience…including Mrs. Munteanu, who at the end of my presentation, basically stormed out the door, clearly disturbed by the information on such matters.

If I remember correctly, the word she used was:"Blasphemy!"

Yeah, that day I did some serious beliefs system shaking on her. It was funny though, how she took that so personal. But to my surprise, the rest of my audience was really into it. I even got some flowers from the other teachers, as a sign of appreciation.

"I tell you, something's changed in her after reading those books. It's like she was discovering the world for the first time."

"I bet, she did." I knew how I felt going down this path myself, only in my case, I was actually looking for it. I was in search for answers of things that neither my parents, nor my teachers or society, could offer any. Luckily for me, Mrs. Tudose—who ironically, was a teacher—was on the search, too. As well as somebody else in my family. My aunt Tina—Laura's mom.

Today the group was bigger; I had to add my sister Raluca to the list and even my mom—now that she was retired and had enough time to appreciate the knowledge. Apparently, the bug of 'there's-got-to-be-more-than-this,' ran deep in my family, al-though, each and every one of us, had their own timeline to deal with it.

Something had happened to me, back in 2005 that forever altered the course of my existence.

It was the end of July, and I was done with exams and the two weeks internship—which marked the end of the academic year and the beginning of the summer vaca-tion. It was now my favorite time of the year, when I could read other things than just my crazy condensed school stuff. Summer vacation was a magical time when, I would reconnect with my spiritual books and practice.

One night after reading something very powerful, I was trying to fall asleep when my crown chakra started buzzing. Literally. I could feel the vortex spinning and making this unsettling noise that woke me up. I had no idea what was going on, but I was sure it had to do with something I read. I did my best to ignore the whole thing, trying to go back to sleep only to find myself in an even more complicated situation.

I was already drifting when a pull took over the buzzing. I felt as if something was sucking me into a hole, but I couldn't really worry, because it was like a trance that paralyzed all my senses. It was pleasant in a weird kind of way. Yet, after a short while, I heard a voice urging me to wake up. And to do it straight away, or I was going to die if I didn't.

It was *sooooo* hard to open my eyes. It took me all the will power that I could muster. While I was pushing myself from the inside, I received an image of a huge snake coiled up in the middle of the room, busy harnessing my life force. That was the moment when I broke the trance, got out of the bed, reached for the light switch only to find it didn't work. No lights.

I immediately tried the lamp on my desk. It didn't work, either. I almost peed myself. Crazed with fear, I pressed the light switch over and over again. In the middle of my desperation, finally the lamp lit up the room. I turned to see if the snake was still there. To my relief, there was no sign of it anywhere.

I knew it wasn't a dream, because I'd been attacked before, but this time was different. It was as if somebody was monitoring my latest activities, warning me not to play with fire. 'Cause if I did, I would end up dead.

A lot of the people I knew exploring the spiritual realm, didn't have such experiences as mine. None of the books that I was reading at the time, was mentioning anything of this sort. They were all talking about paradigm shift, raise in consciousness, ascension, and love and light. That was when I knew it couldn't be all that simple, all that airy fairy. And I was right, but it took a few more years after that, to see *the big picture*.

That night, afterwards, the horrible fear started to lose its power on me, but still couldn't go to sleep. It didn't feel safe, so I turned on my TV and stayed up in bed until the sun came up, and only then allowed myself to drift away. For three or four nights in a row, I did the exact same thing, only to find myself completely exhausted. This was actually how my sleeping with the lights on, began.

A week later, I was in the bathroom brushing my teeth and washing my face with cold water when I caught with the corner of my eye a scar on my neck, right under my left earlobe. I touched it gently to see if it hurt, but it didn't. It was about five centimeters long and it looked laser made, a very thin reddish line that marked a very palpable trench.

I didn't know what happened to cause that. All I knew was that, that week I was praying for a different life. To break the circle of pointless numb repetition, and…to ascend. That's when it hit me. The scar wasn't necessarily an accident, or a coincidence. Added to that, that day I had this strange and peaceful feeling that somehow I was going to be okay, that my life was going to be okay from now on.

My scar was visible only for a week. Luckily, that week I had visited my parents and implicitly my aunt Tina—my spiritual confidant in the family at that time. She'd examined the scar, and after explaining her my latest *nightly adventures* and spiritual intentions, she came up to the same conclusion. That it was no ordinary scar, and something big had happened.

It was only later, when I would come to understand how big this *something* was.

Truth of the matter was, when I had started on this path—on this search for answers—I had never ever imagined it would unfold like it did. Or where it took me.

To this day, I was still in awe.

chapter / TWO

"Miss Ducas, I am really impressed!" Mr. Tellman said, with such conviction that made me basically jump up and down for joy. Thank God, he couldn't see me through his phone.

He continued. "I believe Clara will be thrilled, when she'll see this. Do you think the house will be ready, by then?"

"If you give me the okay on the design part, I don't see why it wouldn't. I've contacted already a good construction firm. They've already sent me an estimate, for what you're are seeing right now, on your computer screen. And, it's under the budget limit. Fifteen percent under, to be exact," I added, quite pleased with myself.

"Miss Ducas, could you please send me an email with the estimate. I will have a look at it, and this evening I will communicate you my decision."

"Certainly. You'll have, it in no time. Is that all?" I hated it when I had to talk so formal.

"That would be all. For now. Good bye, Miss Ducas!" He ended abruptly.

The thing with Mr. Tellman, was that you never knew whether he was cold by nature, or that he liked to play it cool with a tint of mean. Either way, I always had to play stiff with him. I guess some people like to live that starchy.

Every time after we ended a meeting or a phone call, I still wondered, why he chose *me*. I mean, I was aware of the quality of my work and that alone should be enough to quiet my mind. Though, it was still hard to grasp—due to the fact that he was how he was…plus he was an insurance high up CEO guy—how it was possible for our worlds to intersect. But maybe I was wrong, and he was a good judge of character, and he knew all along that I was worthy of his time and money. After all, his profession forced him to analyze the risk factor, very thoroughly. Anyhow, it felt good to be back working for myself full-time, and not having to put up with pointless crap from *others*…

Since Jan and I had moved to Hamburg, I had worked several jobs. All design positions; first in a small but very ambitious corporate events studio, then in a big advertising agency, and afterwards, in an architecture office. Alongside that, I kept my freelance work but to a minimum, only for special projects, that besides paying good money, were meaningful to me.

I had never estimated the impact of my professional path here, on my emotional and physical health, though. It was a rough journey. I was under a lot of stress working in Bucharest for a Big Pharma company, opening pharmacies around the country, but I had never had to deal with the discrimination of being a foreigner and/or a woman in my field. Or being paid less, because I was a woman.

Yeah, truth sucks. And, the worst was, I had to find out, experiencing it firsthand.

It was so naive of me, to think that people were less ignorant and better informed, now that we lived in the era of fast internet, and just one click away from everything and everyone.

Wrong.

People were still ignorant, and in the dark. And most of them were quite content to stay that way, as long as they got what they wanted, which was not a lot. A roof over their heads, and an income to pay the bills. For more, they'd have to exercise imagination and creative thinking, which was an atrophied muscle. Because what fueled most people, was fear. Fear of not having enough, fear of not being enough, fear of failure, fear of new, fear of death, fear of…fear itself.

Speaking of fear, remembering those jobs I'd worked, a lot of frustration and pain comes to the surface. I know time heals everything. It's just, I wish I hadn't gone through those experiences. It wasn't easy to navigate everyday through work assignments and stupid prejudices from co-workers, and on top of that, my out of the ordinary aspects of my life—which were a closed subject.

What had hurt the most and made me spiral into a *very* deep and ugly depression, was the fact that no matter what I would say about myself, about my life before coming to this country, and about my professional background, or anything about me in general, would not be taken seriously. Or I would be made fun of behind my back.

It felt as though my life was one huge joke, a tasteless caricature. I knew now, that those who chose to do so, were first: ignorant, second: jealous of my skills, and third: afraid of my strong personality—as I had been told many times before. The thing was, I was never really a follower, or a joiner. I did things only because I really wanted to. I could think for myself, and I was certainly not afraid to express an honest opinion and stick with it. Not that I got to do that so much at work… They needed my work, not me.

I had resisted heroically, even when the back pains had started. Like, really bad. But no matter how stoical I was, I couldn't escape death. Yes, DEATH. I died. Twice, actually. Of good old broken heart. My heart gave up because I lost the will to live; I saw no point in carry on. I still struggled with that, but I was in a better place today. I felt better, and not thanks to the people here, but because of what I ate. Ironic…I know.

I was vegan for some time now, and for many, many years before, vegetarian. And I saw the immediate improvements by just doing that, by being vegan. But the moment I went raw—closer to one hundred percent—I was pulled out of the depression almost instantaneously. In a matter of days. I couldn't believe the clarity in my head, the giddiness, the joy of having new thoughts, and finally starting to feel something…other then nothingness. Boy, was I in a really dark place. And that was not so long ago. It had been two months now, since I came back from the dead. Mentally and physically.

I took notice of the fact, that here in Hamburg, the weather was particularly bad. And naturally, it influenced people's behavior. Somebody once told me—more like a joke—that people here in the North, were cold because of hundreds of years of bad weather. He was right. But it wasn't just the weather.

Recently I had discovered that nearby, there was a HAARP installation. Which confirmed my suspicion for some time now, that something was going on, which wasn't natural or normal. Plus the chemtrails…which was the cherry on top. All in all…a lethal cocktail.

The mood swings, the depression and suicidal tendencies, had been making victims left and right. And to make it even more evident, for some time now, whenever I would go to the cinema, right before the film started, they would play a commercial about a hotline for people with these kinds of problems…

Yeah. It's as real as it gets, too bad most people don't really connect the dots.

Anyways. Long live the green smoothies!

Oh, crap! I forgot to talk to my sister yesterday. "I have something important to tell you," she had said, but I so was busy with the damn presentation, that I had to blow her off. I promised, I would get back to her later, though. Later, was already tomorrow. Today. A day later. Shit. She was online.

Ducas80: Sorry!!!!!!!!!! I forgot completely…but I have a good excuse.
RalucaD: I know. So how did it go with the Mr.Icicle?
Ducas80: Tellmann you mean.
RalucaD: Who else?!
Ducas80: He's happy, just sent him the estimates, he'll get back to me tonight. So tell me, what's up? Please don't scare me with some horrible news. I had enough for the last two days.
RalucaD: I had this weird dream about you, and you know that some dreams are not just dreams.
Ducas80: I know. Go on…
RalucaD: You were in a strange place with people I didn't recognize and you looked sad like something bad happened to you, and you didn't know what to do next. You held a pendant in your hand. I couldn't really see exactly the shape but looked more like a teardrop. And one of these guys was explaining you something about it, but I don't remember what.
Ducas80: This doesn't sound so bad…
RalucaD: No, but the energy of the dream, was so strong, I really felt it was important to tell you this.
Ducas80: Yeah…strange. But what's not strange about my life…
RalucaD: Look, maybe it's nothing. Give it time to see what unfolds.
Ducas80: Honestly, I really don't want to focus on crap anymore. Actually I want to forget the last few years of my life…but who knows. Time will tell. Anyhow, it's Friday!!! Yay!
RalucaD: Yay!!! Anything fun this weekend?
Ducas80: Got to go to Tim's show. They perform tonight at the Opera House, so it's quite a big deal for him and his company. I'm meeting Jan there.
RalucaD: Sounds fancy. Have fun! Got to go know, I still have some errands to run. Fill me in later… hugs.
Ducas80: Sure. Hugs back.

These past few years since I had moved here, I had kept quite a tight contact with my family, mainly due to the internet. Especially, me and my sister. We talked on a daily basis. I guess not a lot of people could say that about their siblings relationship. In our case, a huge factor would be that we have a lot in common, even if we had developed somehow differently. When we were small, she was more of an aggressive kid, and couldn't understand why I would prefer books, to her.

Right about when she had turned twenty one, one of my spiritual books got her hooked on the subject. Since then, she had absorbed a lot of information, and got herself to experience firsthand things that people only read or heard about. She got to understand *my perspective* on things, on life, on what most people label as *weird*, *freaky*, or just plain nuts.

Although she had been living in a big busy city like Bucharest, managing an Events Agency, what would ground her in all the noise around, would be the same as it was for me. The unseen. The magic of life, the wonder, and the possibility of a new, completely different reality. Time, books, and *out of the ordinary personal experiences* had brought us closer, and today she had become the closest friend and confidant I had, aside from Jan.

$$\infty$$

"Hey, you came!" Tim called out in our direction waving his hand, then headed through the crowd in the foyer toward us. As he reached me and Jan, he almost knocked the air out of my lungs giving me a tight, bear like hug.

I could only exhale. "Great show!"

"I want you to meet someone." Tim added, barely containing his excitement, and before I could say anything, this someone appeared from behind him smiling shyly.

"Hi, I'm Andreas, nice to finally meet you!" he spoke a little louder to cover the noise around us, and shook my hand then Jan's, nodding in recognition.

"Nice to finally meet you too?! ...I guess you know more about me, than I about you," I replied, not knowing how much did Tim told him about me, given the fact that Tim is kind of the fourth musketeer in our small *clique*.

"I met Andreas like a month ago" Jan said, more to me than to the others. "He came to our lab to pick up Tim, and this is how we actually met for the first time. Sorry, I guess I forgot to tell you…"

"Well, Andreas, obviously you have an advantage over me, tonight. So tell me, how's Tim treating you?" I asked, curious about this new development in my friend's love life. We hadn't seen each other in a little over two months, we only conversed briefly on the phone or on messenger, promising to get together soon. But it didn't happen due to crazy schedules on both sides. And…evidently *other* reasons.

Since Tim had showed up in Jan's lab, two years ago, they had become really good friends—and I by extension. One time I was visiting Jan at work, and that's all it took for me and Tim to connect, and realize how much we had in common. He, a scientist, who in his free time did ballet, and I, an architect who battled unseen forces at night… or at any other time of the day. Two misfits navigating between worlds, dealing with daily jobs and stuff, but truly focused and interested in all things *new agey* by some standards.

I was lucky, that although Jan was new to the subject of spirituality and all that encompassed it, he was very accepting of me and my experiences. Actually, this opened the door for him, to a realm that made him question a lot of the things that we consider real. Which was good. That got us closer even faster. It made our soirees with Tim to seem very captivating, and wondrous.

"Great. We're still very new. But I feel lucky already," Andreas answered, eyeing his boyfriend.

"So, his not afraid to share his feelings," I said, looking at Tim who had a smile spread to his ears. He looked definitely happy.

"I know. And that's not even the best part!" Tim concluded.

Jan interrupted us. "I am kind of thirsty, why don't we continue over there at the bar."

"Of course!" Tim nodded, and then pointed with his hand where the drinks and the buffet were, and started leading us through the crowd.

When we finally made it through the sea of people, I was already sweating and glad for some refreshments.

"Here you go!" Jan spoke from behind me, handing me a glass of Champagne.

"Thank you."

"I think it's time for a toast," Andreas said, joining us with his drink.

I nodded in agreement. "To what should we toast to, then?!"

Tim glanced at the three of us. "To new directions and…to the element of surprise!"

Very interesting I thought. "Amen to that!" And a joyous glass clink made our eyes sparkle with anticipation.

Half an hour later, another glass of Champagne and some strawberries—that's all I could find to eat in that mountain of cheeses—the initial awkwardness of meeting Andreas for the first time, faded into laughter and genuinely funny jokes. I found out that he was a freelance journalist, writing for several big financial newspapers, but like us, he was exploring a different side of himself and that lead to…meeting Tim.

"You ok?!" Jan whispered in my ear, as the others were battling for some sandwiches on the buffet table next to us.

"Yeah, I'm fine."

"I mean about last night. I read your message this morning. I'm really sorry I had to work again overnight, and couldn't be there for you…"

I shrugged. "Well, I'm here. Aren't I?"

He looked at me sad and caressed my face with his free hand, trying to get the nuances of what I just said. "I mean it. You know I don't like to see you hurt. Physically, or in any other way."

"I know. So any luck last night with your cells?" I asked, trying to change the subject.

"Actually, yes. I got some really nice results, which will make *the iron lady* jump for joy." By 'the iron lady,' he meant his doctoral studies professor, who was a huge name in the Neuroscience world, but had a highly unpredictable *personality*, which wasn't easy to ignore.

"Well, at least it was a productive night for you. Which I hope gets you closer to the finishing line." We wanted to get married right away after his doctoral graduation, which we hoped it would be soon… But what I'd learned from my previous experience with my Ex. and his PhD studies, later or much later, was a more probable timeline.

"Hey! Since when did you lose faith in me?" he replied, pretending to be hurt by my remark.

"Sorry. Bad night. I think I need more food to cheer up," I avoided, not wanting to explain *again* flashes from my past.

"Let me see what I can do for you. Be right back!"

And before I could say anything else, he disappeared in the mass of people circling around the food area.

Trying to disperse the cloud of unpleasant thoughts forming in my head, I scanned the foyer to see where Tim and Andreas went. Right when I spotted them talking to some people, whom I recognized as being more lab colleagues, my phone began to buzz. I slid my hand in the bag resting on my left shoulder, and grabbed it.

"Mr. Tellman! Nice to hear back from you," I answered promptly.

He sounded relaxed, and friendly for a change. "Miss Ducas, as I said earlier, I really liked your proposal, and the numbers didn't hurt either. What I am trying to say here is, that, from my part, you have the okay to move on to phase two."

"Glad to hear that." I was genuinely filled with enthusiasm, but for some reason I didn't have any more power left in me for business related topics. I was pleasantly drifting, at the thought of a good night sleep.

"I think we should set up from now, a regular weekly meeting. This way you can keep me up to date on the whole process. And whatever little inadvertencies might appear, will be easier to handle. And this is not in any way thought, as a doubt in your skills to manage the project. But I really want everything to turn well and on time for the big day." The 'big day' was his daughter's wedding.

"Absolutely. I was going to propose the same thing." I said, honestly, no sarcasm whatsoever. "It's just, first I have to meet up with the construction firm to see if they will handle all the permits that we need, in order to build. If yes, which most probably will be the case, I would have to confer with them about what other drawing pieces they need from me, to get the process moving. Then I will know more. How's next Thursday or Friday sound?"

"Thursday it is. Friday I'm out of town." That was actually, very courteous of him to

let me know his motivation for choosing one day over the other. It made him almost…
human.

"It's settled then. Have a nice weekend Mr. Tellman!"

"You too, Miss Ducas. See you next week. Good night!" He ended.

Just as I looked up, after I dropped my phone in the bag, Jan stood in front of me, smiling and having both hands full with food and drinks. "Am I a miracle worker, or what?"

"I see, you've been busy… So what do we have here?" I asked, already happy at the prospect of more food into my system.

"Believe it or not, these are some vegan meatballs," he said it very enthusiastically. "Here you have some avocado cream, some salad and a few crispy slices of wholegrain rye bread."

For an event like this, it wasn't bad at all. "Well, I think I love you. Is that still water?" I saw he carried two glasses with different contents.

"Yes. I figured you want this, or orange juice."

"Definitely the water." I replied, already scanning the area for a free table to place our plates on. At my right, thank goodness, a couple just left. "Over there!" I said, pointing to that table, and basically teleported myself right next to it. In the absence of tables with chairs, this would do.

Jan walked slowly toward me, trying not to spill the food or the drinks on the people that kept popping up out of nowhere in front of him, making his way to me, an acrobatic number.

"Sorry, for not taking at least the drinks with me. I saw the opportunity to get a table for us, and…" I said, as he laid the plates, already feeling guilty for not helping him.

"It's okay. That's at least I can do, *for last night.*" He gave me a wink, and then started to bite into his sandwich. With a mouth full of food, and a happy grin, he remembered what I almost forgot. "Isn't your cousin supposed to come to us next week?"

"You're right. The workshop thing!"

"When are we supposed to pick her up from the airport?"

She told me on the phone two days ago, but my memory was somehow blurred. "I think Wednesday. But I will call her tomorrow and ask her again."

"Good. Where was the toilet again?" he asked me, with a pained look on his face. "I really got to pee. Like *now*!"

I stood on the tip of my shoes trying to see over the sea of people, and then pointed in the direction of the cloakroom. "Next to that reception desk, is a hallway. Go there, and head toward the end. It's there on the right."

"Thanks. See you in a bit," he said, and started surfing through the crowd, until I lost him.

Left alone, again, with just my thoughts, I wasn't a happy picture. So instead, I focused on what was on my plate, and thanked to whoever thought of people like *me* who would attend the event, and didn't have to starve.

I suspected Tim had something to do with it. Anyhow, I was grateful.

Halfway through my salad, I looked up and around me to spot a familiar face, when next to a pillar, a few meters away from me, this tall blond man was looking at me with an intense stare in his blue eyes. For a moment, I didn't know what to do, so I turned the other way and took another big bite from my food, trying to ignore the awkward moment. I had had enough in the last two days. When I thought that he wasn't staring anymore or left all together, I turned again in his direction only to find his eyes still observing me. Silently.

And that was the least strange part of it.

When I dared to really look at him, I saw that he was completely inappropriately dressed for the occasion. He was wearing a simple dark blue t-shirt with white short chino pants and some white sneakers, plus he looked tanned. Normally this wouldn't be bad for summer, except here, there wasn't summer anymore. If ever. Or too much sun for that matter. Although for late September in Hamburg, it wasn't bad, but tonight was chilly enough to wear at least a jacket.

Then, I saw something even more strange. At the edge of his body, the air was vibrating, creating a smudged contour around him.

Holy crap! This is not good. I am not crazy. The pulsating air spread, and was dissolving the reality behind him, only to bring forward another one. Now I could see that he was actually standing next to a tree, outside in a garden. In the background I spotted red rock formations, and some wild scattered vegetation. In all the weirdness,

I couldn't help to notice, how beautiful the light was on everything. A stunning sunset that made everyone and everything look warm and familiar. I just stood there with my mouth hanging open, mesmerized by what I saw. I couldn't move or say anything.

Wow...

Lost in the view, I was brought back instantaneously, when somebody pierced through my screen, moving fast toward the buffet table. The image of the *mystery guy* and his environment was fading really fast. It was like the man who walked through it, broke the spell.

Noooo...

The last I could make out of it, was that he was smiling, but more with his eyes, then raised his right hand and waved at me. He opened his mouth to say something, but it never left the lips. The image was completely gone. Dissolved like smoke in the air...

Inexplicably, I felt sad and empty after it disappeared. For those few moments, it felt like I was connected to *something* and *somebody* really familiar. I had no idea why and how that was possible.

"So, what're looking at?" A voice came from behind me, and it took me a few seconds to realize that Jan was back and talking to me.

I didn't know what to tell him. "Nothing really. It's just I thought I saw...*something*."

"Something like one of those things you see at night?"

Definitely not one of *those* things. "I saw something...interesting. Good interesting. I guess?!"

"You guess? You mean, you don't know what you saw?" he insisted, and I wasn't sure if more details would satisfy his curiosity.

I myself was waiting for an explanation for what just had happened here. I mean, I could come up with some theories, but none of it would quiet my mind or the sense of deep longing that was activated in me. It would only make it worse. I decided it was better to drop it...for now. "Look, it's not like this happens to me every day. Yes, a lot of weird stuff happens to me regularly...but this is...it's hard to explain. I saw—"

"You saw what?" Jan asked, obviously annoyed by my inability to give a straight answer.

"Ah, forget it… If it happens again, I will pay more attention, to the details. Okay?"

"What details? Do you hear yourself? It doesn't make sense," he added, looking miserable. "You know, sometimes I feel like you really don't want me to understand what's happening to you. I really want to help, to understand. But you have to let me. You have to trust me more…"

I was already wishing that the whole thing never happened. But I had no control over *it*. Apparently over a lot of other *things* in my life. "I trust you. Don't think that. I don't know exactly what I saw…that's the problem." I answered, and that was the truth. Even more, I had a million questions, and no one to satisfy my hunger. A *different* hunger.

"So, what did you see, or not see?" Tim spoke from behind me, with a cheerful tone in his voice.

People should stop doing that. Pop up out of nowhere and startle me. "Not you too. Please. We'll talk about it when I know more. Thinking this is not a one time event… based on my previous experience. I should know more next time. So everyone relax!" I said, almost losing my cool, and all three looked at me as if they saw an alien for the first time. And then more regrets flooded me.

Why isn't this night over yet?!

Tim put an arm around me, and gave me a squeeze. "Hey, I didn't mean to make you uncomfortable. You know, you can talk to me about anything."

"With me, too!" Jan put in.

For a second, Tim looked at Jan, gave him a smile and then continued. "Anytime. If it's one of those *subjects*, we could meet up and dissect the whole thing."

"Yeah, I know. I wish I had more to say. For now, I will dissect alone in my head. Who knows, I might dream about it and get some answers…"

I wasn't sure, why I couldn't tell them the little that I'd witnessed. Maybe because it impacted me much deeper, and more intimate than I would care to share—with anyone. I felt that the message was for me, and me alone.

I always liked the city better at night. Everything seemed more magical. Like the veil between worlds would be at its thinnest, and I could glimpse into the other side. Into the possibility of something else, other than this opaque, callous, boring, and repetitive reality around me.

I was already drifting into my dreams looking out the window, hypnotized by the buildings and the night lights, that would pass us by. We were driving back home. Finally the day was over.

"Hey, are you still in there?" Jan asked, touching my hands, and that pulled me out of my reverie.

"Sort of. I am glad that soon I will be in bed, and hopefully I will have an eventless sleep. I really need to sleep. This last month has taken its toll on me. Not to mention these last two days. I truly feel like I need a break. From *everything*. Especially, from this place."

Jan furrowed his brows. "You mean from me?!"

"I didn't say that. It's like nothing makes sense anymore. All the motivation I had before, it's gone. Nothing left." I exhaled, tired.

"This hurts, you know? Nothing left?! What am I then, a—"

I stopped him before he would jump over board with his assumptions. "No, silly! It's deeper than that. That's what I've been trying to explain to you all these months. I feel better than I did even a month ago. But ever since I *came back* the second time, I have a hard time connecting to this reality. It's like whatever my purpose was, it's not there anymore. And I don't know what to do with myself."

"What do you mean, you don't know? You promised you will marry me!" Jan scowled, and I burst out into laughter. "I don't do rejections well. And that's not funny!" He pretended to be offended by what I let out, but I could see that even if he was trying to put up a straight face, the corner of his lips were already arching into a smile.

"Yeah. It's not funny. That's why I need a break. A different perspective on things. A fresh start..." I replied, meaning every word.

He turned his head for a second in my direction and gave me a beautiful smile, then turned back to watch the road. "Let me see what I can do about that! Okay?!"

"Okay. Feel free to surprise me." I said, not really believing that he could give me what my soul was longing for, but I made a promise to him. And I always kept my word.

Jan spoke very sure of himself. "I will!"

I am flying...I am flying...I feel so free and peaceful here. Wherever this is.

Around me, I see endless bright sky, no clouds, just beautiful light blue washed by the sun. Under me I see mountain peaks, and lush green everywhere. I spot a panoramic deck where I decide to descend.

Wow...how beautiful this place is! For some reason, it feels so familiar, even if I don't remember coming here before. I put my hands on the wooden railing and look around inhaling the intoxicating beauty emanated by every element. Then I bend over, and discover to my surprise, this out of this world turquoise clear water, that sparkles like a gem stone. It's crazy, I can't take my eyes from it. It's like I'm under a hypnotic spell.

As I look down fascinated by it, I feel how I am being pulled into it. I fall...I just fall. Resistance is futile. I don't fear it. This is soooo...weird.

I hit the water, and realize the texture is different from the water I know. This feels more like air. Liquid air. Normally I am afraid of the water, or to be under it like I am now. But this is something else. I don't find the words... It feels so safe here. I feel safe here. And protected.

I am suddenly cuddled by arms that I can't see, and kissed by...water. I see nobody else around me. I'm not afraid. I have never felt so safe and loved before. Wait. It feels familiar though. How is this possible?

How come I never got to be kissed like that before? It's unbelievably sad, that I lived so long without this. I am surrounded with sooo much love. It's overwhelming. Ironically, I am bathing in it. Literally.

I want to stay here. Forever.

chapter / THREE

"You have to let the clutch slowly go back up, and at the same time, *slowly* press on the acceleration. Try to relax. Don't overthink it." Jan was giving me patiently instructions on how to start the engine. My *biggest* problem since I had decided to drive again. More like relearning it all together.

A few years back, before I had moved to Germany, I had already gotten my driving license, due to my job. I was working for a big Pharma chain, designing pharmacies around the country, and I was traveling a lot, so the firm had decided to give me a car. I thought it was cool, so I had managed somehow between work and school to slip in some driving lessons. Miraculously, it worked beautifully, and I got the license in three months time.

Just as I was happy to have this behind me, the last day with my Ex before him heading back to Germany after a short vacation at home, we went to the movies. He had insisted I drive, to get used to it, but that day I'd felt that it wasn't a good idea. And normally my inner voice would always have primacy, but I ignored it. Only to regret it later...

As I was driving, completely nervous and stressed out, my Ex had decided to give me driving tips. "You are too close to the side walk! Stay more in the middle." That was just the opposite of what my driving instructor taught me. And having someone almost yell at me, was not my idea of 'getting used to it.'

"But this is not how I learned it," I said, completely frustrated.

"Look, I am driving for many years now, what the instructor says and what happens in real life, is another story. I *said*, stay in the middle!" This time he definitely yelled, and I lost even the little concentration I had before.

"Let me be! Or I will do something stupid."

He chose to ignore my protests. "You will do that anyways, if you don't do what I say."

My vision was already blurred with anger, when I had realized that I was now behind a bus, which stopped—at a bus station—in front of me. With little space between us, I'd had to swerve left to continue on my path avoiding collision. It almost had worked. Instead, I had brushed the right side of the car against the bus. I was petrified with shock and the scream that came from next to me, was just a background noise. "*Nooooo*! I told you! You didn't want to listen! Pull over."

I stopped the engine, got out of the car, the bus driver, too. We checked the bus first. Barely a scratch. Nothing really noticeable. Our car, a different story. Well, not exactly bad…but still a visible dent in the front door, and of course the paint was peeled in some places. Overall, nothing really dramatic. But the mental trauma of the whole incident, had kept me away from driving for years after that.

Until a month ago, I had never thought I would give driving another try, even if Jan was always very supportive of that. Something always pulled me back.

What I had learned in this short time—since I'd made this big change in my diet—was to never underestimate the power of a green smoothie. Literally.

This magical drink pulled me out of the dead zone. I was a shadow after I *came back* the second time. A walking corpse. Lethargic, empty of life inside, and paralyzed by fears. But now, thanks to this awesome *discovery*, I could finally see a light at the end of my tunnel. It brought me back to a place where I could dream again, where I could hope, and see possibilities. It even made me curious about driving again. But mostly, it brought back joy in my hazel brown eyes, which made Jan so happy.

"Okay. Now try again. You have good instincts. You just need to get over your fears. It's only us here, no real traffic, no pressure." I honestly thought his encouragement was really sweet and gentle. It's what I actually needed to overcome my internal blockages. And time.

For this *new* endeavor, we had decided that Sundays were the best, to come here to this driving polygon close to our home. It felt more relaxed, plus the nature that surrounded the place, made me think I wasn't in the city anymore. All in all, it was a win-win situation.

"You're right. I need to relax. How do I do that?" I said, turned to Jan with more of pained grin than a smile, my hands still tight on the steering wheel. Why was I so tight?

He chuckled. "Okay. You *do* need a break."

"Thank you for pointing the obvious…"

"But seriously, just find a comfortable position in your seat. Relax. Okay, from the top."

I can do this. I sat as comfortable as I could, then, followed the instructions slowly, one by one. Like in a trance, no thinking involved. To my relief, the car came to life. "Yes! Finally…" I exhaled.

"See? That was easy. Now watch out for that car on the right. Turn left here," Jan pointed in the direction of a less used route. That was clever. I needed space to loosen my fears. If Jan was really good at something, it was that he knew how to give me or create a space to heal my wounds. His gentle way was like a very powerful salve over my bruised soul. It worked miracles. I should tell him that more often…

Almost two hours into my training, and I could sense that my concentration weakened. For me, this was a sign of 'enough for today.' It meant I was tired, and more driving wouldn't improve anything. "At the next intersection, I will head back to the exit. I'm done for the day.
Plus, I'm getting hungry. You hungry too?"

"You know me. I can eat whenever… Speaking of which, how about tonight, you and me, at Leaf?" He looked at me brows arched in expectancy.

"Did you make a reservation already?"

He shrugged. "I might have… So, yes or no?"

"Sounds good. That means we can't eat too much now. I'm in."

"Good. Pull over there. Let me pay this stuff and we're out of here." Jan opened the door ready to step out of the car, when he stopped and turned to face me. With no warning, he kissed me, making me forget about food and…pretty much anything else.

"What was that for?" Was all I could manage, when he pulled back from the kiss.

He gazed into my eyes smiling. "Nothing, I'm just proud of you."

"Proud of what?" I didn't understand what he was trying to say. Sometimes he had this way of saying and doing things, totally surprising. Not that I was complaining.

"You're so cute when you're clueless."

"What's that suppose to mean?" I was even more confused now.

"All of the above. Be right back." And then he jumped out, heading at a quick pace toward the small tickets building, leaving me with a puzzled face.

"I didn't think it would be that full Sunday evening. Clearly, the business is doing well." I nodded observantly. I liked it here. It felt safe, like in a cocoon.

Leaf was a small cozy place in Altona. We had discovered this vegan restaurant a little over a year ago, just as I was at the beginning of my vegan path—at least the diet part. Since then, we had been coming here pretty regularly. Weekends mainly. The ambiance helped too. A bunch of different pieces and styles of furniture, which went together really nice, formed a very pleasant and relaxing eclectic mix. But that wasn't the only good thing about this place. The food too. Which changed monthly and encompassed recipes from around the world. Not to mention the cool music and the friendly staff.

As I was going through the menu, fighting to decide which goodies to taste first, Jan interrupted my culinary fantasies. "I thought I would wait until dessert to tell you this, but I'm too excited to hold it any longer."

I looked up from my very yummy reading, brows raised in confusion. "Please tell me it's not something bad. Sometimes *exciting* for you, can have a different meaning than for other people. Can't this weekend have a happy ending?!"

He laughed. "That's the thing. It does."

27

Now I was curious.

"Remember Friday?"

How could I forget? This week was a marathon of all things Area 51. Not to mention the apparition and the dream, that has shaken my mental and emotional pillars. "Remember what about Friday? I mean there was a lot going on. "

"The part where I surprise you?!"

I leaned back into my chair, arm crossed. "I thought this is the surprise. The dinner, tonight…"

"Yeah, but that's like an intro. You said you need a break. So I got us a break." He pulled out from the inside pocket of his jacket two tickets. Plane tickets.

"Okay… I'm surprised." My eyes considerably wider now. "Where is the surprise taking us?" I was all ears now.

"Paris," Jan answered. "I thought, what better thing to do than have a pre honeymoon. Right?! Why wait until I finish my PhD? The word I'm looking for is, *spontaneous*. And please no excuses why we shouldn't do it. Plus, the tickets aren't refundable. We're leaving in a week from now. So you have to clear your work appointments, 'cause starting next Monday, we're out here…"

I was speechless. A million things would fly through my head, ranging from why this was coming at the worst time possible, just as my project was taking off and the fact that the client was…*difficult*, to why I *should* grab the opportunity to wash away the last few months if not years, of struggling basically for nothing. My responsible side would normally pull me back to my senses. But the thing was, the little voice inside me that *screamed* all this time for a change, didn't want to play nice anymore. It got stronger. It demanded my attention.

To heck with the consequences… I want my break.

I didn't realize that I went to my overthinking position. With both hands covering my face, breathing heavily, until Jan spoke again. "Are you, okay? Please tell me you like my surprise?!" He pulled slowly my hands away, then removed a dark rebel curl from my eyes. "It's just five nights, I'm sure everyone will understand. I mean, if the *iron lady* was okay with me taking a week off on such short notice…"

"Wait. You already spoke with her? When did you have time to—"

"*Surprise* remember? I emailed her yesterday morning while you were still sleeping. Luckily she didn't. But that's not really surprising, she runs on klingonian batteries." Jan smiled. "She answered lightning fast. Of course I didn't tell her that I want to take my fiancée to Paris right in the middle of a big experiment. But I thought since maybe this is the last chance until Christmas for some free quality time together, I fed her the family stuff excuse. So the road is clear."

"I guess I have no choice, but to do the complete opposite of what I would do normally," I said, already relaxing at the prospect of a short getaway. Away from the grey and the heavy.

"Thank you. So we're going."

My eyes glowed with joy. "Yes!" And I felt my face lighten up into a smile.

I guess a week away from here and my daily routine wouldn't be such a bad thing after all. Even if I had to explain to one probably-not-so-happy client, that we would have to interrupt our new agreement of weekly meetings right in its infancy. The project would still be here when I would return. And the crappy weather. Why not live a little?

Three courses later and one appetizing dessert placed in front of me, I was one happy stuffed duck. But I didn't care. The good thing about eating vegan and mostly raw, was that I could eat to my heart's content, and only good things would happen to my body. From losing weight by eating—which was never really a problem—to clearer skin, sharper eyesight, gone asthma, lung capacity improved, not to mention a ton of energy.

The evening was a surprise in itself. A very pleasant one. Jan had delivered as he promised. But I couldn't help of thinking of the dream I had two days ago. So much love. I felt so loved. So *magical.* I'd never experienced anything like that ever. Not even with Jan. And that started to make me uncomfortable. *What the heck is the meaning of this?*

How was it possible for a dream and an apparition to change so much in me? It's like somebody opened a door into another realm and forgot to close it back, and I was standing in the doorway wanting to cross over but not knowing how or why. Weird.

Thank God, for awesome food to numb my mental chatter. "This is *soooo* good. Want to try mine?"

29

chapter / FOUR

Like the previous time I was here—at the construction firm I was working with on the project—the people seemed nice and very prompt. I didn't have to wait too much in the lobby. "Would you like something to drink?" the young assistant asked very politely as she accompanied me into the conference room.

"Some water. Still water, if you have?" I wasn't really thirsty, but drinking water was one of my good habits.

"Yes, of course." She left, then I randomly chose a chair, sat down, and placed my large bag on the table. I opened it and dug in for my folder. I brought with me as much papers as I could carry. Being prepared was one of my many traits that made *some* to love me and others to hate me. Maybe not hate, but definitely somewhere in the area of envy mixed with pure contempt. A nasty cocktail that I had endured to many times before. But now that I was my own boss again, I didn't care about that anymore. I answered only to myself and of course to my client.

"Here's your water. They will be right with you in a few minutes. Do you need anything else?" the assistant asked.

"Water is perfect. Thank you," I said, taking the glass she put in front of me, then took a sip. For some reason I felt nervous. I didn't understand why, given the fact that I already had a meeting with someone from their team. He sent me an estimate to my proposal, and that made Mr. Tellman very happy and willing to go through with the whole thing.

But tell that to my brain...

"Miss Ducas, nice to meet you!" a voice said, and I turned my face from the glass wall that was letting in a warm sunlight making the conference room a friendlier place.

Surprisingly, the voice was not who I expected. The tall red haired woman in front of me was maybe ten years older than me, and exuded a cheerful vibe which I liked instantaneously. I shook her hand. "Likewise. I'm sorry but I don't know your name. I was expecting..."

"You were expecting Armin," she spoke over me. "Unfortunately Armin had to take care of another project, and I was briefed shortly yesterday in the afternoon. I have to excuse myself for not being able to send you feedback sooner. I was in meetings all day these past two days..." She looked slightly embarrassed, which was a clear indication that she was telling the truth.

"It's alright. I myself know, sometimes things get really hectic and it's hard to prioritize," I said, and she nodded in agreement.

"How rude of me. My name is Martina Weber. Please, call me Martina. This is Cristina and Ben. My team." She pointed across the table to a woman with dark hair held in a ponytail and a medium height chubby man, who were smiling friendly at me. Both of them carrying a notebook and something to write.

I extended my arm across the table, and shook their hands too. "Nice to meet you both. I'm Ariana Ducas. In case the short briefing wasn't covering my name," I said, and they all laughed at my irony, and then we all sat down.

"I am the newest addition to the firm," Martina began. "Right now I'm still in the process of learning the ins and outs of it. I've started a month ago, and since then it's been quite an adjustment ride. But I'm really thankful to Cristina and Ben. They made my life easier here." The way she spoke made me realize she was under a lot of stress. I knew too well this state of things. Not fun at all. But the good thing was, she at least had the support of her team. Unlike me, back when I was working for other people.

Martina continued. "Last week I was assigned an ongoing project and since then, it's just one sitting after the other, meeting the clients, introducing myself to our

31

suppliers and all that comes with taking over a new project. Not a single dull moment. And yesterday…well, that happened very spontaneously. Armin took over a new client. So here I am. I hope you aren't very disappointed with us…"

I was glad to see that my new business partner was displaying *human* qualities. This was a rare thing around here. Plus she was a woman. A rare trait, in this field and in this country where women were still being paid less than men. I guess now, after living a few years here, I understood better the exacerbated forms of feminism that were being enforced. We had men and Catholic Church to thank for that…

"Actually, I'm happy. It's the first time in a long time when—"

I was now frozen in place and staring at a man who pierced through the wall behind Martina's chair.

What the… Pleaseeeeee not now…

Weird was back. It couldn't have picked a better moment than popping up in the middle of a business meeting. I was to optimistic thinking I could manage a relatively normal life and a career. What a fool.

"Miss Ducas, are you okay?" Martina spoke, breaking the trance.

I made an effort to focus. "Call me Ariana. Sorry, didn't sleep well last night. Just tired…"

"Can I get you something? An aspirin, perhaps?" She looked concerned at me.

It was hard to ignore the tall man in the black suit who was approaching, his eyes fixed on me. I wanted to run. But I couldn't. I was in a meeting, God damn it. What kind of professional would I be, if I were to rush out with no believable explanation to these people?

"Maybe some tea. Herbal tea always helps." I finally composed myself. "If it's not too much trouble," I said, rubbing my temples.

Cristina was already standing up ready to comply. "No problem, it'll be a minute," and she started at the door.

"If you don't feel well, we could reschedule the meeting," Martina suggested.

I shook my head. "I'll be fine, in a few minutes," I lied, trying to smile as the man in black—ironic or not—was standing beside me. And then the dreaded happened.

"You can see me, right? And hear me," the man spoke to me, obviously ignoring concepts like walking through doors or being visible to everyone, or the fact that I was in a meeting for Christ sake…and talking to *no one* wouldn't make such a good first impression.

"Tomorrow I have a meeting with Mr. Tellman. Friday he's out of town, and I'll be gone the entire next week. So, rescheduling it's not an option." I tried to seem calm even though the man was still hovering over me.

Cristina came back holding a big white cup, completely oblivious to the fact that there was somebody else in the room, other than the three of us. *Lucky her.*

She placed the cup of tea in front of me. "We only have a sage-mint combination. I hope it's okay."

"So where are you going Ariana?" the man asked, with no consideration whatsoever to the context. I think if I were less afraid and less stressed out, I would do…*something.* Instead, I continued with my 'ignore-and-it-will-go-away' strategy.

"Absolutely, fine. Thank you." Although, I didn't believe that my tea was *that* magical, to make certain things disappear. "We could go over the papers that I brought with me and see where we go from there."

"You are stubborn, as they said," the man insisted, then leaned down to whisper in my ear. "No worries, I will find you wherever you are." Suddenly, I felt the blood drain from my face and cold sweat coming through my pores. My breath was slow and heavy. It was like the air got sucked out of my lungs, leaving my chest constricted with fear. "It's going to be fun working with you. See you around." And he was gone. All of it. The challenging voice, the suit, the man that I couldn't really look in the eyes. No noise, no warning. As if it never happened.

"Are you sure you can do this?" Martina's preoccupied voice made me come back from the dark and cold place where I was locked a moment ago. Realizing, that my hands tightened around the folder that I dug out of my bag. When did I do that?

"Sure." But I wasn't sure, so I masked my shakiness taking a few gulps from my hot tea. Surprisingly, the tea did help. It brought warmth into my body, and slowly I recovered all my other senses. Funny how a small thing like that, could bring so much comfort. A powerful antidote, to shake away gloomy experiences.

"Mr. Tellman has finally decided upon a certain design version. The estimate from

Armin helped a lot. So thank you. Especially to Armin," I underlined, consciously trying to put behind, what just happened only a few moments ago.

"This sounds nice. I had a look at it myself this morning. And I will definitely tell him that," Martina replied very cheerfully. Her good mood was starting to melt the murky vibe around me.

I began to unfold the larger drawings. "I was wondering if you guys deal with the permits too? That would make things a lot smoother."

She nodded. "Sure. That's why I'm here. This is more my department. My area. Although I oversee other things too." And I was thrilled to hear that. It would save me a big chunk of time. Dealing with authorities, was the *least* of my favorite activities to do.

Forty-five minutes later, we were all dissecting floor plans, the most cost-effective— of course, durable—structure, and slowly, moving into the exterior materials and fin-ishes, that would best represent the design. I had to admit. It was fun working with them. My new partner team, was an unexpected gift.

I worked in the past, with a lot of people that put ego above everything else. And it made all too hard and unpleasant to deal with. Tiring and exhausting. Life sucking.

The idea of meeting with these people on a regular basis—except for next week— was actually, something to look forward to. Who would've guessed?

I always found airports to be somewhat cold and impersonal. Especially, if you had to wait a lot. Sure, there were many cafes and restaurants to pass time, where you could sit and enjoy something to drink or grab a bite. But actual sitting and waiting in a relaxed manner, it was another story, entirely. Probably because I knew the problem from the inside, I was so critical. In the end, it was all reduced to how much money they—the airport—could make off of you. Whether you would fly somewhere or waited for someone to arrive, it was all about consuming.

"Are you sure it's the 19:40 flight?" Jan asked a bit confused.

"That's what she texted me before taking off." I pulled my phone from the right

34

pocket of my jacket, and flipped through the messages. "There! See? 19:40 from Basel. But you can go check again. I'll stay here." I needed to sit down, and luckily there were a few free seats right outside the baggage claim. Perfect to spot the one I was waiting for. My cousin Laura.

"Okay. Do you want me to get you anything? We still have an hour left," Jan suggested.

"No, I'll be fine. Maybe, later," I said, and Jan started toward the big screen placed on the right side of the baggage claim exit.

My cousin was coming over to attend a three day seminar. Something about self development, overcoming past issues, dissolving traumatic events and other stuff. This sounded pretty interesting. She'd asked me if I would like to join her. When she had, I was very much inclined to do so, given the fact, that at the time, I was coming out of my last job completely demoralized. Actually...more like deeply depressed, with no prospect of *ever* see the light again.

Yeah, my last job working for an older—and old school— architect was like a train wreck. One that couldn't be anticipated. But with life altering consequences.

It was short-li-ved, only a month. I had never imagined, to what length someone would go to, just for money. Now I could. Once more, I was confirmed that being older, didn't necessary mean that the person was wiser, better, nicer, or *trustworthy*. Nope. On the contrary. More like, the person—the asshole—was a very experienced perverse mind that spent a lifetime accumulating skills in the art of bullshit.

The guy needed someone like me, highly skilled in the area of design, presentations, and three dimensional representations that he could use to land a big—and by big, I mean retire young big—project.

He had the connections and I had the skills. A match made in heaven. Or...hell. I had honestly believed, that this was the job where I would finally establish myself as an architect. But wanting this new job to work, *so badly*, I hadn't smelled the trap. *Use me for getting the project. Get rid of me afterwards, and then hire cheaper people to work on the details.*

After all, he had warn me in the beginning. He'd said his record working with women, wasn't a *happy* one. I had wondered why, back when he'd interviewed me for the job.

35

Now I understood why. Unfortunately, too late for me. I was out of my old job, and out of this new one. Then I spent three months fighting to get the money he owed me.

This was the last drop that sent me into the deepest darkness. All the way to the bottom. I thought I would never recover.

"Okay. I have two things to tell you. Please don't scream at me." Jan was back looking pained.

"What now?" I asked calmly, like in a trance, expecting all sorts of crazy things.

"I forgot the key in the car…"

"You did what?!" Obviously, I wasn't expecting *that*. "Seriously, sometimes I think…"

"But the good news is, the plane is delayed for at least twenty minutes. If I go home now and take the spare key, I'll be back before your cousin arrives."

I had no power to argue with him, for losing or forgetting stuff for the *millionth* time. The plan he had, sounded logical and doable. "Fine…go." He turned, ready to leave and catch the S-train. I grabbed his left arm and stopped him. "Hey, do you at least have the apartment keys?"

Jan checked his pockets, found them and then dug it out. "Here. See?! Now, can I go?"

"Just checking. Go, and try to be fast," I said, knowing that telling him won't guarantee he would make it on time. "And make sure you don't lose or forget these ones somewhere else."

"Ha, ha, ha…" His face twisted in a funny grimace, then he left speeding through the crowd.

Yeah, that was Jan. Sometimes I thought it was cute, endearing actually, to see him go all chaotic, for misplacing stuff, or losing them altogether. But I realized, that *sometimes* was actually more of a regular thing. A lifestyle. One that I had to adjust to.

One and a half hour gone by, there was still no sign of my cousin, or Jan. Great. I was already losing patience. I should've bought a magazine, or a cheap book. Now it was too late.

The arrivals screen indicated that the plane already landed. Which only meant one thing. She was waiting for her luggage. I positioned myself strategically, so I couldn't miss her.

Patience.

In my head I was still debating whether today's *happening* was real or not. But the icy fear I felt back in the meeting, was still reverberating through me every time I was attempting to make sense of the whole thing.

Why me? And who were *they*? Who, the hell was behind this? Whatever this was. I wished I had told Jan about today but I stopped myself sensing somehow that this was *waaay* out of his powers to protect me. I mean, if people would go through walls during the day now, to come and find me, there was little he could do. I was basically on my own.

I was screwed.

"Hey, over here!" a familiar voice shouted in my direction. "Ariana, over here!" When I focused better I saw my cousin Laura. She was waving her arm energetically. Ironically, she spotted me first.

I moved as fast as I could, surfing through the people that whether wanted to sit down or stand up. The narrow space between the long seating benches was pretty challenging for so much action.

After I successfully freed myself from the entanglement, I closed the distance between us, in just a few steps. We kissed on the cheeks and hugged tightly. "I'm so happy you're here!" And I meant it.

"Me too," Laura smiled. "There was some turbulence just before we were about to land. And we stayed in the air a few more minutes. I hope you didn't have to wait too long."

"It's okay. Actually your delay was perfect. Jan forgot the key in the car. *Again.*"

"Hey, who forgot what?" Jan's cheery voice sounded from behind me. "I'm back, aren't I? Key and everything." I turned, to see him all sweaty from running. He smiled at my cousin and leaned forward to give her a hug. "Welcome to Hamburg!" he said, and before he could do anything, Laura planted two kisses, one on each cheek. By the way, he was still adjusting to our greeting custom.

Funny, how a small thing like a kiss on the cheek could be misinterpreted here in Germany. I had no idea in the beginning when I was introduced to Jan's family that my gesture was seen as an *exotic* thing. Especially, when I met them for the first time. I could sense the awkwardness around it. And later in other circles. Slowly I became shy of my own upbringing. It made me feel weird for something that had *no* sexual connotation whatsoever.

No matter, I kept being me. And what do you know? Things started to shift. Now, more people around me would perform this ritual. In the meantime, some read, or found out from others, that cheek kissing had other symbolism than romantic or sexual. Like a greeting, or to indicate friendship, to congratulate, to show respect, or to comfort someone.

"Okay, let's get out of here. The car is parked, not very far. I hope you're hungry," I said to my cousin, and Jan took her suitcase. "I know *I* am, and definitely Jan." He chuckled, and nodded at the same time.

"Yeah, something to eat would be great. And a bed to crash. I think I'm more tired than hungry," Laura admitted.

To comfort her, I put an arm over her shoulder and squeezed her a bit. "We have both."

chapter / FIVE

It was always interesting, whenever I took the subway, to observe people. How life affected them daily. What was imprinted deep, in their subconscious? Why would they *still* choose to comply, with a system that was pushing us all into stress, anxiety, and depression?

Lifeless expressions, empty eyes, sunken shoulders…that was pretty much the usual picture. With *few* exceptions. Whenever some noisy kids or teens would hop in and break the monotony, with their loud conversations, and laughter at someone's joke. Or some eager tourists, busy with their maps, trying to figure out where they were.

"Excuse me. Could you help me with something?" I turned and saw an old lady, surprisingly tall. She had a big smile and her energy was up.

"Yes, sure!" I wanted to match that energy.

"I'm trying to get to Rödingsmarkt. Do you know how far is it?"

"At the second stop. I'm heading in the same direction. Actually, I'm going further, but I can let you know when we're there," I answered, trying to be helpful.

"Thank you. You're really kind," she added, and then she looked up at the panel above my head that was displaying the different train routes.

I was already in a good mood, but the energy coming from the old lady gave me an extra boost. Interesting. Usually it would be the other way around. *Other* people would feel energized around me.

Twenty minutes ago, I left Mr. Tellman's office. A decent space, on the eleventh floor in Astra Tower, very close to the riverside. For an insurance company, the design inside was pretty clean and light. Of course not overly optimistic, but enough to spread a pleasant vibe.

Mr. Tellman had surprised me again. He reacted unexpectedly well, when I gave him the news that I too, will be out of town for a week. No questions asked. I guess, the fact that I brought so much feedback from the meeting yesterday, made him trust me even more. I saw it in his eyes. He allowed me a glimpse inside him for the first time since I took this job.

It was nice to be appreciated and… *trusted*.

"I think, I'll stop here. But thank you anyway," the old lady said out of the blue, right when the train stopped. A station before Rödingsmarkt.

"Okay…" Weird. "But this is not—" She disappeared before I could finish. Literally. I blinked once and she was gone. I looked out the window to see if I spot her on the platform. Nothing. Vanished.

Wow!

Talk about *weird* in a row. I should be thankful, that nothing happened while I was with Mr. Tellman. I didn't even want to imagine how that would go. Most probably, not good. But at least this weird today, didn't give me chills, or would produce future nightmares. There was something nice about the old lady, that I couldn't put my finger on it. Besides the cheerful vibe. Something safe.

For a few minutes, my mind drifted, somehow in a positive direction. I was wondering if the old lady was one of the *good* guys, trying to protect me. Or I was just imagining that. But if she did, this raised even more questions.

The train stopped again. Quickly, I realized that I reached my destination, the City Hall. I stepped out, and started toward the exit.

My cousin and I were supposed to meet at Café Mélange, next to the City Hall and directly situated at the Alster. It was one of my favorite places to grab a bite while being in the middle of the shopping area. Which was always very busy.

Today the weather was good, that meant one thing. More shoppers. Plus it was lunch time, and the people that worked here—right in the heart of the city—were pouring out of their offices and into the streets. Ready to take over, all the places to eat available in this perimeter.

Normally, having so many people on the streets, it would be a positive thing. It would make everything more alive. More human, and less artificial. Except, it didn't. It just appeared busy. In part, the consumerism culture was to blame for narrowing the possibilities of how to experience the city. After all, Hamburg was a trade and industry city, not to mention an important financial center.

Due to the fact that the emphasis was *always* on buying, acquiring, whether you'd need it or not, Hamburg couldn't be labeled as bohemian. For that kind of vibe, you'd have to look for hidden places scattered throughout the city. And let's face it; the weather wasn't much of a help either.

My phone started buzzing. I opened my bag and pulled it out. It was a message from Laura. She was running late. It didn't matter; I was already in front of the Café.

Surprisingly for this time of the day, I spotted a few free tables outside, and headed toward one close to the water front. I sat down, exhaling relieved that the most *difficult* part of the day was over. Mr. Tellman was satistified by my performance in such a short time. Finally, I could start to fantasize about my upcoming vacation.

Before I even had the chance to browse through the menu, still lost in thought, a very tall man, popped next to my table. By what he was wearing—a white shirt and a black apron around his waist—and holding a small note pad and pen, I realized that was the waiter. "Can I get you anything?" His voice sounded familiar.

I looked up, but the face wasn't anybody I knew. Anyhow, his appearance was very laid back. Though, his uncombed sandy gray hair was contributing to that, there was something unusual about him. His intense green eyes made him stand out. Like I couldn't place him in any visual typology.

Realizing that I was staring, I tried to refocus on his question. "Uh…I'm waiting for someone to join me. I would like to order then."

"Okay. Something to drink maybe?" He now stared back into my eyes; like he was daring me to come up with an answer on what was so unusual about him. "Water?"

How did he…*do* that? That's what I was going to say. "Yes. Still please, with

Hmm…it wasn't *really* common to be asked if I would like lemon juice.

Too much had happened lately. And I was starting to think that I was reading too much into it. Into anything, actually. But how could I not? People appearing out of nowhere, and from where you'd least expect, breaking all barriers of mainstream science. Not that I had a problem with that. At least with breaking the barriers part.

Science…that thing that most people would accept it blindly, was no more valid and full of *absolute* truth, than any mainstream newspaper or TV station, that were paid loads of money to spread disinformation, fabricated facts, and turn the tables always in favor of those few unseen in the background. The *master puppeteers* of this screwed up version of a world.

Since I moved to Germany I didn't even have a TV anymore. At first, what really threw me off, was the fact that everything was in German. All movies were dubbed. I tried, as many locals advised me to watch TV and especially the movies in German, to learn faster the language. But the experiment didn't last too long. I couldn't stand to hear inept voices and badly translated jokes. I mean, come on… How could you really appreciate an actor, or the quality of his or her performance, if you would muffle it with questionable, and in many cases ridiculous voices? To ask yourself that, you'd have to know the *difference*. But for that, you'd have to have the choice first.

Ironic how that works…

Coming from a country where everything would run in original with subtitles, whether it would be a Japanese movie, or a Spanish one, an Indian or a Swedish film. I would have the possibility to hear the real voices of the actors. I would get to enjoy *their* acting, and as bonus, I would familiarize myself with all those different languages.

Funny, if not tragic, that *I* was the weird one here, for wanting something normal. Apparently, normal just to me. And to a few others.

"Hey! Sorry to be late," Laura said, marching toward me. In another few steps she reached my table and was now pulling out the chair across from me preparing to sit down.

"I got here only a few minutes ago. I thought you'd need more time?"

"I thought so, too. My train had to wait for another one…I heard something about repairing some stuff. But luckily, it went fast. Plus, I wasn't sure how easy was to find this place," she added.

"And how was it?"

"Which one?" She smiled. "The seminar or finding the Café?"

"Both."

"You said this place is left from the City Hall. I saw the sign from a hundred meter or so... So it was pretty easy. And the seminar...really good. I cried a lot."

My brows rose. "Meaning?"

Laura dropped the bag on the chair next to her, then unbuttoned her trench coat. "Can you believe it's so hot today?"

I sniggered. "Yeah, it's probably HAARP... They're getting ready for the national day. Let's give the obedient slaves—a.k.a. citizens— some sun..."

My cousin seemed confused. "What do you mean?"

I forgot she was not really in the loop with the big picture. "It's a weather modification tool...among other things. Military program stuff... Let's just say, we could talk for hours about the subject." And frankly, I didn't have the energy to go into this. "Forget it. So, you were saying there was a lot of crying today?!"

Unconvinced by my explanation of 'what-the-hell-was-wrong-with-the weather-patterns-lately,' Laura continued. "This guy is brilliant." She meant her seminar teacher. "You know, when we were children? It's the first time in years, when I feel so light and free. He's basically teaching you how to break free from the past using a family tree healing method."

I was all ears. It sounded like some other methods that I'd tried in the past. "Go on..."

"You go down the family tree and see who had issues with whom, and then you say 'I forgive you,' 'I release this and that,' and other stuff. It's sounds cheesy but—"

The very tall waiter was back, interrupting our conversation. "Here's your drink," he said, placing the glass, the bottle and a small cup with the lemon juice in front of me. "I wasn't sure if you wanted it mixed or not." He then pointed to the juice cup. "Here is juice from two lemons."

"Thank you. No problem." I looked up and smiled. "I will do it myself."

"Anything else?" he insisted. And every time he was speaking to me, it was as though he was trying to connect with me. It wasn't flirting. It was something else. His voice inflection was sending a recognition signal. I had *no* idea what I was supposed to get.

"What do you have?" Laura asked me. "I'm having what you're having."

"Um…I haven't decided, yet. I just got here only a few minute before you, remember?!" I wasn't really hungry but chewing some food was better than chewing crazy thoughts. "But,I can recommend you some nice Mozzarella Panini," I told her, knowing it was a great dish—especially, for those who still ate cheese—, then I turned to the waiter. "I will have the tomato soup without the cream, and the vegetarian pizza without the cheese. Maybe you could add, more garlic?" I said to the waiter, already excited, just by thought of garlic.

"Sure," he replied, smiling back.

"And a Pizza Margherita for me!" my cousin added, from behind the menu. "And another glass, please. We'll share the water."

"Good. Great weather today!" the waiter remarked.

"Yeah." We both said at the same time, me and my cousin. But probably, both having different opinions on how this weather was possible.

The waiter left, and I wanted to know more about her workshop. "So, you were saying…"

"Right." She ran her fingers through her hair. "The technique is very easy, but you need a partner who asks the questions. Basically I had to pair up with a woman, Linda, and we asked each other the questions. I *never* imagined how much crap I've accumulated from my parents, especially from my mother. But then I discovered that she *herself* was carrying crap from her mother, and it goes on and on… With every releasing and forgiving, I teared up so badly… Rivers pouring out of me. It was crazy."

"I'm sure, nobody was judging."

"No. That was the whole point of this exercise. To get it all out. To free yourself, from these mental and behavioral patterns." She sounded so excited and yet so centered.

Laura and her husband Patrick, were interested in opening their own family business. A personal development practice. He was a psychiatrist, open to explore *new* avenues—less by the book—and my cousin was a nurse, who had wider interests than her job.

"I'm happy for you. I should've registered, too. But now it's too late," I admitted.

"No worries." She rummaged through her bag, then pulled out a business card and handed it to me. "Here, you have the e-mail and the website of this guy. The phone, too. He will repeat this module in two months. In case you're interested."

"Thanks." I took it and read it. I couldn't help to notice the happy logo. "I will consider it." And I *really* was considering it. But what had always stopped me from doing this or any other classes of this sort, was my reluctance to share with others the *peculiar* part of my life.

I wasn't ignorant to dismiss these kinds of tools. On the contrary, I was a big supporter. I mean, even these classes and workshops were still very much alternative by most people. But *my* stuff, was *way, way* far out for both categories.

These kinds of classes were operating in the area of the subconscious, helping you live a more free and meaningful life. But what I was going through, wouldn't qualify for it. People walking through walls, psi attacks at night, apparitions and other yet uncategorized facts, weren't exactly things easy to fix with a bunch of questions.

I wish it were.

Our waiter was very prompt ,even if he seemed a little too laid back for this job. But then again, who was I to judge.

The food was delicious. We totally stuffed ourselves, but we didn't care. Laura even ordered some ice-cream for dessert, and I decided to try their fruit salad. Both of us were pleased how the day unfolded so far. I was *finally* free and ready to go on vacation, and Laura was feeling like she had a major breakthrough.

"Let's go buy some shoes!" Laura suggested very enthusiastically, as I was getting the money out of my wallet to pay the bill. I chuckled and shook my head.

"What? What's funny?" she asked.

"Nothing. I wondered how long you'll last. Here, shopping is like a national sport," I added, somewhat sarcastic.

"So, what?" My cousin seemed undisturbed. "I don't shop as much as I should. Besides, I'm looking for some winter boots. I spotted a few shops down the street. In Basel I see a lot of boring stuff, and I thought while I'm here, maybe I have better luck."

"Sure. No problem." I didn't want to ruin a perfectly good afternoon debating other people's addictions. "Just let me pay this and we're out of here." I spotted the waiter, and waved my hand at him. In a few strides he was by our side. I put the money in the bill holder, handed it to him, then stood. "Thank you. The food was great!" I said.

"Yeah. Really, loved it!" Laura added.

"Glad to hear it. Thank you, too!" he replied smiling, obviously surprised by the nice tip.

My cousin and I started toward the exit, when I heard his voice behind us. "Have a safe trip!" he shouted.

I swirled my head in his direction. "Thanks!" And then I turned back and continued walking, slowly realizing that I hadn't told this man anything about my upcoming vacation. And whatever conversations Laura and I had at the table, that he might've overheard it, didn't even touch the subject.

Hmmm... Very strange.

We walked into the first shoes store that crossed our path, my cousin already spotting a few models of boots to her liking. After a few more scanning she grabbed one. "Nice! I think I'll try this one."

"Do they have your size?" I asked.

She checked a few boxes from the model she chose. "Yes. Hold this for me. Better yet, put it back. I found my size!" she said, full of exhilaration.

I took the boot and placed it on the shelf where she originally spotted it. Then, *I* saw something that I liked. *Really* liked, in fact.

I snorted. *How ironic...*

They should put a sign outside that said: "going inside, my cause serious damage to your bank account." At least this way you would be warned, and you'd stay the hell away from it. As I would normally do.

I didn't want to shop, yet, there it was. A very cool short flat boot. Just, perfect. For *me*. Like it was expecting me, all along. And had the right price too. Crap!

I could summon my will power to ignore the rush. I did it many times before, not allowing myself to fall prey to impulsive shopping. So I turned to my cousin to see what she was doing.

Laura had the new boot on and she was checking herself in the mirror. "What do you think?" she asked me.

"I think it looks good on you. What do you think?"

"Yeah. My gut feeling tells me to buy it. But then, there are still a lot of shops to march through. Unless, you're tired?" She grinned at me.

I didn't want to spoil her fun. "We can go and see other shops, if you like? But if your gut feeling it's telling you to buy it, why don't you? Is the price okay?"

"That's the thing. It is," she replied, still looking at herself in the mirror. "I like the design, and the price too."

"So what's stopping you?" I tried to make it easier for her…and me. "*I* like it on you. You like it on you. The price is right. What else is missing? We could go into other stores and not be happy with what we see, and then we would have to come back here."

"You hate shopping that much?" She giggled.

"You got me! But, seriously now. Where's the problem?"

"There isn't any. I just feel like exploring a little bit more. But you do have a point," Laura admitted. "I'll take them!"

"I don't want to force you, or anything. We can explore more. I have no problem." Even, if I hated when there were *so* many people around, especially in small spaces. She was family, and I wanted to make her stay a happy one. We saw each other sporadically as it was.

"I believe you. But I've decided. I'll buy them." She seemed happy. "Did you find anything you like?"

"Please, don't ask me that. *You* wanted to shop, not me," I insisted.

"If you like something, tell me. I'll buy it for you. A gift from me. Oh! We could get something for Jan also." Her eyes started to glow.

"You don't have to… And as Jan goes, I just bought him a pair of shoes last week."

"Yes, but this is a present from me to you both. It's enough that I see you every half a century. Let me do something nice for you, for a change," Laura pleaded. "Please?!"

47

I didn't want to argue with her. "Fine. But you really don't have to."

"So, show me which one you liked!" Clearly, there was no changing her mind about the whole gift thing.

Twenty minutes later, we were standing outside on the street, each holding a bag of shopping. Hers with her boots, mine, with *my* unexpected perfect boots, and a pair for Jan.

"What do you want to do next?" I asked her.

"Get something for Patrick?!"

"Of course. What do you have in mind?"

"A suit. We have a wedding coming up. And I thought I could buy him something nice to wear to the wedding," Laura explained, and then she pointed at a fancy clothing store across the street. "Let's go there, and have a look."

And all I could do was nod my head in agreement. "Let's!"

We were standing at the traffic light waiting for it to go green, when my phone began buzzing. I pulled it out of my pocket. It was Martina. "Hello?"

"Hey, Ariana. Martina here. Do you have a minute? It's quite *important.*" The way she emphasized important made me go into fighter flight mode. I was a problem solver, and whenever the word *important* or *deadline* entered the conversation, my adrenaline would kick in.

Please, be nothing really major. I want my vacation...

The light went green, and my cousin was preparing to cross the street. I used my free hand and tapped her on her shoulder, then whispered. "Go ahead. I'll be with you in a minute. I really have to take this. It's work." Laura nodded, and left heading toward the clothing store, as I remained on this side of the street.

"Sure," I said to Martina. "What's this about? By the way, the meeting with Mr. Tellman went very well. The things we dissected and solved yesterday, made him very happy."

"Oh, good. Sorry to bother you, but we have a tiny problem," she replied. "Could you check your notes from yesterday regarding the cladding part?"

I was already going through my bag. "Just a second."

"We sent a few emails out to different suppliers, and only one had what you wanted.

Well, not quite. But, very close. The question is, would this item have a *B* option, or should we ask further?"

I checked my notes, but nothing there was very restrictive. "You know what? Send me an email with the samples and I'll let you know in a couple of hours. Okay?!"

"Sure. Sorry to be so panicky about this. I'm still new here and trying my best."

I could totally relate to that. "I know. Don't worry, will figure this one out. Okay?!"

"Okay. Thank you. Later then. *Ciaooo!*" Martina ended.

"Ciao."

I dropped the phone into the bag, and then I looked up. It was green again. I took two steps, when an aggressive noise made me jerk my head. A navy blue sedan was roaring to life, and was now on a collision course with…me. It was inescapable. It was too close for me to do anything.

Oh, God! Oh, God!

I was going to die…

In a blink of an eye, the car was next to me, already feeling the impact of the headlight on my right thigh, when two strong hands grabbed each of my arms. After that, everything went in slow motion and didn't seem real anymore. People, buildings, other cars, all disappeared from my awareness.

The car went right through me. Just like that. Like I was air. As if I wasn't corporeal…or really there. A mere observer, watching it with no power to move, or anything else. I felt like in a trance. I had no idea what was going on, or whether I was still alive or not.

Only when the car passed me and disappeared from the view, I could regain full sensation in my body. Becoming solid again. Those strong hands were still there. I looked up, left and right, and saw two men. They were bald and very tall. And dressed kind of strange. But this wasn't the time to think about fashion choices here…

"You should be more careful, when you cross the street next time," the men on the left said to me, in a neutral voice.

I was still in shock and couldn't articulate anything. If there were people on the street that saw what happened, I couldn't see or hear them. My grasp of reality was completely blurred, muted. They sensed that, and escorted me to the other side of the road.

When we got over there, I wanted to thank them. Plus, I had a million questions running through my head. I wanted answers. What the hell happened here? *Who are you people?* And why someone was trying to kill me *deliberately?* In my sleep, or otherwise.

I turned around to face them. They were gone. I was left speechless, again. But eternally grateful for being alive and unharmed.

For what seemed like forever, I just stood there unable to move. My mind agitated, trying to make sense of it all.

"Everything okay with work?" a voice said from behind me. It was Laura.

I didn't know what to say to her. Explaining what took place a few minutes ago—or so I thought, because the sense of time was completely altered now—wasn't exactly in the realm of her experience or understanding. "Yeah…everything is fine." My voice sounding shaky.

"You don't look fine to me." She scanned my face for signs of 'not fine.' "What happened?"

I wish I could hide it better. "Just minor details. I wanted a certain type of material, and they asked around about it a few firms, but only one came close to our needs. Really, nothing major. But in two hours I promised Martina I will give her feedback. She sent me an email—"

"But this doesn't sound bad," Laura agreed.

"I told you."

"But you look *truly* pale. Maybe it's the food?" She was trying to come up with a logical explanation for something that was defying logical. But I couldn't really tell her that.

"Maybe. Yeah…" I mumbled.

"Now that I think about it, I kind of also feel a little bit…off."

In her case, it might be true. All that dairy… "It could be the food. These days you don't know anymore what they put in it." And that was also very true. "Unless you prepare it yourself, using the cleanest ingredients, well… all is possible." That, and non food related facts. Like me, surviving death in the most unusual way.

Laura nodded. "You're right."

"Now let's buy that suit you wanted, and go home. I have an email to read." Actually, more than anything, I wanted to dissect the whole thing with my sister. There were too many *very* tall people involved in my life in less than a few hours. I began to see a pattern there.

chapter / SIX

Saturday was basically free for Jan. But today was one of those exceptions—though lately more of a regular thing—when Jan had to isolate some proteins or something of that nature, which normally could take longer hours during the week. For a lot of PhD students, the weekend became a useful time to prepare in advance for next week's experiments. So instead of going directly to the restaurant as planned, we had to stop first by the lab.

"That over there is the new hospital wing," Jan explained to my cousin, who was actually quite interested in where he spent lots of hours during the week, and apparently weekends.

"The complex is huge!" Laura exclaimed. She wasn't exaggerating.

"I know. Here is a small football court. Mostly people from the hospital play in their spare time. Over here," he pointed to the left, "it's my building."

"Nice. It looks new," Laura noticed. The white building was five-stories high, not really big, but with large windows giving the impression of transparency, and openness. Yet, it really wasn't.

"Relatively. It's maybe ten years old," Jan said.

We stopped in front the gate to the underground garage. Jan rolled down the window and pulled out his access card to open it. A few seconds later the card reader beeped and the gate started to move to the side.

Security was a great deal here. In part, because of the expensive equipment and all sorts of substances and things, but that wasn't the only reason. Research and research results was another, one I would estimate even bigger than the rest.

Apparently in science, things ran like in any other industry. The more valuable your project was, the more you had to protect it from the competition. Secrecy was implicit. A good research meant not only money, but prestige as well. Career were made and unmade this way.

On the third floor—where Jan's lab was— things looked pretty quiet. We passed a few people on the hallways that looked like they would rather be anywhere else but here. I could totally relate to that. Especially when it came to work interfering with the free time. But other than that, I felt somehow at home.

Probably having a mother as a psychologist, and wondering a lot the halls of the clinic where she used to work—she recently had retired—the medical environment had been deeply imprinted in my subconscious. I guess it reminded me of her. Being around her. Being safe.

"I don't believe it!" Tim shouted at us from the kitchen's door holding a half empty casserole and a spoon. "What a nice surprise. What are you doing here on a Saturday evening?" he said, walking toward us, pretending to be scandalized.

I grinned. "You have to thank Jan. He forgot to do some stuff. You know, the usual... So what do *you* do here on a Saturday evening?" I asked, more rhetorical than actually being surprised to find him here. "Don't you have a boyfriend?!"

He gave me a big hug. "Yes. And his coming in—" he looked at his watch. "Forty-five minutes to pick me up. You know, dinner and all that fun stuff."

"Good. I was worried you made him go away." I giggled. "By the way this is my cousin Laura. And we're *too* on our way to dinner. A place in the Portuguese quarter."

He shook her hand firmly. "Nice to meet you. I'm Tim. Friend and colleague. Sharing misery together..."

"Likewise. Not the misery part though," Laura replied. "So forty-five minutes it's too long?" She gestured to his casserole.

For a split second he looked confused. Then a smile widened on his face. "...Oh, this. Yeah. It's just a pre-snack. I still have twenty minutes to kill before I check on my cells. Plus I can eat a cow right now. I'm just warming up."

"Let's go in the kitchen. We have more chairs there," Jan suggested.

We followed him inside. The kitchen was fairly spacious and tidy. It looked similar with the one on the first floor where they used to work. A few months ago they had to move on this floor, due to some administrational issues.

Three out of the four walls had cabinets stocked with all sorts of dishes, glasses, mugs and several kitchen appliances. And of course, a giant coffee machine. In the middle of the room two tables joined together formed a longer one, which could serve at least sixteen people—counting by the numbers of chairs around it.

Except Jan, all three of us took a seat, Tim already munching on his leftovers.

"I have to go to the microscope for a while. You guys are going to be okay here? Unless you want to join me," Jan said, turning his head toward my cousin. "Laura, you still interested?" Jan asked.

"Sure. I get to visit you rarely as it is. You're coming?" Laura looked at me waiting.

"No, go right ahead. I've already had the pleasure of taking the tour. My feet won't move anymore anyway. I have to save some energy for later." We had a busy day again. The small stroll into the city turned into another heavy shopping session. I needed my rest.

"Okay," Laura said smiling, then stood. "See you in few minutes." Then she and Ian left the room.

"Oh, good. Now we can talk. Something's not right with you." Tim searched my face. "So spill."

I almost forgot how perceptive he was. "Yeah…I don't even know where to begin," I said, rubbing my face. "Whatever happens lately is beyond everything I've experienced before. And believe me, I've been through a lot of insane, hard-to-digest crap."

"You don't have to tell me that. You know I believe you. It's me you're talking. Hello?! So what's going on?" Tim was trying to make me comfortable.

"A lot. For starters, I am still in awe, that I'm alive and well after what happened yesterday," I admitted.

"Don't make me ask you again. We're alone." He glanced around. "You can talk."

I wasn't sure where to start. But it didn't matter, he would inhale whatever details I would give him anyway. My stories were to him, what gossip was to people that thrived on that.

Thank God for that. . .

So I decided to tell him first about the meeting I had a few days ago with Martina, and about the man that popped out of the wall scaring the *crap* out of me. Then I went on about all the strange encounters from yesterday, ending with the sci-fi type of rescue that *forever* shattered for me, the laws of physics. At least the ones taught in schools.

Tim didn't seem to be affected by my confessions, he looked rather fascinated in fact. "Did you tell Jan? Or your cousin?"

"Only you and my sister know. I wanted to tell Jan, but I saw him worried about me lately. I simply couldn't find the words. And to be honest, I really don't know how he can help me. I mean, now that the *weird* it's not restricted anymore to night time. Whoever wants to find me and. . .hurt me, they have no trouble doing that during the day." I waved my hands at him in frustration.

"I hear you. But you still have to tell him. What if something happens? You disappear or something. I don't want to even think about that. But let's say something happens. He won't even know where to look for you. No one will, except me and your sister. And involving the police is just plain stupid. It will get us all committed."

I snorted imagining a scenario like that. "Yeah. You're right."

"Of course, I am. But other than that, I think it's really interesting," he added.

"Just interesting?" I looked at him in disbelief. "If you mean that getting almost killed, and then saved by some strangers with alien freakin' type of capabilities. Then, *yeah* it's interesting." I unleashed my sarcasm at him.

Tim took my hands in his, looking straight into my eyes. "I didn't mean it like that. But don't you see a pattern here? All these strange stuff happening to you is like a sequence."

He was right. I saw it too, but I didn't allow myself to believe that it was more than just what it was. That meant that all my personal searches weren't anymore just words in a book, or random experiences that made no sense. It was definitely something real. "Of course I see it. I just pretend not to. This way I still think I can have a semi normal existence."

"But don't you want to know where this all leads? What's the purpose of it?"

"Why do you think I spend all that time reading, researching? It's like my second nature. Of course, I want to know! I want to understand. It's just…I feel alone, and helpless…" I admitted frustrated.

"Hey, look at me," Tim said, holding my chin forcing me to see the worry in his eyes. "I'm here if you need me. I know it's not much what I can do, but at least you can talk to me when you're like this. You don't have to wait until we decide we have time for each other. And you have Jan. Don't exclude him from this. Even if you think he's not really equipped to deal with this sort supernatural *freaky* stuff. The man loves you more than life itself, for Christ's sake."

I hated when he was right. But that didn't comfort me as it should. "What should I do now?" I exhaled, running my fingers through my hair.

"I tell you what you should do." And then he pulled out his phone from the back pocket of his jeans. "We're going to have fun tonight. All five of us." He was already dialing.

"What are you doing?" I asked him, but he brought his index finger to his lips silencing me.

He was calling Andreas—his boyfriend. Very succinctly, he let him know about the change in plans. Judging by the happy face Tim made, he took it pretty well. "It's settled. He's coming in twenty-minutes or so. I'm afraid you're stuck with us, whether you like it or not."

I laughed. "The more the merrier."

"Exactly. Okay, I'll go finish my stuff. You stay here and tell the others about the 'more' part." Tim stood and walked to the sink dropping the empty casserole and the spoon there. "Would you like some music? I don't want you to feel alone in here."

"Sure."

He walked up to one of the two fridges. On it, there was a big stereo system. He turned it on, and then switched through different stations. "You like this?"

It was something happy, but not over the top. "Yeah. Thanks."

"No problem. There's tea if you want something to drink. Or water. I had earlier some orange juice but you came too late." He grinned at me.

"I'm fine. Music it's perfect. Now, go. Watching you eat made me even hungrier."

"Okay, see you in a bit." Then he left.

$$\infty$$

The restaurant ran at full capacity when we arrived. I was really surprised to be able to change the reservation on such short notice. Especially, on a Saturday evening. If that didn't work, we were prepared to go to the place Andreas picked for him and Tim.

Though not really small, the restaurant appeared truly cozy. The fresh paint on the walls suggested the place was recently renovated. The happy orange bringing Mediterranean warmth and the metal decorative objects hanging on the walls next to some commercial paintings—though not kitschy—giving it character. For a regular restaurant in the Portuguese quarter, it was more than okay.

It wasn't just the tourists that were eating here—close to the Elbe—but locals too. In the evening or at any other time during a sunny day, the area would be buzzing with life.

Ironic or not, our restaurant was Spanish. The Portuguese quarter was actually a mixture of Spanish and Portuguese restaurants and shops. Everything here, had to do with fish in one way or another.

We were still at the entrance, when a friendly face welcomed us. "Good evening! Welcome to Casa Rodriguez! Do you have a reservation?" a tiny half bald man asked.

"Sure. Ducas. Table for five. I called earlier to change the reservation?"

He went to check the info with somebody at the bar, then he came back. "Yes. Follow me, please," he invited us gesturing with his hand, and we did.

Three hours later, we were all complaining from having *too* much to eat. And some of us, too much to drink. But our faces said something else. Underneath all that stuffing we did, we were glad that somehow tonight brought us together. Each of us, for different reasons.

"I shouldn't have ordered dessert." My cousin shook her head in complaint. "These past few days I ate like a pig. Now I feel like I have to unbutton my jeans."

I chuckled. "Welcome to the club. Although, I don't worry anymore," I said, looking at the check to see how much we had to pay.

"Yes, because you eat only grass," she added, pretending to be annoyed.

"It's not true." I snorted. "Nuts and seeds, too. And let's not forget the fruits and the veggies."

"Whatever. It's not fair," Laura insisted.

"I tell you what. Let's go home, and I'll get you some water with fresh squeezed lemon juice and I promise, you'll feel much better."

"Sounds good. But what about them?" she asked, tilting her head toward the others.

Across the table, the guys were involved in some political debate. Andreas brought up the subject. It was something that he was writing about. They looked like they could keep it going for a while. I waved my hands at them to get their attention. "Sorry to interrupt the fascinating topic. But, what if we continue this at our place? Unless you're tired. Laura doesn't feel too well, and I can solve her problem much easier there."

"We don't have to leave, right away because of me," Laura insisted. "I'm fine." She tried to move the focus away from her.

Jan jumped in. "Actually, this is a good idea. Why don't we? Tim? Andreas?"

"We don't want to bother you," Andreas tried to be polite.

"Nonsense. It's Saturday night, and obviously none of us wants to go to sleep right away. But some of us *do* want to seat more comfortable. Or wear larger clothes…" I added. "So the fun doesn't have to stop. We just move it to a different location."

"She's right," Jan backed me up.

"Okay. Great," Tim said overly excited, and Andreas nodded in agreement.

"Who's driving?" Jan looked around. "I could, but…I've had more than one glass of wine."

I already knew that all three of them had something to drink. Some more than others. "No. Maybe I should do it. I have to practice either way." I tried to be brave, although I didn't feel quite sure of myself yet.

Laura put a hand over my arm. "Let me do it. You don't have to drive if you don't feel comfortable. You can do it another time."

I didn't want to admit, but I was relieved to hear that. "Fine. Then let's hit the road."

Ten minutes later, we were all standing outside of the restaurant in the crisp air, waiting for Jan to bring the car from where he parked it earlier. The street was full with cars when we arrived, so he parked wherever he could. That was two streets away.

"Now I'm really grateful for that extra sweater you made me bring with me," Laura admitted, her teeth chattering.

"Live here long enough, and you too, will develop a sixth sense when it comes to weather," I said.

"So, you feel better?" Tim turned to me. Obviously, we couldn't continue our little talk we had earlier in the kitchen, once we got to the restaurant. Plus, throughout the evening other topics were the focus of our conversations.

"About?" I teased.

"You know what." He arched his eyebrows.

"What are you guys talking about?" Laura demanded, her eyes pendulating between me and Tim. Andreas was busy with a cigarette, so he didn't pay attention to us.

Before I could answer to any of them, my eyes caught something across the street. A man in a black leather jacket was staring right at me. I didn't recognize the face, so I looked away. Only to realize, that the sly vibe I got from him, was somehow familiar. I now stared back at him and he was smiling satisfied. I acknowledged him.

Oh, crap! It was the same guy from the meeting with Martina. The one I didn't dare to look at his face. Now, avoiding was simply not a choice anymore. So I looked.

The street was well lit, not just by the street lights, but by all the busy restaurants on each side of the street. It made it easy to read his features. He seemed Mediterranean with his short dark hair and very piercing black eyes. He wore black as last time, only different type of clothes. More casual. And if it weren't for that cold cunning look in his eyes, he could almost pass for a normal person.

Something totally unexpected, had me froze in place. As he leaned against the car behind him, arms crossed, he started talking in my head. Then I realized I couldn't move or speak. The freeze was literal.

You know, just because you're protected it doesn't mean I can't get to you.

What the hell was he talking about it? What did he want from me? And what protection? A very abrupt realization, brought back to the front of mind, the car incident. I was protected indeed. But, by whom?

"Is that him?" Tim whispered in my ear. Then I understood, that the man who took over my mind and physical functions was visible to everyone.

Look at you. You have no idea what's going on. His smile widened.

Was he able to read my mind, too?

They say I should give you some time to get used to the idea. But I don't like to see potential go to waste.

There's that they again. What idea should I get used to?

I don't want to hurt you. Not at the moment anyway.

A car approached him and stopped. It was Jan. He got out of the car and waved at us. "Hey, let's go people! Let's move it! Laura, here's the key!" He approached and dangled it in front of her, completely unaware of what was happening.

That must've broken the focus of the guy in black, because I could move again. "What took you so long?" And my voice was back. It felt like an eternity had passed since I last had any control over my body. I didn't know exactly how he did it, but there was a certain resemblance between this situation and the one where I was rescued by those…*beings*. Something that had to do with time alteration. Or how we'd perceive time.

"What's going on?" Tim whispered again in my ear. "Did he do anything to you? Did he hurt you?"

"We'll talk about it later." Then I moved passed him heading for the car keenly not looking at the man in black. "Are you coming?"

The others were already in the car, and Tim insisted I take the front seat. I didn't argue. I just wanted the get the hell away from here as fast as possible. And as far away as possible.

"Everyone here?" my cousin asked, looking up in the rear mirror, ready to start the engine.

All of us answered in unison. "Yes!"

Relief washed over me, when the roaring engine put the car in motion. We advanced maybe a few hundred meters or so, when *he* appeared in front of us not very far—a distance that would be closed in seconds. The man in black just stood there, in the middle of the road. Waiting with daring eyes.

It took me all the energy I had left not to react at his sudden apparition. Clearly, the others didn't see him, or somebody would've said something.

I closed my eyes wanting the whole thing to go away. Then I heard him again in my head.

See you soon...

I opened my eyes. The road was clear.

chapter / SEVEN

Four rows in front of us, the flight attendant let us know that in a few minutes we would land. The flight from Hamburg to Paris was one of the shortest. Approximately thirty minutes. Ridiculous, how the actual flying time was three or maybe four times shorter than the getting on the plane. Which was why in many cases, I preferred the train.

Drinking earlier, a glass of Champagne they served us—and on an empty stomach—made me a little tipsy. I wanted to put behind me the last couple of weeks, and simply enjoy the vacation—or at least the illusion of it. So when the flight attendant came to our side to offer us drinks, Champagne seemed like a good idea. Plus, having alcohol on a Monday afternoon had something rebellious in it.

On the plane, everyone seemed to be in a good mood. It might've had to do with the fact that we were all going to Paris. Whether it was for business, or pleasure.

"This damn air-conditioning!" Jan muttered, and I understood him. "I didn't catch a cold driving my bike to the lab in the rain or cold weather. But now, sitting in this plane for half an hour it might just happen."

Normally, I would be the one complaining about being too cold, or never really having summer since I moved to Germany—at least in the north where we lived. But sometimes a little alcohol worked wonders. Not only was my mind a little slower, but I didn't really feel the cold anymore—thanks to my bubbly drink. "Well, in a few minutes prepare yourself for another weather adjustment," I said.

It was his first time to Paris; and in the fall, as well. So he had no idea, what to really expect. Except for what I told him from my previous trips.

Weather wise, was like in Bucharest. The beginning of October could go as high as thirty-degrees Celsius. Of course, rain could be very much in the picture. But with the weather modifications in the last years, I would expect nothing less but an overall pleasant time, away from worries and...things that defy logic.

After we landed, the moment the exit sliding doors opened, a wave of delicious hot air washed over us. Instantaneously, pulverizing the cold out of every cell in our body. Stiffness and contracted, was replaced by ease and relaxation. "I told you," I said with with a huge grin on my face, and we started toward the bus station.

"I hope it stays like this. At least until Saturday. Then, I don't care. We won't be here anymore anyway," Jan added, enthusiastically.

"I have a feeling, that the weather is the last thing you need to worry." Although I hadn't read the forecast for this week. "But, what we're going to do here. While, we're here."

"What do you mean, what we're going to do here?" He gave me a mischievous smile.

My cheeks flamed. I didn't need to hear the words for what he had in mind. "Besides, *that*." My brows arched.

"You mean, there's more?" Jan pretended to be surprised. "More than being naked with you, and food and wine?"

I snorted. "Yes, as a matter a fact. Some culture, too."

"I thought the whole point of going to Paris was to just enjoy, you know...the *simple* pleasures in life," he replied, and I couldn't help but laugh.

"You have no shame, do you?!" I teased.

Jan tried to keep a straight face but the arched corner of his mouth said something else. "I don't know what you mean."

I chuckled, then shook my head.

Taking the bus from the airport was a good idea. We spent the same amount of time in traffic as we would have by taking a taxi, but for less money and actually got to see more.

Jan was taking in every bit of the city. The streets were bustling with life, with people everywhere going about their lives, hurrying God knows where, or slowing down, enjoying a late lunch, or just a cup of coffee. This way he could see the *real* Paris, not the overly romanticized perspective you would find in about every travel guide book. Chic next to crumbly, breathtaking next to dirt and haste next to perfect laziness. Still, Paris was Paris. Fun. It reminded me of Bucharest.

An hour later we had arrived at the hotel, and were now in our room, unpacking. Luckily for us, the hotel we chose, was very well situated. A five minute walk to Gare de l'Est and to the closest Metro Station, and ten to twenty minutes Metro ride to any important places downtown.

The hotel had been recently renovated, so it looked decent enough, although for a three star establishment, I thought it was a rip-off. Especially, when it came to the size of the room, actually the size of everything. I guess paying attention to details like that, was professional deformation. I was an architect after all.

When you entered the room, more than ninety-percent of the space was occupied by the bed, with two tiny nightstands at each side. Next to it, there was a very narrow wardrobe—with a safe inside—and the door to the *of course* small—but functional— bathroom. Across the bed, adjacent to the entrance door, was a luggage rack flanked by a miniscule table and a chair. In contrast to everything small around us—apart from the bed—a huge plasma TV, was floating on the wall. Which I was absolutely certain, it would be ignored for the entire stay. At home, we didn't even have a TV anymore. We had decided to get rid of it. And that was probably one of the best decisions in my life.

The view was… There was no view. Across from our window, we could see into the neighbour's room. Two meters away. Instead of having the window facing the exterior, the light, the sun and all that…well, we had the unpleasant surprise to have nothing to stare at, but an old couple in the next room. So much for our romantic scenery.

Anyways, at least the room was clean, unlike last time when I visited—with my Ex. Or the fact that the online pictures of the rooms of that hotel, were actually pictures of the best room in the hotel. Which we got to stay in, due to shower malfunctions. Yeah, it was quite the experience.

"You hungry?" Jan asked. "I'm starving." That didn't surprise me one bit. Sometimes I had the impression that food was more important to him than anything else. He was very much an emotional eater. I had a theory about that, but thank God I took over the kitchen and prepared a lot of healthy stuff.

I placed the big chunk of cash from my wallet into the safe, and kept enough for a day. With Jan forgetting things and other unexpected circumstances, I was the bank. "Yeah, sure. Let me change into something more light, then we can go directly to that vegan place in Saint-Michel."

"I thought we'd go someplace on Champs-Élysées first." He looked at me confused.

"You're right. But then I thought, why go there, buy an overly priced sandwich or something like that, in a crowded place—and not good crowded— when we can actually enjoy eating and not feel miserable. We can do that later anyway." I grinned.

"When you put it like that, it sounds very smart."

I huffed, slipping into a pair of orange ballerinas and grabbing a thin jacket—just in case we weren't going to come back to our hotel room until late in the night. "Thank you! I'm ready."

"Oh, don't forget the camera. I want to take some pictures today," Jan insisted.

I opened my bag and showed it to him. "See?! Already here."

"You're like a magician, you know?" Jan said jovially. He was not far from the truth. "How do you do that anyway?"

"Do what?" I smiled. "Guessing other people's needs?"

"Yeah, that."

I blinked my eyes theatrically. "Since you ask, we have to stop by a supermarket. We need water."

"You still haven't answered my question?" Jan demanded.

"I don't know, really. Even before I became an architect, I could see and compute complex situations in my head. Observing details, the necessary steps. The same goes for how I've accomplished things in my life. First I define what I want. Then, I learn everything I can about the subject. Then, I break it into steps that I follow. And I adjust the course as I go, until I reach my target. That's it basically," I concluded, waving my hands in the air.

"Yeah, but it's more than just that," Jan said, and I knew what he was implying.

"I thought you can't think on an empty stomach." Trying to change the topic, not exactly wanting to dwell on it, too much. I came to Paris to forget about the less than normal *features* of my existence. I wasn't sure I was going to succeed, but I was at least going to attempt this.

I gently turned and pushed him toward the door, and he barely resisted. "I hate, when you play with my weaknesses." He frowned, now opening the door for me.

"Hey, it's not my fault you're so easy." Barely containing my giggles, I stepped into the narrow hall, and he followed me closing the door behind him.

$$\infty$$

The warm night air was a blessing for us. After all that maddening cold and rain months in a row, this was an entirely different world. For Jan, at least. For me, was just… deliciously *normal*.

It wasn't just the temperature that was so pleasing, but the atmosphere, the life that was happening all around us, as well. Laughter, trees, smiles, loud talking, car honks, some singing on the corner of the street, exploring curious eyes…joy. All blended together.

After inhaling half the menu from the tiny vegan restaurant in Saint-Michel—even Moby ate there a few times—we were now crossing the bridge to Notre-Dame, heading home. To our hotel. And a stroll seemed like a great idea.

"Man, that apple pie was good!" Jan said, rubbing his belly with his free hand. With the other he was holding mine. "I wish I could eat like that, every day."

"I don't want to interrupt you culinary fantasies, but now that you're finally full, how about something else than food," I added, inhaling deeply into my lungs, the intoxicating scent of the trees, that I missed all these years since I had moved to *the north pole*.

Jan broke my reverie. "Ooh, I like when you talk dirty."

I shook my head, choking on a laugh. "Ah, if life would be that easy, wouldn't be great?!"

"It is," he assured me. "But seriously, what you're talking about? You have that look again. Remember, we're here to have *fun*. That's what I've promised."

"I know, and I wasn't going into those dark places with my thoughts. On the contrary. I was actually thinking, maybe after you're done with you PhD, I thought maybe we could explore other places. Like, warmer places…" I implied, gesticulating with my hands at the scenery around us. "Of course, I know it's not that easy to find a job in your field…or mine."

Jan stopped abruptly, forcing me to slow down and come to a halt, as well. He took two steps and turned to face me, now holding both my hands. "Yes, it's not easy. But you forget one thing." He was now gazing intently into my eyes.

"Which is?" I said, eyebrows raised.

"You know that you are my home, right?!" And for a second I couldn't breathe because of the intensity of his words. He shook my hands. "Home, is where *you* are. So no matter where you want to go, I will follow. Is that simple."

The certainty in his eyes was unmistakable. Waves of heat from somewhere deep inside of me, threatened to pulverize me into tiny sparks of light.

I stood on my toes and kissed him.

I came to Paris to forget the lurking danger around my existence. So I welcomed everything that was the opposite of that. Everything that was light and hopeful and… love.

chapter / EIGHT

What am I doing here? I don't remember wanting to come here. How the hell I end up in places like this?

I can't say what this place is, but I'm standing outside in front of a building. It's too dark to tell if it's a cathedral or a castle. Definitely stone walls. I'm in front of an entrance, and the door is opened. I don't dare to enter. In there, it's even darker than where I'm standing. Actually it's pitch black.

Unseen arms snatch me from the ground. I don't see anyone, but I feel a shape. Definitely a him. He carries me like a child in his arms, and starts to run. Run. Run. Run. Wait… Where are we running? This is not good. Why do I feel so paralyzed?

A tiny, weak voice inside me, screams for help. The situation feels familiar.

Oh, shit! It's real. I'm not dreaming. I mean, I am, but not really. I am being hijacked again. Wake up! Go back into the body! Wake uuuuuuup!

I want to cry but the desperation strangles me. I don't know how to go back. Somebody is running away with my soul, for Christ's sake. Oh, God! Wake up!

Heeeeeeeelp! Heeeeeeeeeeelp!

I forgot Tuesday the Louvre was closed. So yesterday, we went to visit Musée d'Orsay instead. It was actually perfect that way. After the first day with the flight, and the weather adjustment, plus the long walk into the city, I wasn't sure I was going to survive another marathon.

Yeah. Visiting a museum like the Louvre, was a marathon in itself. Especially, if you wanted to see everything in one day. Not that you would actually be able, to enjoy each piece of art exhibited there. But at least, you would get to march through all the halls of the palace, and bonus, you'd receive an extensive neck workout from turning left and right, trying to absorb as much art as you can on your way through.

Musée d'Orsay was more like the warm up before the race. Nevertheless, worthwhile visiting. Even if only just to see the Impressionists. Or just Van Gogh alone.

"Is it always like this?" Jan asked, tossing his head around, completely stunned by the monster line to the tickets and info desk. Not to mention, the huge glass pyramid high above our heads through which we entered. He was completely taken by the whole underground giant size hall, swarming with people everywhere. Whether going or coming out of the rest rooms, or grabbing a snack before proceeding to the exhibition halls, the place was buzzing with life. And it was just nine-thirty in the morning. The usual.

I nodded. "Pretty much... I take it, art hasn't been all that important to you?" Not that I needed an answer to that. I knew his background very well.

"Well, if you count watching stupid shows on TV as a form of enjoying...art," he gesticulated with his hands, "I guess that's as far as I go."

I couldn't help but laugh at his honesty about it. "That's why we're here today. To remedy that. Now you get to see the *real* thing. I'm sure, even you are curious to see *Mona Lisa*."

"Is that, the strange looking woman, everyone pretends to be so transfixed when they stare at?" he said nonchalantly, looking over the crowd in front of us.

I chuckled.

"I guess you could say that." Totally getting his irony. "Not everyone understands it, but they act like they do. You know, cultural programming. Besides, it's a *da Vinci*, so yeah...lots of fake onomatopoeia goes with it. But if you don't like it, or don't get it, you don't have to pretend anything. I promise not to be such a snob. Even if my backgrounds in arts might tempt me to do so. To be perfectly honest, even I, don't like everything. I don't care how famous or old it is. So you're perfectly safe with me," I reassured him, giving a brief squeeze to his hand.

"Do you think I will like it?" Jan asked, somewhat unsure.

"What? Mona Lisa?"

"No. Yes. That, too. I mean the whole thing. The Museum. What it's in it."

"What now? Museum anxiety? It's kind of late for that, don't you think? Was that bad yesterday—"

"Noo… I mean, it's all this hype around places like this one, and sometimes it's just a waste of time and money. When in fact we could do…you know, *something else*," he said, eyebrows raised.

I frowned. "Again. Was that bad yesterday?"

Jan shook his head. "No. Never mind. Stupid question."

"Exactly. Even for the most art illiterates, there is something to appreciate. Trust me. It won't suck."

"So what, now I'm an art illiterate?" Jan played the offended card.

I groaned in frustration.

He glanced at me, giving me a crooked smile. "I'm just, messing with you. You're easy too, you know?!" Jan laughed, and I shook my head in disbelief.

"I should've seen it coming…"

Ah, distraction at last.

Just what I needed. I almost forgot about the night before.

I swore to God, if this were to become a regular thing—which it did lately…—very soon I wouldn't be able to pull myself back to reality. Or life. It was bad enough that I had to pretend to be normal to the people around me, and share with only a few what was really going on.

In a way, I made peace with that. Walking this path of searching for the *truth*, was full of surprises, to say the least. But I wasn't about to give up. I was *that* stubborn. I just wished, that, in truly scary moments—life force drainage situations…literally— that, there was someone not only to talk to, but to tell me how to deal with it. How to defend myself…

70

Over the years, I had learned different tricks, techniques, to strengthen myself and build protection. But, obviously wasn't enough. I, didn't know enough, or the right thing. I just felt like a blind person, walking in the dark, wanting to trust whatever piece of information, that could supposedly help. And lately, I was growing desperate. Not a good thing, all things considered.

"Right, then. Tickets, checked. Maps, checked. What else?" Jan said, eyes browsing through the pile of papers we got just a minute ago.

"That's it. Okay, now would be a good time, to pay a visit to the bathroom," I suggested, knowing what was coming. "We have a long day. Or should I say, a long *road* ahead of us. Full of art and stuff..." I smiled, expectantly.

Jan folded back the papers and slid them into my bag. "Pee, it is. We meet up back here, in five." Then we split, heading in opposite directions each facing another long line in front of the toilets.

Lovely.

Fifteen minutes later, finally we managed to get out.

"Ready?" I asked, still deciding where to go first. I had already visited once, and had a pretty good idea where each section was.

"Sure. So, where to?" Jan said, waiting for me to direct our tour.

I pointed to the three main entrances. "To the left, we have *Richelieu* wing, where among other things, we will see Napoleon's apartments. Directly in front of us, we have *Sully* wing, with 17th, 18th, 19th century French paintings as well as Greek, Etruscan, Roman and Egyptian Antiquities and many others. To the right, we have *Denon* wing, with Italian and Spanish paintings. Also, Italian and Spanish and Northern European sculptures, and of course lots more. These are just some highlights," I insisted.

"I think I want to have the whole Mona Lisa thing behind me, by lunch," Jan said, eyes squinted, after a moment of weighing the choices. "We will have some lunch, won't we?!"

I snorted. "Sure. Don't worry, I don't plan to starve us. Jesus! Stop thinking about food, every five minutes. We just had breakfast," I huffed, in exasperation.

"Good. Just making sure," he replied, grinning at me like an idiot. "So, have you decided yet?"

71

"You wanted to see Mona Lisa by lunch?! Denon it is."

"After you…"Courteously, Jan invited me to take the lead.

"From here, I'm sure, you can go by yourself." I pointed to my right. "In there, is your Mona Lisa… A tiny painting, on a big wall, in the middle of the room. It's impossible to miss. There is always a big crowd, hover over it. Not to mention, the sea of gadgets, desperate to immortalize the life altering moment. Go and pretend like you get it." Then I pushed him gently toward the entrance. "I'll be here, when you're done."

For a second, Jan turned his head to me, amused by the idea. "It sounds very… *religious.*"

"It is. For some… Now go. And try keeping your irony to yourself." A chuckle escaped his mouth, and then he left.

Finally.

I was *sooo*…tired. I needed to sit down. Too much input already.

In two strides I reached my target. A free seat, on one of the many—but not nearly enough—visitor sofas, strategically planted along the very long hall, entirely dedicated to Italian paintings from different centuries.

This thing was so luxurious and decadent. Rich, burgundy velvet cover. Soft. Heavenly. I was beginning to melt, sinking in my seat. God…this was so good.

For two and a half hours, we'd roamed the halls of Denon wing. To my surprise, Jan turned out to be very impressed. Especially, with the Italian sculptures. It was sweet to see him all so…undone. Eyes glowing, with pure admiration for those elegant shapes and proportions. Of course, you didn't need a Master in Arts to appreciate fit, athletic, naked bodies, with majestic features posing graciously.

Moving further to the paintings—Italian 13th-15th c. and more—a whole new world opened for Jan. Although, he didn't possess the language to express himself like someone with an art background, nevertheless, his comments were convincing and to the point.

Right about that time, my feet stopped obeying me. So, when we had arrived by the da Vinci segment—which was close to the adjacent hall where Mona Lisa was displayed—I decided, a little conservation of forces was necessary. After all, we still had two more sections to go through. And this one, wasn't quite over yet.

"The similarities are astonishing," I heard a voice beside me, but I was too much into my blissful trance to care. "Don't you think so?" the voice insisted.

I would have ignored it further, if it weren't for the warm breathing, very close to my ear. I turned. An unknown face, with an intelligent smile, was staring at me. "Excuse me?!" I didn't want to seem rude. "Are you talking to me?" Already, rearranging my sitting position.

The man sitting next to me, dipped his head toward the painting across from us. "Sorry. I couldn't help but notice, certain characteristics you and da Vinci's *"Saint Jean Baptiste"* share." Then his eyes started pendulating, from me, to the androgynous being on the canvas. "Insightful, warm brown eyes. Majestic face. Clean, elegant features. Not to mention the hair. Your dark curls. Even the same demeanor. Hmm…interesting," he said, rubbing a hand down his jaw.

Interesting, indeed.

The only other person, who said something similar—surelly not in so many words or so…*eloquent*—was my Ex. The last time, I was with him, visiting the museum. Standing in front of the exact same painting.

The words I heard today, weren't meant to be flirtatious; the last time either. They came from a place of surprising realization. Today I would add, even some sort of confirmation.

Weird.

I looked at him closely. Medium long dark hair, that was reaching his shoulders. Aquiline nose, thin lips, dark circles around the eyes. He wore a grey suit—a good quality one—and a black shirt, unbuttoned at the neck. Legs crossed, I couldn't help but notice the *really* nice, black velour leather shoes. The man had taste. And probably, money.

"Are you an artist? Or an art lover?" I asked, intrigued by his whole mysterious vibe. I couldn't tell if he was tired, or stressed, or maybe both.

"The second one. But not really. At least, not in that fanatical sense, like, throw away ten millions on a painting. Keep it in a safe room. Where no one would *ever* be allowed in, other than myself. And go there, just on special occasion to stare at it. No. I think there are more important things, to use these kinds of resources on."

I chuckled. "Like what?"

"Books, for instance. Old, rare manuscripts. I like to collect *knowledge*." He gave away, a mischievous grin.

Ah, a man after of my own heart. "Now, that you mention. I too, am a book lover. Bookworm, you could say. I like to read. A lot," I said, gesticulating with my hands.

He laughed. "I'm Pierre, by the way," he extended a hand to me.

Frenchman. I wouldn't have guessed it. His English was good, no French accent whatsoever.

"Ariana. Nice to meet you," I said, shaking his hand. "What brings you here, then?" I gestured toward the room slash location. "Unless this is your first time. And you had to cross that off your 'once-in-a-lifetime' to do list. But, to be honest, you don't seem to be *that* kind of tourist. Or tourist at all."

"Very perceptive," Pierre said smiling, crossing a hand through his hair. "I was supposed to meet someone here," his tone changed, a bit. More serious. "I live here. I'm a local."

"Business or pleasure?" I asked.

Pierre seemed somewhat uncomfortable, face changing color. He opened his mouth to say something, but words didn't leave his throat.

"I'm sorry. I don't mean to be nosy. You don't have to answer. Just making some conversation..." I said, realizing, he didn't ask me anything about myself. Or, why I was here. So, I continued, trying to overcome the awkward moment. "My fiancée, is in the other hall." I gestured to the huge chamber, where Mona Lisa was displayed. "He, however, has, a sort of a once-in-a-life-time to do list. And that includes taking Mona Lisa off the list by lunch," I said, shaking my head and laughing at the thought of it.

"How do you tell a complete stranger, something... *important*, without them freaking out about it?" Pierre blurted out, eyes on the painting in front of us.

His words took me by surprise, completely. Whatever train of thought I had, it froze. My body, too. The whole thing had the effect of an adrenaline shot. Making me alert, but in the same time unable to move.

"*You're* the one, I'm supposed to meet. And please, don't freak out." He turned to face me, lips twitching, eyes begging to trust him.

"I—"

"I know. This is weird," Pierre retorted, hands held up in defense. "Also, I'm sure this is not the first strange thing that happened to you, so far," he said, determined to break my fear.

How ironic…and *true*.

Nonetheless, I couldn't stop the hysterical laugh in my head.

I wanted to say something, but he continued. "You have questions, I have answers. Things happen to you that are…out there. Well, for most people."

Tell me about it…

Pierre crossed an arm over his chest, and with the other propped against it, started to rub his temple. Whatever he wanted to say, it wasn't easy. "A million things must be going through your head right now. What I'm trying to say, is that, I'm not most people, or…the enemy."

I glanced around, realizing for the first time since he dropped this…*thing* on me, that I was in public area. With hundreds of people swarming around me, going in all directions, busy taking pictures of the paintings, or of themselves in front of the paintings. "Who are you?" I managed to ask.

"A friend."

I snorted, breathing heavily.

"And you're too smart and intuitive, to know I'm not lying." He turned toward me, eyes intently on me.

"Really?! 'Cause lately, I don't feel like that."

"You're scared and in the dark. I know how it feels," Pierre added.

"Do you?!"

He looked me in the eyes, with this dead serious expression. No words. Just staring.

He's not kidding.

I glared back at him. "I had one of the worst nights in a while. I am lucky, to even be *here*—as in alive—and not on the *other* side. If you know what I mean…"

"I do. That's why I'm here."

I ignored his words of reassurance. "So, excuse me, for being so reluctant to trust a stranger…" I said, anger and frustration spilling out.

Pierre smiled, then corrected me. "A friend. A *new* friend. A friend you need. Whatever life you have, or you might think you have, without answers…it can get pretty intense.

"Look. I came today, to introduce myself to you. No real conversation, is going to take place *here*. There are too many eyes and ears around us. And I don't mean the visitors." He gave me another hard look.

That didn't sound reassuring. But I think, I knew what he was implying.

"You intend to eat tonight, right?!" he said, and I looked at him, somewhat amused.

"If you think that—"

"That you're going to accept an invitation to dinner from me?! No. I don't expect that. I was thinking more of the opposite. Why don't *you*, tell me a time and a place, and I'll show up there. Hopefully for you, I will have more answers." He rose to his feet, already buttoning up his suit jacket.

"I thought you had the answers," I replied.

"I do. But depends on the location, how much I can…share," he said, eyebrows raised.

I stared at him, not knowing what to say, really. The fear was gone, but that didn't mean I trusted him. What he was proposing, sounded pretty safe though. A meetup in another public area.

"So… have you decided yet? Pierre looked at me expectantly.

"Absolutely not! Have you lost your mind?!" Jan said, completely enraged. "I leave you a few minutes alone, and you decide to trust a stranger with your life?!"

Yeah. That didn't go well.

I didn't expect anything less from him after I told him about my earlier encounter, and the fact that I agreed to let Pierre join us later at the vegan place.

"What is wrong with you? You won't tell *me*, your *fiancée* all that troubles you, all that is crazy and weird in your life. Because you think I won't understand, or I wouldn't be able to help. Do you know, how this feels?" He stared at me, pained.

I wanted to say it wasn't like that. But the fact was, agreeing to this *thing* tonight, was saying something else. I wanted to comfort him. I wanted to comfort me. I wanted many things.

"I know how it feels. You feel excluded," I said.

Jan huffed. "Exactly."

"Why do you think I told you, all of this? To keep it away from you?! No. I wanted you to be a part of it. Yes, I think that there are certain things, that you cannot help me with. And not because you don't want to, or you don't understand. But because, it's so out of your hands…and mine. That's why, I *need* more information. More answers. I know, it looks like I'm crazy. And maybe I am. But last night, I almost died. Again. And honestly, I don't know how long this *stuff* is going to happen to me. I have to understand what's going on. I have to learn how to defend myself against this. Do you understand? Tell me you do?!"

"Of course, I do. But which part, is supposed to make me feel better? Because *nothing*, you just said or did, makes me feel better. It only makes me feel, *more* helpless, and useless. Unable to take care of you. To *be* there for you. In every situation…" Jan blurted out his frustration.

God, this was hard.

"I know. And I know, you're tired of me saying, I know… Look. We're going to be there together tonight. That's already something. I won't be alone to face…this. I only said yes, because *you're* going to be there with me. So, look at the bright side…" I said, squeezing his arm.

He shook his head, hands on his hips.

"And if something goes wrong, and I'm not saying it will. Hey, you get to punch somebody! How's that for helping me?" I grinned, sliding my hands around his neck.

Jan was now gazing into my eyes, a timid smile forming at the corners of his mouth. "You think, I can take him?" his voice less tense, than a moment ago.

I laughed. "Oh, absolutely."

chapter / NINE

Pierre was sitting at a corner table, busy with his phone, when we walked up to him. He had arrived only a few minutes before we did. He looked rested and genuinely happy to see us.

Before I could say anything, he introduced himself very politely to Jan—who was like a ticking bomb…ready to go off at the slightest suspicion. Fortunately for us, no reason presented itself.

We exchanged a few words about our day so far, and the fact that we were dead tired and deliriously hungry, then ordered right away—already knowing the menu from the previous nights.

I was surprised to find out that Pierre as well, was a fellow raw-foodist. Who occasionally—like me—enjoyed a cooked vegan meal with a glass of wine. Not so astounded though, to find out, he was older than he looked—he was forty-eight, but looked early thirties. Given his diet and all…

Totally relating to that.

Whenever asked to tell my age, I would get this astonished look on people's faces. A thirty-two year old, but looking no older than twenty-two.

Yeah. That was an advantage…in some situations.

Professionally, not so much.

In my twenties, I really struggled to be taken seriously. Still am. Especially, in my profession—where things were still very much patriarchal. Thank God though, for opening my mouth to speak…That compensated a lot, for my less than *ripe* appearance.

"Thank you both, for showing up tonight. For being so brave." Pierre raised his glass to us, and continued. "I wish we could've met in less *radical* circumstances. In a different context, all this…*distrust* hanging in the air right now, wouldn't even be possible," then he took a sip of wine.

Around us, the small restaurant was running at full capacity. People of different ages and backgrounds—mostly tourists like us—were enjoying a nice dinner, a glass of wine and lively conversations. Still, the noise level wasn't so high, to have to raise our voices in order to hear each other, but high enough, not to be overheard by the others.

Jan was chewing passionately on his food—still very guarded toward Pierre, but calmer now—when I decided to break the awkward silence. "I'm known to be a straight forward person. Not that it brought me too many benefits, but at least, this way I got a lot of unnecessary crap out the way," I said, and Pierre smiled. "Another thing, you have to know about me, is that, I don't like to waste time, either."

Jan chuckled and nodded at the same time. "Very true."

I frowned at him, then turned to Pierre. "Let's start somewhere."

"Sure," he said, hands still playing with his glass.

"How did you find me? And, who do you work for?"

Pierre cleared his throat. "Both, good questions. I will start with the second, if you don't mind? It's easier to answer." He paused shortly, and when no objection from me or Jan came, he continued. "In a strictly professional sense, I work for myself. I have a few businesses."

I was right. He had means.

"So, this is a front for something else?!"

Pierre chortled. "You could say that… It's… It allows me to pursue other *things*. More important things."

Great. More vagueness.

"To answer your first question, now. Well… You needed help," Pierre insisted, arching his eyebrows. "And I was asked, to come and meet with you at the museum."

I was already alarmed. Who was following me? Who the hell asked him? Then I answered my own questions, remembering the less than *normal* encounters I had lately.

At this point, anything was possible.

"You see, you're *special.* Your DNA codes have been activating in you certain functions, abilities. Because of that, and the value they carry, you have appeared on many *radars.* Mostly, on the ones you don't want to be. Lucky for *you*, you were close to me, and I could intervene."

Huh, I was not crazy after all. I felt I was transforming, but couldn't estimate how much, or the implications of that. Although, always had my own suspicions. "I see. Still, too unsubstantial for me to trust—"

Jan jumped in. "So you're saying, all these insane things happening to her, it's basically her fault. Not on purpose, though."

"Technically, yes. But things, are not that simple. *That* black and white. I'm sure she figured that out by now. Right?!" Pierre said, eyes intently on me.

I simply nodded.

Of course, there was more than just biological upgrade here. I didn't spend most of my life searching for the TRUTH—that thing that sets you free—and having those crazy experiences, to believe anymore in that new-agey 'love and light' crap. No. I lost that naïve part of me, a long time ago. Now, I just believed, that a *true* seeker, was going to bump into nasty stuff from time to time—lately more often than I cared for.

"I suppose you're familiar by now, with the whole Ascension story. Stories. Theories," he added, gesticulating with his hands.

Of course, I was. Was he for real? I was starting to feel mocked. "I'm sure you know that, too. Or this conversation would be that…wrong." I pressed my lips into a smile, brows raised.

Pierre laughed. "Right. Well, it's true. Ascension is real. Not that the actual truth about it, is out there. Just bits and pieces. More or less distorted. But, I'm sure you know that, as well."

Nothing new so far. I gave an annoyed smile.

He caught that, and continued. "You're what we call a Christic."

"Who's *we*?"

"We'll get to that later. Aren't you curious, what a *Christic* is first?" Pierre asked, hands clasped under his chin.

"Sure. I would be very grateful though, if you could just stop tergiversating. Give me some credit here," I waved my hands in the air. "I can take a lot in."

Pierre leaned forward, arms crossed resting on the table. "A Christic is somebody with a specific genetic structure. Somebody who is able to hold eternal life. There is a big difference between *immortality* and *eternal* life."

Now he got my attention. Apparently, Jan's too, because he stopped chewing. "Go on."

"You see, there are *finite* life forms and there are *eternal* life forms. Both can have immortality. Or better said, very long life spans, to the point of indefinite. A finite life form, in order to sustain itself for so long, they need to take energy from other life systems. In that regard, they are like vampires," he said.

"From what you're saying, I gather, we *too,* are like that. We need external sources of energy to survive," I replied, a little bit confused.

"True. But that's only because of the *distortion* in our anatomies." As if he was anticipating what I was going to ask next, Pierre added. "I will explain that later, too. Now. Going back to the difference between eternal and finite; as an eternal life form/system though, we generate our own energy. We multiply it."

"I still don't see where the part of me being *Christic* or eternal, fits into the picture."

"It will. I'm not done yet. There is a lot of information, and it's hard to compress it without making it sound kind of abstract," Pierre said.

"Don't worry about that. So far, you haven't lost me."

Great. Now I felt like peeing.

I am not going to the bathroom now.

"On the other hand, as a finite life form, although you might get to live for thousands and thousands of years, after many life cycles, the template—the structure behind of what you perceive as physical—gets so distorted, to the point of disintegration. This is called a space dust return. As in, return to Source," he said.

"Wow. This sounds so *drastic*," I said, a billion of questions swarming in my head already.

Pierre nodded. "Something definitely, to avoid," he said, swirling his glass, then took another sip of wine.

I thought everyone was eternal. Good or bad. However that relative it may be. I mean, I knew one day we *all* would reunite with Source. But not like that. "So, basically what you're saying is that, there is such thing as *definitive* death. Like, for good."

"In a sense. But not really. Because even in that moment of complete dissolution, you still are inside of God. The Source of all things. So, you're not really lost or dead. You just don't remember yourself anymore," he added, lips thinning.

Wow. Horrible. "This sounds like death death, to me."

Pierre waved his hand. "There is however, a special procedure, to be reassembled back again. But that's a topic for another time." Sensing an objection coming, he spoke further. "Let's not digress, too much. I'm trying to give you the most relevant information to you, at the moment."

He had a point.

"So, back to being eternal. And Ascension," I said, realizing that Jan finished eating, and kept quiet the whole time. Probably as curious as I was. Or just analyzing in his head what he just heard, most probably brewing some skeptical remarks.

"You need a certain amount of your internal anatomy to still be able to work as intended in the Original Design," Pierre explained. "To *even* have a shot, at Ascension. Which is another way to return to Source, but with your memory intact. It's a natural process of going back. But that's just one aspect."

"Assuming what you say it's true, how do I know, I'm still *functionable*?"

Pierre chuckled. "Well, your extrasensory abilities for starters. Which, I'm sure you've noticed them by now. Then, all your experiences, which most people call them 'paranormal.'"

Of course. *Obviously.*

Note to myself: stop asking stupid questions.

"So, if Ascension is just a *natural* return home, why all these crazy things around it? Why do *I* have to go through this nasty stuff?" I asked, frustrated. "And I'm at a point, where I moved way past the 'love and light' crap. And that whole *mind-numbing* passivity."

He laughed. "Good. You're a fast learner." When he spotted a "Gee, thanks" expression on my face, Pierre added. "I mean it."

"Since I was eight, I've been on this *personal* quest. To find answers, to existential questions. I have to say, that after so many years, hundreds, if not thousands of books, workshops, lectures, interviews, you name it…nothing seems to create a clear picture of why the world is the way it is. I mean, I have a *much* better and wider understanding of the *'Big Picture'* now. Of what's really going on. With us, in politics, socially, economically, spiritually. I know that, now you don't need war to conquer a country. You just buy it. You create an artificial economical crisis. Then trick people into buying the whole *bailout* bullshit. Make them think they have no choice but to borrow more money. Fake money. Creating even more debt. To the point, where you bail out countries—which is code for buying them. The whole—"

"The whole thing is just sick, and beyond disgusting?!" he added, and I shook my head. "I know."

I rubbed my hands up and down my face. "It's so insane… Most of the time, I feel like I live among zombies."

"It's good that you know. Saves me from talking about it," Pierre said. "Or what I like to call, level one of *general* knowledge.

"We're at the beginning of a new time cycle, and right in the middle of the Star Gate Activation, in a *hacked* Time Space Matrix. So yes, a lot of action is taking place right now. Good, and bad." He exhaled, with two fingers pinching his chin. "Overwhelming at times."

"Tell me about it…"

I knew we were living in a holographic reality. No shock there. Science—quantum mechanics, even biology—was already backing this up. "I heard, read, lots of stories about the Annunaki. Or the 'Gods' as mentioned in the Sumerian, Babylonian and Egyptian records, as being at the root of the problem. There's a whole encyclopedia about them on the web. Videos, articles, books…you name it. All basically saying, that they created us—altered us genetically—as a slave race to mine gold for them. They were after monatomic gold, to rejuvenate and extend their lives, among other things."

Pierre stared at me pleased. "That's just a very small fraction, of what happened. But yes, they were, *are* involved. Not going into a lot of details, the last big *nasty hit* on the planet and on us implicitly, happened during the Atlantian times, when the Eternal Life Grid lost two-thirds of its quantum."

Since my childhood, Atlantis was one of those big obsessive mysteries that had haunted my imagination and my dreams. Whatever I could get my hands on—information wise—I would devour it. So I knew a thing or two about it. Obviously, not everything. Or, one hundred percent accurate. "Care to explain, what an Eternal Life Grid is?" I said, already intrigued.

"You know how in different religions, it is mentioned the Tree of Life?"

"The Tree of Knowledge, of good and evil in Christianity? Or like the one in the Kaballah, the Ten Sefirot?"

"Yeah. But it's not just there. It's everywhere. It's a universal symbol, carrying more or less the same meaning," Pierre said, crossing a hand through his hair.

"Go on."

"Funny you mentioned the Ten Sefirot. The Eternal Life Grid is kind of like that, only it has twelve points—centers. Actually they are thirteen, because the twelfth repeats itself at both ends. It's a symmetrical construct," he gestured with his hands.

Hmmm.

When he saw me trying to picture it in my head, Pierre took a pen out of the inside of his jacket and started drawing on a napkin. Then turned the piece of paper to me.

Okay, *that* was something new. "So you're saying, the Kaballah has it all wrong?" I asked, arms crossed.

He shook his head. "Not at all. It's just they have the representation of a finite Tree of Life. It has to do with the *distortion*, I mentioned earlier. Their mechanics model shows the truth about something based on a finite system. Not to mention, ran in reverse."

Wow. Definitely food for thought.

"Every person, animal, tree, object, has this structure at the core. The Tree of Life.

It's like the hard drive of a computer. We all have that. More or less, working properly at the moment."

That actually made sense. Browsing through my head, the image of this channeler girl—which I'd discovered years ago on the internet—popped into my mind. In one of her videos, she was talking about something similar. Then, I remembered this blind woman *Valentina*, back home in Romania. She could see these geometrical shapes behind everything. Literally. She knew when the sun set, or rose, or whether if it was cloudy, or any other type of weather situation, but not limited to that, solely, based on these abstract shapes and forms she saw. As if she was reading code.

"So basically, an Eternal Life Grid is a Tree of Life, minus the distortion," I concluded.

He nodded. "In a nut shell. Yeah. And *all* the Eternal Life Grids connect to the Unified Field, or the Lattice Grid."

Huh! Interesting. "You mean something like *'The Grid'* in the movie Tron?"

Pierre's face lit up. "That's exactly, what I mean. I wouldn't be surprised, if the guy who wrote the script, knew *certain* things. You know, certain movies, aren't just entertainment…"

No shit! I gave him a mocking look.

Of course, I knew.

He caught that, and held a hand up. "Sorry. Didn't mean to offend you. It's just, most people are clueless about this stuff."

"In case you forgot, I am not most people," I said, a little bit annoyed. "I thought that was like the first requirement, for us to even have this conversation…"

Pierre laughed. "You're right. Sorry." Then the buzzing of his phone interrupted whatever he wanted to say next.

He received a text message. When he finished reading it, he looked up. "I'm afraid, I have to go."

What? *Now?!* Just when it was getting interesting… I still had a million questions. Not cool. Not cool at all.

He read my disappointment. "But if you're both free tomorrow for lunch, we could continue our conversation then," Pierre said, and took a business card from his wallet. "Here's where I'll be at one o'clock."

I took the card, and read the name of a restaurant: *"Carte Blanche."*

Hmm. Interesting name, for a restaurant. Carte blanche meant, unconditional authority, full discretionary power. What this had to do with food? I had no idea.

I wanted to say something, but he was faster and already standing up. "I'm sure you would like to know more. As I would like to know more about you."

I looked at Jan, eyes basically begging to agree.

He smirked. "Looks like I don't have a choice," he said, and I grinned happily.

"Good, then. One more thing," Pierre added.

"What's that?" I asked.

"Please, allow me to pay for your dinner tonight. I feel like this is the least I can do, to repay your trust. I'm sure before coming here, took some serious convincing," he said, glancing shortly at Jan.

You bet, it did. "Oh, you don't have to. But thank—"

Jan put a hand on my arm and spoke over me. "Actually, that's really nice of you. We would happily oblige you," his eyes locking with mine, giving me an evil smile.

He behaved throughout the entire dinner. No threats, no sarcasm, no caustic remarks. Now, he wanted compensation.

I was speechless. My face turned red.

Pierre laughed. "All right then! And in case you wondered, the place we're going tomorrow, is vegan, too."

Awesome.

We said goodbye to Pierre, and when he was out the door, I turned to Jan, eyes squinting. "You have no shame, do you?"

He gazed at me innocently, barely containing a smile. "I don't know, what you talking about?"

"Uh-huh." I rolled my eyes.

chapter / TEN

Jan put his arm around my shoulder, and steered me toward the window of a small jewelry shop. "I think, I saw something for you," he said, enthusiastically.

"*I* think, we're going to be late. And as much as I would love a cool piece of jewelry, we're on a budget. Last time I checked, it didn't cover extravagant purchases," I added, flatly.

He shook his head. "Ah, you're no fun. When did a little window shopping hurt anyone?"

"Unless you're masochistic, well…*me*. I don't like to be teased. I want—"

Jan stopped, spun me around, forcing me to face him. "*Really*?! I thought you like it, when I do this," he leaned in, cupping my chin. His cheek, gently brushing mine. A few rebel strands of his hair trailed down my face, sending chills down my spine. Warm lips startling me. Gentle at first, then, more demanding, and before I knew it, my hands ended up tangled in his hair. He moaned against my mouth, then pulled back. Breathing heavily, Jan was now watching me. His electric gaze, piercing through every cell in my body. "Well?"

I was left reeling.

This was supposed to be a romantic getaway, but actually, very few romantic…*activities*, happened so far. More like, *random* moments. Not because I wasn't on board with that, but because whatever I ran away from, followed me here. Not allowing me, to really get lost in the moment. Be carefree.

"Well, what?" Eyebrows raised, pretending not to get what he was implying.

Jan groaned. "Oh, you're so going to pay for this later..."

I laughed.

I knew what he had in mind... My stomach fluttered.

Against my protests, we approached the display window, where a black mannequin face wore a pair of *striking* drop shape emerald earrings, set in rose gold. Now I understood how he spotted them. The contrast between the black of the mannequin and the sparkling green, made it *impossible* to miss. Even from a fairly large distance.

"I was right, wasn't I?" Jan said, reading admiration in my eyes.

I snorted. "So what. It's not like we can buy it, or anything."

"What if we can? What if I can?" he added.

I peered at him in confusion. "Did you win the lottery? Got a new job, I don't know about?"

He chuckled. "No. To both your questions."

"Then?"

Jan cupped my face, looking straight into my eyes. "I want to spoil you. You've made already too many sacrifices, all these years. With my PhD studies, and everything. It was hard for both of us. But *especially* for you," he said, removing a rebel curl from my face. "I will be *forever* in awe, of your courage. Of your kindness. Your strength. And the fact that after all the problems and the setbacks, you're still here. By my side."

I swallowed hard.

His words, touched a very sensitive spot in my deeply bruised soul. So much, had been bottled up. Frustration. Humiliation. Anger. Disappointment. Disgust. When shit happened, I had soldiered on. Picked myself from the ground. Kicked myself in the ass, and moved on. Hoping, thinking of a brighter day. A new beginning to make things better... *God* I was so tired of doing that.

"I wanted to surprise you. You know, a pre-wedding gift. But nothing so far, seemed worthy of you—"

I could barely contain my tears.

Damn it.

"Don't want to spoil your *admirable*—not to mention swoon worthy—intentions. But you still haven't answered, how you're going to pay for it," I managed to say.

"When my grandmother died… Well, she left me and my brother some money. Enough for a down payment on house. Or an apartment. Or build something. You, being the architect and all." He couldn't stop grinning.

Total surprise. I knew his grandmother passed away—several years ago, before we even met—but no financial detail ever entered our conversations.

Unable to say anything, he continued. "This, and by this, I mean the whole thing with the money. Was supposed to be a surprise and my wedding gift for you. But couldn't wait that long. So I decided to do a little *carpe diem* thing."

Say something, damn it!

"Wow." I shook my head, eyed widened.

Jan laughed. "So, let's get them," he said, tipping his head toward those gorgeous earrings.

As nice as the whole unexpected chunk of money was, I couldn't help to feel certain unease. "Maybe we should use it for a house then. Or as a safety net, in case we move somewhere new, and we need to start over." I was talking from experience now.

I took the phone out my bag. "And as predicted, we're late. Let's go. We can talk about it later. After we're done with Pierre." I tried to steer him away from the whole expensive gift thing. Not that I minded a really *really*, nice pair of earrings.

"Yeah… Nice try! But I won't back down. I came prepared for that." He chuckled.

I frowned. "Fine. Whatever. Let's go now. And later…I won't stop you from doing that. Promise." I gave an exaggerated grin, secretly hoping he will forget later. As he usually did, with many other things. At least, I could count on that.

Bag on my shoulder, I grabbed him by the arm, and forced him to move away from the display window. Apparently, "Carte Blanche" was maybe fifty meters away, across the street from the jewelry shop.

Thank God, for that. Because, this morning when we'd looked it up on the internet, it had seemed much further away.

Even from the outside, you could see that the whole interior of the restaurant was *white*. Not cold though. As many would complain.

I love white. Very soothing.

We walked in, and looked around to spot Pierre. This place wasn't very big either, but seemed more spacious, and clean and happy. White tables, white chairs, white sofas, white floor, white walls. But each element had a different texture. Here and there, small accents of color—like some picture frames, or the flowers on each table. All and all, a pleasant space to eat and socialize.

To my surprise, Pierre wasn't here, and all the tables were full. "Shit. I think we're, too late. I whirled my head around, already a little jumpy. "Or maybe, he said a different time?"

"Or maybe, he stood us up?" Jan thinned his lips, brows arched.

No. It couldn't be that. "He doesn't seem the type of person to do that. Plus, he came earlier yesterday. Something came up. I think we should just wait for a little while."

"Maybe next time, you shouldn't trust every stranger that comes your way." Jan's sarcasm wasn't really helping.

"I don't trust every stranger—"

He cocked his head to the side with a slight frown. "Really?!"

Whatever.

I was starting to get even antsier when a very cheerful voice stopped the mind chatter. "Bonjour Madame! Bonjour Monsieur!" A tiny dark-haired woman in a spotless white shirt, with a black tie and a black apron over her jeans, spoke to us. She was caring a tray full of empty glasses.

Her infectious smile, made me smile. "Bonjour! Uh…we're waiting for someone. We were supposed to meet here at one o'clock. But—"

And just like she had a sudden realization, she nodded. "You must be Mr. Rosin's friends?" she said, switching now to English—little to no accent.

Now I felt stupid, for not even asking Pierre's last name. "Pierre?!"

She laughed. "Of course. Mr. Pierre Rosin. He's waiting for you," she confirmed, in a warm voice.

I giggled. But for an entirely different reason. "*Of course*, he's waiting for us," I said, grinning at Jan, who was now holding his hands up as to tell me "fine, you're right…"

I was too excited to rub it in his face, so I let it go.

We followed her to the bar where she dropped the tray, and placed the latest food order. Then she walked around it and strode through a long corridor, with her hand gesturing us to keep up. On the right, there was a staircase, and ahead in front of us, was a door to the back of the restaurant.

I thought she was going to take us upstairs, probably to another part of the restaurant, when she opened the door inviting us to follow her outside.

Okay. Maybe to a terrace?

I wasn't wrong, entirely. It was more like a patio. Three sides of it, were flanked by walls carrying ivy, almost to the top of the second floor. A few plants in pots here and there, were creating a cozy atmosphere. In the middle, three tables with chairs were completing the setting.

Pierre was sitting at one of these.

He seemed busy, only this time he was writing something on his laptop. He looked up, and gave us a big, sincere smile. "Hey! You made it." Already standing up, he crossed a hand through his rather messy hair, and greeted us with the other. "Please, take a seat. I hope it wasn't hard to get here."

"Not at all. *We're* sorry, we're late. We passed by a shop and got a little…carried away," I admitted.

Pierre laughed lightly. "Yeah, that can happen. So, did you get anything good?"

Before I could say anything, Jan spoke first. "I would've. But she wouldn't let me buy her something *really* special I saw for her. And then she insisted on being on—"

I stopped Jan before he could go any further with the story. "Okay. Why don't we order something to eat? I saw some interesting things on someone's plate. It looked really yummy. How's the food here, by the way?"

Pierre seemed amused by the whole situation. "It's good. I eat here everyday. Except, when I'm out of town. I hope it's okay we came out here. I mean not sitting inside. I thought it was more convenient… Plus, I really like it out here. To eat and work," he explained, then closed the laptop's lid.

"No. It's absolutely fine. I mean it's nice inside too, but here…" I glanced around.

"It's actually perfect."

Jan just nodded in agreement.

Pierre picked up the laptop and got up. "What would you like to drink? I'm going to get someone from the bar to come back here. And while I'm at it, I'll take this upstairs." He meant, his laptop.

Jan peered at him, in confusion. "Wait. You live here?!"

A wide smile splashed across his face. "I do. I thought it was practical to live and work at the same place."

"Wait. You work here, too?"

"I own the place. The restaurant and the apartment upstairs, they're mine," Pierre admitted, completely at ease.

Jan couldn't hide his shock and admiration. "*Niceee.*"

Yeah. Nice.

He mentioned he had several businesses, but still didn't see it coming. Like I didn't see it earlier with the whole inheritance story—this reminded me, later I'd have to have a chat with Jan about stuff like that. But that explained the whole familiarity of his name around this place.

"By the way, this little *oasis* here, is actually just for me and my staff. So we won't be bothered, if we don't want to," Pierre added, and then left.

The speechless phase didn't last very long. As he announced earlier, a minute later, a young waiter showed up, bringing glasses and tableware. "Mr. Rosin says to tell you that you are his guests. So, if you have any special whishes that are not on the menu, please tell us, and we will do our best to make it for you." Then he addressed me specifically. "Mr. Rosin told me you saw something you would like to try. If you could describe it to me, I would most certainly recognize it," he insisted, now placing in front of us the menus.

I couldn't help but smile.

The man was *sharp*. And fast. I liked the fact, that Pierre paid attention to details. That said a lot about how he ran things—in private or in business. When I came to think of it, that sense was extended even to fashion. Not that he was exaggerating or anything, but you could see that he knew what he was doing. Well, wearing.

Pierre came back, right after the waiter took our order and left. Somehow, it felt as if they all worked in tandem. One came. Another one left. Like clockwork.

"This is from my personal cellar," he said showing us the bottle of wine he brought with him. "It's one of the wines I sell here and in some…other places."

Of course, he made wine. He was a Frenchman. "So, you're making wine too… among other things. My father also. Of course not at this capacity. Now that he is retired—he is an engineer—he spends more time with the vine my grandfather left him. In Romania, winemaking is old tradition like here."

"Romania. I knew there was something about you, I couldn't quite put my finger on it. You're *Romanian*," he acknowledged me, the corner of his lips curving up into a tiny smile.

"I thought you knew everything about me," I put in, a little surprised. "I mean, given the circumstances of how we met."

His eyes were glowing with something, I couldn't define yet. "They said we had things in common. And it would be easier—" he stopped, changing his mind about what he wanted to say next. "Funny how this works."

I was confused. And there it was, that *they* word again—that was driving me crazy. He wasn't the only one who used it around me. The thought of the other person who mentioned it—and the potential significance—sent cold chills down my spine.

I wanted to ask him to clarify that for me, instead, I let him continue.

"My great grandfather was Romanian."

I stared wide-eyed with surprise. Jan, too.

Pierre started pouring wine in our glasses. "He came here when they were build- ing the Eiffel Tower. He was an engineer. Most people have no clue, that the Eiffel Tower was built based on Romanian technology with Romanian steel. From Reşiţa and Govăşdia—Hunedoara."

I was impressed. Even *I* hadn't know, until recently.

"He was part of part of Pănculescu's team of engineers. Actually, they were quite close. They worked together at the end of the nineteenth century, on the railway that was connecting Bucharest to Predeal. Previous to that, Pănculescu worked in Eiffel's company making a name for himself.

94

"Anyway, while my great grandfather was working on this project, Eiffel paid a visit to Pănculescu in his home town—Valenii de Munte. Eiffel became interested in Pănculescu's innovation—and despite a five-year contract initially, the railway was completed in less than a year. Long story short, my great grandfather ended up working on the Eiffel Tower. Fell in love with a French woman named Elise, got married, had kids, and basically settled here. And this…" His hands gesticulating in the air. "This was his house and office. And now it's mine."

Wow. That was a page of instant history, right there.

"Beautiful story," Jan managed. Then went on to say something, which *completely* didn't even cross my mind. "This means you get free rides up to the top of Eiffel Tower?"

I let out a soft laugh.

Pierre chuckled. "Actually, it does. Why? You want one?"

Totally shameless, Jan said innocently. "It's still unchecked on my Paris to-do list…"

I shook my head giving Jan a scold, and then turned to Pierre. "Thank you. But, there is no need for that. We can—"

"It would be my pleasure. We could do it later today, if you have nothing scheduled in particular. Plus, it will give us a little more time to fill you in on *certain* things," Pierre insisted, eyebrows raised.

Jan looked at me, grinning like an idiot.

I saw no point, in obstructing fun for Jan and more answered questions for me. So I let it go. It was a win-win for both us.

The food arrived and we dug in right away. Jan was *clearly* having some sort of religious experience with the food—judging by the onomatopoeia coming out of his mouth. Couldn't blame him. Everything we tasted was beyond *scrumptious*. And the stuff I saw earlier, and wanted to have it as well. Suffice to say, my taste buds would cherish these moments forever. And the Tomatoes and Coconut Soup…was to die for. By the time the dessert came, we were wondering, *how in the world* we hadn't discovered Pierre's place earlier. Not that we were complaining with the one we went each evening…but the *food* here was simply…perfection.

"I've been meaning to ask you since yesterday. What happened *actually* on December 21 2012? I'm sure something happened, because I felt it. Obviously not the doom and gloom scenarios. I mean, I see a lot of change happening, good and bad. Stuff coming to the surface. Hidden truths, pop up where least expected..." I peered up at Pierre, expectantly.

He took another bite from his slice of raw vegan chocolate cake—a.k.a. holy mother of chocolate goodness. "What happened on December 21 2012, was a major turning point. There were moments throughout 2012 when the negative agenda, gain a few more points. Turning the odds in their favor. Luckily for us, things didn't stay like that for long. Not going into a lot of technical details—because that would take hours and hours...—but Earth has reclaimed its ability to ascend. And we, with her. Well, those of us who still can."

"Because of the distortion," I put in.

"Right."

"So, what now?"

He stared into my eyes for a second, then dragged a hand through his hair. "Now, we heal."

Jan didn't look like he was paying attention to our conversation at all. He was still lost in the culinary experience—*orgasm*. Already devouring a second portion of Carrot Pasta with Creamy Zesty Garlic Sauce. After the dessert he *just* had.

"Meaning?"

"Ascension is a process. Doesn't happen overnight. And we wouldn't even be here today without help," Pierre said.

I knew what he was implying. "Like help from other beings? Other races?"

"Eternal races," he added.

And then I realized. He was referring to those beings that had their anatomies intact. *Christics*.

"What you're really asking is, where we go from here? What reality we will experience? Right?!"

I had read about different Ascension scenarios. Most of them, talking about a New Earth. Or moving up to the fourth and settle into the fifth dimension. But I was curious to learn what *he* had to say about it. So, I simply nodded my head.

"If you expect a black and white answer, I'm afraid I don't have one. The path each of us will take, is determined by the quantum of Source energy we hold in our life form. Some will manage to accrete so much energy, enough to leave this Time Space Matrix and return to Source, at the end of their life time. But some, will want to experience other reality systems and continue the process of ascension, of healing.

"Your choices, determine the place you will ascend to. You will however, always find a place to call home. There exist an uncountable number of reality fields, which you already know. So nowhere, we'll seem foreign to you. You will always reach those you know, those you remember," Pierre concluded.

Somehow, his answer confirmed what my intuition—my inner guidance—already told me. But I was sure, he could be a little more specific than that. "I see. But after all that you said, I assume, you have already a destination in mind. A place where you want to ascend to. So, what's it called?"

He hesitated for a second, clasped his hands under his chin, then spoke. "Aurora Earth."

chapter / ELEVEN

"Cool! Sounds like a name for a vacation place," Jan startled us. And just when I thought we lost him, he decided to join in the conversation. Popping up with a bubbly remark.

Ironically or not, the name reminded me of a *real* vacation place back home, at the Black Sea. A sea resort called Cape Aurora. Where actually I spent a summer vacation with my family, when I was kid.

"What is this place? How do you *get* there?" I asked, excitement coloring my voice.

Pierre looked at me, mirroring my emotion. "I want to show you something," he pushed his chair back and got up. "But we have to go upstairs to my office."

"Sure," I said, and turned my face to Jan who was still *eating*—unbelievable...he could eat and eat...and eat some more. "You coming?"

"Go ahead," he talked with his mouth full. "After I'm done. It's too damn good to—"

I frowned at him. I felt kind of embarrassed.

Pierre smiled kindly, holding a hand up. "Take your time. And if you want more, please feel free to order whatever you like. You are my guests. I want you to feel at home."

Jan looked like he was on cloud nine. "Thanks. Maybe I will. Um...could you tell me where the bathroom is?"

I was under the impression, than Jan was not *just* feeling at home, but kind of abusing Pierre's hospitality. I think he was still making me pay, for dragging him into this.

"Of course. Go back to the bar, and on the other side of it there's a small hallway. And there you'll find it, " Pierre explained, and then pointed to a window above the back entrance. "Feel free to join us anytime. It's the first door on the left."

Jan nodded, chewing happily.

I was quite surprised, to see how his vigilance toward my personal safety, was easily swayed in favor of more *food*.

I sighed lightly. "Okay. Let's go," I motioned Pierre to lead the way.

When Pierre opened the door to his office, a *sea* of books welcomed me. They were everywhere. On the walls, in the floor-to-ceiling bookcases. On the coffee table— between the two couches facing each other in front of a fire place. On the couches. On the window sill. On the working desk. On the floor. *Everywhere.*

Normally, I didn't like the clutter—it affected my internal clarity—but I did *love* books. *Really* passionate about books. There was just something magical about them. That, and the fact I was an avid knowledge seeker, slash consumer.

I took three steps and stopped, swirling my head around. "Wow! Now I get what you meant by collecting knowledge…" I managed, my voice filled with admiration and a hint of *envy*. Most people drooled over other people, cars, expensive watches, different modern toys. I drooled over books.

A chuckle came from behind me. "This is just a small chunk. It's basically what I need to have around for my day to day work…research," he added, nonchalantly.

My jaw dropped.

"Excuse me, but what is your *real* profession?" I said, already intrigued.

He was now standing next to me, hands in his pockets. "I have a degree in history and political science."

"So you teach?"

"I used to. Now, only occasionally. Small lectures, here and there. Given the *exotic* nature of my interests, I try to keep a low profile. I write books, mostly. Of course, under a pseudonym."

"Why use a pseudonym?" I asked, intrigued.

"Because what I write about, it's powerful and dangerous, too," his brows arched.

Now that he mentioned those two attributes, it gave me a *pretty* good idea about the nature of his writings.

I braced myself and looked him straight in the eye. "I've got to ask you this now. Because I'm losing patience. And we don't have forever. Who's *we* and *they* in this equation? And please, no more evasive answers. I want specific."

Hands still in his pockets, he mirrored my stare. "My Vertical Family."

I blinked once, completely puzzled. "Your what?"

"You wanted specific. I gave you specific."

"I meant no more going around the bush. Not *cryptic*," I retorted.

He started toward his desk. "Now, see? I thought my approach was better," then settled into the chair behind the desk, gesturing me to take the other available one across from him. Which I did.

"And what approach was that?" I said, hands crossed over my chest.

"I tried to give you a context. A bigger picture. So when I'd come up with a term like that, you wouldn't have this reaction."

Okay. He had a point.

Pierre continued. "That's why I brought you here. So I can *enlighten* you…"

I left out a sigh, then started to rub my hands up and down my face. "I'm sorry, I'm so jumpy. It's just…a lot has happened to me lately. I came to Paris to escape for a few days, those things that terrified me. But I was wrong to think that was possible. They followed me here."

He leaned back in his chair, looking at me attentively. "Care to share? I'm here to help you, remember?!"

Shoulders slumped, I began to tell him about everything that troubled my days *and* my nights. About the last attack from two nights ago, when I almost died again. And the ones prior to coming to Paris. Then I went on, and summarized my encounters with the guy in black. And the fact that he also, mentioned a *they*, which spiked my paranoia when I heard Pierre say that with no explanation. Of course I couldn't omit the event with me ran by a car and turned all ghostly, while being saved by two very tall—and bald—men. Then, all the other uncountable weird situations I could remember.

After that, I gave him a compressed version of my life so far. Including the depression episode, which killed me twice. And basically, my journey of discovery. My quest for answers so far.

When I was done spilling out, Pierre leaned forward, arms resting on the desk. "So, you're an architect?!" he said, more to himself than to me.

I frowned. "That's all you got, out of everything I've just told you?"

"No. It's just…it's very interesting. *You* are very interesting. Your story. The whole thing," Pierre admitted.

"Interesting won't make me sleep better at night. Or safer…" I said, pressing my lips.

For several seconds, he empty stared at me. With a sudden move, rolled his chair backwards, turned to a shelf behind him, and pulled out a rather *large* book. Then rolled himself back, and placed the book on the desk. "How many chakras do we have?"

Come on, that was basics. "Seven." Was that a test?

His hands began browsing through the book. Then brusquely stopped, when he found what he was looking for. "Nine embodied, but two dormant—until very recently—" and rotated the book so I could see what was written there. "Actually, we have fifteen."

Huh?

I leaned over. On one page there was a drawing showing a human silhouette encased in a fifteen layer capsule. On the other, the silhouette in profile, showing the exact location of the chakras and some other *things*. "What are these?" I pointed to the little star signs in between the chakras.

"Crystal Seals. They serve as frequency separators. Or seals. They modulate the wave spectra between particle and anti-particle Reality Frequency Bands," Pierre responded, as if this was common knowledge.

Only it wasn't. Not even for me. Not yet, anyway. But I was hungry for new knowledge, so I pretended to be totally unfazed. "Okay. But what this has to do with what we've talked earlier?" I said, looking up from the book.

Pierre tilted his head to the side, pinching his chin. "You know how over the course of history—well, the official one…not the *real* one—there were spiritual teachers who said that if you want to find God you have to look within? Well, that's literal."

Of course, I knew. Meditation was one of those practices that changed my life forever and for the better. "I think this is an established thing in the 'spiritual community.'"

"Yes. But what I'm referring to, is much more substantial than anything what's out there," he insisted.

"I'm listening."

"What you see here," he placed a hand on the opened book between us. "It's just a tiny fraction of our spiritual anatomy. Although that term is not entirely correct. *Divine Architecture* would be more accurate. But for the sake of the argument, let's call it *Spiritual Anatomy*. As in the part of ourselves which is invisible to most people."

"Go on."

Pierre's fingers were resting now, on the encapsulated human silhouette. "Like these layers here, our Spiritual Anatomy has more parts than just the Chakra System. We have a Light Body, a Luminary Body, a Radial Body, Vertical Pillars, Shields, Merka-ba Fields…etc. *Each* is composed of other elements. *Each* has a certain structure. A geometrical configuration."

I was an architect. Of course everything had a structure. There was no such thing as *random* in my world. Everything in nature was intelligent design. So it made perfect sense. "You mean that thing call Sacred Geometry?"

He nodded. "Yes. Although what's out there, *barely* scratches the surface. And mostly, if not everything, has to do with *fallen* systems. Finite life systems."

"I see."

"Anyways. Going back to connecting the dots…our spiritual anatomy holds the key to Ascension. To going to other worlds. To other planes of existence. And ultimately, to *freedom* from the distortion."

I like the sound of that.

"But in order to do all these things, you need to repair your Spiritual Anatomy first. There's no way around it. Especially, if you want to take this body with you. You have to transmute it," Pierre insisted.

"And how do I do this?" I asked, curiosity—and something which I would describe as recognition?—burning in me.

He leaned back in his chair. "They're called *Techniques*. Or simply put, they are very specific exercises."

"What kind of Techniques?"

"They are similar to meditation. Only they operate with particular symbols and energies. Directing them to different parts of the anatomy, to perform various tasks. Very much so, like computer programs. So first, you must get to know the *language*," Pierre said.

Seems logical.

Only I wish I would've learned about them sooner.

"In May of 2012, a critical mass of energy was reached, which created a separation within the planetary energetic grid. So naturally, this affected us all. Not just the people. But *every* life form. On December 21, 2012 our planet anchored the final three Pillars—and before that, Pillars one through nine. Having all twelve Pillars turned on, made it possible for the planet to rise really high in energy, shutting down the access of the Fallen Systems to Earth's energy."

"So, basically it stopped the hacking." I said, more to myself.

Pierre ran a hand through his hair, and then continued. "Yes. But there is still a lot of work ahead of us. Events to take place that will aid the healing process. That will help sort this mess we're in."

The more he talked, the more I had the impression I knew nothing about this... *subject*. "Care to expand on the whole *mess* issue?"

He checked his watch quickly.

That had me wonder. What the hell was Jan *doing*? I mean, I knew he liked to eat—okay...I liked it, too—but even for him that was a little exaggerated. Not that the conversation with Pierre bored me—completely the opposite. In fact, I could stay here and listen to him for hours...days...weeks. Okay. For an unlimited amount of time, until my curiosity would reach a satisfaction point.

"The abbreviated story," he said, clasping his hands, "is that, during the Atlantis Time

Cycle—more than 26000 years ago—*the Fallens* have inserted a 'virus program' into the planet's second dimensional frequency band. What we currently perceive as solid, is the second dimensional frequency band seen from the third dimensional frequency band—where our consciousness resides."

Okay… *that* I really didn't know. "If I get this right, this means that what we *always* perceive as real, solid, and very much physical, is the plane *below* our consciousness. Or, consciousness is always one plane—one frequency—band above solid."

"Exactly."

Wow. This was mind blowing. Made me think on *Avatar*—the movie. And how they inserted their consciousness into another body, yet keeping their original body alive. The ramifications of *this* idea alone, opened a door into something that would forever shatter our perspective on what it meant to experience living.

"The second dimensional frequency band is also our Emotional Body. Our physical body—entirely—represents our emotional body. The same goes for the planet. What we see through our physical eyes, is the Emotional Body. So the virus was inserted into the Emotional Body of the planet, where it allowed a mathematical program to manifest a pattern called by many the 'End Time Drama.' Which was an attempt of various fallen races to take the entire planet and its energy quantum, into their Black Hole System. This was always a matter of survival for them. We, the planet, were just fuel. Simply food," Pierre explained calmly.

Holy crap!

"So whoever incarnated here on this planet, automatically picked up the virus program. They intended for this End of a Time Cycle—December 21, 2012—to have their last battle for Earth's energy. Without the End Time Drama, the end of this time cycle was supposed to be just that. The end of a time cycle. "

I exhaled heavily.

For a few moments, I didn't know what to say. Too many emotions, running through my system. I just sat wordless, looking out the window.

As if he knew what was going through my head, Pierre broke the silence. "How was this possible? Well, for eons of time the planet's life force was stolen. Ran in reverse, and used to create more distortions. All, to serve one purpose.

"The planet couldn't access the original information, encrypted in the Divine Program. So for a very *very,* long time, things like Ascension, not having to die, being in direct communication with your Higher Family—"

And then something clicked. "You mean the Vertical Family."

He smiled. "Exactly that I mean."

Ha! I giggled inside, for figuring that one out.

"We couldn't access real joy, happiness, living in balance, having healthy relationships, abundance. These codes didn't have enough Source energy to turn on."

"How do you know this stuff? I mean, where do you have this knowledge?" As he stated, he *really* had substantial knowledge. Nothing like I had heard, read, or seen anywhere. And I bet, what he just shared, were just...peanuts.

He huffed. "This is another long story. Another—" but when he saw my disappointed eyes, Pierre made an effort. "Some was passed on to me, from my family. Some, was from other sources. And lately, I have my own direct link to—"

"You mean your Vertical Family," I put in.

He met my eager gaze. "Yes. And right now, a lot of the info coming through my own connection, is overwriting some of the previous knowledge. Because of the distortion and all. Now that more Source energy is available, some things that are described to be in a certain way, are not exactly like that anymore. But not entirely wrong either. So at the moment, I'm in the middle of sorting out a *huge* body of information."

I was right again. "Wow." Now I understood the dark circles around his eyes. "You don't get much sleep lately, do you?"

Pierre smirked, confirming my suspicion. He straightened in his chair, hands leafing through the pages of another book, he just picked up from a pile on the window sill—next to him. "Before you leave, I really want you to do this," he extended his hand offering me the opened book. "Here. Have a look at this."

Without hesitation, I took it. "The 12D Seal, or the Maharic Seal," read the title on the left page. Under it, there was a beautiful drawing, followed by text. They were steps of a visualization exercise. "I'm assuming, this is a Technique?!" I said, still reading through.

"Correct." His response, coming a little too sudden, startling me. "Not just any

Technique. The Twelve Dimensional Seal is a keystone tool. It does a lot of things. For instance, it begins the process of activating the higher chakras of the personal Eternal Life Grid," he said turning the page on the book with the chakras. His index finger, pointing to another human silhouette which had drawn upon the schematics of the Tree of Life. The one he showed me at the restaurant yesterday.

I took a closer look, absorbing every details.

"Used regularly, this triggers and activates the DNA Template. Causing other parts of the Spiritual Anatomy to work properly. Like having again a full 12 dimensional Merkaba for instance," Pierre added.

I remembered reading about Merkaba somewhere. But, I didn't pay too much attention. "You mean the spiritual vehicle to transport yourself to other worlds? Realities?"

"Yes. Now go back to the Technique, and read it thoroughly. Then I'll explain, the things you find unclear," Pierre insisted.

"Okay."

"And when you're done, we'll do the Technique. Well, you'll do it. I'll just guide you through it."

Awesome!!!

I nodded, excitement rushing through me. This was Christmas and Easter two-in-one for me. Not that I was celebrating either one of them anymore. At least not in that traditional sense.

Not wasting a second more, I devoured the words. The drawing was a Symbol Code—apparently a very important one called the God Seed Code—which I was supposed to place it visually at the pineal gland first.

The steps didn't seem that complicated to me. Only a few things here and there needed clarifying. Which Pierre did, like a very good teacher. Methodical and with easy and logical analogies. The rest, was just like any other visualization meditation. "I think I'm ready," I said, decidedly.

"Good. Now put the book down, and try to find a comfortable position to sit in. Back straight. Arms resting on your legs. And close your eyes. But more importantly… try to relax." Pierre's commands were firm, yet calming. Like a professional.

I took a few breaths until my mind and my pulse slowed down to an imperceptible rhythm. A feeling of peace settling over me.

Now, I was *really* ready.

chapter / TWELVE

A final blast of energy rippled through my entire being. Leaving every atom in a state of pure bliss…

I was shivering when it ended. It felt as if I had just immersed myself in ice cold water. This was some strong…badass Technique.

"Wow…" I managed.

Eyes still closed—trying to compose myself—I heard Pierre's soft chuckle. "Welcome to the Eternal Life path."

"It feels pretty damn awesome," I replied, joy filling me. "Now what?"

Pierre's amused glance welcomed me when I finally opened my eyes. "Now, you do that every day for a while. Until I can show you more. You need at least a couple of weeks of daily practice. This way you'll build 12D energy, gradually. Until it stabilizes. Otherwise it will overwork your energetical grids. Then, we can do more and faster."

I was completely ecstatic at the prospect of 'do more and faster.' But how was that going to happen? "Wait. What are you saying? 'Cause I don't intend to come back to Paris…that soon." Or in the foreseeable future. This was a vacation. And a pretty expensive one. "Plus, I've got work to do. Like work, *work*. You know? The kind that pays the bills?!" I added, a little panic starting to strangle me.

Pierre's clear features seemed unaffected. "Some things are more important than others. I'm sure we'll meet again. Our—"

"It's easy for you to say," I interrupted him, annoyance stepping in. "You have what normal people call *financial freedom*. I or Jan, don't have that." Even if earlier, Jan's confessed about the inheritance, still wouldn't count as financial freedom. That was to start a life together. Nothing more. "I really don't see how that will happen?" Frustration and helplessness adding to the whole array of toxic emotions circling in my head now.

I let out a heavy exhale.

How was it possible? A minute ago I was flying. And now, I was about to crash into negativity.

Pierre leaned forward, elbows resting on the table, palms cupping his face. "I thought you knew by now—"

"Know what?"

"Thoughts create reality. The whole holographic reality stuff…"

I snorted, rolling my eyes, face swirling to the side.

I wanted to laugh actually. More to free myself—from all that garbage accumulating in every crevasse of my brain—than anything else. "Of course I do."

"Then?" he said, gesticulating with his hands.

Okay. Now I felt embarrassed again. Not for Jan. But for me. I was supposed to know better. God *was* a better mathematician than me. So much, for being *enlightened*…

"Look. I understand. You have a life you have to go back to," he continued, when he saw me lost in my own *translation*. "But there are certain things set in motion. And they won't stop. You are just at the beginning of a long and sinuous path. Something *entirely* different. You need to prepare." His tone carrying an unspoken warning.

"Prepare for what?" I asked, an unsettling feeling rushing up my spine.

Gazing at me as if I were a kid, Pierre explained. "What has happened to you up until this point, it's only the beginning. And as more things activate. Planetary, as well as individually. You are not safe. You're protected, obviously. But not really safe."

This makes me feel so much better. Looking forward going back to Hamburg…

"And how am I supposed to react to this?" Frustration resurfacing. "I get it. I'm *special*, and all that. But I still don't think, I'm *that* important to constantly watch over

109

my back."

I knew I was contradicting myself by saying those things. I didn't need to be run over twice by a car, or to experience all the other freaky stuff, to see a pattern there. That's why I was here. I knew, I was being unreasonable. But, couldn't help it.

I was holding onto my little piece of 'normal' life that I had. If I'd let go of that, I would be lost. Fear would win. And then what? Back to depression? Death?

Pierre's laugh had a scattering effect on my very loud thoughts. "That's the thing. You *are.* I haven't figured out your mission, yet. Your role to play in all of this," he said, twirling his left hand. "But make no mistake. If you managed to attract that much attention so far. Things won't stop here."

I swallowed hard.

He opened his mouth to say something. Then closed it back. He started rubbing his eyes and face, concern spilling out. "I want to make you a proposition."

I'm listening.

"I'm sure you'll say no. But I will say it anyway."

I really had no idea where he was going with this. "Shoot."

"I want you to extend your stay here. Two more weeks. You will be staying with me, of course. So you don't have to worry about extra costs. I just need more time to see who's behind your attacks."

Absolutely no—

He saw my big objection coming, and pushed further. "Don't give me an answer now. I want you to think things very carefully," his tone very serious now.

At this point *absurd* seemed a word devoid of meaning. And Jan was the first thing that came to mind. How he would react. What he would say to this. I didn't have to stretch my imagination. I had a *pretty* good idea of what to expect. And "sure" or "yes, go for it" were none of those things. Just the opposite. Followed by a long lecture on how my judgment was *clearly* not working anymore, and that I shouldn't be trusted with decisions like this one. To put it mildly.

And then, there was the job—the only project I had, momentarily. I would most definitely lose that, for not delivering on time the final product. Mr. Tellman wasn't the kind of person to be interested in matters of the soul. I couldn't just explain to him that

I was on an existential quest, and apparently hunted by *things*, people, for which I had no names. Yet. He was just not built like that. For him, life was something very concrete and predictable. Any events out of the ordinary, would most probably be filed under 'errors' that need to be avoided.

Yeah.

Or I could just invent something, and work on the project from here. But what? I had a feeling that no matter how good the excuse would be, he would still be pissed.

Two more weeks, was not a long time to be away. But would definitely generate even more chaos in my *already* disturbed existence.

Hmmm…

$$\infty$$

"Oh my God! You didn't." Shock traveled through my words.

Jan was holding in his right palm a small black box. He opened it, and two emerald earrings were staring back at me. "What? You thought I would forget?" My silence was his answer. "Of course you did—"

"I—"

"You thought I was eating like a shameless pig. Which I did," he admitted, laughing. "But actually, this was the perfect opportunity."

I was standing there, speechless. Waiting for him to make sense.

We were on the second floor of the Eiffel Tower. For some reason, less tourists than expected. Night already falling on the city. And a light breeze messing with my curls.

"When Pierre asked you to go with him into his office, and I was still having food on my plate. It hit me." He couldn't stop giggling. "And Pierre telling me to order more… was pure genius. I was just going to use the bathroom excuse…at some point. All worked out *brilliantly,* by the way!"

"But you did order more," I said, remembering the fact that the whole time I was upstairs with Pierre, he didn't even bother to come and check up on me. To make sure I was safe and all that crap he was pestering me earlier with.

"I did. And it was *awesome.*" He looked like his was still savoring it in his head.

"You're sick. You know that, right?!"

He chuckled. Barely containing himself.

"Anyhow…with both of you going upstairs, I realized. *This* is my chance. I ordered first, of course. And man, that *Raw Parsnip Mushroom Alfredo Pasta* and *Lasgna…*" he exhaled, pleasure drooling from his words.

"I get it. It was epic," I said, kind of annoyed. We were still talking about food.

Jan shook his head. "No. Not epic. We need *new* words for stuff like this—"

"Okay, moving on now—"

"Right. And after that, I jogged across the street. Bought the earrings. The man who sold them to me, was actually really nice, and gave me a discount. I *might've* said something to him about a 'special' anniversary, to get the discount. And it worked! So, do you see it now?!" he emphasized, brows raised. "It was meant to be."

"But—"

"No more buts. I'm not going to return them. They were *made* for you. They're yours. Period," he said, decisively.

"But—"

Jan raised his left index finger. "Agh-agh!"

Hands on my hips, I looked into his happy eyes. "I was going say, and then what?"

"And then I ran back. Went to pee. And back at the table, waiting for the next dishes. Which didn't take very long. I was worried, it took too long. And you might suspect something," he grinned at me, idiotically. Well, cute. Idiotically cute.

"You lectured me the whole time, before going to Pierre's restaurant. Not to mention yesterday, when—"

"Yesterday, I knew *nothing* about the man. Not that now, I trust him completely. Or his motivations. But it's a public place. And, if anything would've happened, well, there were witnesses."

I groaned.

Funny, how his mind worked. On one hand, he would forget and or lose a lot of stuff. And on the other, he would just have this *weird* reasoning—which made total sense.

"Still. If I follow your logic, you chose to risk my well being. For which you have proclaimed your *'violent'* devotion. See the disparity here?" I retorted.

"And I stand by my words. If he gives me any reasons, I won't hesitate to hit him." Jan's eyes glistening with some sort of evil pleasure.

In the night sky, with his tousled hair and that expression in his eyes, he looked fierce. Beautiful in a dark way.

"You're crazy..." I sighed, shaking my head.

"Look who's talking!" Jan's brows shot up.

We stared at each other for a second, and in the next, we both burst into laughter. Healthy, deep, unrestrained, laughter. It felt so good. So liberating.

"I want to laugh, too. What's going on?" Pierre's melodic voice, brought the moment to a halt.

We completely forgot about him.

Both of us, turned our heads at the same time. Jan was still chuckling. I on the other hand, started to feel a little pang of guilt, and stopped. We weren't *exactly* laughing at him. But he was part of the whole story, which had us react all sorts of crazy. This particular moment included.

Then I remembered his proposition from earlier in the day, anxiety and more guilt surging through me. I hadn't told Jan about it. Not that I didn't want to, but—. Fine, I chickened out. Things were complicated as they were. I didn't need more...drama. Not now, anyway.

"We've just realized, we're both crazy," Jan's answer came, now glancing at me.

Surprised by his honesty, I smiled.

"Crazy is good. It's a sign of sanity," Pierre said, resting his hands on our shoulders, giving a quick squeeze.

So much truth in those words...

For a very brief moment, I didn't know what to say. Apparently, not Jan. "Hey, could you take our picture? We don't have that many. Somehow we didn't have time to record much of our trip. It would be a waste, to miss this opportunity."

"Sure. Gladly." Enthusiastically, Pierre grabbed the camera from Jan, and took a few steps backwards. Then started shooting. He took more than one, to Jan's satisfaction. The whole time telling us to smile more. Actually, that was for me.

I was sort of in a trance. Being there, but not really. Dreading the moment when I had to answer him.

After had we finished our little *initiation* session in his office, we went downstairs. Where of course, Jan was pigging out, happily and undisturbed. Since then, nothing was ever mentioned. We had just tackled the mundane, and he was nice enough to give us a personal tour of the city. Showing us special places, which you wouldn't find in any guide book. That made it even more charming. Not to mention cool.

And as promised, he took us to the Eiffel Tower, too. Apparently having a great grandfather working at the tower, came with benefits.

"Why don't I take a photo of you and Ariana?" Jan offered. "And then you and me."

Pierre seemed thrilled, and complied immediately.

They exchanged places, and when Pierre was standing next to me, he slid his hand into the inside pocket of his jacket and took out something. "I want you to have this," then put it in my palm. "It's important. Please, accept it." It was a silver chain with a pendant.

Without any objection, I looked closely at the jewelry piece. "It's beautiful. Why? Why is it important?" I lifted up my eyes.

Pierre placed a hand on the small of my back, already prepared for the picture. "Did you make up your mind?"

I did. "Yes."

"And?"

Jan was grimacing, waiting for the group of tourists who was crowding in front of us, to move along.

"I'll have to say no," I answered, feeling all sorts of guilty and stupid. "I'm sorry. It's not the best time for me right now."

I expected Pierre to convince me otherwise. Or at least to object. To come up with more reasons, for why I *should* stay longer. None of that happened.

"*I'm* sorry. Could you please, do something for me?"

"Sure."

"Please, wear this every day." With his free hand pointed to the chain in my palm.

"It will help you with your transition—"

"Ready?" Jan called out to us, having now a clear path to take our picture.

We both said yes, and that was that. Moment immortalized. Then I took one, with them together.

"Now the three of us," Jan insisted, obviously in a very good mood.

I stopped and asked an older lady to do it for us. She was kind, and accepted.

I went back and decided to let Pierre in the middle. He patted us gently on the back, before putting his arms around our shoulders. "We're ready!" Pierre shouted toward the lady.

Afterwards…all went kind of blurry.

chapter / THIRTEEN

Hamburg was exactly the same, as we left it. Grizzled, rainy…cheerless.

Even just a little sun, would make such a huge difference. But, we had no such luck. We had decided to take a taxi from the airport. Which was a better idea than the S-train. I didn't feel like walking the entire distance from the S-Bahn station to our home.

"Welcome home!" Jan said, as he held open for me the entrance door of our apartment building.

I snorted, and walked in. "Yeah. I kind of missed all that gray and depressing vibe. Who needs sunny and joyful?"

Jan laughed at my sarcasm. "You have to admit. It has a certain charm to it."

"Right." Shoulders slumped, I started climbing the stairs.

When we reached our apartment's front door, Jan set our luggage beside him, looking for the key.

"I got this," I said, grabbing the key from my bag. "Somebody's cooking something nice." The smell hit me the moment we entered the building. Now it just got stronger. Our building was from the fifties. Modernized and with better insulation. But I guess some smells traveled through everything. Or maybe my sense of smell got really sharp.

"Yeah."

Apparently I wasn't the only one.

"This reminds me," Jan peered at me. "We need to eat. Like, right now."

I laughed.

"This smell comes with good music." I put the key into the lock, sudden realization coming over me. "Oh my God! It comes from our apartment." I turned to face Jan, eyes terrified.

He snorted. "It's not possible. We checked everything together when we left, remember?!"

My face even more constricted with fear. "Exactly."

"Step aside," Jan ordered me calmly. "Let me do it."

I did, and Jan unlocked the door swiftly, pulling it open. The music and the cooking smells were indeed coming from our place.

Okay. This was really absurd. What kind of thief—if this what it was—would do that? Cook and listen to music?

"Alex?" Jan called out. "Is that you? Mama?"

Of course.

His brother and his mom received each, a spare key from us. Just in case. Emergencies. Family stuff. And apparently this?

"Surprise!" an entirely different voice, answered.

Raluca?!

My sister came out of the kitchen, with a dish cloth, wiping her hands in it. "Anybody hungry?" she said, wearing a big smile.

A surprise for sure. And a good one, too.

"Did I tell you, how much I love your sister?" Jan said, stopping for a moment, then went back to inhaling the food my sister prepared for us.

"About a dozen times?!" I said, shaking my head.

Raluca burst into laughter. "I don't mind. There is more if you want," she reassured Jan.

I snorted. "That's basically what he did this entire trip. Eat."

"That's not totally accurate," Jan spoke, mouth full of food. "What about those earrings I bought for you?"

My sister, who was sitting beside me, pushed a strand of hair behind my ear. "They're gorgeous. Where did you get those? I mean, I know, Paris. But, was it an antique shop? They look vintage."

Good question.

Since we came back, I realized that some parts of our trip didn't make sense. Plus, a lot of blanks in between.

"Don't remember exactly. It was on our way to eat somewhere. That's what, two days ago?" Jan answered. And it was clear to me now, he had the same problem. Not being able to pin down events, not to mention the details.

"Enough about us," I changed the subject, annoyed by the fog on both our minds. Which now in retrospect was getting suspicious. "What really brings you here? Besides this," gesturing to the whole surprise thing.

"An event. For a friend. Do you remember, Peter?"

"Not really."

"Okay. I met him a while ago. At one of our events. He was one of the guests. And he liked it very much. The event, I mean. And us. So, next thing I know, I get his card and a phone call from him, a week later. Telling me they want us to organize something for his company. He owns a big advertising agency, and for three years now, has been living in Bucharest. The main office is here in Hamburg, but he runs the one in Bucharest. He fell in love with the city," my sister said, cheerfully. "Well, I guess the weather and the people helped, too."

I smiled. It was nice for a change to hear about normal people, doing normal things. And most of all, to see Raluca happy.

"I'm not surprised," I concluded.

"We've decided, we're doing the wedding there. Hey, did you put some rosemary in the soup?" Jan spoke, in his usual manner of jumping from one thing to another. No transition in between.

"That's great news! And yes, there is some rosemary in there," Raluca replied,

118

then turned her head to face me, eyes squinted. "When were you going to tell me this? I do this for a living you know?!"

I held my hands up in defense. "Whoa... See, now you're doing it, too."

"Do what?"

I sighed lightly. "We were talking about you, and then you fell into Jan's trap."

"Now I feel insulted," Jan said, pretending to be hurt, but barely containing a smile.

Lips pursed, I gave him a light shove.

"Hello, people?! Wedding, in Bucharest?!" Raluca's eyes pendulating from me to Jan.

Then we both spoke at the same time.

"It's no big deal," I said, waving a hand dismissively at her. While Jan nodded, eyes wide open, a huge grin splashed across his face. "I know..."

"You can't be serious. Not a big deal?! My sister is getting married. *Of course*, it's a big deal! Are you out of your mind?!"

I leaned back into my chair, rolling my eyes. "Jan likes to start shit."

Jan chuckled, confirming my point.

I continued. "We were on the plane, on our way back home. And that's when we talked about the *possibility* of doing the wedding in Bucharest. Next summer. Because of the weather, the atmosphere..."

"It would be more festive and fun," Jan put in, voice filled with excitement.

"Exactly," my sister agreed, clapping her hands like a little kid.

"So it's been only a few hours, since we've actually considered it. No need to get crazy," I assured her. "And you *are* the first to know about the *possibility*. Happy now?"

"This calls for celebration. I'll go get the Champagne." She pushed her chair back, and got to her feet.

"Wait. You got us Champagne, too?" Jan asked, eyes glowing at the prospect.

"What do you think?"

Jan got up from the table. "I think, I love you. But you know that, already. Now, you sit down. I'll go get it." And then went into the kitchen.

"It's on the second shelf!" Raluca called out after him.

"Back to you now. So, tell me about the event that you're supposed to do here," I said, happy to change the subject. Not wanting to obsess about the wedding with her. For me, wedding meant something very personal. Something small, intimate. For my sister…well, that was her job. Not that her agency was specialized in weddings or anything, but she would see it like one of her projects. Nothing wrong with that. I too, saw it as a project. Only different. Not long ago, I was doing corporate events and exhibitions for a living. Well, the design part.

"Yeah, about that… How would you feel about working for me on this project?" She shifted her weight in the chair, curling her legs underneath her.

"Oh."

"Actually, it's more like a 'please-help-your-sister-and-no-is-not-acceptable' situation." Raluca practically begged.

I took a deep breath, and exhaled. "What's this about?"

"I need you to make the place prettier than it is. It's at this new hotel close to Astra Tower. We reserved the restaurant on the top floor. It has a terrace and everything. It looks good. But, I don't know? It misses something. So, here you come into play. I need you to work your magic," she explained, an exaggerated grin, confirming that she was in over her head.

"When is this thing going down?"

"Friday…"

"As in *next* Friday?"

She nodded, face contorted. Uncomfortable.

"Of course, next Friday…" I shook my head in disbelief.

Raluca leaned closer to me, eyes like a puppy when caught doing something stupid. "That means you'll help?"

"Looks like I don't have a choice. But thanks, for the courtesy." I couldn't help the sarcasm.

"You're the best!" She grabbed me, almost suffocating me in her embrace. "Thank you! I mean it!"

I hugged her back. "What are sisters for?!"

Then we heard a popping noise. Champagne.

"I'm coming!" Jan yelled from the kitchen.

It seemed, Jan was again lost in some 'mission impossible' in the kitchen. Transforming *yet* another simple task, into something that would cause headaches. At best.

"Take your time!" I yelled back, rolling my eyes.

My sister giggled, completely entertained by the whole situation. She'd heard from me how Jan was a master at this kind of stuff. Now she was experiencing it live.

Eyebrows raised, Raluca placed a hand on my arm. "By the way, I've negotiated a very *generous* sum for your services. Peter wants the best. And I told him, that *the best* comes at price."

I sighed, dragging a hand through my hair. "What, now you're trying to motivate me? You've already got me agree to this. No need to sweeten it. You know how I work. First, I have to get to know the challenge. Then, the rest follows—"

"I heard somebody is in need of a little motivation." Like a cat, silent and unexpected, Jan popped up at my side, holding three glasses full with the bubbly drink. Handed one to each of us, and then sat down.

I snorted. "Yeah. Only the right kind."

"I think I know exactly what you need," Jan said, placing his glass on the table. Tugged my chair closer to him, carefully taking the glass from my hand, setting it next to his. Then cupped my face between his hands, and leaned in, our noses almost touching. I opened my mouth to speak, and before I knew it, his lips were on mine stopping my unspoken thoughts.

And just like that, he deepened the kiss, forcing any resistance out of me, and for a few moments there, I almost forgot that my sister was there with us. Watching us feeding from each other's mouth.

Raluca cleared her throat. "*That* is definitely the type of motivation only you can provide." Then broke into a cheerful laugh.

I drew away, cheeks flushed.

Jan's hands were now hanging around my shoulders. "I know," his gaze on my lips, his words still carrying the heat we just shared.

I was not a prude, but somehow I couldn't escape feeling embarrassed in front of my sister. So I gave him a gentle shove. "Yeah. Okay lover boy, play nice," I said, trying to diffuse the awkward moment. "Let's hear what this is about."

Jan readjusted the position of his chair, which was now basically glued to mine. So now he could really, sit next to me. With an arm across my shoulders, he gave me a tight squeeze. "See, it worked. My method is *flawless*," he said, winking at my sister.

I elbowed him in the ribs, making him groan. "Mine, too."

Jan held his hands up. "Now she's all yours."

Raluca broke into an uncontrollable laughter. "You guys are hilarious!"

When she finally came down from it, she began telling us more about the event on Friday. It was, *exactly* what I feared. A ten year anniversary of the company. Awards gala. Hundreds of guests. A music show. And many more other details, for which I had only three words: a huge production.

Insane.

She assured me that, most of it was already taken care of. She had been working on it for at least two months. But they needed a concept to unite all elements. A vision to make everything come together. Then she shared some of the ideas which Peter found *sexy*, but so far, none of the people she'd contacted in regards to design, delivered what they envisioned.

When I asked her why she didn't tell me earlier—like immediately when she got the project—she said, that at the time I was unavailable. Just coming out the depression. I was still tending to my emotional wounds.

She was right. I was a mess.

I was mentally and emotionally, unavailable. Not that now I was completely healed, but I was in a good place. Mostly because of *green smoothies* and other *rawsome* foods. Which most people won't even consider for turning their life around.

She said, she thought she could manage, with the people she had hired in the first place. She had never expected to get this chaotic and unresolved so close to the finish line.

I *definitely* saw a pattern there—knowing things from her previous projects—but I didn't want to rub it in her face. Working with deadlines and managing multiple parties to a contract, was never easy. Not even for me. I simply handled it differently. Not that she wasn't doing a great job, or making it all work in the end. But the *detour*…that was what made my stomach clench up in knots. Bonus, I would get headaches, neck pain, back pain, and nightmares. Especially, when I would be called in for a rescue mission. Like now.

She went to pick up something from her bag on the console table down the entrance hall. When she returned with a big folder under her arm and another in her hands, Jan lost interest in our discussion, motivating he had to do the dishes. Which, we didn't complain.

My sister and I were still going through papers and numbers when he came to tell us an early goodnight. Soon after finishing tidying up things in the kitchen. Sleep was another vital component to him—next to food and…me.

Utterly envious, that he was about to plunge into the dream world—and I was already dealing with unplanned work, five seconds after we arrived home—I kissed him goodnight. Raluca gave him a tight hug, and then he was gone. To blissful sleep.

Ah…life was so unfair.

After a while, seeing me all quiet, staring blank at the wall behind her, Raluca knew I was lost in my head. Assessing the situation. "Look, let's call it a day. We can do this tomorrow. I'm really sorry, I had to dump this on you," she said, now voice filled with real remorse. "I admit, it was very selfish of me to do this. You've just got back from vacation, and didn't even have time to readjust to your own life, and here I am, forcing more deadlines down your throat." Then she began picking up the sheets of paper spread everywhere on the table and put them back in her folders.

Her words forced me back to reality and out of that web of new data.

"Well, thank you for realizing that," I retorted, no guilt whatsoever.

She smiled sadly. "I'll understand if you change your mind. I'll just deal with Peter my own way."

Very tempting idea.

"And what way is that?" I asked intrigued.

"You know me. I'll find something to make it work," she said, voice a little unsure.

Yeah. I wasn't fooled. She needed my help, and as much as I would love to say no just because I could. I simply couldn't.

"You know me too, right?!"

Still organizing her papers, she nodded. "I'll be fine," Raluca insisted.

I shook my head at her denial. "Yes. You'll be fine. Because I won't desert you. Now let's go to bed, before I *really* change my mind for lack of sleep," I said, already standing.

In an instant, my sister's arms clung around me, her head resting on my shoulder. "You're the best," she whispered, then kissed me on the cheek.

We stayed like that hugging each other, a little longer, then she pulled away wiping tears from her eyes. I patted her on her back, then went to make the bed for her in the living room, and she hit the shower.

Our three-room apartment, though not very big, was very well organized and clutter free—thanks to my obsession with having space. So while the workroom or home office, was also a dining area, the living room was mainly a guest room. Due to the fact that we were using the workroom for all our daily activities. Less the sleeping, which was always in the bedroom. The only room with one clear designated function. Well, besides the kitchen and the bathroom.

I was almost done when she came out of the shower, wearing a plaid printed pajama pants and a t-shirt saying "Keep calm and call your sister."

I broke into an uncontrollable laughter.

She peered at me innocently. "What?"

I managed to point at her t-shirt. "No way! Where did you get that?" I asked, still laughing so hard, almost peed my pants.

Raluca tipped her head down, hands tugging at her t-shirt. "Oh. This you mean?"

I nodded between laughs.

"It's my favorite sleep t-shirt," Raluca said matter-of-factly. "It makes me feel safe," she added sheepishly, her face flushed.

I could hug her just for that, if I could only stop laughing so hard.

Earlier I was tired and annoyed. But now, it was all gone. Just like that.

A lesson to be learned. Never underestimate the power of a good slogan t-shirt.

"This reminds me. I got you something from Paris. I was going to send it to you in the next days," I said, and then went to get my bag.

Raluca settled comfortable under the covers and was now waiting for me, eyes curious and filled with excitement.

I came and sat on the edge of the bed—expandable sofa—and put the bag on my lap, and started digging. When I finally found what I was looking for, I pulled it out. "Here. This is for you. I hope you like it," I said, handing her a small shopping bag.

She took it, and looked inside. "Wow, this beautiful!" Raluca exclaimed, her hand holding now a silver necklace with a big tear drop shape pendant.

Oops. "Sorry, *that* is actually mine," I replied, smiling uncomfortably. "But if you really like it, it's yours. There is more in the—"

"Where did you get this?" Raluca asked, her fingers examining the pendant very closely. Then she looked up, with this expression in her eyes, like she uncovered a great mystery. "Do you *know* what this is?"

Mouth half-opened, wanting to tell her what I remember about this necklace, Raluca went on. "*This* is the pendant from my dream. The one I've been telling you. Where you'd have to make a difficult choice?!"

I was rapidly going through my brain, searching for that piece of information. Lately, I had a lot of blurred moments. Not quite sure whether I'd dreamed about it, or really had experienced it. Ironically, most of my dreams recently, weren't just *dreams*. So crazy...

"Um... Oh! You're right. You did, tell me about it. Right before that ballet thing with Tim. That was, what? Two weeks ago?"

Raluca nodded. "Something like that."

We were now both staring at each other, waiting for the other to go first.

Eyebrows raised, Raluca broke the silent moment. "So? Where did you get it?"

I exhaled heavily letting my frustration out, and began telling her the bits and pieces of information my brain had. It wasn't much. I had this memory of me and Jan at the Eiffel Tower with this guy—I forgot his name—who took pictures of us. At some point Jan had decided to take one of me with this...person. And this guy had asked me something—which I found weird in retrospect—about making a decision. I told her that I remember saying no—not sure why though. And that afterwards, he gave me the necklace, telling me I should wear it every day, which it would help me with my transition.

When I was done spilling, I noticed that Raluca's face went all serious. "So, yeah. That's pretty much, what I've got."

Raluca shifted her position, steadying herself on her elbow, head resting on her arm. "And you don't think it's weird? I mean, you just confirmed some parts of my dream. If, not all of it. You said you felt sad, when you said no to him. In my dream you looked sad, and you had to make this important decision—"

Another wave of frustration bubbled inside me. "No, it's not weird at all," I answered sarcastically. "Of course, it's weird. Ever since I left Paris, I've been squeezing my brains out to figure what the *hell* happened. To me. To Jan. 'Cause obviously, the both of us have the same problem. We don't remember certain things. Or places. Or names."

"Hmmm… You know what? You should see a hypnotherapist. Do some time regression hypnosis. See what really happened. That'll give you some answers," she said, already leaning back on her pillow, stretching her arms like a cat.

Not a bad idea.

"Right, because my scheduled has cleared, and next week I have nothing else to do, but retrieve lost memories," I retorted instead.

Raluca snorted. "Not next week, obviously. You know, what I mean."

I did.

If I would survive next week's storm, I would most definitely try that option.

"We really should get some sleep. Your *surprise*, comes with a huge price tag. Besides work, tomorrow we have to go to Lydia. That means 'goodbye' lazy Sunday morning for me, and 'hello' unwanted brunch." Not that Lydia—Jan's mom—wasn't great. But since I had changed my eating patterns…brunch wasn't on my menu anymore. Plus, I really *really*, loved sleeping in on Sundays.

I leaned in, and kissed Raluca goodnight on her cheek ."Do you want me to turn off the light?"

"No. I think I'll read a little bit," she answered, her hand already grabbing the book on the side table next to her head.

Bag in my hand, I stood. "All right then. Have fun. Nighty night," I said, and started toward the door.

Not looking up from her book, Raluca said, "I love you!"

I smiled. "Idem."

chapter / FOURTEEN

It always begins like this. And then… God knows what follows. Most of the time not good things.

I am lying in bed, yet I can see through the bedroom's door into the hallway. And it's dark, as usual. No problem though, discerning the shapes of what's around me.

Out of nowhere, a light pierces through the darkness, and a ghostly shape—white and thin like smoke—flies toward me. It's very tall, and from what I can make out of its contour, it looks human. But barely.

I am afraid, and already panicking. Yet, can't do anything. Run or hide. It's as if I'm merely a spectator. Only, this is really happening, and is happening to me.

The white smoky silhouette is above me. All my emotions are frozen in place. The dread, the fright… they are just distant voices. Nothing can save me now.

Paralyzed and eerily fascinated, I see a tube of light descending upon me and into my solar plexus. Next thing I know, I feel this thing drilling inside me. Going up, and down. Going up, and down. Up, and down…

I register a very uncomfortable sensation. This reminds me of when the dentist drills into your tooth down the root canal. And although you had anesthesia, you can still sense an unpleasant feeling. It's not real pain, nonetheless is very disagreeable. And I want it to stop. Now…

. . .

It stops. After what seems like forever.
All of it.

"He's a cheater!" Jan called out at his brother, his arms tightening around my waist. "See, that's why I don't play with him anymore. He's an asshole." Then placed a kiss on the top of my head.

"Ah, but an asshole who wins!" Alex exclaimed, voice filled with child like satisfaction, to the dismay of his mother and his wife.

Raluca chuckled.

My sister seemed to enjoy the game of cards as much as I did watching them play.

Back against Jan's chest, I was lying on the sofa watching four adults gathered around the coffee table, becoming children again.

I couldn't believe, how fast time went by. Just a few hours ago—which felt like minutes—we had arrived at Lydia's, as requested—more like ordered—by Alex. Raluca and Alex upon her *surprise* arrival, made a deal. He would provide the key to our apartment, and she would have to come to brunch. Us included. Mandatory.

Emotional blackmail. Alex was good at that.

Since Jan had got all caught up into finishing his Ph.D. thesis, didn't get to see his mother as often as he used to. Actually we both didn't. Myself now being involved in this new project, plus the fact that I needed my space to heal. So now, his brother and Meike, had the weekly task to come and keep her company for a few hours. Maybe eat together. Take her for a walk in the park.

A year before Jan and I got together, his father had died of cancer. An ugly battle, which his father lost. That made his mom spiral into depression. In time she got better, but she'd started to feel lonely. Alex had insisted that she moved to Hamburg to be closer to them. Easier to reach, in case something would happen to her.

She hadn't followed the advice right away. She was afraid to leave her brother and sisters, and friends in Osnabrück. Her whole life was there. However, more than a year ago, going through a health problem, she had realized, that maybe it was about time to make a change. And so she had moved to Hamburg.

Only to develop another depression.

I wasn't surprised. Hamburg did that to many people. Me included.

Thank God, I was now out of that deep black abyss.

So the whole weekly routine, was the only way she'd cope. Lately she got better. In fact, today she was practically *glowing* with happiness to see us all crammed in her small, but cozy living room.

Meike pulled herself up to her feet. "I think I need more sugar. Or I'll hurt him, for sure. Anyone, more cake?" she asked, already slaloming through the sea of legs and arms, heading toward the kitchen.

"Yes, please!" Alex raised his hand.

The rest of us declined, including Jan. Which was nothing short of a miracle.

Meike stopped, hands on her hips, shaking her head at her husband. "I wasn't asking you. You don't get to cheat, and then want to eat my cake. It doesn't work like that." And then she strode out of the room.

"Oh, come on..." Alex called after her. "You know, you love me! Me! The love of your life?!"

From the kitchen we heard the door to the fridge opening and closing with a slam. "Keep telling yourself that. See if I care..."

Except for Lydia, we were all laughing. "Play nice, kids!" she said. "Now, you've upset Meike." Her smiled faded, allowing worries in her eyes.

"Nah..." Alex waved a hand dismissively. "She's just a little pissed, 'cause I didn't let her win. Right, *Schatzi*?!" he said, tilting his chin up, waiting for her reaction. "You know me! I'm an asshole sometimes..."

Still, nothing came from the kitchen. Silence.

Yeah, this was about to get uncomfortable.

Meike was the most sensitive one in this family. And apparently, Alex didn't really get that. He would see everything as a joke. Expecting everyone, to understand that. Well, Meike wasn't tailored that way.

Jan was shaking his head, trying to contain his chuckle. "Tonight, he'll sleep on the floor with the dog."

I elbowed him lightly in his side, and then turned so I can face him.

"What?" he asked innocently."It's true. If he doesn't apologize…"

I stared for a second longer in Jan's eyes, passing a silent message to him, then repositioned myself comfortably in his arms.

"This is so unfair. I didn't do anything, and *I* get the 'dirty look,'" Jan huffed in frustration, his arms encircling me.

My sister shifted her position, wanting to stand up. "I'll go, check on her," she said, her voice a little anxious.

"No. I'll go." Lydia put her hands on the coffee table to steady herself, mirroring my sister's intention. "Alex, you're *so* insensitive sometimes, you know that?" she continued, her words carrying a reproach.

Jan held up a hand. "No need. Both of you, please stay where you are. Let him solve his own shit. This is ridiculous." Then gestured toward his brother. "Alex, get off your ass man! And go apologize. Unbelievable—"

"You people, have no sense of humor," Alex retorted shaking his head, while pulling himself up, from the floor.

Without even looking at him, Jan spit more irony. "Tell that, to your wife—"

Alex stood, straightening his pants and shirt, and regardless of everyone said, he was still smiling. Like I said. He lacked a sense for potentially 'hazardous' situations.

He took one step, and before he could take another, my vision did something *totally* unexpected.

In an instant, the room and everything in it, became a two-dimensional image. Without warning, or time to assess the situation, the image deconstructed itself in smaller pieces. Just like a puzzle. Next thing I knew, pieces started to vanish one by one, leaving behind complete blackness.

In a blink of an eye, I was surrounded by nothingness, complete darkness. Like a power failure. *Total* shut down.

What the—

And just like that, what just happened a few…milliseconds ago? I was reliving the whole process in reverse. Reality was reassembling itself right before my eyes, just

131

I blinked a few times, unsure of my vision. I rubbed my fingers over my eyelids, and then opened my eyes again.

Everything seemed to be normal. Except, that now, *Meike* was back in the room. With her back pressed against Alex's chest, and she was talking and smiling at us.

Holy crap... What was *that*? Did I lose consciousness? Did I faint?

No. It couldn't be.

The whole thing couldn't have been more than a split of a second. How did this happen?

Before I could stop myself, I blurted out. "When did you get here so fast?"

In the next moment, all five pairs of eyes, were on me. And judging by their look, my question seemed ridiculous. Or more like, *idiotic.*

Meike tipped her head to the side, a hand pointing at me. "You're funny. Ha-haha…"

The others were joining her. Amused by my *joke.*

I wasn't kidding.

Me looking completely confused and frustrated, didn't help the situation either. They were still giggling. "I'm being serious. One moment Alex was there," I said pointing to the place I last saw him before the 'lights went out.' "And now, you're both here. Happy and smiling, like nothing happened—"

"I know, what you're trying to do," Meike gestured with the index finger at me. "But you're still coming to my party. Especially, now. Since, Herr *Arschloch* here," she swirled her head in Alex's direction. "Will pay for a beautiful evening out by the Elbe."

Seriously, Lydia was a *cool* lady. Not many mothers of boys, were so casual about insulting their sons in public—even if just jokingly. I was always amazed by her ability to take each situation for what it was. And that was one of the many reasons, why I loved her so dearly.

"What party?" I asked, even more bemused.

"Meike's birthday party. You fell asleep, didn't you?" Jan's words brushing by my ear, sounding amused by my presumed activity.

Oh, crap. I forgot she had a birthday coming up.

Still, it didn't deter me from wanting to make sense out of the whole weird…time space blackout.

"Am I *that* boring that nobody pays attention to what I say?" Meike, pretended to be insulted.

"*Schatzi*, you know I always listen," Alex rushed to add.

She huffed. "Liar."

Then realization dawned on me.

Holy mother of crap!

Did I just time traveled? I knew it was possible. Real. Hell, a few weeks ago I went all incorporeal, when that car went through me. Why would *this*, not be just that? Time travel.

But why?

Why now?

More question that needed answers.

Excited and terrified at the same time, I sat up, swung my legs over the couch, and pushed to my feet.

Before I could move any further, Jan caught my hand in his. "Are you okay?" His gold-brown eyes filled with concern, and *something* else. Not sure what.

I hesitated for a second. "I will be in second. I just need some water. You know me, 'weird' is my middle name. I just had one of *those* moments," I replied, giving a faint smile.

"I'll go get it for you. You stay here—"

"You don't have to. I need to stand for a bit, too. To get myself together."

"I'm coming with you. You look pale."

"I'm fine," I insisted, and left.

I made it into the kitchen, glad that nobody had the *slightest* idea of what had happened. They were back to discussing the party on Thursday.

Crap.

Next week was already crammed with work, *thanks* to my sister. How we were going to get everything done in time for the event on Friday, *and* go to the Meike's birthday party on Thursday, was a big mystery. One that I would *not* dwell on it, right now.

I simply refuse.

I pulled the door open to the top cabinet where the glasses were. A sudden wave of nausea, traveled through my body, leaving me weak, and causing me to lose balance. I stumbled against the kitchen table top. I managed to steady myself before I could do any damages to the clean plates piled on the counter, or to hurt myself.

Whoa… This is not good.

I shook my body shortly. Wanting to get rid of the unpleasant sensation.

It only made it worse.

Bad idea. Bad idea.

This made me rethink the whole idea of having a glass of water. The queasiness, had an unexpected effect on my stomach. I stuffed myself earlier with food, but with my kind of food. Which was a big green smoothie and a huge salad. And a few minutes ago, I was doing great. Now, I felt that the whole thing might come back up. I could feel my throat ready to make just that.

Oh, no. No, no, no…

I made it to the bathroom, and locked the door behind me. In the next second I was over the sink, pouring the life out of me. An uninterrupted stream of…

Ugh…

When it finally stopped, I turned on the faucet, letting the water wash down the contents on my stomach splattered over the sink. Then I cleaned my face well, and rinsed my mouth to get rid of the smell. I felt that wasn't enough, so I picked up the tooth paste, and one of the extra tooth brushes that Lydia kept around for guests, and cleaned my teeth and mouth. And again the sink. I didn't like to leave a mess behind me.

When I was done, already felt much better. I splashed more water on my face to resuscitate myself. But my head was still spinning. So I lowered myself, until I reached the floor. I sat down, back against the bathtub. I pulled my knees up and my head back resting on the edge of the bathtub. My hands finding the coolness of the tiles, a blessing.

I simply let myself drift, eyes blank staring.

Minutes went by. I don't know how many.

A brief knock on the door, broke my trance. "Ariana? Are you okay?" Behind the door, Jan's voice sounded really worried.

Startled, I rushed to answer. "Yeah. Sure. Just need a minute."

"It's been half an hour. I thought, something happened to you. Can I come in?"

How ironic. Something *did* happen earlier, and nobody bothered to ask then. Not that if I told them, they would believe me. Well, except my sister and Jan. But I wasn't going to explain him this now. "I'm fine. Just had a little indigestion problem. Ate something that didn't agree with me. I'll be out soon. Promise," I said, my head turned toward the door.

"*Oh*. Okay. But if you don't feel good, we can go home," he offered.

"Sounds good."

"I'll go tell Raluca to get ready." And then I heard him walk away.

I pushed to my feet, and surprisingly the queasiness was gone. But I still felt a little weak, and on top of that, I had to pee.

I unbuttoned my pants and was now pushing them down my thighs.

"*Nice…* I wasn't expecting this. But I'm not complaining. Please, keep going," a voice said, and I froze in place.

I would recognize that voice anywhere.

Not because it had a nice timbre, or it brought back warm and fuzzy memories. But because it represented everything I dreaded the most.

And now I was terrified. Again. I wasn't going to give him the satisfaction, though. "Do you get off, on people urinating?" Already pulling my pants back up, letting my shirt cover the open fly.

He never appeared to me in a private place before. Well, not in my home anyway. *Thank God for that!* But who was to say, that that was not going to be where the next encounter would take place.

I looked up and saw the guy in black, wearing a teasing smile, as if all was fine with the world, and his popping up in Lydia's bathroom, was a natural occurrence. "Not that I recall. But I bet I wouldn't mind seeing *you* do that."

I had two words for him: *sick bastard.*

Then I did something I never thought I would have the courage to. I stared at him

135

defiantly. "Who the hell are you?" I asked, coldly. "What do you want from me?"

He spread his big arms. "I thought you'd never ask?" Then he let them fall beside him. "I'm Lorenzo. Your new partner." He tilted his head to the side.

I huffed. "My partner? Partner of what?"

"How was Paris?" Amusement playing in his dark sly eyes.

If I was horrified a few moments ago, now, the amount had tripled. The way he said it, triggered an icy realization in me. My eyes widened. "It was you, wasn't it? The night when I was attacked in my sleep. In Paris. You tried to *kill* me." I might've not remembered much from my vacation, but *that* was definitely one of the things I did.

He nodded, impressed. "Very good. And no, I wasn't. I was just testing you. We've been doing it for a while now. I'm sure you remember a lot of—"

Indignation boiled inside me. "Test me? *For what?* Don't tell me, military? Black Ops? Or it's too cliché to—"

"Close. But no. We're not military, but we work in that area, as well. In fact, we're involved in all areas of life," Lorenzo said firmly. "We've been called many names, but one that it's popular these days, is *Archons*. I'll let you, do the homework on that one."

The name sounded familiar, and even without research, I could sense a negative vibe from it.

He closed the distance between us in two steps, and was now towering me. He was at least a head taller than me. Though not extremely big, he looked very much athletic. "Something is different about you," he said, sniffing me—literally. "Anything else you'd like to share with me?" Lorenzo arched his eyebrows.

"I thought you can read my mind?" I replied incredulously.

"Not exactly. But this doesn't stop me from finding out what I need to know." His words carrying an unspoken threat.

"Why not just kill me, get it over with. Isn't that where we're heading, anyway? 'Cause I'm pretty sure, I'm going to say no to whatever you have to propose," I replied, foolishly.

Lorenzo chuckled, his hands clasped behind his back. "First off, I can't kill you. Yet. I don't have the order," he said, his eyes wondering over me.

I swallowed hard.

He leaned in, his mouth whispering in my ear. "You reek of fear, yet, you have little consideration for your own life. I think I like you, already."

I shrugged my shoulders. "I guess, dying twice and coming back, might have something to do with it. Or, I simply don't value my life, as you said."

"Yet, you fight for it, when the threat is real," Lorenzo added. "What motivates you?"

For a second there, I wasn't sure what he meant by it. Then I understood. Truth be told, I wasn't sure either, what motivated me to fight. Maybe just my natural survival instinct. Maybe something else, entirely different. Whatever it was, wanted me to stay in this body.

"Why are you, *here*? In a private bathroom. How did you find me, if it's not much to ask?" I said, gesticulating.

Lorenzo planted his hands on his hips. "Well, that thing you did earlier back there," he swirled his head toward the door, in the direction of the living room. "Was enough to alert us. To find your location."

I gazed at him, totally baffled.

He continued. "Come on… You're a smart girl! Figure it out. *How* did I find you?" Lorenzo was grinning, like that was supposed to help me or something.

And then, it did.

No way. No way. It can't be. Or can it?

I had read about it, in articles, books…you name it. A myriad of technologies were using that already. But I guess until you knew for sure, you couldn't truly say it was so.

I mirrored Lorenzo's stance, and then answered. "Brain waves."

Lorenzo smiled pleased, his eyes gleaming in acknowledgment. "It' going to be a pleasure, working with you." He turned his back to me, and took one step toward the door. The air around him seemed to vibrate, smudging his contour. Then he fissured out of my reality.

chapter / FIFTHTEEN

"How do you know it was time traveling, and not you falling asleep, and dreaming it?" Jan asked, his hand pushing back a strand of hair from my face.

I stared at him in disbelief, my mouth half opened.

Hadn't he witness me having other uncountable *special situations*, to know that I was perfectly capable to make that distinction? Okay, I admit, certain *things* were harder to set apart, because a lot of my dreams were not just *dreams*. Things happened in that realm. They were as real as it got. Like what I'd experienced last night. As unusual as it was, not to mention uncomfortable, it was real. How did I know that? Because it started as a dream, and all of sudden, I was awake and aware in my body. The only thing that was *different*, was the fact I couldn't move. I was trapped in my body. A silent observer. Then, throughout the whole day, I had this sensation of lightness around my belly. Like a blockage was removed. And my mind was at peace.

Well, until *this* thing happened.

Seriously, sometimes I felt like there was no point in sharing this stuff with him anymore. On the one hand, he would be open to understand this strange world I was operating in, and on the other, his science mind side, would kick his naturally intuitive mind to the curb. Very frustrating.

"I believe her. I have my own share of *weird*," Raluca put in.

We got back home from Lydia, a few minutes ago, and I was telling both of them,

138

what really had happened with me back there. What I saw. How everything disappeared and reappeared again in a matter of seconds. Or less. Didn't even reach the Lorenzo part yet, and seeing how this was going, I was starting to doubt myself for wanting to spill out the whole thing.

I sighed, and let myself drop on the couch. "This is not about believing or not believing. It happened, alright?! And the way things stand, more is underway," I snapped at them.

Jan glanced at me standing, while my sister took one of the rolling chairs in our home office, and sat down. Then, both spoke at the same time. "What do you mean?"

The boiling sensation was back. Frustration, anger, and helplessness, were brewing a toxic cocktail. And all of it, wanted out.

Against my better judgment, and my ever cautiousness regarding this subject, I blurted out the rest. The part where Lorenzo popped in Lydia's bathroom, and scared the crap out me. The part where he told me he was my partner, and also being the one responsible for the astral attack in Paris. To which Jan reacted at once. "*What*? What kind of partner?"

I shook my head in response. "That's something I still have to figure it out. Although, it's not hard to imagine where this goes. Considering the fact that he travels through walls. And apparently, space and time is not a problem either..."

Jan dropped on the other rolling chair opposite my sister. He dragged his hands through his hair, then rubbed them up and down against his face.

"Did I mention he can appear invisible to others?" I added casually, crossing my arms over my chest.

Raluca nodded. "Oh, yeah. I remember from the last time—"

"What last time?" Jan's eyes pendulating from me to my sister and back, looking for answers. "You two, better start talking now. 'Cause this is getting insane."

I gazed at my sister incredulous. She was supposed to keep her mouth shut about that one. She knew a lot more than Jan. Things I'd sensed they were *too* out there for him. But I guess now was a good a time as any, to let it all out. Unload this *weight* I had been carrying—mostly alone.

"Let's put it this way. I'm pretty sure Lorenzo—or his people—are behind that car running over me," I said.

Jan's eyes were dilated. "*What*? When was this?"

Raluca jumped in. "When our cousin was visiting you. They were out shopping—"

"So you're saying, all three of you knew this whole time?" he asked, exasperation coloring his voice.

"No. Just me and Raluca. And Tim," I admitted, feeling a pang of guilt.

He shook his head, letting out a nervous snort.

I continued. "I know how this looks. But, believe me, I've always wanted to tell you everything. It's just… You made it clear, that *some* stuff was too hard to swallow. Or you just, dismiss it entirely. And sometimes, I need to communicate with people who understand what I'm going through. That have similar experiences. Or at least who are open to accept, that *maybe* reality is stranger than what we're taught."

"This is crazy," Jan said, in defeat.

"I agree."

"No. I mean *you* thinking that if you don't tell me certain things, we'll be fine. Look around, does this look like fine?! You getting yourself in life and death situations. You being chased by men that can walk through walls. You being—"

Legs crossed, I clasped my hands around my knees. "What changed, in your perspective?"

"What do you mean?" he frowned.

"A few minutes ago, you were still debating, if what I've just said was perhaps a dream. Dismissing basically, my experience. Then you go on, and give me this speech of me acting all irresponsible. Like you actually *believe* these other wacky occurrences—which personally, I find harder to process. Though, they really happened. So which one is it? It's very frustrating to navigate through what is possible or not possible for you."

Jan placed a hand on the table, his gaze locking with mine. "You're right. My science mind sometimes overrides the rest."

"Thank you," I remarked sarcastically.

"But lately, I had my own share of *inexplicable* things."

That was new.

"So, yes. I pay attention a lot more than you think. It's just—"

"You refuse to look like a fool for believing stuff at the fringe of reason," I added.

"Yeah, something like that," Jan responded, a weak smile forming at the corners of his mouth.

"As a passionate scientist, you should be open to a lot more. I don't have to tell you, how far science has come. You know that already. You have an insider's perspective. The technologies we use in our daily lives, are simply children's toys. The real progress is being constantly blocked, so the big corporations can prosper endlessly," I emphasized.

Jan shifted in his chair. "True. But—"

I held a hand up and continued. "And there are *things* outside of this slavery mechanism that can't be quantified and sold. And they are afraid of it. They are afraid of people waking up to their power. They are afraid of *consciousness*. And whenever one of us goes through this process of awakening, we're being ridiculed, marginalized, isolated. Or worse."

My sister nodded in agreement, then placed a hand over her heart. "*I* know how it feels."

"And you're afraid of ridicule," I point it out to Jan.

Jan pushed his chair closer to the desk, leaned forward, his arm resting on it. "I can't afford right now to be ridiculed. I still have to get my PhD." He let out a snort. "But that doesn't mean I'm not curious and open to explore the unknown. Especially, when your life is involved. I want to keep you safe. I want to be there for you…"

"Then *be* there for me. Mute your skepticism. Turn down a little your distrust. And then you'll be there for me," I replied, my frustration pushing the words out of my mouth. "And if you simply can't, then don't wonder if I keep quiet about certain facts."

My sister chuckled.

Both Jan and I, moved our gaze on Raluca. "I don't understand, what's funny?" I said confused.

Raluca sighed. "You two are *so* lucky to have each other. Do you know how many people would love to have a relationship like yours? Do you?"

Jan's intense gaze was now on me. "*I* certainly do."

I rolled my eyes. "What this has to do with, anything?"

"Obviously you're both blind," Raluca replied, flatly. "So, let's concentrate on the problem at hand. What's the deal with this guy. Who is he?"

"The correct question is, what is he?" I emphasized.

Jan spoke before Raluca could form her question. "What is he?"

"An Archon."

They looked at me, as if I said the name of a tree species in Latin. Or something in Chinese. No idea what that meant.

Raluca shifted on her chair, playing with the ring on her finger. "Sounds familiar. Don't have a clue what it is, though."

"Sounds like a character from a computer game, or something like that," Jan added.

When he put it like that, didn't seem as threatening anymore. Or real. Except it was, and I had to figure out what the hell this was.

I scratched my head, then leaned back on the couch. "I was going to do some research online. But then I had to explain myself to you and—"

"Okay. Let's not waste time anymore," Raluca suggested, went for her bag, and picked up her tablet. Jan and I followed suit. He opened the laptop in front of him, and I took the one sitting on a shelf in the bookcase next to the couch.

All three of us started working.

An hour later, scrolling down throw countless articles, fragments from several different books, and some personal experiences splashed on personal blogs, then comparing it with my own, I got a pretty good idea of what an *Archon* was. All saying basically the same thing.

As I suspected, nothing good though.

Nothing good at all.

Archon meant "Ruler" or "Lord" in Greek. A frequently used term in the ancient world, for the governor of a province, or any religious or governmental authority. Only those, weren't the Archons I was dealing with. Though they called themselves that, because they saw themselves as the rulers and enslavers of humanity. The term Archon was used first by the ancient Gnostics to refer to inorganic, parasitic beings, which intrude upon the human mind and deviate our consciousness from its natural design.

After the burning of the Library of Alexandria—which was run by Gnostics—several texts mentioning these mysterious beings and what they were about, survived. But until recently, the powers at be, had taken care of in the last two millennia to write out the Archons from our history.

Gnosis or 'inner knowing,' was a path of mysticism that ultimately led to self-realization of one's own divinity. And as usual, because this path led to *true* FREEDOM, the opposing forces thrashed it. Misinterpreting it. Getting things out of context. Demonizing it.

Fortunately, some irrefutable proof made it to the present day.

Gnostic texts dating back from 100 BC—more than 2000 years old—had been found in December 1945 in Nah Hammadi, Egypt. Though it wasn't until 1947 when a French scholar by the name of Jean Doresse, had identified their great importance.

Among many other *highly* interesting things, the Nag Hammadi material had recorded visionary experiences of initiates, as well as, first-hand encounters with these parasitic beings.

These inorganic beings had emerged in this solar system prior to Earth being formed.

These *cyborgs* were a genuine species inhabiting the planetary system—sun and moon, too.

A cool fact was, that even back then, the Gnostics knew that we lived in a holographic reality, except that these beings were constructing it by imitating, duplicating, the geometric forms emanated from the realm of the Generators. From the Original Source.

According to these teachings, around 3600 BC, an invasion occurred that was like a virus. And the beings invading were called Archons. They infiltrated into the web of our reality Matrix as well as, into our minds and souls, creating disconnection from God. From Source.

So for thousands and thousands of years—if not tens of thousands or more—we were not ourselves anymore. We were lost in distorted copies of life and thought patterns.

Yeah. Heartbreaking.

I looked up from my screen and shared my findings with Raluca and Jan, more curious to hear what they uncovered.

Raluca went first. "Apparently they are envious toward humanity, because we possess the intentionality they lack. They feed on our fear. We are food to them. Above all, they attempt to keep us from realizing our 'inner light,' from claiming and evolving our divine essence. Which they don't possess either."

I nodded in agreement. Nothing new so far.

"I found a physical description of Archons," Jan added, enthusiastically.

Somehow that part escaped me.

Arms crossed over my chest, I raised my eyebrows, waiting for him to continue.

"According to the Gnostic codices, there are two types. Embryonic and a draconic or reptilian type," he said.

My sister's eyes widened in realization. "Which totally explains the whole Greys and Reptilians alien situation."

Then a question rose in my mind. "What about the Annunaki? They seem pretty Archontic to me, too. All that genetic manipulation they did to us. Not to mention, that they are shape-shifters after all…"

"It doesn't say anything about that. But it might as well be so," Jan added, and went further. "It says here, they can penetrate the terrestrial atmosphere and terrorize humans. But they can't remain for very long in the biosphere," a smirk escaping him, like he couldn't believe what he was reading. Or the fact that he was actually considering it to be true. "They exist as an alien species separate of mankind, but also as a presence in our minds. Something like a set of programs operating in our mental environment. Invading our mental software is far more effective, than any physical breaching of the biosphere."

The more he read, the more his face lit up in cold realization. As if for the first time, things sunk in, and made sense. It wasn't anymore just me saying weird stuff to him. He was actually *getting* it.

Raluca scrolled down on the screen and stopped. "Archons use telepathy and suggestion to attempt to deviate us from our intended course. The most successful technique they use to infiltrate and substitute our mind-set with theirs, is through religious ideology. For instance, the Judeo-Christian Salvationism is the primary ploy of the Archons. The whole thing is nothing more than an alien implant."

Her words reached inside me knowledge I never knew I had on this subject. I mean, I knew that all organized standard religions were nothing but a tool to keep the masses ignorant and busy fighting each other. But that was just an intellectual understanding. This was different. Couldn't explain how I knew that what she was saying was true. But every cell in my body recognized the truth in it.

"*Error* is the key word," Jan punctuated, his face focused on the screen. "The Gnostics say, that the Archons are agents of error. They aren't evil in the sense that they possess autonomous powers of destruction. Rather, they *need* human complicity to gain power over mankind. Yet, they are predatory. Archons exploit our tendencies to let mistake go uncorrected."

"Basically they use our real co-creative powers to create the reality, the context they want," I added flatly.

My sister simply nodded.

Jan rubbed a hand up and down his face, and then continued. "Anyone who assists them willingly or unconsciously is in fact a kind of an Archon. One way is by accepting their programs, their mind-set, and then implementing them in our society. The other way is by actively or passively conforming to the imposed agendas."

I smirked, and instantly, Lorenzo's face popped in my head. What kind of an Archon was he? Not hard to guess, though. As for his physicality—and his ability to pop up in the most unexpected places or realms—well, that area was still covered in mystery.

He read further. "In society, the Archontic forces manifest through authoritarian systems—belief-systems included—in ways which make humans to turn against their innate power and potential, thus violating the symbiosis of nature."

Yep. Sounds about right.

"Okay. One thing is sure," I said, determined.

Jan and Raluca looked at me, expectantly.

"I need help."

"What do you have in mind?" my sister asked, preparing herself to treat this like one of her work projects. Which kind of made me laugh. 'Cause that would be my approach, too. Which in a way was a good thing. It would keep me moving. Instead of just being paralyzed with fear, waiting for the worst to happen.

Jan stood up really fast, his hands on his hips. "I know what I have to do. From this moment on I will keep a night watch and during the day—"

"*You?*" I chuckled.

He frowned, looking insulted.

"You *do* realize how ridiculous *and* improbable this sounds to me. You have trouble just *staying up* late. Which in most cases is 11 p.m.—with a few exceptions which include working overnight in the lab. And I work at night most of the time. That's my most efficient and productive time. I try to go to bed earlier only when I feel like my batteries are empty. That's why we have basically different sleep cycles. You know that, already. And during the day, you're going to do what? Guard me? I don't think so. You have to be in the lab. You have to work on your experiments and write on your thesis. And finish this God damn thing," I said, frustrated.

Jan's defeated gaze, told me he knew I was right. "But how can I help, otherwise?"

"Yeah, how can we help?" Raluca insisted. "You are not alone in this. I know it feels like it. But who knows, tomorrow it could be me, or Jan, who's targeted. I want to be able to do something about it. You taught me, we have to fight until the last breath." She spoke the words with such conviction, that I felt tears forming at my eyes.

I guess I taught her well. Usually I would be the one doing the moral support speech. But this time, the situation was reversed.

My throat felt dried, and hoarse. "We have to find a way to stop Lorenzo or any of these *people* that are after me, from reaching me. Awake or asleep. As long as they can track me by my brain waves, it's pointless to run away and hide."

"Brain waves?" Jan repeated.

"Yeah. And apparently the little *incident* earlier, spiked my signal and that's how he knew where I was. My exact location. The rest, how he actually travels through space and time, well, I can only speculate. So unless we come up with some protection mechanism...I'm screwed."

For a few *long* seconds, silence fell over the room.

"Alright." My sister started up beat, her palms slapping her thighs. "We have to find some form of clouding you. Well, your brain patterns," she said that, like it was the most easy thing in the world to do.

"Did this guy or any of the other *freaks* reach you here, at home? Did *anything* appear to you in our home? Manifesting physically?" Jan asked.

I didn't need to think too much to answer that. "No. Only in the astral, or whatever plane that might be."

He dropped again in the chair, his hands moving through his hair, his eyes searching for answers.

"Maybe the space of your home is protected, only the astral has holes in it," Raluca, put in.

Hmmm.

Never really thought of that.

She continued. "I mean, these physical encounters with Lorenzo happened in a public place. Right?!"

"Except, today," I said, my lips forming a straight line.

"Right."

"She has a point, though," Jan said. "It's seems the encounters are always in a public place. Well, not here anyway. Which brings me to my earlier proposition. To watch over you when you sleep."

I arched my brows. "I usually go to bed when you're about to wake up. And every time when I was attacked at night, in the astral, and you were here, lying beside me, it didn't change a thing. Need I say more?"

"You sure know, how to make me feel useless," he said, bitterly.

"I am simply, stating the facts."

We continued like this for a little while, going around in circles, thus becoming increasingly frustrated. Then, decided to start searching again online for some sort of method, technique, device, anything...that actually could shield me from these *beings*.

We discovered several different solutions that shielded our brain from electromagnetic radiation, but nothing remotely helpful to my situation. They all basically had to do with protecting us against the electrosmog—from TVs, computers, mobiles phones, microwaves, radio waves, etc.

Not Archons.

At some point, exhaustion crept in all three of us. Protection or not, we needed to take a break. I was too tired, to care anymore about a possible attack. Finding a solution would have to wait until tomorrow.

All I wanted in that moment, was just to crash in my bed, and drift blissfully off to sleep.

And that's *exactly* what I did.

chapter / SIXTEEN

"Jan! Jan, wake up!" I called for the fourth time, my voice reaching that fine line between loud and downright shouting. I grabbed his arm, and shook it vigorously. "Hey! Wake up!"

He barely budged.

Yeah, that was basically our morning ritual. Waking up Jan, was like trying to get someone out of a coma. *Good luck with that.*

Very early on in our relationship, I'd decided that his method of waking up, was not going to work for me. Before we'd moved to Hamburg, while we'd still lived in a student dorm, he'd had a ridiculous alarm clock—with a *horrific* sound—which kept terrorizing me, six days a week, at five in the morning. Bonus fun, the alarm was set to ring three times at ten minutes interval.

Horrendous.

Naturally, this madness had a very important purpose. Make Jan go to work. Back then, he had a mini job as a bread packer at a local supermarket. And had the worst shift ever. The one, no man in their right mind would want it. Between six and eight in the morning.

Apparently though, for Jan was the perfect time frame to squeeze it in, then head to university, get to classes, and for the rest of the day, be in the lab.

Like now, back then, our working schedules were quite different. At the time I was doing graphic design for the university—for the music department. So most of my work was done from home. Which was good, as I didn't have to deal with strict working hours. Just deadlines, and show up at certain musical events organized by the school, playing host.

And because most of my work happened at night, and I *usually* crashed right before Jan would wake up, I'd decided to take on the role of the alarm clock. Firstly, because I couldn't take that hearing mutilation anymore. Secondly, because I was fast, and never needed special tricks to get up. And thirdly, after Jan left, I would go right back to sleep. So I was trying to keep the interruption of my sleep as short and painless as possible.

In order for this to work, I *really* had to make sure he was fully awake.

One time, my vigilance was out the window, and it resulted into a funny situation—well, in retrospect anyway. The previous night we'd had a party on our floor, in the common room, and Jan had stayed up later than usual—which was pretty uncommon—as I was the one going to bed last.

So when five a.m. came, and my phone's alarm clock rang, I sat up automatically like a zombie, went for the phone and shut it off. Then shook Jan vigorously, repeating loudly in his ear a few times to get up, and went right back to sleep.

At some point, like in a dream, I heard Jan's voice. "What a beautiful sunrise. The sky is *so* clear blue…"

"Ugh-uh," I heard myself answering, my eyes still shut.

"Just beautiful. Isn't it?" His voice insistent, tricking me into to opening my eyes and see what he was talking about.

The sky was remarkably clear and beautiful, indeed.

It too-k me about a minute to realize what had happened. At that time of the year—beginning of March—at five in the morning, was still dark outside. No sun rising at that hour. No blue sky.

Shit. He was late.

Two hours late.

Luckily for him, one of his work colleagues, covered for him. And honestly, no one was ever fired from a job that nobody wanted. Actually they were always understaffed.

Yeah…

Miraculously however, sometimes he would be able to get up all by himself. Mostly, during the time of the year when the days were longer. And since we had moved to Hamburg, and our bedroom was facing east—the light would come in pretty strong in the morning—that alone was a stark factor in the process of getting Jan up.

But today wasn't one of those lucky days.

"Jan, get up!" I tried a last time, and finally he opened his eyes, a smile forming at the corners of his mouth.

One of the positive things about being his alarm clock—or not—he would always wear a smile for me every morning. Sometimes even before his eyes would open.

I always thought it was sweet. Not because it was forced. But because that was Jan's nature. Naturally happy.

The downside was, he felt like chatting, and I would still be between realities, not fully awake, yet not really sleeping. So I had to come up with a rule, of 'no-talking-in-the-morning.' Just a kiss on my cheek, or neck, or whatever body part might be exposed and close to him.

"I'm really sorry for yesterday," he whispered to me, his arms encircling my waist, my back now against his chest. "I shouldn't have doubted you."

Oh no. He wanted to talk.

Sometimes the 'no talking' rule wouldn't always apply. Due to factors I couldn't control.

"Great. Thank you. Now go, and let me sleep for another two hours," I muttered, already pained that now I had less than two hours before I would have to wake up again.

Jan chuckled, his warm breath tickling the back of my neck. "You're so cute, when you do that."

I wanted to cry. "You mean, pissed."

He drew me closer in his arms, until there was no space left between us, burying his giggle in my hair. "I promise, you I will find a way to protect you. I know you don't see how I could help you—"

He was right. I didn't.

"But I will." He sounded so convinced, that I didn't want to ruin it for him.

"Great. Now let me sleep."

He barely contained his laughter, kissed me goodbye a few more times, and left the warmth of the bed.

$$\infty$$

The place Raluca chose for the event on Friday, wasn't bad at all. It had definite potential. When she had mentioned the hotel, I'd had something else in mind, but this one I found it to be even better. It was a new hotel, built during the time I was working at the event agency—the office was very close from it. A five minute walk.

Set in the heart of St. Pauli, and only a few hundred meters away from the harbor and in the opposite direction from the Reeperbahn Street—where a lot of the tourists would wander for fun—was a perfect place for a city vacation, or business trip. But what was most appealing to me, aside from the modern architecture, was the actual place where the whole production would go down. The hotel's very own rooftop restaurant slash lounge, with a generous terrace, and a view over the Elbe and the port area that was just...*spectacular*.

"I told you, I have it under control," she said, reading my pleased expression.

"I wasn't doubting your abilities. It's just, we don't have much time until Friday."

She nodded in agreement, her hand patting my shoulder. "That's why you're here. To make sure we'll pull this off."

"Thanks for the vote of confidence," I huffed, whirling my head around, my mind already working on details. Measuring the space, sketching with my eyes, simulating situations, browsing through colors and lights schemes.

After a short while, she started fidgeting around me, her impatience growing. "So what's the verdict?" Raluca asked, interrupting my relentless calculations.

"Interesting. I wasn't expecting this place to be so inspiring. I could actually, see a lot happening. Design wise."

"Good. I'm sure, Peter will be happy to hear that."

I turned to face her. "By the way, where is he?"

She peered around, scanning the faces of those at the tables and at the bar, and then checked her phone. "He texted me earlier. He's running a little bit late. He has a big meeting today. Why don't we sit somewhere, and have something to drink. I'm kind of thirsty. And hungry. I'll order something to eat, too. And screw Peter and his meeting. I was all morning here, to make sure the room reservations and the catering part are on course." Decidedly, she strode to a table across from us, pulled out a chair and sat down. Her bag and the two big white folders ending up on the chair next to her with a thump.

I snorted, understanding her frustration, then followed her.

Not that I minded a bit of a break for the day. But the day wasn't over for me.

After Jan had left this morning, I'd struggled to go back to sleep again. Only the too vivid memory of the previous day with all its *craziness*, wouldn't let me. Kept tormenting me. And when I'd realized, that it was pointless to insist on keeping my eyes closed, I got out bed and went over the stuff I had to discuss with Martina. Which was my first meeting today.

So far, the day was going great. Martina had her team order enough samples of tiles—which I was now carrying with me, in a rather large box and quite heavy, too—for the four o'clock meeting with Tellman. And while I was on vacation, she got most of the authorization drawings ready. Which was a big plus. More reasons, to make Tellman happy.

I had a little over two and a half hours time in between. I really hoped, Peter wouldn't show up, too late. I was going to help, but my first priority was still Tellman.

I placed the box on the table, slipped into the chair across from my sister, and hanged my bag over it. "I better eat then, as well. I don't know when I might get the chance, until later in the evening."

Raluca grabbed a menu, and began browsing through. "Last night after you both went to bed, I stayed up longer. And found something really interesting. "

I lifted my eyes from the screen of my phone, and then set it on the table. "Oh. Anything helpful?"

"Not in the way you expect. But nonetheless, important."

153

Eyebrows raised, I waited for her to go on.

"Remember the time, when you told me, that throughout your entire life you had this *nagging* feeling? Or more like a voice at the back of your head, telling you to keep going. Search further for the *truth*. That there's got to be more. Pushing you to dig deeper, and deeper."

"How could I *ever* forget? It's ever present. Never leaves my side."

Raluca shut the menu, set it aside, and clasped her hands. "Well that *thing* has a name. It's called Epinoia or 'After-thought.' It's a term I found, that the Gnostics used. Epinoia's main function is to awaken. To correct faults in the creation. Or to preserve hidden knowledge, as a means to rectify ignorance and forgetfulness. Basically, to awaken the others.

"It derives actually from Ennoia or Thought, which takes the form of Forethought (Pronoia) and First Thought (Protonoia). And of course a third form, as Epinoia. Anyways, there's a big explanation about how Source, the One, formed the Trinity, and how it expands itself maintaining unity. Something along the lines of…in the beginning, the One, thought upon itself. That mental reflection resulted into a two-fold extension of itself. One part, as the Father, who is the mind (Nous) or thinking, and the other as the Mother who is thought (Ennoia). From these two generated the Son (also Nous), who completed One's reflection upon itself. And through the Son, the thinking had a thought of itself thinking. And that's how Source, expands itself, over and over again. Never losing unity.

"Each new being that 'knows' Source (the One), becomes a part of the creation that reflects Source to itself. Like a series of mirrors. And these mirrors are called Aeons. It goes further than that. Explaining the mechanics of how this actually works. If you're interested I'll give you the link later—"

"Please do," I replied, already intrigued.

"Anyhow, the point I was trying to make, was that Epinoia was seeded into Adam, to remember his true origins. Which is in the Upper Aeons. To help him find his way back home. But then the androgynous Adam got split in Adam and Eve by the chief Archon."

"Wait, wait, wait. Go back to Aeons. You said Aeons are mirrors, I read somewhere that Aeons are cosmic cycles," I said, getting a bit confused.

Raluca shifted her body, now leaning back in her chair. "Both. In fact, in Gnostics teachings, Aeon means God, also. But not in a theological way. More like in terms of the Physics of Consciousness. Aeons are not beings. They are processes, which may be best depicted as immense currents. But currents that are alive. Self-aware. Intelligent. They are gendered, too."

Something clicked inside my head. "*Now* I get the whole thing with Goddess Sophia becoming Gaia. She is an Aeon. Aeon Sophia."

Raluca nodded, satisfied. "And her male counterpart is Aeon Christos."

Somehow yesterday being interested only in Archons, what they were, and even more pressing, *how* to protect myself against them, I overlooked other details, the other parts of the story. Of how Archons actually came to be. Or the biggest story of all times. The story of creation, according to the Gnostic texts.

Well, my sister apparently was curious enough to dig this info up. And I was grateful she did.

I gestured to her to continue.

"Ironically, the Archons are an unfortunate consequence of Aeon Sophia plunging unilaterally from the galactic core. When she went after her experiment—meaning us, the humans. Well, not this human today. The original androgynous humans. Again, the exact process, it was too complex for my brain to recall all the specifics. But it had something to do with fractal impact in the dense elementary array of the galactic limbs. Which resulted in these inorganic creatures. And because they emerged in the solar system prior to earth, they consider themselves Gods. Or Lords. Anyways…these are just a few of the stuff which stuck with me. Which is weird. Because my brain normally refuses to absorb this type *highly abstract* info," Raluca said, rubbing her temples. "That's actually your thing."

I sighed. "Interesting. This confirms, so much. Of what I knew from other sources. But this thing with Epinoia being placed in Adam, how does it work? Since now we have male and female."

"Right. Almost forgot my point. So, Epinoia was placed in the female part of Adam. And when the being was split in two, Epinoia went with the female. She became the key player in helping Adam and herself to remember who they were. And where they came from," Raluca concluded.

I sniggered. "It makes total sense."

"About?"

"About the whole fake story with Adam and Eve. About the human prototypes. The whole female created from man's rib. We have been fed so many lies. And what's worse, some truth has survived in form of a distorted story, which served one purpose. Keep us trapped in 3D. That's why the female has been so demonized. Because of her power to awaken herself and the male counterpart. I'm referring to the whole feminine principle in general."

I was getting angry, frustration bubbling in my throat. "That's why, women were kept powerless. On such a short leash. And the organized religions, have done a terrific job to enforce that. But what's even more perverse, is the opposite."

Raluca raised her eyebrows. "What do you mean?"

"I mean the whole promiscuity propaganda. Double standards for men, which turned them into the smaller enforcers of this sick agenda. Until now, basically women had two alternatives. Be submissive, don't ask questions, and serve the man. And the other, to be promiscuous. Which is another form of control. For both, men and women."

My sister sighed heavily, nodding in agreement.

I went on. "Take pornography, for instance. It's another tool. A very powerful and efficient one. The more people become addicted with deviant, aggressive, grotesque sexuality, the slimmer chances are that they will *ever* wake up from this mess we're in, and ask themselves important questions. Like why are we here? Why the heck do we keep massacrating each other? Why are we *unhappy*? And depressed most of the time…"

"You're absolutely right," Raluca agreed. "The ramifications are endless."

I huffed. "I mean, look at how many couples have problems because of that. It's *insane* and dreadful at the same time. And men, well most men, and some women too, fall prey to those images and ideas and lose the ability to connect with their partner in a sacred, respectful, *truly* intimate way. In a *real* way. And what's even scarier, this is the norm for so many out there."

Raluca dragged a hand through her hair. "Don't I know it…"

Sadly, I knew that she knew. This problem had affected her last relationship, in such a manner, that since then, she had lost almost, if not all hope in men. Trusting someone again. Opening herself up to the possibility that *maybe* somewhere out there, there's a soul for her after all. Someone, who would be on the same wave length with her. Someone that would see *her*. Love her soul. Respect her. All that, all was presently blocked, and filed under: 'not-for-me' category.

"Look around. Society in general, doesn't really support *truly* healthy and loving relationships. True partnerships. All my life, I felt that. Like a highly disagreeable reminder, of what the future has in store for me. So much *unhappiness* around us. And I swore to myself, I won't settle for less than what *I* think is acceptable," I said, shaking my head.

"And you did." Raluca gently patted my arm. "You have Jan."

I snorted content at the realization. "I do."

I exhaled relieved at the thought, that, even though my life wasn't *exactly* how I—or my parents—envisioned it to be, at the end of the day, I would have at least one reason to smile. That reason, was Jan.

My eyes wandered over to the harbor. The sight from here, was just incredible. As if, from up here, the city would breathe a different air. Some type of *freedom*, which, once you would go back down there, you'd fail to attain.

That only made me bore into myself, with more existential questions.

I sighed, my shoulders sinking.

"Are you ok?" my sister's voice pulled me back from wherever my thoughts wandered.

Still quite unfocused and lost in the horizon, I answered. "Yeah… I was just thinking—"

"*Obviously*. You always have that face, when you think. Especially, when something worries you," Raluca insisted.

"What look? I'm not worried," I answered perfectly calm. "You and Jan say this about me—"

"Because it's true?!"

157

I chuckled. "I was thinking about Epinoia. The message for us. What we have to do."

Raluca pulled her phone from her bag, now checking for new messages. "And that *is*?"

"And that is, what?" An unfamiliar but happy voice, made us both, turn our heads at the same time.

Raluca's eyes brightened in recognition, at the sight of the man standing next to our table.

I guess, that was Peter.

chapter / SEVENTEEN

He extended a hand to greet me. "Truly sorry, for being this late. I'm Peter. Nice to finally meet you." His smile widened, showing perfect, white teeth.

At a first glance, he seemed to be the same height as Jan. Without a thorough examination, I could identify Mediterranean traits on his face. High cheek bones, strong prominent chin, the skin a slightly darker shade. His dark straight short hair was perfectly styled. And his cold blue gray eyes, were contrasting with his warm vibe personality. He wore a well tailored modern navy blue suit, with a white shirt, and a matching navy blue skinny tie. Stylish.

I shook his hand, not sure what to make of him, besides his sense of fashion— which reminded me of someone else I couldn't really identify. "Hi, I'm Ariana. Raluca's sister. Well, obviously, you know that already. I guess—"

"I guess, you should be sorry. Because at four o'clock, she has another meeting," Raluca spoke over me, her tone leaving me to wonder, what kind of business relationship they had, or how well they knew each other.

Peter took the seat beside my sister, a crooked smile, never leaving his face. "Ariana, please tell me, what do I have to do, to convince your sister to go out with me?"

My jaw dropped.

Whoa...

I was prepared for *anything* but this.

My eyes went on to focus on Raluca, who seemed completely unfazed by the whole thing. As if nothing had happened. Like this was some old news, which didn't deserve much attention. Except it wasn't. Not for me anyway.

I stared at her, eyebrows raised, waiting for some sort of explanation.

After a few uncomfortable seconds of silence, I was prepared to say something funny, to break the awkward moment, but she beat me to it. "I told you I am professional. This is a business meeting," Raluca urged, her eyes never leaving the papers spread in front of her. "Both of us," she said gesturing with her hand between me and her. "We are here to make sure Friday is what you paid for. So let's get to today's things, to check off the list."

Peter unbuttoned his suit jacket, leaned forward, his clasped hands resting on the edge of the table. "See what I mean?!"

His tone had me smile.

"I tried *everything*, to convince her I'm worth her time. I have no clue, whatsoever, what could tear down the big wall around her. I get it. She got hurt really bad last time. And I'm really sorry for that. But she isn't the only one, to ever go through some awful, shity relationship." Peter raised his hand. "I admit, I have my own flaws. And I might've hurt one or two women in the past. But, I also got burned a few times. It's never pleasant. But hey, I'm willing to move forward," he concluded, his head turned toward my sister.

Raluca snorted, her fingers fidgeting with the pen. "That's the thing. They *always* move forward. To the next one. Like a virus in search of a new host."

Peter, waved his hands in exasperation. "See what I'm talking about?!" His eyes asking for my help.

"Stop talking about me, like I'm not even here." Again Raluca beat me to it. "I really don't appreciate, being put on the spot here. We're here to discuss work. Not my love life."

"That's the thing. You *don't* have a love life. And I'm trying very *very*, hard to remedy that," Peter retorted, frustration coloring his voice.

I couldn't help but burst into laughter. Hard. Wholeheartedly.

Both of them glanced at me, confusion reading over their faces.

I kept at it for a few more moments. And they let me, watching me in silence.

This was so good. Oh, how I needed some sort of release, to shake off the last few weeks. Especially, yesterday…

"Are you done?" Raluca asked irritated. "Can we now, please go back to work?" her eye's pendulating between me and Peter.

I cleared my throat, attempting to gain composure. "Next time, give me at least a little warning. I mean, if you think you can't share with your own sister this kind of stuff—"

"There is nothing to share, because there is nothing going on. Period," Raluca insisted, her annoyance obviously growing.

Peter shook his head. "She's so stubborn." He sighed heavily, dragging a hand through his hair. "Three months ago when I saw her for the first time at this event she organized, I wanted to go to her and just tell her—"

"Tell me what?" Raluca asked. "That I'm *the* one?" she retorted, smirking. "Oh, please…"

Peter focused now on me, ignoring her sarcasm. "I felt like I knew her before. Something so familiar. It felt like, I finally arrived home."

My heart skipped a beat. Because I knew *exactly* what he was talking about.

He continued. "As if I've been traveling all this time through life, never really finding that place, or person to call home. Until, I laid my eyes on her. When she turned to me, and smiled, in that moment…my chest felt too small."

I was choking. I couldn't understand why my biology, and my soul would react so strongly to the memory of an apparition. I felt ashamed… But my shame couldn't diminish the intensity of what I felt. *That* kind of recognition. That sense of belonging. How right it felt. How natural. Home.

The image of *him* standing in that garden… I could almost smell the warm breeze playing with his blond curls.

Crap. Now I was fantasizing about a ghost.

So not good…

"This sounds great and all, but we have work to do," Raluca said matter-of-factly, breaking my trance, for which I was more than grateful. Lingering over an apparition,

161

wasn't doing me any good. It only increased the feeling of being stupid, and pathetic. Not to mention, the sensation, that somehow, I was cheating on Jan. Which was horrible. Especially, since I'd *never* possessed a gene for cheating. Never really understood, why people would come up with so many stupid excuses to do that, instead of taking responsibility for their feelings, their actions.

Now I felt like one of them.

Ugh...

I leaned forward, my arms resting on the table. "Can I say something to both of you, before we begin?"

Peter nodded shortly, his eyes curious and expectant. Of course, Raluca reacted in her usual annoyed manner, when something would take too long. "*What?* "

I leaned back in my chair, crossing my arms over my chest. "Look. I really don't know, what's going on between you two—"

"*Nothing* is going on. How many times do I have to say it?" Raluca's irritated voice, turned all squeaky.

"Whatever." I raised my hand to stop her from protesting any further. "I think after we finish here with work, and I'm gone, you should *really* talk. And find some sort of common ground. Open a channel of communication. Hear each other out."

Mouth half opened, my sister wanted to object. I stopped her again. "I'm not done, yet. If you don't do that, I will lock you out tonight."

Peter chuckled.

"What?" she asked in disbelief. "Are you insane?" she glanced at me, unable to grasp what I was trying to accomplish with this.

My hand still held up, I turned to Peter. "In the case, she decides to give you a chance—by some sort of special *miracle*. If you hurt her in any way. You deal with me. And don't think, I can't hurt you. Are we clear?!"

My sister kept staring at me, eyes wide open, while Peter was smiling from ear to ear. "I think I like you already," he said extending a hand to me. "She was right, about you."

I shook his hand again. "About?"

"You know what you want. You don't beat around the bush. And you're not afraid to get confrontational. You have a strong character. I like that."

"Thanks." Not knowing what else to say to his concise description of me.

I clasped my hands. "Okay then. Let's begin, because we don't have too much time left."

"*Finally*," my sister said, exasperatedly.

$$\infty$$

I couldn't believe my luck, today. All went so smoothly. Well, excluding the episode with my sister and Peter. When I had left them, I made sure they actually stayed and talked. So I'd asked Peter to call me afterwards, to confirm, and of course, fill me in with the *details*, too. Obviously my sister didn't feel like sharing this stuff with me, so I had to do something. To find out, what was going on in my sister's head lately.

Apart from that, all three meetings had zero interference. Perfectly uneventful.

Oh, how I loved this day.

I was standing now in front of a mirror wiping my face with some paper napkins, in the ladies' bathroom in Tellman's office. I looked tired, but I felt good, and that seemed to show up in my hazel eyes. The fire which Jan loved, was back up. He used to say, that whenever I was feeling happy, my eyes would brighten up like two blazing suns. Radiating power and strength. Something which he found extremely sexy.

The thought of that, caused me to smile. From ear to ear.

I was really surprised earlier in the meeting, when Tellman let me pick out my favorites, out of the wide selection of samples I brought with me. His trust in me and what I was doing, was indisputably growing with each meeting. That, or and he was very busy this time, and he was in fact expediting our meeting, and the whole house building process. The man was all about efficiency.

In a way I couldn't blame him. We had that in common, even though at times I'd felt his approach to be a bit too dry, and mechanical. But other than that, he'd started to grow on me. As if we had an unspoken common understanding of how things get done. And get done *well*. Which would make our skill-sets work in concert, to realize the shared goal. His daughter's wedding present.

I really liked that part of our working relationship.

I gathered my things and left the bathroom, heading toward the elevator, happy that I was done with Tellman for the week, and only had to let Martina know, what I'd decided with him. And then she could start up, ordering the amounts for each tiled space.

"Miss Ducas! Miss Ducas!"

I stopped just before the elevator doors, and turned around. The tiny red headed receptionist, strode toward me.

"You forgot this," she said, handing me now an envelope.

I frowned, confused, and took it from her hand. "What's this? Everything, okay?"

She giggled, her eyes smiling under a thick dark burgundy glasses frame. "Yes. This is the payment confirmation for this month," she replied conspiratorial.

I exhaled relieved, expecting of course something else. Not something this light… But I wasn't complaining. "Oh. Great. Thank you."

"Mr. Tellman says, that if something really unexpected comes up this week, you should call him at this number," she said and then gave me a business card.

Again, confusion rose within me. "Thank you, but I have his number. For a while now—"

"This is his private number."

"I have that one, too. It's for special emergencies."

"This is a *different* private one. Mr. Tellman shares this one, with very few people, and only in very special circumstances," she insisted.

Now I was intrigued.

"He also suggests that you memorize it, and then destroy it."

"*Okay…*" I didn't know what else to say. This sounded too much like spy stuff. Or just pure paranoia. Both sounded very Tellman.

This was the part, where I couldn't really get him. I knew he was wealthy, and didn't want to be bothered by normal folks, and kept a very strict privacy policy. And now I was being given a *highly* private information.

I really didn't know what to make of it.

I looked at the white card, reading silently the number. Nothing else was on it. No address. No name. Just a number.

Holding it in my hand, I asked the receptionist. "Mrs. Müller—"

"Oh please, call me Ute."

I glanced at her unsure. "Okay, sure. Thank you. Do you know what kind of *special* emergencies? Although, I hope there's not going to be one. At least, I don't think there's going to be one. But just to be sure."

She pushed her glasses back up her nose with the index finger. "Mr. Tellman doesn't give details when it comes to this number," her reply came, thinning her lips.

At this point I was staring at her like a crazy person. The whole thing didn't make sense to me. She had no more information, than I did. What was I suppose to do? If something came up, which would qualify as emergency? Would that count as special *special* emergency? Or should I use the other number?

I shook my head, in defeat. And another time just in my head.

Let us hope, nothing would come up.

Or else…I wouldn't know what to do.

I slid the card into the inside pocket of my suit jacket. "Anything else?" I asked Ute.

She was fidgeting with her hands. "No. That was all. I thought maybe you have other questions. Today Mr. Tellman has a very busy schedule. And I thought perhaps, he wasn't clear with certain things. Which I could help with."

So he was indeed busy, not just me imagining it, or other things for that matter. "Apparently the only question I have, you don't have answer for it. So…"

"I'm truly sorry. Here, let me at least help you with that." She pressed the button to call the elevator.

I completely forgot that I was carrying a large and quite heavy thing—the tile samples box. "Thank you. That's very kind of you."

The elevator's doors slid open, and I stepped inside. Turned to face the entrance and pressed the ground floor button. "I guess I'll see you next Monday. Have a great a week. Goodbye."

She waved her hand shortly. "You, too." The doors started to close, but she managed to throw in, "Don't forget to destroy the number—"

The doors closed, and the elevator began to descend.

Great. Finally I could go home.

I exhaled relieved.

Then I realized, I was still carrying in the other hand the payment confirmation. I let my bag fall to my elbow, and dropped the envelope inside.

This actually gave me some ideas.

Groceries shopping.

I could go and buy some extra things, which I didn't have at home, and cook something really nice and fancy for dinner. For all three of us. I'm sure Jan would *love* the idea. And my sister would probably stop being pissed at me, for what I basically forced her to do today.

chapter / EIGHTEEN

Yeah. That's what I was going to do. Just stop home first, drop the box, and then go to the supermarket.

I leaned against the elevator wall, my mind working on some recipes I read about a few weeks back, but never had the time or fun to do it.

Strangely enough, after a busy day today, things looked pretty relaxed, and positive. I was in fact realizing, that *maybe* it wouldn't get extremely hectic until Friday, after all.

The elevator stopped.

Somebody else must've called it, too.

Oh well, I wasn't in a hurry anymore. Or stressed about what to get done next, aside from shopping for food and cooking. My thoughts were pleasantly drifting into a realm of domestic bliss.

The elevator doors opened.

And from bliss, I plunged straight into freeze zone.

I... I just...couldn't believe who was standing on the other side of the doors.

Lorenzo.

Only this time he was not alone. The tall blond woman beside him, seemed to be very much aware of his presence, so it couldn't be an innocent victim.

Both wore black suits. How surprising. I mean, I got used to his look. But, she also, seemed to follow the same dress code. Or, vice versa. The only thing that was different about her attire, was the white shirt under the suit jacket, and the heels. Her hair was pulled back into a tight bun, and clean make-up was completing her smart look. In other circumstances, I would find her flawless. Now, just terrifying.

I started pushing all the buttons. I wasn't going to stick around to find out, how terrifying.

"Miss Ducas. It's pointless. It's not going to work. We only want to talk to you." Her voice wanted to be reassuring, but there was something in her tone, that was just metallic, and cold, and empty.

Either way, this transformed the short paralysis I was feeling in my limbs, into pure rage. "I don't want to talk to you. Leave me the *hell* alone, people! I don't know what you want from me. Or who the hell you are. I don't care. I just want to live my life in peace. Stop harassing me!"

"I'm afraid that won't be possible, unless we talk," she replied evenly.

"Are you deaf?! Didn't you hear what I just said? I *don't* want to talk to you! I don't know who you think I am. But trust me, I'm a nobody, with a *very* boring life." Well, my life was *anything* but that. But I was simply using everything I could, to get myself out of this predicament.

Lorenzo smirked. "I told you. She'll put up a fight. She's a big ball of fire."

The way he spoke, it carried something dirty and sleazy in it, which made me want to throw up, if I wasn't that enraged and scared at the same time. God, how I could slap that son of a bitch...

He winked at me. Like he knew exactly what I was thinking. And apparently that only made it worse.

"Miss Ducas. The elevator won't budge, unless I say so. You have no saying in this. I was just being courteous earlier. But if you insist, we can use other methods of persuasion," she replied clasping her hands.

Lorenzo was right. I wasn't going to give up that easily. So I went on the stupid side of things. "If you want to kill me, go ahead. I can't stop you, can't I?"

She crossed her arms over her chest, her eyes shooting ice. "No. You can't. Still, we are not here to terminate you. I wouldn't even have to be present, for that to happen. I am here to offer you a job."

I have a job." My tone mocking her.

"Not for long. Do you really want to spend the rest of your life struggling? We can make it, really difficult for you. No matter how hard you'll try to make it better, we'll always be twenty steps ahead of you. We can make *everything* in your life crumble. Do you enjoy having a Sisyphus type of existence? Is that what you want?"

"I didn't choose any of that. As you said. You are *way* ahead of me. So why don't we just end it here?" I insisted, moronically.

She shifted her weight, from one leg to the other. Then she planted her hands on her hips, clearly losing her cool. "Very well, then. I will let you in on a little secret. For the time being, you are more valuable to us alive, than dead."

The weight of the tile samples was starting to weaken me. I set the box on the elevator floor. Then I stood up fast, and mirrored her stance. "So for now, *I* have the advantage. Yet, *you* threaten me."

"We just want to talk. That's it. Then, you are free to go."

I stared at her incredulous. "So talk. I'm listening." Anger and annoyance rolling out of my mouth.

"Not here. It's not the best place to have the conversation we're about to have." She whirled her head and made a hand gesture, which I could only describe as drawing a square in the air.

Behind them, the air began to vibrate. The walls, the floor, everything, turned into one smudged background. *Holy crap...*

In less than a split second, everything came back. Only different.

Now this was all a little too familiar.

My experience in Lydia's apartment. The previous encounters with Lorenzo. All seemed to have that in common. Time and space bending. Or better said, time and space dissolving. Something to do with modulating the frequency. Only in my case, it happened involuntarily. She and Lorenzo, did it at will.

Before me, laid a spacious white conference room with floor-to-ceiling windows, displaying an aerial view of the city.

Wait a second. This was not Hamburg, anymore.

Were my eyes deceiving me? It couldn't be... Or could it?

169

Frankfurt?!

"Is this, what I think it is?" I mumbled completely stunned, pointing with my left index finger toward the window.

She moved quickly and gracefully along the lengthy table, that was dominating this space, and settled into the last chair next to the head seat, close to the window. Lorenzo followed her and sat beside her, a sly grin never leaving his face.

Both turned their heads in my direction, obviously waiting for me to join them.

"Miss Ducas, I assume you want to resume your activities today, *right*?!" Her tone implying irritation, but trying her best to diffuse my mistrust.

I had to give it to her. She was good at this mind game.

Cursing in my head in advance for being so idiotic to accept this—not that I saw any other alternative—I stepped out of the elevator, walked over to the other side of the table, and took the seat opposite her. Out of the two of them, I'd rather face her directly in the eye, than endure Lorenzo's sleazy expression. Although, he sat next to her, so it was close to impossible not to.

"You got me where you wanted. So talk," I uttered coldly.

She extended a hand over the table. "I'm Sabine."

I stared into her piercing grey-blue eyes, then crossed my arms over my chest.

"Very well then." Sabine ignored my refusal at civility, and with her hand still hanging in the air, she made that square sign again. The elevator opening disappeared, leaving nothing behind, but a plain white wall. And something that I thought as décor objects. Two black octagon cubes. Probably fifty centimeters tall. And the strangest part… there was no door anywhere to be seen. A room with no doors.

Great.

"Would you like something to drink?"

I looked at her like she was a crazy person, my mouth hanging half open.

Undeterred she stroke the table a few times, and the surface came alive. Red symbols, letters—a language that reminded me of an ancient writing—filled up the white background.

Sabine touched a few of those, and in the next instant, three glasses were generated on the table. Then two bottles appeared. One filled with water and one with what looked like orange juice.

"I wasn't sure, what you like. I can make tea if you want," she said, now pouring herself a glass of orange juice.

I was still processing.

Lorenzo seemed to be amused by my reaction—or better yet, by the lack of. "Too much? We lost you already?" And filled himself up a glass of water.

I snapped out of it. "I thought you know everything about me."

"We do. It's just sometimes you are very unpredictable," Sabine replied, then took a large sip. She put down the glass, looking over the window. "You're right, that's Frankfurt."

I rotated my head toward the city view. From up here it, looked pretty astounding. "I'm an architect. It's my business to know that."

It was clear to me, that I was in one of those financial towers. Frankfurt along with Hamburg, were known to be important financial cities. But what made Frankfurt easy to set apart from Hamburg—architecturally speaking—was this exact money district. The contrast between these sky-high glass and steel structures, and the rest of the city. Whereas Hamburg, though going through a lot of modernization and plenty of new architecture additions, had a more homogenous skyline.

"You should drink something. You're going to need it," Sabine said, with her eyes motioning me to get the last glass.

"What's that supposed to mean?"

"You're going to take part in some important negotiations. So I don't want you dehydrated," she said matter-of-factly.

I huffed loudly. "Thanks for your concern. I'll pass."

"Don't say, I didn't warn you." Not wasting another second, she began hitting a few of those red symbols on the surface of the table.

The room disappeared.

A suction force locked into my solar plexus. On each side of my head, above ears and going down my spine and into my right shoulder blade, a strong current united all these points creating a sequence that was now crushing my skull and paralyzed my right arm. And felt like I was cut from oxygen.

I wanted to struggle, to do something about it. But for some reason, I just couldn't put up any resistance. I felt really small inside my body. Like I was barely there anymore.

And even if I was able to escape all this, where the hell would I run? I was in the *freakin'* void...

I blinked a few times praying for this to be over. I didn't want to die like this. Crying was obsolete. I would have done it if I could've. Even that capacity, was stolen from me.

Lights and noises overwhelmed me when I finally opened my eyes.

Reality was back.

Thank God!

"Do you have the file? I think it's time we use it. To talk some sense into these people." A man at my right spoke directly to me.

For a second there, I forgot who this person was. Then all came back to me.

Of course. He was my boss.

I nodded curtly. I lowered my left arm and pulled out a yellow folder from my bag sitting on the floor next to my chair. I set it on the table in front of me. Waiting for more orders, I scanned the room.

With twenty people—including myself—around a large round table, the conference room seemed small and crowded. Not to mention chaotic, since everyone was talking to everyone at the same time.

Across from me, on the opposite wall, a large screen was displaying numbers and financial graphs. On my right, blue curtains pulled shut covered the entire wall. Behind me, there was a table with drinks and snacks, and two servers ready to cater to everyone's needs. The exit was on the left, which was part of an entire glass wall. Outside of the room two security men were guarding the door.

So far the negotiation was going nowhere. The eight African delegates weren't satisfied with what the Chinese investors had to offer, and were growing impatient, to the point of leaving the negotiation all together.

Agitation grew inside everyone.

"I think it's time," my boss said.

I nodded compliant.

I took my phone to check if there were any messages before I started. On the reflective black screen, I saw my face and my short red hair. I smiled at myself. I looked sharp and ready to do my job. I was a mediator. And a damn good one.

I clicked the side button, the screen lit up. No messages.

Good.

I cleared my throat, and asked everyone to calm down, at the same time opening the yellow folder and getting the documents, as well as the report I had prepared three days ago. I gave a copy to everyone, already sensing curiosity rising among them. Only I and my boss knew about the latest data, so my other two colleagues were as clueless as the rest of them.

I pulled the chair closer to the table, rested my elbows on it and then clasped my hands. "Before I begin, I have to inform all the parties involved, that we have contacted an organization inside of our Group, and they are willing to supervise the entire process. To ensure that you all, get the best out of this deal."

One of the African delegates—the one from Rwanda—spoke. "I don't care what organization you people have hired, or contacted. As long as the royalty plan stays the same, we have nothing to negotiate anymore. We have natural resources, and you, *they*," the man said pointing toward the Chinese. "All you care is that your economies stay healthy, while we squirm in poverty. Your solutions are nothing but more poison for us. More suffering for my people. For our people," gesturing with his hands toward the other African delegates. "We know corruption has been a plague over our countries. But make no mistakes. We, the ones standing here before you, we are here to serve our people. Our countries. All previous deals with our countries have done nothing to change the situation. We are tired of your hypocrisy, and your well mannered lies. We have studied at your schools, we have learned your way of thinking, your way of doing business. It's crystal clear, what we are being offered. *Crumbs*." The last word, basically spitted out.

The other African delegates agreed with him, getting loud, vociferating and gesticulating heavily.

He was right. On all accounts.

173

But we had a business deal to close, so it was time to intervene and do my job.

Once more, I asked for calm and reason. It wasn't as easy as the last time. Now the Chinese were getting ready to leave the table, threatening us with a lawsuit.

After what seemed an *eternity*, I had again everyone's attention. Words were pouring out of me masterfully. They were invisible arrows, with poisoned heads, sent to annihilate all and any remaining opposition. Clever words covered with ideas of fairness, of respect, of integrity. All of which, this deal was not. The extra clauses, our organization was stipulating, were only meant to give hope. A few more percentages here and there for the African part, more environmental projects, investments in the infrastructure, help for the farmers, schooling, protection for women and children, etc. The usual. Only better formulated, more solid, and with immediate results. But not the ones they were aiming for. Not the ones that mattered most.

I really didn't know where this energy was coming from, but it felt I could go on all day, until there were no more words to be spoken. Until any objection, distrust, and skepticism would be crushed. Until they would sign. It had to be done.

At some point, the African delegation asked for a short break to confer with each other. While the Chinese wanted to be reassured in private, that our previous agreement was still being honored. The ice was really thin…

One and a half hour later, the Rwandan delegate, holding a pen between his fingers looked up from the papers laid out in front of him. "I should never again, doubt the ability of an intelligent woman, to demolish even my strongest objection. Today you have earned my respect Ms. Schumacher." And then he signed.

A wide smile flourished on my face.

chapter / NINETEEN

I shook hands with everyone after the documents were signed by all parties. The tension which was hovering over the room, was slowly dissipating. Especially now, when the servers were making rounds with the Champagne.

I took a glass myself, and went out of the room to find my boss.

"There you are!" he said. He obviously found me first.

I whirled my head, and saw my boss coming out of someone's office. The usual stern look, that was all too familiar to all of us, was now gone. He seemed very pleased with how things worked out. And why wouldn't he be? I was one of the best out there, at these types of situations.

"You have outdone yourself today. I have to give it to you. Brilliant job!" he exclaimed extending a hand to me.

I shook it somewhat vigorously. "Thank you sir! But that little extra help we had today, didn't hurt us either." And all of the sudden, the words coming out of my mouth seemed vitiated, foreign. Not mine.

"True," he replied, his eyes carrying a strange gleam in them. Something or someone I'd known before. But just couldn't pin it down.

"You should drink that now." With his head nudging me to my glass. "You need it. Of course, water is always better."

And then it hit me.

Eyes wide open in the shock of the realization, I opened my mouth to speak. But it was already too late.

The void swallowed me again.

∞

I don't know how long I was out. But when I finally opened my eyes, I was back in the white conference room. Back in Frankfurt, above the city. Beyond the glass panel, the obsidian sky was starless and heavy. Just how I was feeling right now.

"You should really drink something now," Sabine's perfectly calm voice interrupted my visual exploration.

I whirled my head fast. Which was a bad idea. That only made me even dizzier than I already was.

Whoa...

It was just Sabine and I in the room. No Lorenzo in sight.

She pushed in front of me, a glass filled with water. Without giving it a second thought, I grabbed it and emptied in a few big gulps.

"More," I said, still burning with thirst.

She complied silently.

I down the second one, but the thirst was still there. Like a scorching fire, maddening to my senses.

"With a little training you should be fine next time. The first time is always...well, like you feel right now," she said, a soft chuckle escaping her elegantly long neck.

I put the glass down with a slam. I wasn't sure why it didn't break, given the fact it looked so thin and fragile. "What did you make me do?" I basically shouted at her. "What the hell did I *do* in there?" This anger rising in me, and the very still present fire in every atoms of my being, were melting together into a dangerous combination. I wasn't sure, I would survive it.

I crossed my hands through my hair, my eyes closing, trying to gain composure. My thoughts were all over the place, torturing me, consuming me with guilt and shame, and fire.

176

"You need to drink more," Sabine said. "A whole lot more."

No need to be told twice.

I opened my eyes, and there it was, another full glass. I drank it. More like inhaling it.

Then put it down. Before I could say "more," the glass was again filled to the brim. I didn't have enough energy and clarity to understand how this was done. Later. Now I was busy with reassembling myself. Getting stable again.

This whole drinking and automatic—out of thin air generated—water refill, took another five or six glasses, until I began to feel a little more like myself. More in control. The burning sensation was gone, but was now replaced by this weary feeling. I couldn't quite describe it. I just felt off.

"I want answers. And lots of them," I said firmly. For some reason, the angst I had when they trapped me in the elevator, seemed a distant thought. Maybe I was crazy, for not fearing them now. "You can start with what just happened."

Expecting more of the same luring crap I was told before—nothing concrete—I was determined to use my advantage, to squeeze every information I could out of her.

But she surprised me.

Without losing another second, she proceeded. Calm and cold. Emotionless. Like a machine. "Today was your first unofficial mission. Time is of the essence these days. And we need all the help we can get."

"You mean, all the help you can coerce." I smirked ironically.

She continued undisturbed. "We had to see if your abilities have matured enough, in order to proceed to more complex missions."

I leaned forward, resting my arms on the table. "And what exactly are those abilities?"

She mimicked my stance, her cold eyes boring into mine now. "It's surprising how oblivious you are of your own gifts," she said, pausing for a second, then continued. "You can make things happen. Impossible things for most people. You have the power to influence important outcomes. Plainly put, you can change the world. Literally."

I chuckled. "Funny, you said that. Because so far, I feel like I've failed at life."

"That's because we made sure, you won't create those things that would destabilize our course. You have been watched closely your entire life. In fact, even before that."

"This *really* sounds like a serious case of stalking. Or paranoia," I joked bitterly.

She didn't seem to think so, judging by her cold stare.

"We simply ensure that things go accordingly to plan. No loose ends are allowed. And frankly, you have given us quite a hard time," Sabine admitted.

"*I* gave you a hard time?!" I laughed hysterically. "Are you kidding me?!"

"And I must say, your resilience is nothing short of astonishing. For that, you have my absolute admiration. Unfortunately, you are not permitted to freely pursue all those radical ideas of yours."

"Please explain, what is so radical in having a normal life? A job, a family, something to live for. What is radical in *that*? How is my life interfering with your 'master' plan?"

"We both know, that you are *anything* but ordinary, Miss Ducas," Sabine said.

I huffed. "I'm sure you can do better than this."

"Very well." She leaned back, keeping her clasped hands on the table. "I have no doubt *whatsoever* that you've realized by now, you don't play by the same rules as everyone else. By the way, nice try in the elevator, with the clueless act. But it fooled nobody. We didn't get to you by accident. We know exactly *who* and *what* you are. The only one here, who is still in the dark, is you."

"Great. Enlighten me."

Sabine shifted in her chair, and with the left hand fixed a hair sticking out of her otherwise perfect bun. Then took again a very rigid stance. "You were born wired differently. Your coding, allows you to see what others don't. And do what others only dream of, or read in those fantasy and sci-fi books out there—which are becoming very popular among the younger generation."

I snorted. "I wonder why? Oh, wait! Because there might actually *be* some truth in there?!"

She smiled. "Precisely. But this is not alarming to us. We put out there, enough distractions to keep the minds busy. In fact, this and the films belonging to the same genre, are part of the whole 'getting-ready-for-contact' type of situation."

"Wow… So you're admitting to me, that we're not alone. Not that I was doubting it, or anything," I put in.

She tilted her head, giving me a weird look. "Until we have in place a new structure for how things are run on Earth, there won't be any official announcement from any government on this planet. They are simply not allowed. Otherwise all hell, breaks loose."

Again. Wow...

"And having people like you working for us, will ensure our success."

"What makes you think, that I will work for you?"

"Because even before you were born, you were supposed to join our side," Sabine answered matter-of-factly.

"*What*?"

She sighed, in annoyance. "You were tagged previous to, and at your birth. We have allowed certain parts of your original coding to enter this reality, so when the time comes, you can perform at your best. Although at times, we think, it was a big risk on our part."

I pressed my palms against my temples, and started to rub them, back and forth. "So you're saying, you've altered my DNA?"

"That's one level of alteration. There are others, too."

My eyes widened with realization. "You mean, etheric levels."

"Yes."

Holy shit... This was not good.

My mind was refusing to accept this. Not that this couldn't be possible. But just as well, it could be a lie. "This can't be true. You're just messing with me, so you get what you want."

"Check behind your right ear. Touch that area with your finger. See if you can feel a bump," Sabine indicated.

Almost instantaneously, my hand went to that spot. And my fingers began touching gently the area. There was indeed a bump. But then I remembered. "I had this all my life. It's a ganglion," I replied, relieved.

"Exactly. You had it your entire life," Sabine said, her words implying the irony of it. "That is an implant. A tag. Whichever you prefer. You have it, because we put it there.

179

At birth. And in many other parts of your anatomy, since then. They serve different purposes. To monitor your location, for instance. Or monitor your thought process. It can induce or alter states of being, which in turn, can make you do things. Obey specific commands. And many other wonderful and very handy functions. There are simply too many, to go into detail right now. But you get the point."

I began to laugh hysterically, because the feeling of being powerless was growing overwhelmingly fast.

"What we did today, was just testing the waters. You could be great, you know? You could finally begin to change the world like you've always wanted."

"Are you serious?" I said. "Because the change I did today, it's *nothing* I want to do in the future. Or ever again."

"We're not monsters. If that's what're you implying. We are actually more humane than you. We just have a vision. And in the next few years, when all the natural resources of this world will lessen more and more, you'll thank us, for not allowing everyone to consume everything in an instant. *That* is the true insanity," Sabine insisted.

"Today you have invaded my body, my mind. My will. So that millions of lives will be destroyed, lost, damned forever. I have to live with that now, for the rest of my existence. I don't care about your Eugenics crap!" I yelled, my fists slamming into the table.

For a split second, I thought I saw some kind of reaction on her unmovable facial features.

"It's not *us*—the many—who destroyed and continue to destroy the environment. It's *you*. Your big, greedy corporations who are doing it. *You* are the problem. Not us. It's not us who create financial tsunamis. It's not *us* who destabilize the economies of countries around the world. It's not *us* that created consumerism, and forced people in other parts of the world to pay with their lives for the comfort of a few. It's *you*. It's always *you*. So don't even bother to lecture me about the state of the world. Because, I will throw up all over you," I spat out.

I pushed my chair back, and stood up fast. "Now let me out of here! I want to go home! Now!" I screamed at her.

I started to walk toward the wall, where the elevator opening previously was.

"*Now*! Do your trick and get me home!" I demanded, fury spewing out of every fiber of my being.

In front of me, the white wall morphed into two metallic sliding doors. In the next instant, they opened and I stepped into the elevator. When I turned to hit the descend button, Sabine appeared in front of me, just outside the doors.

"This is not over. I will give you a little more time, to do this willingly. You know, it doesn't have to be ugly," Sabine insisted flatly. As if everything I just said, my emotional response to what took place, was nothing more than a capricious attitude, which deserved to be ignored.

For a moment there, I mustered a little control. But barely. "You're right. It doesn't have to be. Because, I won't do this again. Now get out of my face!" And then I lost it again.

The doors closed shut, and the elevator began its descent.

chapter / TWENTY

When I stepped through the door, my sister did all but jump all over me. "Oh my God! Where the hell have you been?"

"To hell and back again," I said in half voice.

"What happened?"

"Shit happened."

"What are you talking about? Stop being so cryptic and spill it out. 'Cause I can't stand this pressure of not knowing," Raluca urged me.

"Just give me a second here, to breathe—"

Then I took my shoes off, and planted them by the door. I even managed to hang my coat nicely in the wardrobe. And in a few long strides, I was in my office chair, by the desk. I pushed my chair closer, and rested my elbows on the table, my hands cupping my face.

My sister was growing restless. "Please don't keep me in suspense, here! Plus, you owe me for today. Peter was *soo* persistent. He kept talking, and talking. At some point, I thought he was worse than me. So, *thank you* for that—"

"I'm sure your talk was better than mine," I said, annoyance rising in me.

"What's that supposed to mean?" she replied. And I could see her, even with my eyes closed, taking this indignant stance with the hands plopped on her waist. Something what I usually do in similar situations. I guess that's another thing we had in common. Body language.

I lifted my face from my hands, looked up, and caught her offended gaze on me. "It means, apparently I was in Frankfurt, and then I don't know where. And then back in Frankfurt. And now I'm home. So that was that, in a nut shell." I spilled the words rapidly, my lips thinning in a bitter grimace.

"Wait. What? Apparently you were in Frankfurt, and then you don't know where. And then—"

"Please, stop repeating what I just said. I'm not crazy. Or maybe I am. But the point is, I know what I just said. It is, what it is. Now could you, please, in fact pretty please, make me some tea?" My eyes begging not to argue with me.

She glanced at me, incredulously. "Are you kidding me?! Jan and I, we're both looking for you for hours. You left me without a key, to enter the apartment. I had to wait around for Jan. And then wait and worry about you. Then you finally show up, and you're telling me this cryptic shit. And now you want tea?" She gesticulated with her hands, as if I lost my mind.

Well, she had the right to be angry with me. I would be too, in her place. Especially, when one doesn't have the whole picture of the situation.

"Please, don't make it harder than it is. Just some tea, and I'll talk more. I promise," I begged her.

Raluca shook her head, crossed her arms over her chest, and silently went into the kitchen.

In the next instant, I heard the entrance door opening.

"Is she here? 'Cause if she's not, I will call the police. I won't wait any longer. This is insane." Jan's words came from the hallway, worry and angst coloring them.

Then I heard my sister from the kitchen. "She's here! She wants *tea*!" The last sentence spoken with annoyance.

"What?" Jan asked. "Where is she?"

"I'm in here! In the office," I managed to say with enough power, so he can hear me.

He stepped into the room, his eyes big with concern and desperation. "Where were you? We were worried sick. I left like a hundred messages."

"I'm sorry. I was detained. I couldn't reach you. Or anybody for that matter," I said.

"She was in Frankfurt. Then she doesn't know where. And now she's here." My sister felt the need to reiterate my words, while carrying a large steaming cup into the room.

She put the tea in front of me. "Now talk. No more excuses."

"Why were you, in Frankfurt? And when did you even, have time to go there? Weren't you supposed to meet Tellman today?" Jan asked, obviously confused by this new information.

"Yes. And I did, meet Tellman today." I exhaled scarcely. "Then, on my way home—actually, on my way out of Tellman's office—my elevator got high-jacked."

Raluca and Jan reacted at the same time. "*What*?"

I continued. "It stopped on my way down. I simply assumed, that someone else had called it. But no. It was Lorenzo and his boss."

"That son of a bitch!" Jan was now getting really aggravated. "Did he hurt you? I swear to god, I will—"

"You'll do what? I don't recall, you getting any super powers in the last twenty-four hours. This guy goes through walls. Time and space doesn't mean much to him, re-member? And no, he didn't hurt me. Per say…" I added frustrated, remembering how powerless I'd felt back there.

"So he did, hurt you. What did he do to you?" Jan insisted, all sorts of emotions gleaming in his eyes. I didn't have to guess what kind. But murderous and 'causing-someone-a-huge-amount-of-pain,' was *definitely* in there.

"It wasn't him, who *did* something to me." And then, words rolled out of my mouth, like an avalanche. I laid out the entire experience. From the moment of intercepting me in the elevator, to then basically being teleported to Frankfurt. To our conversation, which had turned into, me being further catapulted into another location. Into someone else's body and mind. And without my conscious consent, used and tricked into play-ing a major role in a highly important economical transaction, which led to damning millions of lives, to prolonged poverty and slavery. And the fact, that I hadn't realized what was happening until the very last minute—being in that body or mind. To then, finding out that my body was basically, a mined field. An implants field. That I was a puppet, and *they* were the puppeteers. And I couldn't escape them, in this life, or the next. Or even in between. They just…had me.

Strong reactions came from both, my sister and Jan. Interjections, stopping me from time to time. Most probably, if I were to hear that from someone else, I would do the same.

"And then she let me go. Actually, I got so mad, I screamed at her. And had demanded to get me home. Now when I come to think of it, why hadn't it cross my mind to tell her, to *really* get me home? Or at least, closer." I huffed, ironically, thinking about the positive side of the whole thing. Of which I hadn't taken advantage of. "She basically, put me back in Tellman's building elevator. So when I got out and saw that it was dark, I just called a taxi. This is how I got home," I concluded, taking another sip from my cup.

"That's it." Jan's voice got all thundery. "Call Tellman, and say you're done with his project. I don't want you *near* that building. From now on—"

"Again with that," I interrupted him. "From now on what? We need the money. Are you serious?"

"No we don't. We'll be fine. In fact we are. Didn't I make *that* clear for you in Paris?" Jan insisted.

"I have not a *single* clue, of what you're talking about?" I admitted, trying to squeeze my brain out, for information that somehow would seemed to elude me. Because ever since we got back home, there were many questions marks around a lot of things. Only fuzzy, vague memories about certain situations, places, and people we'd met.

He stared at me, as if I was crazy, or just playing a mind trick on him. So I mirrored back his gaze, waiting for the illuminating piece of information.

"The day I bought you the emerald earrings, you were worried that we can't afford it. That's when I told you about my inheritance. Which was meant to be a surprise for our wedding. But that moment felt perfect, because you were so stubborn, and didn't even want to consider it. To buy them, I mean," Jan said, then shook his head. "How is it possible that you forget about something like that?"

"How is it possible, then a lot of *other* things?" I asked ironically. "How is it possible, that Lorenzo shows up in your mother's bathroom? How is it possible, that one moment I am in Hamburg, and the next, I step through a door and I'm in fact, in Frankfurt? How is it possible, that someone can control my body functions, so they use my consciousness inside somebody else's mind? How is it possible—"

Jan lifted his hands in the air. "I get your point. But still…"

"You want to know, what I remember from that day?" I uttered frustrated.

He crossed his arms over his chest, his eyebrows raised.

"I remember walking with you. Heading to some restaurant to eat, and passing by a jewelry store, and then somehow being late. For a reservation or something. And then having a conversation with this guy that was at our table. And then, you disappearing. And afterwards, *a long* blank spot. And later, you showing up with the earrings. That's it. Well, possibly some other hazy details, but I'm not sure if they are real, or not. So that's how *clear* it is for me."

He shook his head in disbelief. "I thought *my* memories were screwed up from this vacation. From too much wine, and godly food. But yours, are definitely worse than mine."

"Thank you, for pointing the obvious," I replied, bitterly.

"I'm sorry. But doesn't anyone here, see a pattern?" My sister intervened. "Don't you, see it?" With her hands gesticulating, like she just had and eureka moment.

Jan and I looked at each other, then shifted our eyes on Raluca. Then back to each other, trying to figure, what we'd missed. Then focused again, on her.

"You both have blank spots in your memory. Correct?" Raluca said.

"Correct," Jan replied, and I just simply nodded.

"Well, then it's crystal clear. How didn't I realize it, before?" She tapped with her fingers at the side of the temple, shaking her head. "Of course, with all this work and appointments, and calls and travels lately, no wonder that—"

"Get to the point, please…" I begged her.

She put her hands on her hips, her mouth ready to voice her thoughts. "Your memories have been altered," Raluca said, matter-of-factly. "But apparently, whatever caused this. *Whoever* caused this, didn't estimate that the results won't be the same on both of you. I mean, you remember something. And he remembers something else. Or other parts which you don't. And vice versa. This to me, looks like a perfect case of memory alteration. Not that I've experienced it. If I did, I don't remember. Anyways—"

She gesticulated with her hands. "The point is, you two have a problem.

"And, you better start looking for answers fast," she urged, then pointed a finger in my direction. "You came back from this vacation—besides those gorgeous earrings… —with a pendant. Which I told you, looks the same as the one in my dream."

I nodded in agreement, my mind already speeding up. Searching for the missing pieces. "Go on—"

"You said, that you got it on your last day in Paris. And you got it from this person, that was taking a picture of you. Or, was part of your picture, or something…" Then she paused a moment. "Well, how did you meet this person? Do you know his name?"

Jan and I, were staring at each other, waiting for the other to speak first.

He hesitated, probably curious to hear my side of this puzzle.

"I told you already, what I remember," I insisted, looking at my sister. "Sorry, no name…" I shook my head in regret. God, how I hated this…

My sister grabbed Jan by the arm, forcing him to turn to her. "And you?"

He took a moment, probably going through his memories, as well. "I *definitely* remember coming with him on the top deck. But his name…it's just not there…" Jan admitted in defeat. "However, I do recall him saying, something about having free rides to the top of the Eiffel Tower anytime he wanted. Which I thought, was an awesome thing—"

"Do you still have the photos?" Raluca asked, impatiently.

"Sure," Jan answered.

Raluca gestured to him. "Then, what are you waiting for? Go get the camera, and let's see this guy, once and for all. Let's shed some light, on this God damn mystery."

Jan didn't need to be told twice.

He went and grabbed the camera from the middle shelf in the bookcase next to the window. In three strides he was back at the desk. He sat down, already going through the pictures we took in Paris. "This one is great. We should definitely frame that," he said proudly turning the screen to me so I can see it.

I leaned over the table, to have a better look at it. It was a photo of us, at the vegan restaurant in Saint-Michel, with the young owner and his friend, who was also working with him there. We basically ate there every night. And for some reason, we became friends with them. I suspected that my usual big tip, might've had something to do with it. "It's great. But, can you just get to the ones we need? To the end, actually. I'm pretty sure, those are the last pictures we took."

He turned the screen back to him, and went through the rest of them.

A few moments later, he furrowed his eyebrows in confusion.

"What is it?" I asked, losing patience.

"This can't be…"

"What, now?"

He leaned closer, and turned again the screen toward me. "This…"

I pushed my chair closer to him and looked into the screen. "I see a picture of us. You and me. What's impossible about that?"

"Look closer. Don't you see?" Jan insisted.

Then the realization dawned on me, my mouth now hanging open. "No way…"

Jan was nodding with satisfaction.

"Stop being so cryptic you too! And tell me, what's going on?" Raluca demanded.

Before I could say anything, she grabbed the camera from Jan. Then scanned the photo with her eyes. "Oh my God! He's missing from the shot entirely."

Between Jan and I, there was a small distance. A gap. And we held our hands as if we were holding somebody. Only that, there was nobody between us. Just the rail, the city's rooftops and the sky above in the background.

"Did you check the others, too?" I asked Jan.

"What do you think?! Of course. There were only two left, that we took with him. And it's the same situation. One with you, holding your arm around…nothing. And one with me doing the same thing," Jan said, complete disbelief reading in his eyes.

"Yep. I checked. It's how he says," Raluca confirmed, then handed me the camera to convince myself that I wasn't going crazy. "There are two more shots, after this one. Same story."

I went back and forth a few times. To compare, to analyze. To understand. But there was nothing, which a linear mind's logic could explain it.

"I think it's pretty obvious," Raluca said.

I looked up from the screen waiting for her insight, both curious and anxious of what she had to say about this strange story.

"This guy. Well, the missing person in your shots. He is connected with your muddy memories, as well as the with the blank spots—the missing parts. Plus, isn't he the one who gave you the pendant?"

I nodded in confirmation.

"I told you, already. That pendant in my dream, is exactly like the one you have. And *this*, connects you to an event. Or something, that will bring an important change slash decision, in your life. I don't know how big, or small it is. But it felt important. And you didn't look happy about it.

"Now, you can ignore that, all you want. But, we both know, this is getting too real, to just pretend, it's simply a dream, and means nothing," Raluca concluded.

She was right.

But what the heck, was I supposed to do about it? This was worse than look for the needle in a hay stack. There was no name. No face. Just *maybe*, some vague idea about someone. This was worse than nothing. This was a ghost.

"No offence. But I think we are focusing on the wrong problem," Jan put in. "We are supposed to find a solution. To stop these God damn bastards, from high-jacking her all the time. Whenever they feel like it—"

His remark brought me back, to this reality. "And what exactly, do you propose we do?" I gazed into his eyes, trying to find a sense of peace and protection. As I used to do. Back, when I was working in an office, and I had to deal with so much nonsense, and ignorance, five days a week.

"We can move," Jan suggested.

"Because that's, *realistic*," I snorted, bitterly. "I don't want to run away. Even if it's so damn tempting. And you *need* to finish your PhD."

He opened his mouth to protest, but I raised my hand stopping him. "I will move someplace else, because I want to. Not because I am being chased by these... I don't even know how to call them, actually. 'Cause they are not human anyway."

"Call them, 'ankle biters,'" Raluca put in, a sardonic smile pulling at her lips.

"Right. Ankle biters. Parasites. Whatever," I said irritated. "The point is, we can't hide forever. I have to live my life." Then gestured, with my index finger between Jan and I. "*We* have to live our life. There's got to be another way. I refuse to think, that's it. That there's nothing we can do, and we have to give up, and run away."

Jan shook his head, disagreeing with me. "You're *crazy* stubborn sometimes, you know that?"

I answered with a smile.

"I will try *everything* before I have to run away from my own life," I added, decidedly.

Jan sighed deeply. "*Fine*. I was going to tell you about this talk , conference thing, that it's happening tomorrow. But then—" He gesticulated with his hands in the air. "*This* happened. And I thought there's no point in telling you anymore."

"What lecture?" I asked, curiosity sparking in me.

"Actually, about this stuff, that happened to you today." He pulled his chair closer to mine, and took my hand between his warm palms. "And ways to defend yourself against psychic attacks, and all that jazz." He snorted, trying to lighten the mood.

"When is it?" Raluca asked. "Maybe I can go with you, so you won't be alone."

"It's in the late afternoon," Jan replied.

I leaned back in my chair, and swirled my head toward Raluca. "I don't think so. Your schedule looks crazy busy tomorrow. Thanks, but no."

"I can't come with you," Jan added, looking pained and uncomfortable. "I have a meeting with the 'iron lady' around that time. But I will ask Tim to come with you. And when it's done, I can come and pick you up, and we drive straight home."

I stroke his face gently, cupping his cheek with my palm, trying to lift this heaviness weighing over his soul. "No need. I can go alone."

"This is not negotiable." And the intensity in his eyes, made that loudly clear.

I smiled at him fondly. "Fine."

chapter / TWENTY-ONE

I hadn't expected, to see so many people at this type of event. Especially, in a city like Hamburg. Where the vast majority of people, *definitely* had other priorities in life. Like taking the pragmatic, and the material world, to a *whole* new level. Blindly, climbing the corporate and social ladder. Eager to fit the norm. Cold, mechanical efficiency, before anything else. Not allowing much, if *any* space for spirit. Or for any type of more... *subtle* essence to shine forth, and have it as part of their life experience...

Ultimately, there was absolutely nothing wrong with being pragmatic. Or, with the exploration of the material. Only when you got lost in it—entirely, forgetting about that tiny spark inside of you—*that* was when the problems started.

But, who knew? There was actual 'life on this planet.'

"Did you see him?" Tim asked.

I turned my head, scanning the crowd. "See who?"

He pointed toward the entrance doors, to the conference room. "The guy, over there. He is the one, I was telling you about," excitement reading in his voice.

Over the sea of heads, pouring from both sides of the generous lobby, I spotted a relatively tiny man. A frail silhouette, standing out in the busy crowd. His long gray hair was pulled back into a pony tail, and a pair of small size reading glasses completed his relaxed vibe. He seemed to be having a very engaging conversation, with an older lady.

Curiously, he reminded me of someone.

I nodded. "Good. Let's see, what these people have to say." Then I grabbed Tim's arm, forcing him to keep up with me, while I was making my way through the crowd, wanting to get better seats.

On our way to this venue—a fancy and recently remodeled hotel at Dammtor, which conveniently had a conference and exhibition center stuck at the back—Tim had informed me that, there were more than one speaker today. Actually, this was the last day of a three day event. A sort of an 'awake-and-aware' type of conference. Where different individuals from around the world, gathered here to share from their own personal experiences dealing with 'unseen' forces, off world races, military black projects, and many other sensitive subjects, which the ignorant mass would categorize as conspiracy theories. And on top of that, there were some, that were discussing the issue of Ascension. A very hot topic these days, in this community.

$$\infty$$

"A soul can't be owned, but imprisoned. Constrained," the second speaker of today's panel affirmed. Albert Nelson was a former member of an obscure black organization, and a *blue* blood. Who had decided, that it was better to live outside of that world, without the privileges that came with it, but with a clean conscience and in service to humanity.

He continued in a grave tone. "This is a prison planet. We are food. We are here to supply energy for these *reptiles.*"

His words spoke the truth. Not just because of what I had experienced, in the last few weeks. Or, because of what took place yesterday, and the confession I got from Sabine.

His words triggered a déjà vu moment.

I heard this before.

Somewhere else. From somebody else. But this annoying mental barrier, I discovered I had—since I came back from Paris—wouldn't allow me to see what was behind it. *Who* was behind it.

"Who would trap a soul, that is leaving the body at death?" Albert asked, then paused for an instant, his eyes piercing the audience expecting an answer. Even if some of us had some theories about it, no one felt the need to answer a question that seemed rhetorical. We were waiting for his insight.

He continued. "Anyone, who has this type of mind control technology. And in this case, somebody who's negative.

"The soul leaves the body, only when the soul thinks the body is no longer able to maintain the soul. The soul will know, when the body will die. And it will leave just before it dies. Then, the soul is intercepted, memory wiped clean, and sent back to incarnate into another body."

This actually, brought back the memory of the horrible terror I felt when I died, those two times. Not knowing what to do, when I severed the connection with my body. Feeling that 'out there' was not safe. And the only way to change that, was to fight my way back, into my body.

"How can a soul avoid the trap?"

I was all ears, for that one.

"Don't head into the 'white light.' It's a mouse trap. You should turn into the opposite way."

So my instinct was correct.

"Seek to return to where you are from. Seek the Source. If you succeed, you reconnect with Source, and remember everything that happened. A lot of these near death experiences some people have of going into the 'white light,' are fabricated by this distorted Matrix," Albert concluded.

A lady from the audience raised a hand to speak. "So, what can we do about it? Everything you say sounds pretty hopeless. Those of us who have children, how can we protect them?"

The question didn't seem to perturb him at all. "There's always help. In different forms. For instance in my case, and in other's too, the soul—the mind to be exact—is being altered. So that you won't be reprogrammed by the educational system here."

Since childhood, I felt out of place, no matter what I did. And in school, was even worse. In life, in general. Because, I felt like a fraud. I felt exposed. Vulnerable. A target. Simply because, I was different.

"Dyslexia is one of those," Albert continued. "I was dyslexic. So the way I would interact with the educational system here, won't work on me. I was not good in math and languages. But I was good for instance, at acting in school plays. I was good at human interaction, expressing high emotional intelligence.

"This was a form of protection. Thus whatever hidden programs are inside school, university education, or inside of any other format, won't have the ability to reprogram me."

It had never crossed my mind, that I as well, might have a subtype of dyslexia, until he mentioned it. A very well disguised one.

Back when I was in school, I was good with languages, even with math. Very good, with all things visual. Visual learning, visual and geometrical representations. Very good at understanding and expressing abstract concepts and notions, yet Physics, was something I truly dreaded it. Very possible, that my secondary school teacher had something to do with it, as well. With her lack of enthusiasm, and the sense that she was on auto pilot. I mean, I would learn the theoretical part, so I could pass the class. But that was, where it ended. Her manner of imparting knowledge to her pupils, was extremely dry and removed, thus whatever she would explain, wouldn't reach me. Between me and that type of information, was a mighty wall. In high school, things had stayed the same. Though, I was lucky to have as my teacher, someone truly open-minded about a lot of things, as well as being passionate about her subject.

However, this was not the main thing that had me thinking, I could be dyslexic, too. I always had this audio gap, which I would get from time to time. Like, I wouldn't hear certain words. As if somebody would mute specific words, in various moments, or contexts. And I would have to replay a few times certain parts, in order to get the missing information.

Also, whenever I would write fast, I would stumble upon certain letters. And that would really annoy me, since I was exceedingly good in grammar and spelling.

Subtle things like that, which I never had thought to question before, but very much present, and hindering my existence.

According to Albert, this was protection.

It might as well be. Still, not less irritating.

"My 'protectors' are giving me information in a very careful manner," Albert said, interrupting my inner chatter. "The way they pass the information, you wouldn't even know who, or what they are. It can't be picked up. That's why they are very circumspect."

And again, my mind flew straight to those peculiar interactions I'd had recently. Like the old lady in the S-train. Or the very strange waiter, at the Café where I'd had lunch with my cousin Laura. Though, on both situations, I wasn't given any type of information. At least, I was not aware of anything in particular, except the fact, that the whole interaction was odd. Something was off, about it. Therefore, it stood out.

Of course...

I sighed, realization dawning on me.

These people, were trying to warn me. Whoever or whatever, they were. And when nothing else could be done, they had intervened directly. And voila, the 'sci-fi rescue' thing.

In the next half an hour, Albert plunged more into the whole world shadow government, and their covert actions and missions. "The Group," as he called them, saw themselves as beyond our small day to day existence. However, they were incredibly educated and very knowledgeable. The holders of magic and power, interacting with us, at the fringe of our reality, through people placed in key positions managing the 'livestock.'

His sources confirmed that not only the military, but the navy and the air force as well, were in fact working with different groups of extraterrestrials. And they had access to very advanced technology, which they were using to suppress the evolution of consciousness.

"The DNA in humans is changing on an energetic level. This process can't be stopped." Albert argued. "A lot of you probably are asking yourselves, how can they still keep us prisoners, then? Well, for them it's about limiting the damages. If they can't stop it, they have no problem destroying the world. The biggest war here, is not physical. It's an energetic war. The real purpose of the Hadron Collider was to stop Ascension. It didn't work. They tried three days before December 21th 2012. And three days after that. It failed. Shutdown. No beam. Why? Because it was taken out," he said, pacing a lot back and forth.

"They will try again in the next couple of years. Because after that, energetically speaking, it will be hard for them to access help from the other side. But that's another story—"

A young man, two rows in front of me, raised his hand.

"Yes, " Albert said, waiting for his question.

"What do you know about 'Inner Earth?'" the young man asked.

Albert stopped pacing, his hands clasped at the back. Then rotated himself toward the audience. "There are cities, on the inside of Earth on the third and the fourth dimension. The people, who come from those cities from the past, have a high knowledge and expertise, which is not acceptable now. But it will be, if humanity changes its values. In fact they are interacting with us. To some level. But in time, they will come out of 'hiding,' and they will take part in the healing process."

When would that day come?

'Cause right now, the way things seemed, we'd have to wait a few more centuries.

"Sooner than you actually imagine," Albert added, indirectly answering my silent question.

"We're not leaving, until you talk with this guy," Tim said decidedly.

Three hours later, and two more speakers, the last day of the conference was officially over. I actually regretted, for not finding out about it sooner. I would've definitely come to the previous two days, if time and *circumstances* would've allowed it. But then again, I wouldn't be here in the first place, if those freaky things wouldn't have happened.

As a matter of fact, I was grateful for attending today. Even though, most of the information shared, was already familiar to me. It was a great reminder, nonetheless. However, something new and unexpected emerged out of it.

I came here for one reason only. And that was to find out something that could

help my situation. Which, I did. Bonus part, was the realization of being somewhat…
dyslexic.

"Look at all those people," I replied, gesturing toward the crowd surrounding the last speaker of today. Mike Kenna. The same man, Tim had made me aware of, before the talks had started. "Does it seem realistic, that he will have time to chat with me, about my predicament?" I said, my lips thinning.

"I'm sure most of those people, if any, are not in the same situation as you are. He will talk with you, even if I have to force him." He then turned to me, and hanged his messenger bag over my shoulder. "Hold this for me. Stay right here. I'll go get him."

I snorted. "You're crazy."

"Look who's talking—" He winked at me, a smile spreading over his face, and then rushed through the sea of people in the lobby.

Left alone, and not believing for a second, what Tim said, might actually have a chance at occurring, I began drifting into my own thoughts. Mostly work stuff, things that needed to be done, when I would get home. Somehow this was calming, and gave me a sense of much needed security. Something to look for. A structure, in all this chaos that was my life lately.

Two strong hands grabbed each of my arms, and I found myself pulled against someone's chest. "Are you okay? How was it?" I heard the words whispered against my ear. These arms encircled me into a tight embrace, then I felt a soft kiss being planted on my temple.

I smiled.

I didn't have to guess who that was. I immediately recognized the fresh fragrance, which on a certain person gave off a very particular woody scent. Something time-less.

Jan.

"I'm fine. I'd be even better, if people would stop sneaking up on me like that." Something which was true. I really, hated that. Always. Even if it was him, and my reaction was the opposite, of what I would normally do.

"You knew, it was me. Otherwise, I wouldn't have done it," Jan tried to explain himself.

I spun quickly in his embrace, now standing face to face, his arms knitted tightly at my back. "And that makes it okay, because?" My eyes looking up in his, for the adequate answer.

Jan smiled. "I'm sorry."

"Yeah… That look on your face, says just that…"

He chuckled innocently. "You're so cute, when you're mad at me."

I shook my head disapprovingly. "And that's why you do it? For the cuteness factor?! There's nothing cute about being scared—"

Jan pulled me closer. "See?! Cute. You, going all analytical and stuff," he said, his chest shaking from laughter.

I pulled back, enough to prop my hand on his shoulder. "It's pointless to have an adult conversation with you. Are you sure, you left kindergarten? I think I'll call your mom, to ask her about your *real* age. I think you've been lying this whole time."

He was still laughing. "Oh, come on! I was trying to lighten up the mood," Jan said, trying hard to come down from his joy ride. "All these people here, look like they're about to experience the end of the world, any moment now. I had to do something about it. But, I still stand by what I said."

Jan had this way of making it hard at staying mad at him, even if I so wished it.

"Whatever…"

"By the way, where is Tim? I do hope, he is nearby. He promised he'll take care of you, until I arrive. Otherwise, I will make sure he'll suffer greatly," Jan said, the tone changing rapidly from happy to serious in the span of a few sentences.

I rearranged my stance, making sure I don't drop the bags—mine and Tim's. "I thought you came here, to just lighten up the mood," I mocked him.

Even if he got my sarcasm, Jan was Jan. "This was part of the rescue mission, too. But seriously, where is he?"

"Over there," I answered, pointing in the direction of the ever growing group of people, hovering over our last speaker. "He actually, *thinks* that he can get this guy, to have a chat with me."

"Good. That means he's doing what I asked him to do," Jan replied, matter-of-factly.

I shifted my weight from one leg to the other, raising my eyebrows. "And what is that, exactly? Because whatever he is trying, it doesn't seem likely to succeed," I insisted, convinced of the waste of time and energy pursuing this.

Jan grabbed me by the hands, his eyes sending me warmth and certainty. "You need all the help you can get. The best help you can get. I'm just making sure you get that." Then he glanced over my head. "Look behind you," Jan demanded.

I turned swiftly. And what do you know?

Tim and the speaker, were heading in our direction.

I was dumbfounded.

Holy crap... He actually, did it.

On their way to us, I saw Tim talking to him. When he caught me watching them, a big grin spread over his face, his eyes blinking theatrically. As if to tell me, "told you, I could do it."

Jan patted me gently on my shoulders. "This is your chance. I hope you're ready. 'Cause I don't know that many people like him. In fact, he is the only one I found. And coincidence or not, he was also in town. So, you better make the most of it."

All of the sudden, I felt like I was again in school. Nervous before an exam. "If anxious counts as ready..."

Jan took my hand and held it tight. "I'm here, with you. I'm not going anywhere. Try to relax."

I nodded. "Got it."

In another two strides, Tim and the speaker were before us. "These are my friends. Ariana and Jan." Tim said, introducing us, then gestured toward him. "This is Mike Kenna."

"Call me Mike," he insisted, while shaking hands with both of us. "It's very nice to meet you."

We reciprocated his greeting.

"Your friend here," began Mike, shifting his posture, already focusing on me. "He says, you have a very interesting story. And urgent help is needed."

I clasped my hands in fronts of me. "*Interesting* is not exactly, how I would described it. More like 'crazy' would suit it. But definitely, in need of help." A pained smile covered my face.

He pushed his glasses up the bridge of his nose. "I have four hours before my plane takes off. That means I can't do much. But I can at least run a scan on you, and give you some tools to work with."

His offer was more than generous. "It's more than I would've expected. So thank you in advance, for whatever you can do for me," I said.

"Great. Let's go some place quiet," Mike suggested, and all three of us agreed, nodding our heads. Without a moment to lose, he started toward the right wing of the lobby. We followed suit.

chapter / TWENTY-TWO

Mike closed the door behind him. We were now in one of those smaller conference rooms. Close to the entrance, there was a desk, while the rest of the room, was populated with several rows of chairs. No windows, in sight. The entire space, was ours. And I was grateful for the privacy.

"Take a seat," Mike invited us, and we all three aligned on the first row. Then Mike took a chair and sat himself down across from me. "I think it's best if you give me a short summary of your story, so I can understand a little better your situation. This way, I can suggest more personalized help—tools."

I took a deep breath, trying to clear my head, wanting to touch on as many significant details as I could. And without much further ado, I dove right into it. I managed to walk him through a few pivotal moments of my life regarding this whole awakening process. Then I jumped to the present time, and elaborated on these past few weeks. Before and after Paris. Not forgetting the main issue at hand, my encounter with Sabine and the whole 'test mission' I was subjected to. And the fact that I was supposed to work for them, whether I wanted or not.

Mike absorbed my words silently, from time to time pushing his glasses back up the bridge of his nose. "Did they give you, an ultimatum?"

"No. But it's sounds like it's inevitable, that they will get what they want. Unless, I find a way out of this mess," I admitted, defeated.

He raised himself up. "I would like to do the scan now, if you don't mind? Could you please, stand up for a minute?"

"Sure," I said, and then stood up, dropping my bag on the chair next to me. "Do I need to do something? Move my hands, or something?"

"You don't have to do anything. Just relax. It's just easier for me to see where you have the implants, if you're in a vertical position."

"Oh. Okay. Go ahead," I said, and kept my hands hanging at my sides.

Mike nodded. He closed his eyes, then did a few breathing exercises, and I felt a very palpable shift in his energy. I remember having the same sensation earlier, when he was on the stage, doing a public demonstration on someone.

His talk was mainly about alien implants in human biology. Mike was one of those people that could see inside bodies, using his Inner Vision to detect foreign objects. His Inner Vision allowed him to detect not just in this 3D physical body/reality, but in other planes, too. His precision was astonishing. As a former abductee—due to his special abilities, as well—Mike had been used against his will, in various black projects. He had managed to escape a decade ago, with the help of some off-worlders, and got under their protection. A group who call themselves *Guardians*.

Eyes shut, his face moved from scanning my face, all the way to my feet, and then back up. "Well, I see they were very thorough with you," Mike spoke calmly.

"What's that supposed to mean?" I asked, dreading what he had to say next. But nonetheless curious, and wanting to comprehend the seriousness of it. No matter how bad it was, I preferred the truth over the ambiguity and unclarity.

"It means, they covered all possible spots, to make sure you will never be free again."

An overwhelming choking sensation in my throat, began taking over my senses.

"In other circumstances, I would say: job well done!" And he was most probably referring to his 'missions,' back when he had worked for the military.

My knees were so weak, I couldn't figure out how I was still standing in a vertical position.

"You have implants all over your body. Head, neck, arms, genital area, ankles… Hands and feet." He gently took my right arm, his eyes still closed. "Here you have a nasty one." Mike brushed with his fingers the problematic area on my forearm. "Do you feel from time to time a metallic sensation? Almost like a blade cutting through, inside your flesh?"

It was frightening how accurate he described, what I felt there, in certain moments. "Yes. How do you know this?" Then I felt silly for asking.

A sad smile colored his features. "Because I had it, too. This type of implants, have often a tough fibrous membrane, which encases the metal object. The physical implants blend with tissue, organs, whatever is necessary. The biological material is taken from the person that will be implanted, to make sure the body won't reject it. But here comes the twisted part. Most of these implants, are triggered by our own emotions. Actually first by thought, followed by an emotional response, and then it does what it was programmed to do. Mostly to block creative energy from expressing itself, or deviating it toward questionable purposes. Or just plain harvesting it," he affirmed, his eyes now open and gently observing me.

Probably, my emotions were all over the place. "I get it. We're food. *I* am food. And apparently, a prisoner in my own body." I breathed heavily, attempting not to lose the last shred of composure, and burst right into tears. I wasn't sure though, for how long I could do it. "Tell me, there is something we can do—"

He slid his right hand into the front pocket of his jeans. "There is. It's not simple. But there are ways around it."

"I remember you talking about Chelation, and some other products that I could use to do a cleanse. Like Chlorella, or Detoxamin," I said, sparks of hope igniting in the darkest corners of my mind.

"This usually helps a lot, especially with the physical implants," Mike confirmed, and then continued. "But you have implants in other planes, as well. Most of the nasty ones are not on this one. A lot of them are on the etheric level and above. And I'm particularly worried about the ones from your genital area, as well as the ones on each side of your head." He touched gently the parts behind my ears, where I knew for sure that I had at least one. "They are connected with a few in your upper back, and they are also entangled with those that start from your right foot, all the way up your right thigh. And from there, further up to your head. Yep. It's definitely not pretty," he nodded more to himself.

Great...

"I will need your permission to remove those in the other planes. That's something I don't perform," Mike said. "Not yet, anyway. I will ask the Guardians for help."

"You have my permission," my reply urgent. "Is it going to hurt?"

"Depends. You might experience, some unpleasant sensations. And usually these are connected to the physical, through corresponding physical implants. Which *is* the case here."

Lovely...

Mike went on. "You will be eliminating physically, those implants. Most commonly for women, is bleeding. So don't get scared, when that happens. It's like having a short period. If you already have your period at this time, then you most likely won't feel a difference."

Weirdly enough, even though I was in a room with three men, and touching the *period* subject, I wasn't embarrassed at all. Just annoyed.

"How is this going to happen?" I asked him, although, I kind of had an idea, how and when this might take place.

"It will happen most likely during the night, while you are asleep. Probably tonight, or tomorrow. I will text you when I'll know it myself. The idea is that, you'll be lying in bed and your body will be relaxed, in order to avoid complications," Mike answered, now pulling his phone from the back pocket. And that's when I noticed, he had some type of device on it.

"I see. Is that, EMF protection?" I asked, because I had wanted to buy some for myself and Jan. But I wasn't sure, I would get something that would actually work.

Mike nodded, checking his phone. "Your phone number? And email, just in case."

"Sure," I said, and gave him the information he needed. "And, for the rest? I mean the physical implants, what should I do about it?"

"Take Detoxamin, or Kelatox. It's cheaper, and just as effective as I.V. Chelation," he suggested.

I remembered, during his talk he had a segment on Chelation, explaining that it wasn't just great for people with blood circulation problems. Chelation was brilliant at removing heavy metals and alien implants, as well. Even Barium, found in chemtrails.

Mike placed a firm hand on my arm, and looked me in the eyes. "I *really* have to go, now. But you will get the help, I promised. Your case, is a delicate one. I need more information from my *friends*. I will I let you know, what needs to be done next. If *they* went to all this lenghts with you, it means, you are here to do something major. And they are trying to prevent that at any cost. I know, it's sounds cliché...but it's not."

I snickered. Simply because, this triggered another déjà vu. I had heard this before. I was quite sure, about the 'more-info-from-my-friends' part.

God damn, this stupid fog in my head...

"To be honest, what I see in your energetic configuration, is nothing short of a miracle. I've seen this—not exactly, but similar—to maybe a handful of people on the planet. And even if you get rid of the implants, this won't guarantee, they won't try to do it again, and again." Mike concluded, worries reading in his gentle eyes.

That choking feeling was back, and I felt as helpless, as I did before I even spoke with him.

"I see." That's all I managed.

How the hell, could I be doing something major, since for most of my life, I'd had one setback after another? How could someone like *me*, who was basically an out-sider of life, was a threat to the plans of some parasitic secret elite force? Even though Sabine herself, had mentioned my *special* talents, and the possible power I could exert if I were to join their side. I still couldn't see it. But I could glimpse into the dark future she had in store for me. And that terrified me to the core. Definitely, I wouldn't want to be part of that.

Mike shook my arm briefly. "I *promise* I will do my best, to help you out."

I just nodded, my eyes barely containing the tears that were rushing to the surface.

After Mike left us, we went back to the main lobby, not sure what to do next. I wasn't ready to go home, just yet. Maybe I could check out the books and DVDs stands of the other speakers—whom I'd missed—from the previous days. But honestly, mainly I wanted a distraction. Something to keep me busy and away, from all those dark thoughts that were creeping in with a vengeance. I was utterly grateful for Mike's feedback, and I hadn't doubted his words, when he'd promised further help. Only, now I felt *literally* like a mined field. Afraid to think anything. Afraid to feel something that would trigger this twisted machinery inside me. Ironically though, this was impossible to stop.

"I would say, the chat was fruitful. Don't you agree?" Tim said cheerfully, squeezing me in a tight hug. He tried to make me feel better, and I appreciated the intention. Still, was hard to quiet down all that noise in my head, and put a stop to my muffled cry. And somehow I ended up getting mad at myself, for being weak. And emotionally unstable. This was so not me.

"Now, let's go and eat something. I'm starving," he added, looking now to Jan.

"You don't need to tell me twice," Jan replied in his usual playful manner, making me chuckle. He put his hands over my shoulders and pulled me against his chest, and away from Tim's arms. "I think among the many duties of a *caring* fiancée, is to comfort my future wife. So why don't you, leave *this* to me."

I wiped my tears with the back of my hands. "Great. Now you've decided, it's time to be jealous." Though knowing that there was no jealousy involved, just the usual banter between them.

Jan chortled, his chest vibrating. "What? I am caring."

"Uh-huh," I shook my head.

"He is," Tim defended him, jokingly. "In his own 'caveman' way. It's part of his personal charm."

I laughed. "True."

"I thought you were starving?" Jan said, pretending to be offended.

Tim slid his messenger back over his head, positioning it to the side. "I am. *Very*, actually. Any ideas, where to?" He glanced at me. "You know this area, better than me."

"It's quite far to go to 'Leaf,' or to any decent Italian place, but if no one objects, we could try the hotel's restaurant. I heard, it's pretty good. It's international cuisine, so we can all have something to eat. I think," I said, hesitant on the last part.

"Great! Lead the way," Tim invited me, gesturing with his hands.

The Conference Center was connected directly to the hotel and its restaurant, through a corridor. So we got there in no time. Surprisingly, the restaurant was packed. Usually, the people that stayed at this hotel, would rather go and explore other places in the city, for lunch or dinner. Most likely, today was different because of the event. After a long day, of back-to-back talks, many found more convenient to come here and grab something to eat.

Lucky for us, we found a corner table, where we sat ourselves down. Fortunately, my intuition was correct, and everyone was able to order at least two courses. Tim was vegetarian, so naturally, he had more choices. But I wasn't complaining. Plus, the ambiance, the décor were really pleasant. Everything looked new, and modern. I could recognize an overall stylized marine theme. A few nuances of magnetic blues, warmed by some tamed wood tones, worked well with the futuristic lamps, as well as with the other sleek accessories, completing a genuinely chic and clean interior. Perfect for a more sophisticated lunch, or dinner situation.

"I see they do New Year's Parties, too," Jan spoke, now looking up from a brochure he found earlier on the table. "And, it's not expensive. Maybe we should celebrate out, this year," he said, winking at me.

I smiled. "Show me," I demanded, and he passed me the brochure.

"If the food is as good as this place looks, why not?" Tim put in.

The idea was actually, not bad at all. In the last few years, we had celebrated at home just the two of us. Or just with family and some friends. Which was nice. But a change of tone, was more than welcome. At least the idea gave me hope; a sense of normality. That there was a future after all, and no imminent coercion was in sight.

I browsed through the brochure. The offer was definitely, appealing. The usual discount included—as long as you would make reservations before the end of November. Which wasn't that far away.

I nodded. "Sure, why not? Hey, you and Andreas should join us," I said to Tim. "Assuming, I will still be alive and kicking, by then," I added, trying to poke fun at my own predicament.

Tim took a sip of water from his glass. "If he doesn't have some surprise planned already, this could be fun. Certainly, it's not my *dream* to spend the last day of the year, and the first hours of the New Year with your 'caveman.' I see him too much as it is—"

Jan huffed. "Right back at you!"

"But, I would do anything for you," Tim joked again. "And you *will* be alive then. Or else, I will send my mother after that *parasite* Sabine, and her gang of smaller parasites. You know how good she is with cleaning and disinfecting. She is a hygiene freak."

I liked his analogy. "She and me both," I replied laughingly.

"Besides, I don't want to be left alone with *him*, in the lab after that," he meant Jan. "He is annoying as it is. You are the only thing, which makes him tolerable. So don't you dare—"

"Keep talking like that, and I will *uninvite* you from my sister-in-law's birthday party," Jan mocked him back.

This was a surprise, indeed. "You're coming Thursday, too?"

"You know me, I like the beach. I couldn't just say no," Tim answered, a big grin spreading over his face.

In that moment, I realized how worried and scared Jan actually was for me. He knew if something would happen to me on Thursday, only he and my sister would be…'in the know.' So he called for backup. Which was sweet, and utterly romantic. And I wished that all of this would be unnecessary. But I wasn't going to pretend, that everything was fine and safe. So I let it be. I let him believe, I didn't get the real motive for inviting Tim to Meike's party.

"Hey, the more the merrier," I replied, finally my voice sounding more excited. "Is Andreas coming, as well?"

"How could I leave my knight in shining armor, at home? I need protection too, you know?!"

I chuckled, shaking my head. "Of course."

Definitely, this banter today was more than just simply poking fun at each other, or teasing between friends. I knew, they liked to do that at work, but still. This could mean one thing. Both of them did their best, to make sure I wasn't completely freaked out, with all that was transpiring lately.

I had no words, to express my gratitude for that. And again, that choking feeling was rising in my throat, threatening to unleash more tears.

This time I kept it in.

Then the food arrived, and we dove into it right away.

It was delicious.

chapter / TWENTY-THREE

Jan was already asleep. We came back from the restaurant several hours ago, but my sister was still at the venue working. She had sent me a text, instructing me not to wait for her with dinner, because she would be eating there. So I went back to work for Peter's project. Jan had managed to stay awake for another hour or so, and then had dropped into the dream world.

How I envied him right about now...

Anyways. Curiously, I was highly productive. By now, I already had three layout versions for the Event's setting. I had modeled them in 3D, and was now rendering for each version, at least one perspective view.

I was tired, but grateful for the distraction the work brought. Actually, it helped me focus, it gave me purpose, and most of all, I wasn't feeling helpless anymore.

By the time I was done with the first two renderings, I got hungry again.

I set the last perspective view, let it render, and then went into the kitchen.

I pulled the fridge's door open, and stood there, considering what to fix up to eat. Fast, easy and delicious. Or simply anything that would quiet the hunger. I was one of those people with weird food cravings. First of all, I was a garlic and onion *addict*. And as long as one of those ingredients—if not both—was part of what I was about to eat, I would be all right.

I snorted, just thinking those thoughts.

"Veggie spread it is," I heard myself saying out loud. I saw the jar was already open, and more than half full. Perfect. I grabbed it, took three tomatoes from the bottom drawer, then closed the fridge door with my elbow. I wasn't fast just with my work. The ninja skills extended into many areas of my life, including the kitchen. Tired or not, when the hunger kicked hard and loud, I went full-on 'light speed.' So in no time, I washed and sliced the tomatoes, peeled and chopped finely a large onion, and placed all of them on a plate. I took a package of rye crisp bread from the top cabinet in front of me, and set it on the tray.

Something was missing. "Of course… Strawberries!" I had spotted them earlier, but somehow I ended up ignoring them. Now, they were just the perfect addition to my usual mix.

I put all the ingredients on the tray, went into to my office, and set it on the desk, opposite to my laptop. Usually, I would eat looking at my screen, which wasn't healthy at all. But this time, I didn't want to slow down my computer by opening another window. So I let it run, undisturbed. I really wanted to be done with it before I went to sleep, at some point.

The sound of the key going into the lock, startled me.

Raluca.

She was back.

I stepped into the hallway, as she opened the door. She saw me, and her eyes lit up. Her mouth opened, ready to speak in her overly enthusiastic tone. I stopped her, raising the index finger to my lips, warning her to be quiet. "Jan is sleeping," I whispered to her. Not that Jan had any problem with us being loud, when he slept. But tonight, for some reason, it just seemed inconsiderate toward him.

Whilst Raluca took off her shoes, and placed them quietly on the shoe rack by the door, I gestured her to come into the office, when she was done.

I'd had already three slices of veggie spread, by the time she entered the room.

"I'm sorry to be so late," Raluca said, while shutting the door behind her.

"You don't have to excuse yourself. I get it, you had to work," I spoke between the bites. "As you can see, I'm still not done myself," I motioned her to look at the computer screen. And just like an excited kid, she took the other chair and sat down in front of

211

it.

Her eyes were glowing with admiration. "I knew you were good, but this… This is *awesome*. And so fast… Peter is going to *love* this," she nodded to herself.

I snorted. "Thanks," my mouth chewing busily.

"And after tonight, I think he is going to love me, even more." When she said the word *love*, her expression changed. A mixture of excitement and embarrassment radiated from her face.

Now I was intrigued. "What happened?"

Still looking into the screen, she paused for an instant, and then answered. "We kissed."

My eyebrows shoot up, and I stopped the chewing, not sure I heard what I heard. "What?"

Raluca covered her face with her hands. "I know, I'm an idiot."

I was still waiting for her to clarify, so I remained silent.

When she heard no remark, no objection from me, she peeked from behind her hands. "What, no lecture?"

"I'm waiting for the full explanation. The context in which this *unexpected* turn of events, took place," I replied frankly.

Raluca took a deep breath, her face reddened with embarrassment. "We were dining with Nuno, the D.J. that we hired for the Event. We laughed a lot… The guy knows music, and has lived life fully, even if he is younger than us. He is Portuguese, and has some amazing stories to tell. And a lot of funny ones, too." She snorted. "And after all this chaos and stress with the Event and…stuff," she meant my situation. "It was a moment, when I just…relaxed," she admitted.

I could totally relate to that.

"He left at some point, but we continued. I mean, we just went on and on about life, and the situations that helped shape us into the people we are today. We got to know each other better. Plus, I think we had too much wine, so I relaxed more than I intended." She exhaled heavily. "To be honest, I was as surprised as you look right now," she laughed.

"He just kissed me. And I reciprocated," Raluca added, matter-of-factly.

"And?"

"And I liked it." Then she let her head fall frontward.

I took another bite from my beautifully decorated slice of spread. "Great."

She looked up. "Great?!"

I swallowed the last piece, happy to feel my stomach finally full. "What do you want me to say?! That it's wrong? That you're stupid?"

"Yes!" she gestured desperately with her hands.

I leaned back in my chair, my head relaxing on the headrest. "You are single. Unless he has some wife or girlfriend hidden away, somewhere…he is single, too. And he made perfectly clear, that he likes you. Well, more than just *likes* you. You kissed. You liked it. What am I leaving out?"

"We kissed more than once. In fact, we kissed three times. The last one, was before I got into the taxi on my way home," she confessed, as if she was talking about some dark, unforgivable sin.

"Yeah. Scandalous," I mocked her.

She looked at me in surprise. "So you're saying there is nothing wrong with this… *situation*? When did you become so *liberal*?"

I snorted, realizing she was right.

Yeah, when did I become so *liberal*? Usually, I was the one with very strict rules regarding these kinds of situations. And I lived by it. "I think the recent realizations, of how relative all is, gave me an edge," I smiled at my own irony.

"I'm sorry. I'm such, an idiot. How was everything today?" Raluca asked, sincere concern reading in her eyes.

I shook my head. "Don't be. I'm actually happy your day was…surprising in this sense," I smiled. "Mine was good. Mostly. Well, all except the part where I found out I am a walking talking, mined field."

Her expression changed, into horror. "*What*?"

"As you heard. But, apparently there is help underway. So it's not all, completely irremediable," I tried to reassure her. Actually, more like reassuring myself, because so far, no text, no email, no nothing from Mike. And as much as I wanted, I couldn't help but wonder, if what he had promised was going to be delivered or not.

Raluca crossed her arms over her chest, her eyes boring into mine. "Detailed explanation, *please*."

I nodded, and began telling her about the conference day. I imparted a few generalities about the venue and how everything went, little bits about the speakers, and what their material had covered. Then moved to the part where Tim had made the impossible possible, and I was able to come in direct contact with Mike Kenna. Which in turn led to an impromptu scanning session, revealing how heavily implanted I was. And not just, physically. However, thanks to his close relation with some beings that called themselves *Guardians*, he had access to a special procedure to remove these horrible things.

"So that's it? Now you just have to wait?" Raluca wanted to know, confused but somehow relieved, that finally, we discovered a viable solution.

"Mainly. I mean, he has to dig a little deeper. Because, even if they remove the implants, this doesn't guarantee that I'm done with the problem."

She sighed, in disappointment.

On so many levels, I felt the same, still, I couldn't let her sense my own fears. "Meanwhile, Jan has already ordered a large quantity of Detoxamin. Which will be here, in two or three days. So yeah… At the moment, I have to exercise patience."

"This sucks," she concluded, bitterly.

"Exactly. But hey, at least now I know where I can spend New Year's," I snorted, trying to lighten the tone of the conversation. "You and Peter, should definitely join us," I teased her.

"Right." Her face beaming red again. Then she looked at the screen. "Your rendering is done. It looks *so* cool. Truly."

I stood up. "Thank you." Then I walked around the desk to see it for myself. Indeed, it looked cool. "Well, you know what they say. Good design is LOVE. Now, if you could just give me back my chair, I will send all three versions to your boyfriend," I teased her again.

Raluca rose to her feet. "He's not my boyfriend." And in a few strides, she was at the door pulling it open. "Yet," she added, and then shut it behind her.

I chuckled, shaking my head.

Finally I was done for today, a peaceful and extremely fulfilling sensation settling over me. Email sent, now I was ready to go to bed. I shut my laptop, and closed the lid. I picked up the tray with the rests of my unusual food combination, and walked toward the door.

My phone buzzed.

I spun around, trying to detect where the noise came from, obviously forgetting where I put it. I checked the surface of the desk. Aside from my laptop, working lamp, two notebooks and a few pens, no phone was in sight. I put the tray again on the table. I looked under it, and found my bag. I opened it, and searched rapidly through. Luckily, my hand found it and I pulled it out the bag, hope and anticipation rising in me.

And there it was.

Mike finally sent me a message.

Tomorrow night. 4 a.m. your time. I will tell you more…when I'll have more. Until then, sweet dreams.

I smiled.

All that toxic anxiety accumulated over the second half of the day, was now gone.

chapter / TWENTY-FOUR

I was standing in front of the door, having the worst time deciding how I was going to say the news. Not easy. In fact *horrible* wouldn't begin to describe it. Especially now, when we just found each other.

I sighed heavily, and pushed the door open. I searched for him with my eyes, but there was no one in sight. All the windows and doors were wide open, the evening breeze gently playing with the white curtains. I loved it how peaceful it made me feel, even though I could swear the entire world was on my shoulders tonight.

I stepped into the adjacent chamber, and spotted him on the terrace. He was gazing down the beautiful valley, his arms resting on the balustrade. This was my favorite spot, to come to relax, let my mind unwind. Or anytime I had to make an important decision. And just by simply absorbing this beauty, the majesty of the mountains and the hypnotic turquoise clear water of the bay, I would find a sense of calmness and harmony.

He loved this spot too, and for some time now, we used to meet up here after a hectic day. I stopped just before the threshold, and for a moment took everything in. Him, peacefully waiting for me, his rebel amber curls fighting with the warm summer wind. The cerulean sky turning softly into darkness, the lush nature intoxicating us with its rich palette of scents. And even from up here, I could hear, the joyous celebration starting down at the shore. How ironic, it all seemed now. How I wished, things were different... But I couldn't back down now. It was done.

Tears were rolling down my face, relieving the heaviness I felt crushing me.

"How long are you going to stay there?" he spoke, startling me.

I forgot, how strong his sense of my presence—in fact of any presence—was.

I started toward him, wiping my tears, with the back of my hands, and dried them on my beautiful forest green satin tunic dress.

In a few strides I was behind him, and wrapped my arms around his waist, my head leaning over his back, forcing back the last drops.

His hands brushed mine gently, sending shivers down my spine. That actually, made it even more painful, because all of *this* and many other unlived future experiences, will cease to exist tomorrow.

"When, were you going to tell me?" His voice carried a suspicious tremor, which managed to send another wave of shock in my mind—already clouded with grief.

I pulled away and turned to face him. And what I found in his beautiful ocean blue eyes…was pure heartbreak. I almost couldn't speak the words. "You know."

He didn't say anything, just stared at me.

I swallowed hard, my body growing colder in spite of the warm breeze. "…I had no choice. I discovered she joined the Guardians for the Rescue Mission. She went in for Mithon. His signal was really bad, in the last three months. And I knew she was worried, but last week she vanished completely. I thought she wanted some time alone. So I didn't bother her. But today, when I went into Operations, they told me what she did. And no one stopped her, because they need as many of us as possible.

"She knew, she might not come back. She knew, her codes weren't that strong, but she did it anyway. The thought of being without him…she couldn't bear it."

At this point my tears were coming back with a vengeance, making it difficult to stay focused, my vision seriously blurred. "When I found out, I couldn't speak… So as usual, adrenaline kicked in, and I decided to go after her. She is my sister. She is the only family I have left. I can't just *leave* her disappear. I just can't. I have to do it," I said, determined. "Tonight is the Alignment, so the next viable time to go in, is in a few hours."

His unbearably sad, yet composed gaze on me, forced me to look away. "You must think, I am heartless…when it comes to us. And I don't blame you. In fact, I am forever grateful for whatever little time we shared together. That's why, I can't ask you to wait. I might not come back myself," and just thinking about it, that I too, might not be able to retain my essence—become star dust, without any memory of me ever existing—made me sick to my stomach.

"...I don't know what else to say. Everything else feels empty and meaningless," I admitted in defeat.

His elegant strong hands cupped my face, forcing me to acknowledge all those intense emotions his eyes were expressing. "I won't wait...because I'm coming with you," he replied wiping my tears with his thumb.

My eyes widened in surprise.

"You gave me no choice," a sad smile forming at the corners of his lips.

I opened my mouth to protest, and before I knew it, he was on me, silencing me with a kiss. A desperate kiss. He poured in it all his fears, all the frustrations, all the things we should have said to each other but we didn't, because there was no more time. But mostly, he was overwhelming me with...love.

My head was spinning.

I let myself fall into this vortex of emotions, knowing that no matter what he'd say after that, I couldn't allow it to happen. I couldn't jeopardize his soul. I couldn't just sentence him to dissolution. No. No. No...

When I regained balance again, I pulled slowly back, putting a small distance between us, and forced myself to focus. Though, it was a feeble attempt. "This is very noble of you. But I can't let you do this," I insisted, trying to steady my breathing.

He chuckled, the fire in his eyes still strong like a scorching sun, threatening to melt any remaining objection that my brain was able to invoke. "I'm not asking for your permission," he said extending a hand. "Come, we're wasting precious time," he insisted.

"I'm serious," I frowned.

His hand was still waiting for mine. "So am I."

I didn't know what to do, or say, to sway him otherwise. All the scenarios I had played in my head before I opened that door, went directly to trash. All the pain and sorrow I was carrying earlier, now transformed into something raw and vibrant. Exciting.

"Where are we going?" I demanded.

"Do you trust me?"

I looked fixedly at him, my heart starting to beat faster again. Of course, I trusted him.

I gave him my hand, and he took it silently, a beautiful smile flourishing on his face.

We rushed down the steps on the left of the terrace, which were leading to the level below. From there, we walked down a narrow path parallel to the arched valley, until we found more steps, and made our descent to the shore. A very long and quite abrupt zigzag of stairs, through lots of greenery. Normally, we didn't use these. There were other ways to get faster down to the beach. But then I realized, these weren't taking us to the celebration area. They were heading in the opposite direction, to the right of the bay.

By now the sky was dark, and beautiful lights were turning up from all dwellings across the valley. Typically, at night the valley looked very pretty, but with the Alignment celebration, everything seemed even more charming and spectacular than usual. Laughter and music, and a general festive atmosphere radiating everywhere.

We reached the beach, feeling a little out of breath.

"I think it's time for a shortcut," he suggested, and pointed to a small boat tied to a short post, only a few steps away from us. "Let's push it, into the water."

I nodded, took off my golden sandals, and in two long strides we were beside it. He untied the rope, and to my surprise, it was lighter than it looked at first sight. In no time, we were in the boat and on the water heading somewhere...

He was paddling swiftly, obviously trying to get us—wherever we were going...—on time, and the only way I allowed to help, was by holding a lit up lamp.

I attempted several times to trick him into telling me where he was taking me, but after a short while, I gave up. He simply had no intention in sharing, instead he was grinning like an idiot every time I asked him.

At some point, we approached an opening at the base of the mountain—which looked more like a tunnel—and he steered toward it. Then I realized, we were heading over the other side, to the adjacent gulf. I didn't say anything. By now, I was simply enjoying the adventure. Not thinking anymore of what was about to happen in the morning.

We reached the other side pretty fast, and that lamp was very useful, helping us not to bump into all the rocks we encountered, spread across the tunnel.

He jumped into the shallow water, and although he rolled his white trousers up to his knees, somehow he got them completely wet. But he didn't seem to mind at all.

I laughed.

He pulled the boat to the shore, until it was safe for me to step out of it. "Don't forget the lamp," he reminded me, then helped me out.

We were now walking hand in hand, on a narrow path, heading into the woods. I was completely clueless; obviously he knew his way around here. We came to a halt when we almost stumbled on a set of stone steps going up to a platform. I couldn't exactly see what was up there, being surrounded by such dense vegetation, and trees and darkness. But the air, the energy of this place, was different.

"After you," he motioned me with his hand, his voice filled with excitement.

I snorted.

Amused by the whole thing, but filled with curiosity, I began walking up the arched stairs, anticipation rising in me. When I reached the top, I saw a short stepping-stone path, and at the end of it, a beautifully sculpted pink quartz arch. A tree on each side marking the entrance. And more trees behind it.

"What am I not getting?" I asked in confusion, and a bit disappointed.

He came from behind me, grabbed my hand, in the other holding the lamp, and we walked until we got in front of it. And then I saw it.

The air inside the arch was literally pulsating, smudging the image behind it.

"Is this, what I think it is?" I said, turning my head to look at him.

He nodded.

"So where is this portal taking us?" I asked, raising my eyebrows.

"It's not just a simple portal. Or *exactly* a portal. It's an old ceremonial ground, which was used in the past by our ancestors. Now only a few, remember its existence," he answered matter-of-factly.

"And why is it special?"

He couldn't stop smiling. "You will see in a bit. Now close your eyes, and imagine a beautiful place," he instructed me gently, his warm gaze set on me. "The more details, the better. And don't forget to add some water. In a form, or another . . ."

"All right," then I closed my eyes, and let my mind see something pleasing, and he started whispering melodic words in a language I didn't understand. Probably some ancient dialect—which made sense, given the nature of this place. Beautiful, nonetheless.

It didn't take very long until the images took coherent form, and I was taking a virtual tour of the entire thing.

"You can open your eyes, now," he said, briefly shaking my hand.

When I did, my jaw dropped open.

"Is this real?" I asked unconvinced.

"This place exists just for us. Once we step through this archway, no one can enter it—aside from you and I," he said, looking ahead. "Ready?" then he whirled his head toward me.

I nodded, still stunned by what I saw.

Beyond the archway, a lovely meadow was spreading ahead of us. Pretty lights in the grass formed a path which led to a white dome dwelling, a large glass door being the only opening from this side. The dome itself was illuminated at the base, making it stand out even more in the darkness.

We stepped through the arch, now walking toward the glass door. On each side, tall trees were guarding strategically this magical spot. But on the left side, the meadow was expanding, allowing us to see the ocean from here.

"Not bad," he said with admiration, holding my hand tightly.

I smiled. "Wait to see what's beyond that door," I teased.

When we reached the entrance, he held the door open, gesturing me in. "Feel free, to give me the tour."

I snorted. "Well, the entrance it's pretty much self explanatory," I said.

Given the fact the glass door was transparent, even before we reached the house, we could see inside. A wooden table top mounted against a white wall, was decorated with a bunch of white Calla lilies in a golden vase. Three spots of light coming from the ceiling were projecting an intimate atmosphere.

The wall was serving as separator between entrance and the rest of the dwelling.

"So from here, we can go either left or right. Both lead to the same space," I explained, gesturing with my hands.

He grinned mischievously. "You go left, and I go right. And we meet in the middle," he suggested.

I chuckled. "Sure," I agreed, each then going in the opposite direction.

The separator wall was arched on both sides, creating a protecting corridor. In just a few long steps, we were on the other side. Both getting here at the same time. The lights in here, even dimmer.

"I must say, I *really* like this," he pointed to the bed in the middle, set against the wall.

I laughed out loud. "Of course you do," I said, shaking my head.

Aside from the bed, two night stands, a lounge bench and a small bookcase filled with my favorite books, there was nothing else in the room. And everything was white, except two golden decorative pillows.

He chuckled, when he saw the bookcase. "That's definitely you . . ."

I shrugged. "What can I say? My own personal signature."

He nodded, then turned his head to the large glass windows and doors, all wide open, showing a spectacular view of the terrace and swimming pool, which was nicely lit by more grass lights. The sight of the ocean, completing the scenery. A gleam of utter excitement ignited in his eyes. "Perfect," he said, then stepped outside, and I followed.

Close to the rectangular shaped pool, there were two more lounge benches, each decorated with white pillows and nicely folded towels.

With his back to me, he pulled his shirt over his head and dropped it over one of the benches. "Take off your clothes," he demanded, already unbuttoning his trousers.

"I have no swimming attire," I said, feeling myself turning red in the face. Then I realized, I could've imagined it to exist in this place. *Stupid. Stupid.*

He then swirled to face me. "Me neither," he replied in challenge, and then his trousers came off, now standing entirely naked in front of me.

I stopped breathing.

This was the first time ever, when I saw him completely naked. Determinately, I only focused on his face. "I see." That's all I managed.

He advanced a few steps, now standing right in front of me, and towering me with his height. "I'm sorry for the extremely direct *introduction* to my anatomy," he said, and I snorted beaming all kinds of red. Thank God, it was dark. Although he had the advantage at this point, because the two moons were behind him, casting shadows on his face. Did nothing though, to hide mine, or the embarrassment I sensed showing. "But we don't have much time left," he pointed out, thinning his lips.

Then grief and sorrow hit me again, like a ton of bricks. "You have time. You don't have to come with me——"

"Stop *saying* that," obvious pain emanating from his words. "My mind is made up. There is no turning back," he said, decidedly.

"*Why*? Why is there no turning back for you?" I demanded, a stupid fury rising in me.

Even though the darkness was covering a lot of his facial expressions, I couldn't miss those raw emotions churning in his eyes. "When you saved me the second time around, during that crazy mission…something changed in me, permanently."

"If it's out of gratitude, you can just simply say 'thank you.' If it's guilt, well, there's no need. You don't owe me anything. I saved many other lives. It was my job."

He grabbed me by the arms, giving me a brief shake. "*Stop* pushing me away. Nothing what you'll say or do will change my mind," he paused for a moment, holding my gaze, with such intensity, I thought I would get pulverized in that instant. "And let me finish, what I have to say."

I almost forgot he was utterly naked in front of me, going all angry and vulnerable. So I let him talk.

He seized, that I was now paying attention, waiting for his explanation, so he continued. "I saw *you*. I saw *who* you are. In everything you said and did. I saw this *incredibly* elegant coherence. I saw this inexhaustible *blazing* light, who refuses to give up. Even when there is nothing left to fight for. To hope for. In fact, the most astonishing thing happens then. Out of nowhere, you ignite even brighter and stronger, until nothing and *no one* can stand between you and what you want. Until you crush any resistance, any obstacles in your way. You're *that* bright. Your *fire* has marked and altered my soul *forever*."

I stood there as if struck by lightning. Hardly able to form anything *coherent* to say. How ironic. And those stupid tears were coming back, demanding to be released.

He placed his hands gently on my face, his head leaning in. "Now you understand, why?"

I swallowed hard.

I simply nodded.

"Good. Now if you don't mind, I want to finish, what I've started. We really, have to get into the water for that," he said with all sincerity.

I burst into laughter, and tears at the same time.

For a second he looked confused, then he got, what I got. He raised his eyebrows. "Well, we can do that, too," he grinned impishly. "But first, I have to make sure, we'll find our way back to each other. No matter what happens," he added, the tone now changing into something urgent.

I sighed heavily, becoming again *painfully* aware of all the implications that came with the decision I made only a few hours ago, and then started to undress. I really didn't want to waste anymore time. I *didn't* have any more time.

When I finally got into the pool, the water was delightfully warm and soothing. In fact I was wondering, why I had resisted so much not to get in it, sooner.

We were now standing, facing each other, a small space between us, the water reaching my shoulders level, and barely his chest. The awkwardness I had felt earlier, was gone, and seemed silly now. Instead a feeling of peace and serenity enveloped me, like a cocoon.

Gently, he placed his left palm over my heart center, instructing me to do the same, to place mine over his heart center. More fascinated than curious, I did what he asked. The intensity I saw earlier in his gaze, was back. Only now, becoming more solemn and ceremonial. Then he began again to speak in that beautiful dialect. From time to time, telling me to repeat certain words after him.

With every word that came out of his mouth, I felt the energy growing inside my chest, and my palm pulsating. A burning sensation accompanying both. And then more energy. More pulsating. More growing. More expanding. And then something wonderful happened.

We now both, were glowing in the heart center. Each carrying a sphere of light inside ourselves. He continued repeating those magical words, and the spheres expanded outside of our bodies until they intersected each other. And now blending into one giant ball of aquamarine light, with sparks of gold and silver. Expanding. More, and more… Beyond us. Beyond the pool. Beyond the dome. Until the entire place was embedded with this energy.

Completely and utterly mesmerized by what I saw and felt, I hadn't realized when he'd moved. "Remember this place," he said with urgency, his hands gently brushing my cheeks. "Come here in your dreams, and find me. Call me here," he pleaded, his eyes swirling with unspoken emotions. "We will always find each other in here."

My eyes widened, and I stared at him open-mouthed, grasping what he just did.

And then he kissed me.

chapter / TWENTY-FIVE

I swear this week it's too long... I mean Wednesday went by fast. But not fast enough. And today...was still Thursday.

Only three days ago, I thought there wasn't enough time to deliver something what would match my own 'impossible-to-please' expectations. Weird, how now I wanted things to speed up, even more. But the motivation behind, it wasn't work. It was this messy *thing* that was interfering with my existence.

I sighed deeply, glancing quickly at the crew that was assembling the stage area, where the awards would be presented. Strangely enough, things were coming together pretty nicely. And at high speed, too.

Total paradox.

"I was right."

I whirled my head, and spotted my sister approaching. "About?" I replied, curiously.

"About the fact that you and I make a *killer* team," Raluca said, winking at me. Then handed me the big cup of tea, I ordered earlier.

Since yesterday, we had basically lived here—at the Event's venue—supervising the first phase of décor installation. I had to make sure that every piece went where I intended it to be. Or simply adjusting the position of some of them, to get the most out of the desired effect. Unexpectedly, the crew and I had worked in true symbiosis.

The people we had finally decided to hire—for the execution and installation—were from an emerging local company, which had a young and very passionate management team.

I had to give it to them. Their reaction time to my final version was impeccable. Especially, when that version arrived yesterday morning in their email box. After Peter overly enthusiastic had said, "Love it. Love it. You choose which one." And I did, without wasting any more time.

When they had realized it was more efficient to finalize the elements on site, the crew brought all the necessary tools with them. Naturally, the restaurant had to close entirely for the public, for the course of these two days, as well. That was billed extra, but Peter didn't mind.

By late afternoon, the first few pieces were ready to be mounted in place. And by fairly late at night, we were looking at two thirds of the set already finalized. That was impressive work. Of course, from time to time, I couldn't help but jump in and offer my direct help with certain details they had felt unsure about it. Especially, since most of the décor pieces consisted of canvas, metal frames, wires, and lights.

Today, in the course of the morning, while I was having a short meeting with Martina via Skype, the crew had put together the last elements. Leaving the stage for last. Which, was now. I really couldn't complain.

I took a sip from my herbal tea, and set it on the table next to my laptop.

"I think we'll be ready, before the party," Raluca said.

I glanced around quickly, and nodded shortly. "It seems so. Meike will be thrilled, that for once we might actually arrive on time."

Raluca furrowed her eyebrows. "What do you mean?"

I snorted. "Jan and I, kind of got this reputation as *late arrivers*. Like late, *late*. For all the family gatherings, and stuff."

"That's…strange. You are one of the most punctual people I know. If not the most *annoyingly* on time person. I don't know very well Jan's record. But you…you are a *machine*. So there's got to be a logical explanation, which Meike doesn't get."

I laughed at her perspicaciously assessment. "There is. Jan is slow. And sometimes he *drags* to get his ass there. Paradoxically though, he likes to be around his family.

But getting there or getting there on time…a whole other story."

"Who drags what?"

My sister and I, we swirled our heads, and saw Peter only a few meters away from us.

He was looking smart in a white shirt, paired with slim cognac chino pants and a pair of navy blue converse, smiling from ear to ear. I was pretty sure that had nothing to do with work.

"Didn't your mom tell you, it's not polite to eavesdrop?" Raluca answered trying to sound offended.

She didn't fool me, or Peter. Her glowing eyes, and the instantaneous blush the moment she acknowledged his presence, were a big give away.

Peter obviously liked the play. "She did. But I do it anyway," he replied, grinning mischievously.

She planted a hand on her waist, forcing herself not to smile. "Well, that's why—" Raluca stopped in mid-sentence not sure how to continue.

Peter shoved his hands in his pockets, eyebrows arched. "*Well*?!"

This was actually cute to watch.

Raluca crossed her arms over her chest, her eyes intently on him. "I bet that's why you are still single."

"How, is that make any sense? And by the way, I thought the single status is no longer accurate," he challenged, shifting his weight from one leg to the other, grin still in place.

"That's what I thought, too." I mumbled.

If a moment ago she blushed, now she was beet red. Her eyes were shooting fire arrows in my direction.

Ups…

My phone buzzed. I picked it up from the table and swiped the screen to unlock it.

Unexpectedly, there was a text message from Jan.

Before the party I have a surprise for you. I will come by to pick you up. Let me know when you're done.

"Yeah, I think I will be late for the party. Again," I said, more to myself after reading the message. "I'm *pretty* sure, very soon Meike will start to hate us."

"What happened? " Raluca asked, happy to change the subject and move the focus from her *thing* with Peter, to something that would not put her on the spot.

"Oh, nothing," I replied, waving a hand dismissively. "Jan has a surprise for me. Before the party. That means I will be late again. We will be late again," meaning Jan and I.

"Things look great here," Peter remarked, glancing around. He checked his watch, then lifted his head. "You two, will be done by then. Go to your family party. I don't want to be the reason, why your future in-laws will ban you from any and every family activity."

Raluca took the chair opposite me. "We only have today and tomorrow until late afternoon. To finish. To check. To double and triple check everything. She can go early. But I might have to stay a little longer. I promised you, a great event. That's what you'll get," she said decidedly.

Peter followed her gaze. "Oh, I have no doubt. But family, is more important than this."

"I have to agree with you, on this one," I said.

"But *this* is important." She gesticulated with her hands.

Usually this was something I would say. But today, and under recent circumstances, I was beginning to reevaluate my priorities.

Peter stepped closer to where my sister sat. "If I would've had anything to complain, you'd know it by know." Then he bent over and surprised her with a kiss.

She definitely didn't have time to protest.

I smiled.

For a second there, I didn't know what to do with myself, so I looked away. Not really embarrassed, but feeling like I was intruding their private moment.

A good time to drink that tea… I sipped slowly a few times from my cup.

Thank God, it didn't last very long.

Peter stood, his eyes swirling with fire. "If I still find you here at six, I will drive you myself to the party," he said, staring into my sister's equally heated gaze. "I have to go now. Meeting in ten." Then he turned toward me and smiled. "Have fun at the party. I'll see you tomorrow?!"

I nodded as 'thank you,' then confirmed. "Absolutely."

He took one last look at my sister, pouring unspoken emotions into it, then spun on his heels and started toward the exit door. "I *will* come and check on you," Peter said, on his way out, and kept going until he disappeared through that door.

"Whatever," mumbled my sister behind him.

I chuckled.

She covered her face with her hands. "Oh, God. What am I doing?"

"Isn't it obvious?"

"That I'm stupid? I already figured that out?"

I snorted. "Falling for someone can make you do stupid things. *That* I know."

She peered through her hands, still flushed. "Am I? I mean, am I *falling* for him? Is this a case of falling? 'Cause right about now I feel like someone gave me a bad flu, and can't think straight."

"Yep. The symptoms are pretty accurate. Although I haven't had a cold in a long while." Which was true. About the cold. I hadn't had one in years. Especially, since I'd started taking regularly vitamin D3.

Raluca straightened in her chair, and let her arms rest on her lap. "I *sooo* wish this week to be over. And then reset. See how things will look, after this weekend."

I huffed. "Funny. I had the same thought earlier," I said, my words sounding bitter.

She peered at me trying to get what I meant by that. Then her expression changed from embarrassment to worry. "Are you okay? In the morning you said everything was great. Now you have that look again. The one, that worries me. Please tell me, you're okay."

I sighed. "I am. It's just—"

"You're not sure if the removal operation worked?"

When it happened I hadn't woken right away. But I did remember floating weight-less in a beautiful realm, traveling, exploring. And at some point, I'd felt as if someone had held me in their arms, and then had laid me back in my bed, finally grasping something solid, anchoring me here in this reality. And that's when I knew I was back in this body. Afterwards, I had drifted off again to sleep.

Jan had tried to stay awake to guard me, throughout the night, in case of *weird* activity. Of course he'd failed...*heroically*. I couldn't blame him, though. He'd had a very long day yesterday. Mine had been the same. We were both beyond tired, when we finally had crashed in bed. Plus, he had to be *again* very early at the lab today, to take care of some cells.

When I had finally woke up this morning, a distinct sensation of lightness and fluidity accompanied me. I'd felt at peace, as though everything in the world was right again. I hadn't experienced this kind of serenity in a *very* long time. Since childhood to be precise.

"Oh, I don't have any doubts that it worked. But the extraction of these things, doesn't guarantee the end of the problem. At least, this is what Mike told me. So on one hand, I'm extremely grateful for the help I got. And very lucky, too. 'Cause I really don't know, how this was possible. I mean, to find someone like Mike and his kind of *connections*.

"On the other hand, I don't have the slightest idea of I'm supposed to do. To erase the threat that is hanging over my head. And taking some Detoxamin, or doing some Chelation, won't *exactly* keep me safe," I admitted, in defeat. Oddly, I didn't feel plagued by fear now. Instead, a sense of inevitability was crawling at the back of my mind. Something that I would have to face. Whether I wanted or not.

"Don't talk like that," Raluca said.

"Like what?"

"Like, there's no hope. You're really, scaring me."

I snorted. "Well, it is scary, in case you didn't notice. This is not a game. This is... real," I returned, my gaze fixed on my hands.

Raluca leaned forward, resting on her elbows. "I don't know anyone in this world that is more resourceful, than you are. And I'm not saying this because you're my sister. I *genuinely* don't know anyone, with your ability to transform the shityest thing or situation into something great." She paused for a second, looking away from me, then continued. "You are my hero. You are not allowed to lose hope. To give up. Period." Her voice carrying a suspicious tremor.

231

I lifted my head, and when I looked closer, she had tears at the corners of her eyes.

I felt my chest constricting with pain.

By now, I had to love the irony of life. I was the one with the sword over my head, yet, I felt I had to protect my sister from my own misfortune.

I stood, and went over to her, and hugged tight. "You know, the hero doesn't always get a happy ending," I tried to lighten the mood, by joking about it.

Raluca returned the hug even tighter, clinging to me with desperation. I think this was the first time, when I *truly* sensed the angst she felt for me. "Promise me you will fight. *Promise* me," she urged, sobbing over my shoulder.

My throat felt dry.

"Promise," I managed in hoarse voice, and kept holding each other like that for a while longer.

There was no more distinction between past and present. Childhood and adulthood. I was again the *big* sister that had to dispel the threatening shadows of the uncertain…future.

chapter / TWENTY-SIX

It became increasingly obvious, that we were heading to Blankanese—which was a west suburban quarter of Hamburg. A beautiful and quiet place along the river Elbe, where a lot of the rich and famous would choose to reside, hidden in luxurious greenery.

"Where are we going?" I asked, for the millionth time.

Briefly, Jan turned his head to me, smiled, then focused again on the road ahead. "Patience," he said calmly. "You *definitely* need to work that muscle more," Jan teased.

I snorted, staring out the window to my right. "You are wasting time by stating the obvious. It won't make any difference, now."

Jan laughed. "I love you," he said, out of the blue.

Eyebrows furrowed, I turned to stare at him. "What this has to do with anything?"

He laughed further.

"I don't think this is the best time, to show me your latest discovery," I insisted, thinking he was trying to get me to check out a new restaurant or café. From time to time he would do that, whenever I felt overly stressed with work, or with life in general. "People are waiting for us, at the party. I'm sure, Meike has black listed us by now," I said, growing really impatient.

Jan put his hand over mine, interlacing his fingers with mine. "You worry too much, you know? You shouldn't do that. It's not healthy."

"I kind of don't have a choice…"

He chuckled. "Everything will be fine."

"Right…"

"…And we're almost here," Jan said, removing his hand from mine, and used it to steer the wheel to the left.

We were now entering a side street from the main road in Blankanese. Left and right the area seemed mostly residential, with a few shops, here and there, a bank branch and a post office. All very well manicured, new additions next to freshly renovated buildings. In fact, the entire Blankanese was like that.

I was quite familiar with the area. This used to be part of our usual tour, whenever we would drive around in our car on certain nights, wanting to escape our myopic reality. Unfortunately, or fortunately…not sure about that part. But there had been indeed, many nights like that, when we'd just let ourselves drift and dream at better times, with futuristic music in the background. Just forgetting for a few hours about the rigid, constricting, mechanical existence forced upon us.

Simply magical.

And *definitely* the cheapest form of therapy.

"Almost where?" I asked, hoping he would finally give in, and enlighten me. But no. Not a chance. He kept grinning—to my personal annoyance—and drove until the end of the street, then veered again to the left. And found a parking space behind a blue Polo.

Now, I was completely in the dark. "Are we visiting someone?" I said, seeing just houses—cute houses—on each side of the street.

Jan took the key out of the ignition. "Maybe," he replied mischievously, opened the car door and got out.

I groaned, exasperated. "I'm *soo* going to get you for this," I said after him, then stepped out of the car, too.

We walked maybe a hundred meters, and on the right I spotted a beautiful garden. Actually, more like a very well landscaped green space. Which I assumed, belonged to the white modern house next to it. "Beautiful," I said, with pure architectural

234

admiration. "Lucky, whoever is living here. And to have this kind of green space in this area…truly a luxury."

Jan stopped right in front of it. "Funny, you said that," Jan replied, holding my hand. "Because *this*," he gestured with his free hand toward it. "Belongs to us."

I snorted. "Sure. In our dreams—"

He turned toward me, smiling, certainty reading in his gold-brown eyes. "The opportunity came so fast, I couldn't say no," he stated matter-of-factly. Then pulled out from the inside pocket of his jacket a white envelope. "Inside there are papers, which say that you and I own this."

I opened my mouth to say something, then pushed the words back down.

I still couldn't decide, if he was pulling a prank, or was dead serious.

"You did what? You bought the house? How…?"

"Not exactly. Most of the area next to it. The garden part," he answered, amusement playing in his eyes.

My eyes widened, eyebrows shooting up. "*What*? You bought a garden? Are you insane? Since when do you need a *garden*? I don't remember you *ever* displaying any inclinations whatsoever toward gardening. I mean, you have problems keeping plants alive," I said, assessing the situation. "*I* have problems keeping plants alive. Well, at least I remember to change the water in a vase," 'cause we didn't own any plants, lately. We tried a few times, whenever family would buy us plants as house gifts. But not a single plant, had lasted more than a couple of months. I really couldn't explain why that was. Especially, since I was a big lover of nature, and trees. But, obviously not in my own home.

Jan burst into laughter.

"What kind of logic is that, to buy a garden, next to someone's home? *How* do you see yourself using it? I really don't think you are the type to plant tomatoes and cucumbers."

And apparently that was even funnier than what I said before, now he couldn't stop laughing.

I planted my hands on my hips, mouth half opened. "This is not funny," I pressed. "Please tell me you're not that stupid—"

Still laughing, he shook his head. "I'm not. I swear," Jan said, raising his hands in the air in defense.

"Then what do you call, this?" I demanded, pointing to the envelope in his hand.

"I call this buying a piece of land for us. So we can build our home. Well, so *you* can design and built it. I will just enjoy the fruits of your hard labor," Jan asserted, chuckling.

My jaw dropped.

Of course, that would make more sense, and not what my stressed mind came up with.

He definitely possessed this ability, to leave me speechless. More often, than I cared for. So I stared at him, silently waiting for the punch line.

It never arrived.

"How?" I asked.

"How what?"

"How is all this, possible? If it's true, what you're saying."

He arched one eyebrow, as if to say that I shouldn't doubt him. "A colleague from a neighbor lab told me about his older brother's misfortune. He lost a lot of money in crappy investments. So he needs to sell a lot of things to get back on track. Naturally, he doesn't want to sell the house. Not yet, anyway. But the garden, that he was willing to sell."

"When did this happen? 'Cause last week we were in Paris. And this week…we all know what happened."

Jan stared at me, his eyes filled with gentleness. "It was part of the surprise. Before we flew to Paris, I'd already made the deal. But the papers came out, only this Monday. And Monday, well, shit happened."

Tell me about it.

"So it was the last thing on my mind." Jan placed his hands on my shoulders, his gaze turning serious. "You scared the crap out of me Monday, disappearing like that."

"It wasn't part of my immediate or future life plans," I retorted ironically.

"I know." He bit his bottom lip, worries emanating from this gesture. "Finding Mike was a miracle. I honestly didn't know what to expect," he admitted vulnerably. "But he kept his promise. And I'm *sooo* sorry, I fell asleep. Again." He shook his head guilty. "By the way, how do you feel today? " His eyes searching for signs of unwell.

"Actually, great." I didn't want to feed any further his concern for me, as well as my own unrest about possible *unhappy* adventures. So I change the subject, pressing further the matter at hand.

"How much?" I asked, knowing that the square meter around here was quite prohibitive for a lot of people. And the size of this thing was pretty generous. "How much did you pay?"

"I doesn't matter. It's ours."

He told me once—or twice…not really remembering the other time though—about the inheritance he got from his grandma. I never asked him about the size of it, though. But to acquire something like *this* required a good sum of money.

I huffed, shaking my head in disbelief. "You are crazy," I concluded.

"That means you like it," he grinned impishly.

"This is not about me liking it, or not. It's just…"

I found myself again unable to reply.

Instead, he continued. "I made you once a promise. That we won't wait for life to happen to us. That *we* will steer it our own way. That's what this is. I know you think I'm slow, and maybe I am. But not because I don't get what you say. It's my stupid fears that sometimes block me," he pleaded, warmth and honesty pouring out of his heart. "But I always *always,* fight against them. And you know that my biggest fear is to lose you. That you'll disappear one day from my life, and I won't know what to do with myself."

I knew all about his fears.

I sighed.

Sadly, lately, the events and occurrences in my life, were pointing in the direction of those fears becoming reality. And the thought of it, was *highly* unsettling to me, to say the least.

He grabbed my hand, our fingers interweaving, his eyes piercing mine with the avalanche of emotions swirling in his. "I know you are scared, too. For different reasons. But I promise you. We will look back one day, to all of this…and we will laugh about it. It won't be like this forever. It just can't."

With his hand that was holding the envelope, he showed toward the green space. "You see this?" Jan asked.

I nodded.

"*This* is our future. Right here. Right now. I will fight for it. It won't be just another unrealized dream. Another disappointment for you. You deserve the best, and I'll make sure you get it." His words were stated with such conviction, that for a moment, I allowed myself to relax and dare to dream with him.

Ironically, and unexpectedly, the actual dream I'd had a night before, surfaced. Wow. It couldn't have chosen a worse time. The memory of it filled me with guilt and shame. Because it felt so real. So loving. So true. And *that* was very disturbing to me. It made no sense. Why? Why me?

Yesterday morning when I woke, I tried a few explanations in my head. Some had to do with Lorenzo and Sabine, messing with me. That wouldn't be surprising one bit. Already had a taste of how it felt to have someone else's mind controlling mine. But then again, the dream was too pure and intimate, to be projected by somebody so cold and disconnected as these two.

The other thing I was contemplating, was the fact that most dreams were not dreams. But messages to be interpreted. For the love of me though, I couldn't come up with anything remotely cohesive. All I knew, was how overwhelming this loving feeling was. Only one other time I'd experience that. And that as well, was in a dream.

"Now, only one thing is missing," Jan said breaking the reflective process going in my head.

"What's that?"

He let go of my hand, and pulled out a pen from the same pocket. "I need your signature also." Then extended the pen to me, and without even glancing at his expression, I knew there was a distinct smile—one that he'd use anytime I needed more convincing.

"I thought it was a done deal."

"Almost—"

I lifted my head, and peered at him. "This is insane."

Jan chuckled, unfolded the papers and handed it over to me. "Sure. Whatever you say. But you still have to sign."

It was hard not to smile. "Fine. Where do I sign?"

"On the last two pages. At the bottom. Right next to mine."

I did as instructed, though I really wanted to protest some more. "Happy now?!" I said, looking up from the papers. I folded them back and placed them in the envelope. Then gave it back to Jan.

"Very!" Untamed joy beaming out through his gaze.

$$\infty$$

We parked at the end of Neumühlen, and from there we walked. Anytime of the week—extremely busy during the weekend, though—this pedestrian area was always filled with life and people that wanted to escape the busyness of the city. A refreshing contrast, to the usual vibe of cold and unmovable. Which was curious, given the amount of new architecture rising everywhere. But hey, I guess people *did* affect a place, and in major way, too.

Thank God, we were only forty-five minutes late when we showed up to Meike's birthday party. She welcomed us unexpectedly joyfully. Pretty sure, our present helped *a lot* to sweeten—her otherwise very easily irritable—disposition. The place she chose—actually Alex did—for the celebration, was a trendy little restaurant at the river side. Inside the décor was tailored to emanate a homey, yet, modern Nordic type of atmosphere. A simple monochromatic composition of grey and blue gray—furniture and curtains— encased in white, and warmed by wood accents.

I hadn't expected, that we were going to be that many people. But when I saw that she'd reserved two fashionably long communal tables, I quickly counted more than thirty guests. At one table her entire family was gathered around her. Her mom, her dad, and her two older sisters with their husbands and children. Alex. And some other friends of theirs I didn't know.

Being the last to arrive, she seated us at the other table. Where among more unknown faces, my sister, Tim and Andreas had already arrived, now enjoying conversation, drinks and some appetizers. Lydia was seated there, too. I didn't mind to stay there to be perfectly honest. When they saw us approaching, Tim almost jumped out of his chair. "*Finally*, you're here! I thought you got swallowed by a black hole," he said in jest.

I snorted. "Close. But no. Just another surprise, from Mr. Surprise himself," I said thinning my lips, pointing with my index finger at Jan.

Tim arched an eyebrow. "*The* surprise?" he asked now looking at Jan.

Of course...

"You too, knew about this?" I said to Tim.

He grinned, all of his teeth showing. "*Sorry*. But I had to keep my mouth shut. I promised him. I hope, you're not mad at me."

"I'm not. Don't worry," I said smiling.

"What surprise?" a voice said, and I turned to see Lydia coming to greet us.

We hugged and kissed on the cheek. "Ah, just that Jan made a big hole in that inheritance of his," I replied casually.

She looked at me, confusion reading in her eyes.

Jan pulled me away from her and into his arms. "I bought us a piece of land so we can build our home," he added, planting a noisy kiss on my temple.

Her eyes lit up, genuine warmth emanating from her face. "This is *so* wonderful. I'm so happy for you. Come here," she said, now hugging us both tightly.

And just like that, Jan and I, ended up being the main topic for a while at our table. Not something that I had intended, but nonetheless entertaining for everyone else. Apparently the whole thing was a generator for all sorts of subtopics about hilarious things. And that made our table seem overly joyous in comparison with Meike's. Which felt quite strange. Not to mention that it started to look like we were at two different parties.

From time to time though, I would catch her glance our way. Not sure what to think about that blank stare of hers. But at least, she didn't seem upset or anything. If she was but not showing, then today she was a champion.

In the meantime, the main course was being served, and the waiters were constantly refilling our glasses. I was really happy that we as well, had something to eat. Like

Alex said, Meike made sure everyone was well fed—according to their own dietary preference. For that I was indeed grateful, and next time a saw her turning her eyes on us, I raised my glass to her.

She smiled.

Then mirrored me by raising her glass, happy that I acknowledged her.

Good.

That gave me peace of mind.

Probably two hours in, the cheerfulness and exaltation at our table, didn't seem to slow down. On the contrary. It became this strong constant stream of good energy spilling out and spreading at other tables, too.

"You should've seen Andreas how he handled those bastards," Tim was so cute every time he couldn't stop showing us, how impressed he was with his boyfriend.

Yesterday they'd had a short altercation with some macho guys when they were coming out of a comedy club on Reeperbahn. This was the busiest street in Hamburg, due to its many tourists type of attractions. Good and bad. Among these, there were as well many theaters. So it wasn't uncommon to run into people that had too much to drink enjoying themselves, singing and dancing on sidewalks or even right in the middle of the streets. Unfortunately, they had bumped into an aggressive bunch. Luckily, things didn't escalate.

"Here's to my hero!" Tim raised his glass. Jan, Raluca and I, joined him enthusiastically with our glasses.

"To your *Iron Man*," Raluca toasted, playfully.

Tim put an arm around Andreas, his head resting on his shoulder. "He's much cooler than Iron Man. And more handsome."

We all laughed, except Andreas. His flushed expression, said that he felt quite embarrassed. But kept grinning, in spite of that.

I whirled my head to my left, where my sister sat. "So, when did you get here?"

She took another bite from her plate. "Maybe fifteen, twenty minutes before you," she answered with her mouth full, still chewing.

"Let me guess. Peter brought you here?"

She furrowed her eyebrows. "Yes." Raluca paused for an instant, swallowing the rest of the bite, then continued. "I couldn't believe when he showed up at six o'clock. He basically, forced me out of there. That bastard…" Raluca shook her head in disbelief.

I chuckled. "Yeah. That bastard…"

chapter / TWENTY-SEVEN

Strange thing the time. I *genuinely* thought Friday evening would never come sooner. Or *ever* for that matter. Crazy wouldn't cover it anymore, what this week had been. Through some unexpected miracles—and acts of good will—though, we were now minutes away from opening the event.

All seemed to be in place. But that didn't stop my sister from being jumpy around everyone. And become *especially* annoying to the people at the bar. I mean, they were doing their best to keep a polite and civilized attitude, but their body language would indicate a different message.

"Hey, watch where you put those," Raluca almost but screamed, at the flower delivery people on their way to the terrace. "I don't have time to replace it, if you break it," she huffed, exasperated.

Obviously, she was on overdrive. She'd told me, she hadn't slept very well last night. Even though she had nothing to worry for today, she'd come in early in the morning to work on the last details. And then double and triple checked everything. Then she went home about two hours ago to change for the event. And now, with only twenty minutes or so left before the first guests would arrive, she was panicking.

This was not like her at all.

I went over to her, caught her by the arm and pulled her into a corner by the entrance. "What's wrong?" I asked, looking straight into her eyes, already searching for the cause.

She peered at me in confusion. "Nothing is wrong. I'm just making sure these people don't mess up my hard work. *Our* hard work," Raluca said, gently pulling away from my hold. "Now what's wrong with you?" Indicating with her head to my recent gesture.

"Usually when you start to get all manic and loud, *something* is wrong. So, what is it? And don't make me ask you again," I urged her.

There were moments like this one now, when involuntarily I would step into my role as the big sister and she had no other choice but to comply.

Lips pursed, she crossed her arms over her chest, but careful as not to wrinkle her beautiful dark lilac silky top. "I had another dream."

Eyebrows raised, I waited for her to continue.

"It's about you."

"About?" I asked.

She shifted her gaze, focusing it now somewhere behind me. "It's probably nothing." Her words meant to dismiss any further questioning. Still, the tone she used, plus her earlier uncontrolled burst, weren't fooling me.

"What did you dream? If it's bad, you know I can take it," I reassured her, knowing that she was probably worrying about a possible vision. A message for me. Something not…good.

Raluca pinched the bridge of her nose with her thumb and index finger, blinking a few times. "You were again—"

"There are my S.W.A.T. team girls!" Peter cheered, approaching us, followed by two men. One was carrying a camera and the other was just carrying himself, very presentable. A press crew, obviously. And the first one to arrive that was supposed to cover the event tonight.

"These people want to talk to you, too. To my heroes," Peter said, then made the introductions. We found out that they were from the ARD, and that they were doing a report for an important show about the advertising industry and new media in general. After all, Hamburg wasn't just a big player in the finance arena, also, one of the largest media centers in Germany.

First they interviewed my sister. Most questions were about her background and how she ended up doing what she was doing as a career. As well as, about the events and media scene in Bucharest. The interviewer—a guy most probably in his early fifties judging by what I found in his eyes, but looking no older than forty—although he seemed to be genuinely interested in what Raluca was sharing, there was something artificial about him. Something false. Which automatically, made me dislike him.

Oh, well. Just another reporter doing his job.

Meanwhile the guests began to show up, and Peter was there to welcome them. He seemed contagiously high-spirited. Which was great for many reasons, and apparently he didn't even notice my sister's outburst from earlier. If he did, well, he simply didn't seem to care. Other things were more important. Like making sure, the evening would be a success.

I looked around, and for the first time I allowed myself to see it through the eyes of a guest. So different. When you are the one creating something, you are so caught up in the process, you invest so much energy and soul, that you tend to focus only on what needs to be done. You see all the imperfections, all the things you would do differently, and forget to acknowledge what's good about it. As a guest, you are an outsider. You like or dislike something based on the final results, corroborated of course, with personal taste and or preference. You are completely detached, by the vision or the outcome.

I liked what I saw.

Elegant shaped metal frames, draped in white canvas and lit from the inside, were populating the enclosed restaurant area, as well as the terrace, creating a futuristic airy type of ensemble. Extra sets of ambient lights accentuating particular elements. We couldn't replace the entire furniture that was already in place, but that wasn't an impediment. In fact, it made my job easier. I brought in a few new pieces as accents—different shades of dark and light blue—which blended very well with the overall white existent ones.

My phone buzzed.

I was surprised that I even registered it, as the noise level was increasing rapidly.

I pulled the phone out my jacket's waist pocket. It was a text from Jan.

245

Sorry. I'll be late again. Now heading home to change. See you in an hour.

I sighed. "Of course…"

"Hey, it's your turn!" I heard Raluca shout at me, gesturing to the press people that were now coming toward me.

For a moment there, I completely forgot what she meant by that, so I stared at her in confusion.

"I have to go take care of the guests." And then she rushed to the entrance, to welcome everyone.

I slipped out of my temporary trance. "Oh. Yes. Sure," I said, forcing a polite smile. "This way," I suggested, wanting to get away from the growing number of people in the reception area. The reporter and the camera man followed me without hesitation.

We moved to a relative more quiet corner, as to be able to hear each other, and speak without raising our voices. To my disappointment—not that I had any particular expectations—the questions the guy asked, were pretty much the same as the ones he used on my sister. Which I thought "*how boring and uncreative.*" Or maybe he had to follow a format. Either way, it felt repetitive and unsubstantial from my perspective. Except one question. Which seemed, to *not exactly* fit into the whole story about myself, career or anything to do with the advertising industry. But interesting, nonetheless.

After we ended our little interview, I accompanied them to the bar, as my sister instructed, to make sure they were served and pampered properly, before proceeding to other guests that were on their 'to-talk-to' list. Because tonight, wasn't just about the party, but the echo in the media, afterwards.

When I was sure they looked happy and had drinks in their hands, I excused myself, and left kind of in a hurry. Dictated by biological needs.

I had to pee. Really bad.

Thank God, the bathroom was near.

In a few long strides I was in, and ecstatic to discover that both stalls were free. I rushed into one of them and found the desperate relief.

Moments like these can feel like…nirvana.

246

Relaxed and a happy grin planted on my face, I was ready to join again the crowd. I washed my hands, dried them with a paper towel. Then checked myself in the mirror. All seemed to look better than I expected. Hair pulled back into a relaxed bun, a bit of mascara, and a very subtle lip gloss, was all I had managed today. And on that note, I'd decided that aqua velvet slim fit pants and a suit blazer with a vaporous white top, was what I would call a happy light choice. The overall result…effortless chic.

"Perfect," I smiled at myself in the mirror.

The door opened and a man came through.

It was the reporter.

"This is the ladies bathroom," I said jovially, thinking he confounded it with the men's toilet. Which was the next door.

He smiled and locked the door behind him. "It is, isn't it?" His tone was weird and creepy. He couldn't be drunk. I just left him with a glass of Champagne.

Oh God, please tell me he is not some pervert.

Adrenaline kicked in, and my mind began racing.

I was in a public space, but with the noise level rising, if anything would happen to me, screaming for help would not work. I looked around to see if I could grab something in case he tried…something. Unfortunately for me, there wasn't much I could use. This was a modern bathroom with a minimalistic design. The walls were covered in matte glass panels, and aside from the wooden countertop where the white ceramic sink was mounted in, and an interesting wooden shape as bin, there was nothing else in sight.

Shit.

I tried to remain calm, and used a different approach to the situation. "Is the men's bathroom, busy? You're lucky, these are free," I pointed to the two stalls. Then I started toward the door, hoping his intentions weren't as shady as I sensed them.

He didn't budge. In fact, he crossed his arms over his chest, eyes carrying a scary glint.

Yep. Bad.

"So, how do you see the future, Ariana?" he asked.

What?

Strange.

Then it hit me. This was the question that stood out. The one he asked me earlier, and at first, I thought he was referring to the future of media or design. But no. He was asking about a general vision of life, world.

I mirrored his stance. "I thought I answered this question earlier. Was not enough? Is this why you followed me in here? Because if this is what you define as dedication to your job, I call it stalking. And it's not cool. Actually it's creepy. Please step aside," I demanded, becoming a little more confident.

He smiled menacingly, and in two strides was in front of me, only a few centimeters separating us. Before I could react in any way, he grabbed me by the arms. "You have been very naughty, lately. I can't say I'm surprised, though," he mocked, then blinked his eyes. When he opened them again, they weren't blue anymore, but black like—

Lorenzo.

I froze instantaneously.

The morphing continued, his face fully forming right under my very eyes. Though my mind utterly refused to accept, what it was witnessing.

No. No. No.

A spark of rage broke my temporary paralysis, and I drove my knee into his crotch. Unfortunately, he caught it before it could do any damage. I jerked furiously then, trying to break free from his hold. I wasn't going to accept passively to surrender.

This only made it worse. 'Cause now, his hold was forceful and stingier than ever. His hands were digging into my skin like sharp claws, piercing through the layers of clothing, pain shooting to my brain.

He leaned in and whispered into my ear. "You smell delicious. And it's not your perfume I'm referring to." As before, his words made my skin crawl with disgust. He was a predator. The mix of fear and rage—and now numbing pain—was like an aphrodisiac to him. "Now, let's try something new," he said, his hands moving lightning fast to my head, thumbs pressing into my temples.

The pain I felt a moment ago, was nothing compared to the wave of maddening lava that was melting my brain.

I lost all feeling in the rest of my body. I opened my mouth to scream, but it died in my throat.

"Now, let's get out of here," Lorenzo said, nauseating satisfaction gleaming in those evil eyes.

Reality began to blur. The room with everything in it was dissolving. And then a horrible vertigo took over my senses.

Oh God, I will throw up...

I closed my eyes, praying for this whirling sensation to stop.

Not only my head was on fire, but I was now barely containing the meal I had three hours ago. Then I realized how ridiculous I was for worrying about messing my outfit.

God...

. . . .

"It works. She's ready. She needs a little training though," a male voice said.

"Good. 'Cause we can't waste any more time, with her. We have to do it, now. Take her to Recalibration," another voice replied. This one was female. Very firm. More like pissed.

If only I could open my God damn eyes...

Through my eye lids, I could distinguish some shadows. Lights and shadows. I was aware of the fact that I wasn't standing anymore. I must've fallen or something. Well, that wouldn't be surprising at all. Despite my best efforts I couldn't move anything. Not even the smallest part of my body. I was merely a thought trapped inside a body.

"I don't think she will survive, if we do it now," the man insisted.

"We don't have time. It has to be done, today. We can't miss the Alignment," the woman argued.

"You said, she is very important to the mission. Do you want to lose your investment, now?"

She sighed, pausing. "No."

"I thought so."

"Give her some glucose," the woman instructed. "I'll be back in an hour."

The pain which was torturing me earlier, as well as the loss of balance, faded away almost entirely. But the queasiness was still strong and scrambling all my senses. I felt being moved somewhere. Which only aggravated the nausea I was trying to control.

Son of a—

. . . .

A violent current ran through my body jolting me awake, forcing my eyes to open.

What the—

"Welcome back," Lorenzo spoke, towering over me, holding a syringe in his right hand. Then set it on a metal tray. "Sorry, to bring you back like that," he added, his eyes expressing some sort of remorse. As if he cared for my own well being...

I was lying on a bed, with clean white sheets. The long side of the bed placed against a wall. Next to my head, there was an IV stand with a bag—almost empty—dripping into my arm. I looked around, trying to figure out where the hell I was. First, I noticed that the room had no windows, and was fairly small. But there was a door—a metallic one with a porthole window—on the wall across from my feet. The ceiling as well as one of the four walls was apparent concrete. A few dimmed spots of light above me, and a LED strip alongside the base of the concrete wall ensured the room with enough light to see the other but still perfect to relax and...nap.

I lifted my gaze to meet Lorenzo's piercing dark eyes.

Under other circumstances, I would find Lorenzo's features interesting. Someone with depth. Someone who knew a lot. Intelligent. Confident. Magnetic. Except, that all his potential, was turned into the wrong direction.

Insane, how normal he appeared now. As if the predator never existed. Or that version of himself was just an alter ego. An evil twin. Ideal for all the dirty jobs he had to do.

"You know, you and I, are not that different," Lorenzo stated, digging his hands in his pockets.

"Really," I scoffed. "Then tell me, how does someone *not that different*, become so twisted and dehumanized?" I asked, trying to sit up. I managed only to steady myself on my elbows. And for the first time since I regain conscience, I could assess my body. I was completely dressed. My party clothes, aside from a few wrinkles—which were caused by the induced blackout—seemed to be spotless. No stain of anything. Still, I could've sworn, that I threw up all over myself on my way...down. At this point I wasn't sure whether I hit the floor, or he caught me before I lost conscience.

He pulled up a chair—which a moment ago didn't even existed...unless my mind was playing a joke on me...although I'd seen this trick before with other objects and fluids. He sat down next to my bed. Then leaned forward and helped me to adjust my position, until my feet were steady on the ground, and my back was resting on a big fluffy pillow against the wall. "Now, that's much better," Lorenzo said.

"Thank—"

I stopped, because I realized, I had nothing to thank him for. He got me like this. In fact the opposite would be the correct reaction. But I didn't have enough energy to start a verbal duel—which I had a feeling I would lose anyway. So I chose conservation of personal resources.

Lorenzo chuckled. "You're undeniably, cute."

I rolled my eyes, growling on the inside.

"Here, drink this," Lorenzo urged, holding in front of me a large glass of water.

Where did that come from? Oh well, enough with the obvious. Magic. Or technology. Or whatever...

I took the glass and down it in a few big gulps, then set it on the metal tray on the bed, next to the syringe. "Where am I?" I asked, my eyes focused now on the light coming—through the round opening in the door—from what I imagined it would be the hallway.

Lorenzo pulled the needle out of my arm and rolled down my sleeve. "I can't answer that."

Of course...

"Not right away. Afterwards, sure. You won't be a risk, anymore."

"After what?" I asked, panic resurfacing once again, making my weak stomach to contract in defense.

251

Lorenzo leaned back in his chair, his eyes deciding what to tell me. "After Recalibration."

A fuzzy memory of hearing this word before, came back to me. I thought I had hallucinated or dreamed about it. Then I looked at the IV stand, and realized I hadn't. Whatever had happened in between, it was real.

"What is Recalibration?" Already assuming something awful, my body reacting silently.

He smiled, then let his arms fall beside him. "You will find out, soon enough. Don't you want to know, why you and I, are the same?"

I opened my mouth to start disputing his claim. But then I reconsidered, choosing to ask something else instead. "Will that change anything?"

"No."

I snorted in defeat. "What's the point, then?"

"To know yourself a little better. Come on, self pity doesn't become you."

Okay, so he was trying to play with me, as if I was his pet. A dog. A little game of throw and fetch, before something that sounded definitive. And...unsettling.

Lorenzo peered at me, most probably scanning my mind and emotions.

I really couldn't care less now, even if he read my worst fears.

He leaned forward, elbows resting on his knees, clasping his hands in front of him. "You're not going to die. Not today. It's been a while since any *others* have been...lost in the process. And we will send you back to the party. Don't worry, no one will ever notice you were gone."

"How reassuring," I mocked, but deep down feeling relieved.

chapter / TWENTY-EIGHT

My sudden shift in energy seemed to amuse Lorenzo, who was now checking his watch. Or whatever gadget he was wearing on his left wrist, that looked like one. "Sabine will be here, any minute now. Are you sure, you don't want to know what things, we have in common?" he teased.

Hearing her name, propelled unpleasant recollections to the forefront of my mind. The metallic, blade like feeling I had around her, was now grazing at the core of my being. At this point I wasn't sure anymore, which one of them was more twisted and menacing.

I decided that no matter what, I couldn't let her win. "I'm all ears," I uttered, blocking the paralyzing sensation I experienced a moment ago.

Lorenzo smiled satisfied. "We share the same blood type."

I raised my eyebrows. "What, AB Negative? *That's* the big news? *Really*?!" I snorted, shaking my head.

"Actually, mine is O Negative," Lorenzo replied.

"Congratulations, you are the Universal Donor."

He looked at me, deciding whether I was completely oblivious or just plainly stupid.

"*What*? I know that I have the rarest blood type, out there. That's, the big mystery?"

He didn't say anything, just stared at me. Which was getting annoying.

"Or the fact that if I get pregnant, and the baby has a Positive blood type, I would need an injection to stop the rejecting and consequently the killing of my future baby. Is that it? Don't worry, I have that covered. I know what to do when, and if, I want to have a baby. But to be perfectly honest, that's the last thing on my mind right now. I'm kind of busy *surviving*," I argued.

He remained silent, lifted his hands, then clasped them under his chin.

"What did I leave out?" Exasperation spilling out.

"What do AB Negative and O Negative have in common?" he asked.

"They're both Negative," I answered, gesticulating with my hands.

He chuckled. "Exactly. Let's do a little more logical reasoning. I see you're good at that."

Asshole.

"Why don't you share your precious insights? And speed this up. After all, Sabine will be here soon and will break our little bonding session."

He laughed. "Fine. But I was really enjoying this."

I squinted my eyes, spitting fire and annoyance.

Lorenzo raised his arm in defeat. "Okay. Okay…"

I crossed my arms over chest. "I'm listening."

"Rh Positive means that you have the Rhesus Monkey Protein in your blood cells. Rh Negative blood type, means you don't have the Rhesus Monkey Protein," Lorenzo said. "This is important because, people with Rh Negative blood cannot take a transfusion of Rh Positive. They do not mix."

I was aware of that part too, but I let him continue, hoping to find something else. Something more significant.

"Modern medicine—well, the commercial one—still hasn't figured out the origin of the Rh Negative Factor. In the official recordings there's only one occurrence, a crossbreeding of a horse and a donkey, which resulted in a new species of sterile Rh Negative mules. The answer that medicine and science currently offer, is that the Rh Negative Factor suddenly appeared in the current blood types pool, around 35000 years ago. Its origin still unknown." Lorenzo paused, he raised his eyebrows, a wide grin spreading over his face.

He was waiting for my input, obviously making me work for what he had to share next.

"So, what you're saying, is that my blood type is alien," I deduced.

He nodded in confirmation.

"And that we are hybrids," I said, voicing further my thoughts. "All of us, Positives and Negatives."

"Correct. But nonetheless, there are significant differences among these two. Never wondered why you have these higher sensory abilities? Why you have so much energy in comparison with most people?" Lorenzo asked. "Or, why you always felt like you don't belong anywhere?"

Of course I had. I spent most of my life digging up information, facts, and proof that I wasn't crazy.

"Rh Negative blood cannot be mutated or cloned. Which in turn, limits the possibility of artificially creating Rh Negative Plasma."

This, I didn't know.

"Simply put, we are a very small, limited *special* club. We are less than seven percent on the entire face of the earth, at the present moment," Lorenzo reinforced.

I snorted. "Great. Which part, is supposed to make me feel better? Or, even see this as a good thing?"

Lorenzo peered at me, reading my emotional barometer. "I've been where you are now. I get your frustration. Your *anger*. You are entitled to it. But after today, this will be…history."

I wasn't sure whether I liked the last part or not.

No reaction came from me, so he continued. "You should feel good about it, because your blood is inherently 'karmic-less.'"

What?

The door to my tiny 'cell' opened with a short loud noise, instantaneously pulling me out my pondering state.

Lorenzo and I, we both whirled our heads in the direction of the door.

Of course…

I huffed.

Sabine stepped in, approaching my bed in a few long precise strides, her gaze impassive. As last time, when I had the *unpleasure* of meeting her—and in spite of the unnatural vibe she was emitting—her face looked immaculate and composed. If I didn't know who, or what she was, I would think she was one of those bank or insurance people. Her eyes paused for a moment on me, assessing my *condition*, then shifted her focus on Lorenzo. "It's time. The storytelling can continue afterwards," she informed us.

Impeccable timing.

Just when it was getting interesting...

"What? No more passing through walls?" I scoffed, gesticulating with my hands. Imitating the gesture she did to jump from one location to another. "Or it's getting boring after a while, to have that kind of power?"

She spun around to face me. Her expression though neutral, it said to me, she was contemplating something in the range of either disdain, or pure indifference. "I have to keep some appearances. I am exercising my humanity, from time to time. As limited as it is. It's important," she replied in a very civilized manner, contrary to my expectation.

"Wow... I would love to have that kind of control, over my emotional apparatus," I confessed with honest admiration. She may be a cold heartless zombie, but this ability was something to be appreciated, especially, in certain situations. Like the one right now, for instance.

She gave me a smile, which I don't recall *ever* seeing it on her distinguished features. "Oh, but you will. It's one of the many perks of Recalibration."

That word again.

I swallowed hard, realizing for the first time since I regain consciousness, the gravity implied in her words.

God damn it! Do something...

Sabine caught that, but the factitious smile never left her face. She clasped her hands behind her back. "A little suggestion. Don't try something stupid, like escaping. You haven't the slightest clue, where you are. We might not even be underground, as you very inquisitively assumed. For all you know, we could be very well, let's say, somewhere in the middle of an ocean," she teased. "Plus, really you are in no capacity to do anything remotely dangerous. Except, to harm yourself unnecessarily. And we don't want that. Not after we've just revived you," she said, nudging her head toward the IV stand. Then moved again her focus on Lorenzo. "Let's go, and be done with this. I have a meeting upstairs in less than an hour, and it would be nice to have something to eat today, before that." Sabine turned on her heel and headed out.

Whether she was lying or telling the truth—about our possible and very remote location, testing my mental and emotional response—if I had the tiniest chance to go back to my sister, to Jan, I wasn't going to sabotage it. Despite *whatever* this Recalibration would do to me—nothing good I'd assume. But that didn't mean I was going to accept this, passively submitting to her will. As long as I was still alive, I had the advantage. I was more valuable to her agenda like this, as she had admitted it to me, that day in the elevator.

"Cruise ship," I uttered behind her. "We're on cruise ship, heading to Hong Kong." The information, simply popping into my head. I couldn't explain how I knew. But I knew I was right.

She stopped in her tracks, right before the threshold. Then whirled her head in my direction, her smile disappearing completely from her face. "So what. It's not like you can swim your way back home," she replied dismissively, and walked away.

You bitch...

In two long strides I was behind her. I lunged at her, eager to do some damage to her arrogant guise. My fist flew outward—

—

I couldn't move. As if someone pressed pause on me. I became aware, that I was frozen in midair, in charging position.

What the—

Sabine turned, her eyes wide in surprise. Startled. Only a few centimeters were separating her nose from my fist. This was probably the first and the last time, when I would have the satisfaction to see her this *small*.

"I've got this!" I heard Lorenzo call out.

"You better," she threatened, and then stomped off.

257

I could hear, I could see, I could think, but otherwise, my body refused to obey me. I was hanging suspended in the air.

Lorenzo…you despicable piece of sh—

"By the way, that was wicked," he whispered in my ear. And even if I wasn't able to see his face, I could feel the scandalous grin. "I told you, we have a lot in common."

Agh…

"Now, I'm going to put you down. And you will play nice until we're done with you. Because you won't have a choice," Lorenzo stated matter-of-factly.

I didn't know how, but I was going to hurt him somehow…

Lorenzo put his hands on my arms, and the effect was that of dissolving the stiffness away, and then I fell. But he caught me, before I would hit the floor. He helped me then to stand up. And for the first time, I glanced around, examining the space I found myself in. We were on the corridor now. A long one, and relatively wide. Very bright too, in comparison to the dimness of the room I was held captive until a moment ago. Quickly, I spotted more doors, and floor to ceiling glass walls—that belonged to wider spaces—on each side of the hallway. And at both ends, one full matte glass door. The floor was covered in something that looked like linoleum. A wood patterned linoleum.

An unpleasant wave of nausea hit me in full, losing balance again. *Wow…*

Lorenzo steadied me with one arm. "Yeah, that can happen… Sorry for that, and for this one."

I didn't have time to process, to form my question, 'cause with the free hand Lorenzo already worked his device, and a sudden numbing feeling washed over my entire being. Everything slowed down, inside and out. Speaking was muted, and awareness of self suspended. My will surrendered to his. "This way," he said, and I followed as if it was my own mental command.

Strangely, how peaceful I felt.

I put one foot in front of the other, and began traversing the distance indicated.

With the little mobility I was left in my neck, I was able to slowly sway my head, and observe what was existing, laterally. Not much. We passed by a few more doors encased in solid walls, followed by the wider transparent spaces, which appeared to be empty. With the exception of a structure entirely of glass, that looked like a speech stand, but the lit symbols on it, indicating some sort of control panel.

"I will definitely miss your *fire*..." Lorenzo spoke, a hint of regret in his voice. "That's one of the downsides of the Recalibration. But I am curious, to meet the *new* you. To see in what all that ridiculously huge potential of yours, turns into."

His words seemed to overlap with my thoughts.

My thoughts? Fire. Recalibration. New me.

"Once you get to know Sabine, she's not that bad. Though sometimes, she deserves to be taken down a peg or two. Or ten," Lorenzo chuckled.

The corners of my mouth raised.

She does...

We approached another segment of those transparent spaces. In the one to the right, behind the glass curtain, Sabine was working on the control panel. Aware of our presence, she turned her head when we stepped in. "The conditions look optimum. This Alignment is particularly helpful," she said, a peculiar gleam reading in her eyes.

"Good. After all, she is your biggest project," Lorenzo replied evenly.

We continued our advancement to the middle of the room, and came to a stop in front of large golden disk, approximately two meters in diameter, and about twenty centimeters high. "Now, please step on it. And stay in the center," Lorenzo indicated, and I followed peacefully the request.

From where I stood, I was looking straight at Sabine, who was monitoring information on her screen. Lorenzo came to her side, and clasped his hands behind his back. "She's ready. You can begin."

Sabine raised her head and stared at me, satisfied. "This has been a very long wait. Finally, you are where I want you to be. I'm pleased to know that after *this*, you won't be disappointing us anymore."

For the first time since I was overwhelmed by nausea, the tranquilizing fog over my mind and senses was lifting. Abrupt understanding of the situation fired through me, my eyes widened in shock.

"Initiate locking phase," Sabine commanded.

Nooo...

A beam of light ignited from under my very feet and pushed through and beyond me forcing my head to tilt back from the unexpected force. The energy traveled to the ceiling connecting with a mirroring disk above me. A second thrust of energy, propelled me a good portion into the air.

"Begin Merkabah reset," was the following command.

A cone of energy spiraled downwards and another from under me spiraled upwards, meeting and locking the middle. My hands flew outward and my legs spread apart, my head returning to vertical position. I lost again complete control over my body. I became *again* an impassive observer.

Across from me, Sabine was busy working with a 3D model of what I realized was my energetic architecture. A *holographic* model the size of a football. I'd read about it, I'd seen drawings about it. *Now* I was experiencing it firsthand. I just couldn't believe that I was staring at a miniature representation of my very own blueprint.

Sabine used her hands, to manually adjust the position of the two intersecting tetrahedra. Which in turn, translated into an immediate shift I felt in the dynamic of the two spirals.

Now, the opposing currents were pumping energy at different speeds. One spun much faster than the other. The energy increasing exponentially. Violently. Unstoppably.

The vertigo I was experiencing, was *beyond* any human tolerance.

The energy whirlpools, generated another field around me. A violet sphere pulsating and growing in size, and finally, encompassing my hands and stopping just above the tip of my fingers. Suspended in the air like Da Vinci's Vitruvian Man, I felt *literally* pulled in all directions, as if to be dismantled piece by piece, by these colossal forces.

If this didn't kill me…

I wanted to scream. I wanted to shout at her, to stop this insanity. Even if just for a moment. To let out of me, all the profanities I was capable of. Unfortunately, that wasn't possible anymore. Because, they made sure that capacity was silenced together with the rest that matter. There was no way out of this. No form of relief… No nothing…

Through excruciating pains shooting everywhere, beads of sweat forming on my forehead, I heard again Sabine. "Commence Life Grid reset." With a pulling a part gesture, she expanded the hologram, and zoomed in, bringing forward another structure. Another layer of my anatomy. Which looked like—

Holly God! The Tree of Life.

I was looking at my *Tree of freakin' Life*. This was surreal…

Wait. This wasn't the Tree of Life I knew.

This was a bit different. Like—

I think I saw this somewhere. Or someone told me about. Oh crap… I couldn't pin it down.

Oh God… What is she doing to me?

Sabine moved her fingers across this structure, and began moving around all the center points. Using the grid's verticals and diagonals. Then a weird static noise started to vibrate into my body, my energy centers—my chakras—reacting violently to it. Another pulling process began, overlapping the ongoing one. This one though, felt as if someone was rearranging me inside. Restructuring everything. A scorching fire roasting every cell, every atom, every particle…

Blood came out my nose.

New levels of agony and lava…

Too much, was a while back.

My tears were pure liquid fire.

Out! Out! Out! Ooooooooooooooooooooooooout!!!!
I want out!!!!!!!!!!!!!!!!!!!!!!!!!!!!!!!!!!!!!

. . . .

∞

Relaxed and a happy grin planted on my face, I was ready to join again the crowd. I washed my hands, and dried them with a paper towel. Then checked myself in the mirror. All seemed to look better than I expected. Hair pulled back into a relaxed bun, a bit of mascara, and a very subtle lip gloss, was all I had managed today. "Perfect," I smiled at myself in the mirror.

The door opened and a man came in.

"Mr. Tellman?! What are you doing here?" I asked, entirely confused.

He locked the door behind him, and then stared at me horrified. I'd never seen him like that before. So undone, so…not like him.

In the next instant, a million scenarios flew through my mind. About all the things that could've gone wrong with Martina, with the project, with the authorization process. With… everything. "Did I forget a meeting with you today? Did Martina—"

"I can't believe, I am too late," he said, his voice low and stricken with dismay.

Okay, he was officially scaring me. "Too late, for what?"

He stepped closer. "Too late, to do my job."

"Excuse me?"

Mr. Tellman placed a hand on my shoulder, his eyes searching for something. "They got to you first. I can't believe, they got to you first," he insisted, shaking his head.

I raised my eyebrows, not having even the *slightest* clue, what he was talking about. "Mr. Tellman who's *they*?" I asked.

He composed himself, and looked straight into my eyes. "Did you memorize the number I gave you for special emergencies? The one, I asked Mrs. Müller to give you?"

"Yes. Of course," I confirmed, panic already rising in me. "Mr. Tellman, if something's wrong—"

"Good." The smallest sign of relief, traversing his stern features.

Good? He wasn't making sense at all.

"There is no other way," he said decidedly, his eyes focused somewhere beyond me, then back to me. "Today is the Alignment, so you might make it. I'm extremely, sorry. It's my fault. But if you have this chance, before the Reset becomes permanent, I won't let it slip away." He paused, a moment. "When you wake, use the number to find me," Mr. Tellman urged.

I was *truly* beginning to think he'd lost his marbles. Or that he was drunk, which didn't seem like something he did often, or at all. Then again, I didn't know the man outside the work environment. Perhaps, he had some personal problems? Maybe he was on some sort of medication, which had this sort of side effects.

"I don't understand," I demanded.

Before I knew it, he pressed a palm on my chest. "I'm truly sorry." A full burst of energy surged from his hand into me. My eyes popped out in surprise.

Another shock wave.

I was blasted out...

chapter / TWENTY-NINE

"Did you make up your mind?" he asks, patiently.

"Yes."

"And?"

I stare across where Jan grows impatient, waiting for the group of tourists who is crowding in front of us, to move along.

"I'll have to say no," I answer, feeling all sorts of guilty and stupid. "I'm sorry. It's not the best time for me right now."

"We've missed breakfast. I can't skip lunch, too. Come on. Please, get up!" a cheery voice insists. "Plus, Peter is coming. We have to discuss in more detail, about the event. He really wants your feedback."

Opening my eyes was 'mission impossible.' I felt as if somebody had dropped me from the top of the highest building in world, and by some sort of magical happening, I was still alive. But, barely. Every cell in my body was throbbing with pain. I had zero power left in my reservoirs.

"Come on," the voice begged.

In the next instant, I felt the covers being pulled off of me. "I shouldn't have let you have those two cocktails. They are deadly. Two hours ago, I felt like you do now. But with enough hydration, you'll be up in no time. Here, drink this," the voice demanded, a hand shaking me vigorously.

Yet no reaction from me. My body refusing to cooperate.

The same strong hand steadied my head, my lips parting , startled at the feel of cold glass. I only managed to semi open my eyes, but was still unable to distinguish the shapes and colors in front of me. "Open your mouth," the voice pressed, and just like that, water was poured down my throat. Lots of it. Repeatedly.

After a fairly large amount, my eyes finally opened.

Raluca.

"Where am I?" I asked, my head still spinning.

"In our hotel room?!" Raluca answered. "Remind me, not to let you get heavy drinks when you're *that* tired. Especially, after the plane ride from hell..."

"What? Where's Jan?"

"Who's Jan?"

I pushed myself up with my hands, and leaned against the headboard. "I don't have time for your jokes, right now."

God, how I hated this dizzying sensation...

"Really, who's Jan? None of the three guys at our table, were called Jan. And one of them was Peter. If I recall, correctly. So snap out of your dream, and come back to reality. We have to go downstairs, in fifteen minutes," Raluca said, then paused observing me briefly. "Fine. Twenty. Because of...your condition. But, seriously. I don't want to be late. So I suggest, you go to the bathroom and freshen up."

I was really struggling not to snap at her. "My *fiancée.*"

She snorted. "What fiancée? *Wow* that drink was strong..."

I decided to ignore her little game instead. "Call Jan to get me...to take us home." Flashes of images of various events were circling my mind and vision. All fusing together, in an undecipherable canvas. Not sure anymore, what was dream or reality.

"I think you need something stronger than water. I'll go get you an aspirin," Raluca stood, and walked around the bed, then dug her hands into an open travel suitcase, searching through a pile of stuff.

"What day is today?" I asked.

"Friday," she replied, evenly.

Maybe it was indeed, a dream? Still, a lot of things didn't make sense.

"How did we end up here, if the Gala is tonight? I *specifically* remember that Jan droves us home after Meike's birthday party. She and Alex took Lydia to their place, and the rest got taxis. And I also recall, the fact that on our way home, we were talking about the flower delivery for today."

Raluca stopped, turned her head and gave me one of her famous weird looks. "Ugh, no. We arrived yesterday in Hamburg, and straight from the airport came here. To our hotel. We had dinner with Peter, and some of his friends. At some point you didn't feel well and left. I came upstairs a little later to check up on you, but you were already fast asleep. So, I didn't disturb you. I ordered some tea, just in case," she said pointing onto the other night stand where a white cup sat there empty. "Which I ended up, drinking it myself. Then I crashed, too. And no. The Gala is not today. It's at least a month away, in the future. We are still narrowing the date down."

"*What*?"

"Okay. I get it, you have a *truly* bad hangover and apparently a very detailed dream," she said, gesticulating with her hands. "But seriously, we need to get going."

"What day is today?" I asked, infuriated.

"I've already told you. Friday."

"What *date*?"

"September 13."

What?

It can't be.

I rose to my feet swiftly. Which was a bad idea. *Really* bad idea. The vertigo came back with a vengeance. "Give me your cell phone," I demanded.

Raluca stared at me, and for the first time, she appeared to lose all of her happy mood, and exhibited something which said *horrified*. "Look to your night stand. It's there. Unless now you're blind, too."

I whirled my head around, spotted it, and grabbed it in a heartbeat. I swiped the screen.

12:22 p.m.

September 13

I huffed. "It can't be…" And kept staring at the screen. "…Just can't be." I lifted my gaze, my eyes traveling around the room. Across from the bed, on the table, there was an opened laptop. I rushed to it and checked the time.

12:23 p.m.

September 13

"No. No. No…" I dragged my hands through my hair. "I can't be losing my mind. No…"

Raluca stood up, with a little plastic bag in her hands. "Okay. Take it easy, now. Calm down. It's just a dream." Then pulled out of the bag, a small box. "I found it. Here, take this." And tossed it at me.

My automatic reflexes worked before my mind could even process. I caught it one handed, and read *Aspirin+C* on it. "I don't think *this* can fix my problem," I snorted, then set in the table.

This can't be happening. It's not real. This is a dream.

I started walking back toward the bed, my hands rubbing sharply up and down my face. In my head, a hysterical laughter accompanying my dismay. I collapsed on the bed.

This is not real. It's not real. It's not real.

When my eyes tried to focus on something other than the ceiling, I noticed my sister standing across from me. Hands planted firmly on her waist, Raluca stared at me evidently annoyed. "This is an important job for me. You can't have one of your freak-out moments, right now. I'm going to call Peter, and let him know that we're running a bit late. And you're going to the bathroom, right this very instance," she reinforced.

Something clicked inside me.

Of course…

It's been there all along, since I woke up and even before that. But the chaos of information swirling in my head, didn't allow me to see it for what it could be. I had to do it, before I would arrive to any satisfying conclusion. Or before, I would *officially* declare myself a nut case.

I jumped to my feet, and grabbed my sister by the shoulders. "Do you, trust me?"

Raluca mirrored my stare. "Usually, yes. But—"

I shook my head. "You have to trust me now."

She continued looking fixedly at me, waiting for an explanation.

"You, go downstairs. There's no need for both of us to be late," I said, at the same time walking her to the door. "Tell him I don't feel well. But I will join you a little later. He will understand," I insisted, then unlocked and held the door opened for her. "Do this, please. For me," I said, my eyes pleading.

Raluca nodded unsure, and walked out.

I shut the door behind her, and immediately went and snatched my phone.

I took one deep breath, and began dialing the number.

To be perfectly honest, I hadn't expected much. Like, not even have someone at the other end, to pick up. Or the number, to even be real. But it was. And somebody, had picked up. Which made me, not entirely crazy. When he'd answered, he only said that he would be here in fifteen minutes. So there hadn't been time to do much, aside from a very succinct bathroom routine, and changing into something I found laying around on the sofa across from my bed.

Now, we stood face to face.

"You did this to me," I said, pointing my index finger in his face. A wave of frustration and anger, threatening to spill over. "Whatever the hell this is...going back in time and messing up my life story—

"Who the hell *are* you?" I demanded, planting my hands on my hips.

Mr. Tellman stared at me coldly, plainly dismissing my outrage. "I'm a Guardian. I make sure that people like you, navigate safely certain corridors and sectors of reality. Realities." He corrected himself. "You didn't just go back in time. You are now in fact, on an entirely different timeline. The you, that you knew yourself on that timeline, doesn't exist anymore."

Son of a—

"So you *did* kill me," I uttered furiously, my mind racing in a million different directions. Trying to grasp the implications of this new situation. "Why?"

"That timeline was compromised. *You* were compromised," he stated, matter-of-factly. "That version of me had to make a radical choice. One that was meant to save you. In the next few hours, the pieces of information you brought with you from the other timeline, will settle in. Eventually, you'll understand the bigger picture. Here," he said holding out two white envelopes.

I furrowed my eyebrows. "What's this?"

"Your tickets," he replied, then handed them to me. "For you and your sister. Your plane leaves in less than three hours. Both of you, need to go. The insert it's still fresh. I'll need to cover your tracks. It's safer, this way."

I shook my head in confusion. "Tickets, to go where?"

"You need help. A different, kind of help. I'm sending you to someone that can give you that, and more answers."

I huffed, imagining the reaction of my sister, when I'd relay the news. "This…the whole thing is purely insane. I'm—"

"I know, how that must feel. Still, you should consider yourself lucky," Mr. Tellman pressed.

I snorted, not sure how to interpret the whole *lucky* thing. "I guess, I am lucky. Out of this messy, erratic whirlpool, at least I still have my sister."

A barely visible smile came across his face. "As memory goes, you will retain your former self. You won't lose that. But you'll get flashes of things that happened on this timeline, too. Either way, I'm positive your sister would love to fill you in, with details about your new identity."

I pressed my lips, nodding my head, a heavy breath escaping my constricted lungs. The emptiness and dread I felt, allowing the thoughts of 'no Jan' in my life anymore to slip in, was paralyzing to say the least. It felt like a death. The death of a loved one.

How does one continue after?

chapter / THIRTY

I had no clue, where I was supposed to go, until we'd reached the airport. Those were very precise instructions, that Mr. Tellman—a.k.a. my Guardian—had given and which I'd followed without question. For my own safety, as he had urged. Though Raluca hadn't seen it that way, when I'd showed up downstairs with our packed suitcases, at the table where she and Peter, had seemed very engaged in a conversation. I had excused myself for feeling poorly earlier, thus showing up so late. Then I had informed Peter about the sudden 'family emergency' which had forced us to shorten our stay and had to leave at once. I hadn't elaborate on it, but I'd expressed the seriousness of it. And had promised him that he would receive feedback from me in a day or two, regarding the project. It wasn't in my nature to invent this type of excuses, but I couldn't very well have said "hey, I've been recently killed, and landed on another timeline," either. Definitely *no*. I wasn't going to jeopardize Raluca's professional path, like that. Plus, I had yet to discover how much '*in the know*,' this version of my sister really was.

Not only Peter had showed veritable understanding and regret for the situation, but as a matter of fact, he himself, had driven us to the airport. The entire time my sister shooting arrows of 'you-have-lost-your-mind-completely' and 'I-hope-you-have-a-good-explanation-or-I-will-murder-you-as-soon-as-we're-alone' at me.

All I could do, was to bluntly avoid and ignore her furious—though silent—

assault, hoping that soon, things would make a little more sense. For both of us. So I'd continued like that for the entire time of our journey to Paris, too. In fact, until we had reached our destination.

When I stepped through the door of the cute and serene restaurant, flashes of me and Jan doing the *exact* same thing, sent a wave of energy into my solar plexus. My legs turned to jelly.

"This way," the petite woman said, and we followed her quietly, down the long corridor.

Without even saying, I knew exactly where she was taking us, as the déjà vu sensation was increasing in volume. She opened the back door, inviting us to step outside into a lovely atrium with plants crawling on the facades, a few tables with chairs populating it in the middle.

And there he was.

My heart leaped, recognition flooding through me.

"Monsieur Rosin, your guests are here," the woman announced.

He lifted his head from the screen, his eyes filled with a genuine spark of joy. "Thank you," he replied, and then she left, closing the door behind us. He rose from his chair and walked to meet us.

He extended a hand to me. "I'm Pierre," he said, clear excitement reading in his voice.

I shook his, staring at him incredulous. "I know. I'm Ariana. This is my sister, Raluca."

Pierre smiled and for the first time since we had left Hamburg, my sister finally began to melt off that ice from her face. "Nice to meet you," he replied, giving her a vigorous handshake. Then shifted his eyes back to me. "For the longest time, I've been expecting you," he admitted.

A storm of questions was circling my mind, threatening to make my head burst. But I had to start somewhere. So out of that chaos, I chose one. The most pressing one.

"Why am I here, on this timeline?" I asked.

"You've been given another chance," Pierre replied.

I furrowed my brows. "A chance, to what?"

271

He paused shortly, then answered. "A chance to ascend. You're on Ascension Timeline."

"What does this mean?"

Pierre placed a hand on my shoulder, his eyes gazing into mine. "It means, we've got work to do."

Acknowledgements

Writing this book, has definitely been a long and strenuous journey. Though, a very special one. I have never imagined the places it would take me. Mentally, emotionally…physically. And I mean this in the most literal sense. It has been a remarkably unique healing process. It has taken me from a very dark space, where I couldn't see anything ahead. Where I was completely and utterly numb inside. To back into the light. And quite frankly, looking back, I thought it would never ever happen again. Me returning back to life… Fortunately I did, and right now I feel like I'm just beginning to power up the internal engine…and who knows what wonderful things will unfold from now on. But all of this wouldn't have been possible without help, from the most unexpected situations, places, and people. I believe I owe a great deal of appreciation to *someone* (that unfortunately I can't name right now…he and I know why) who has literally pulled me from that abyss, and pushed me to write the book. So for that, as well as for other things…*special* thank you!!!!

Also MASSIVE "thank yous!!!" to all of our new friends (that we made since we've moved to this continent), to Min, Chris, Roberta & Pietro, Takashi, Chantal, Lola, Li Ping, Carlos, Velisar, Adina, Cintia. And if I forgot someone, it was unintentional. Thank you for your kindness, and support (with our transition here) and friendship, throughout last/this year.

Of course, I can't forget my family (from Romania & Germany), who has been tremendously supportive (in all ways possible) with our bold move...hahaha. "Thank you from the bottom of my heart!!!" Another special "thank you!!!!" goes to my sister Raluca, for many things, among them, for being my best friend and number one fan, beta reader, and for allowing me to use her name for one of my characters.

Last but not least, I want to thank to my other best friend (and husband) Tom, who's gentle soul, has allowed me to heal, and who never doubted me, my abilities, and the new path I've taken.

Almost forgot...and "THANK YOU" to YOU, whoever you are. Thank you for reading my book!!!

ANA-MARIA THEIS is among many other things
an architect. Since an early age, writing has always been
part of her creative expression. It began with poetry, and
when the right time came, words turned into a book. And
from now on...into more. She is currently residing in New
Jersey, with her husband, books and...lots of trees.

More info: www.anamariatheis.com

Made in the USA
Middletown, DE
01 October 2015